Assassin Nation™

CREATED BY
KYLE STARKS & ERICA HENDERSON

KYLE STARKS

CREATOR/WRITER

ERICA HENDERSON

CREATOR/ARTIST/COVER

DERON BENNETT

LETTERER

JON MOISAN

EDITOR

ANDRES JUAREZ

LOGO DESIGN

CARINA TAYLOR

PRODUCTION DESIGN

image

IMAGE COMICS, INC.
Robert Kirkman—Chief Operating Officer
Erik Larsen—Chief Financial Officer
Todd McFarlane—President
Marc Silvestri—Chief Executive Officer
Jim Valentino—Vice President

Eric Stephenson—Publisher / Chief Creative Officer
Jeff Boison—Director of Publishing Planning
& Book Trade Sales
Chris Ross—Director of Digital Sales
Jeff Stang—Director of Specialty Sales
Kat Salazar—Director of PR & Marketing
Drew Gill—Art Director
Heather Doornink—Production Director
Nicole Lapalme—Controller
IMAGECOMICS.COM

SKYBOUND

FOR SKYBOUND ENTERTAINMENT

ROBERT KIRKMAN CHAIRMAN DAVID ALPERT CEO SEAN MACKIEWICZ SVP, EDITOR-IN-CHIEF SHAWN KIRKHAM SVP, BUSINESS DEVELOPMENT BRIAN HUNTINGTON VP, ONLINE CONTENT SHAUNA WYNNE PUBLICITY DIRECTOR ANDRES JUAREZ ART DIRECTOR JON MOISAN EDITOR ARIELLE BASICH ASSOCIATE EDITOR KATE CAUDILL ASSISTANT EDITOR CARINA TAYLOR GRAPHIC DESIGNER PAUL SHIN BUSINESS DEVELOPMENT MANAGER JOHNNY O'DELL SOCIAL MEDIA MANAGER DAN PETERSEN SR. DIRECTOR OF OPERATIONS & EVENTS FOREIGN RIGHTS INQUIRIES: AG@SEQUENTIALRIGHTS.COM OTHER LICENSING INQUIRIES: CONTACT@SKYBOUND.COM WWW.SKYBOUND.COM

ASSASSIN NATION VOLUME 1. FIRST PRINTING. September 2019. ISBN: 978-1-5343-1329-3
Published by Image Comics, Inc. Office of publication: 2701 NW Vaughn St., Ste. 780, Portland, OR 97210. Copyright © 2019 Skybound, LLC. Originally published in single magazine form as ASSASSIN NATION #1-5. ASSASSIN NATION™ (including all prominent characters featured herein), its logo and all character likenesses are trademarks of Skybound, LLC, unless otherwise noted. Image Comics® and its logos are registered trademarks and copyrights of Image Comics, Inc. All rights reserved. No part of this publication may be reproduced or transmitted in any form or by any means (except for short excerpts for review purposes) without the express written permission of Image Comics, Inc. All names, characters, events and locales in this publication are entirely fictional. Any resemblance to actual persons (living or dead), events or places, without satiric intent, is coincidental. Printed in the U.S.A.

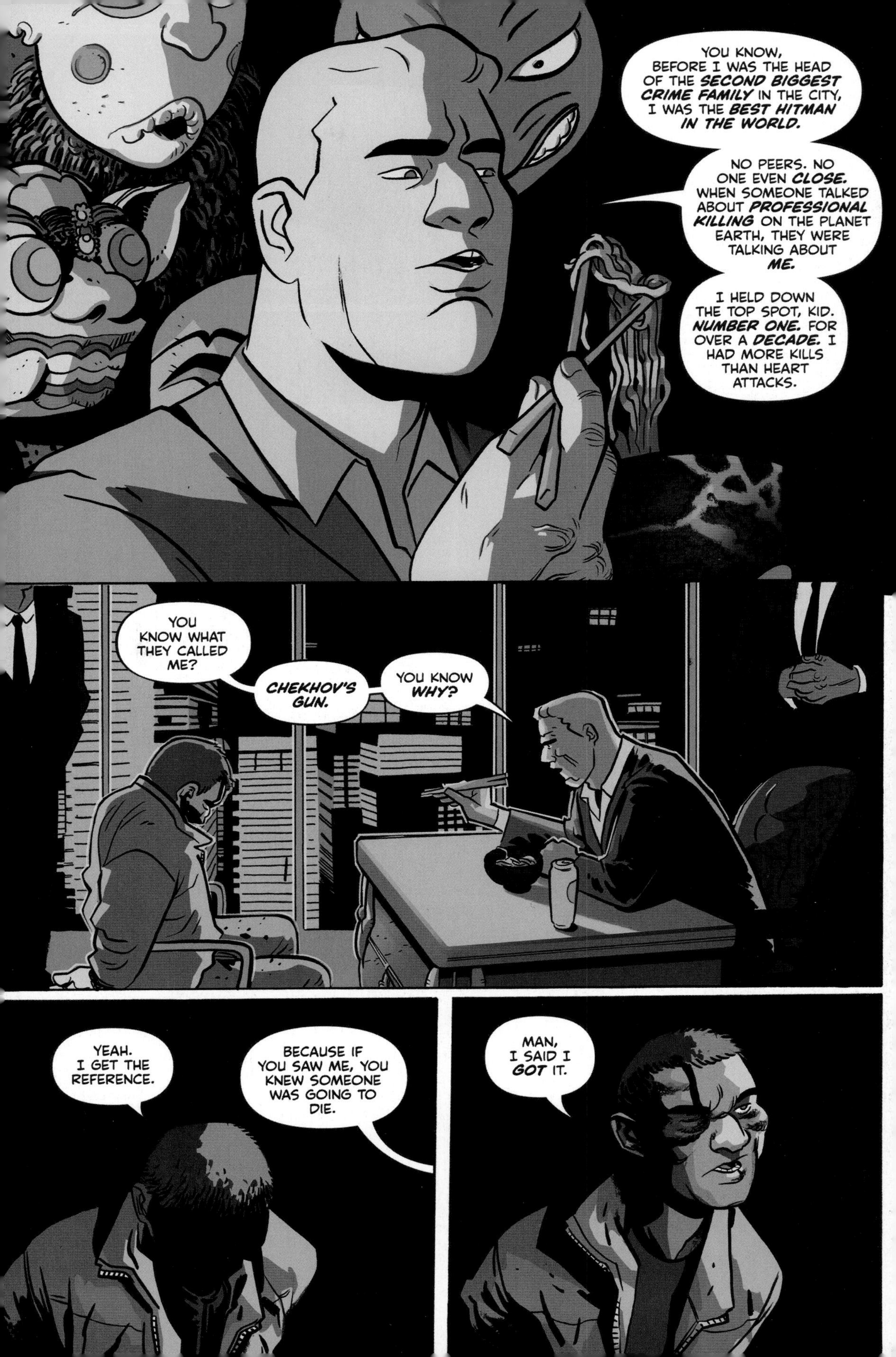

YOU KNOW, BEFORE I WAS THE HEAD OF THE SECOND BIGGEST CRIME FAMILY IN THE CITY, I WAS THE BEST HITMAN IN THE WORLD.
NO PEERS. NO ONE EVEN CLOSE. WHEN SOMEONE TALKED ABOUT PROFESSIONAL KILLING ON THE PLANET EARTH, THEY WERE TALKING ABOUT ME.
I HELD DOWN THE TOP SPOT, KID. NUMBER ONE. FOR OVER A DECADE. I HAD MORE KILLS THAN HEART ATTACKS.
YOU KNOW WHAT THEY CALLED ME?
CHEKHOV'S GUN.
YOU KNOW WHY?
YEAH. I GET THE REFERENCE.
BECAUSE IF YOU SAW ME, YOU KNEW SOMEONE WAS GOING TO DIE.
MAN, I SAID I GOT IT.

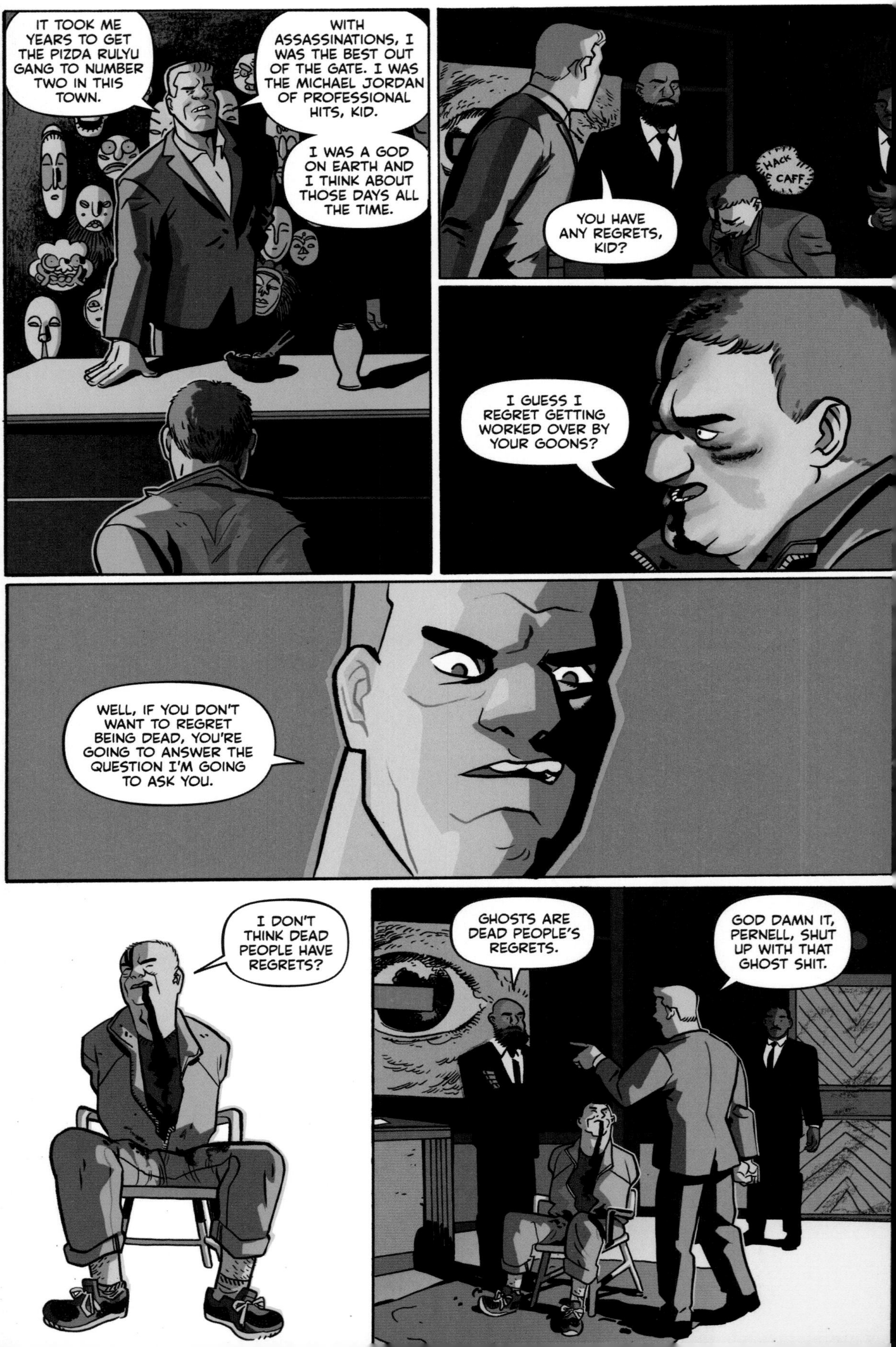
IT TOOK ME YEARS TO GET THE PIZDA RULYU GANG TO NUMBER TWO IN THIS TOWN.
WITH ASSASSINATIONS, I WAS THE BEST OUT OF THE GATE. I WAS THE MICHAEL JORDAN OF PROFESSIONAL HITS, KID.
I WAS A GOD ON EARTH AND I THINK ABOUT THOSE DAYS ALL THE TIME.
HACK CAFF
YOU HAVE ANY REGRETS, KID?
I GUESS I REGRET GETTING WORKED OVER BY YOUR GOONS?
WELL, IF YOU DON'T WANT TO REGRET BEING DEAD, YOU'RE GOING TO ANSWER THE QUESTION I'M GOING TO ASK YOU.
I DON'T THINK DEAD PEOPLE HAVE REGRETS?
GHOSTS ARE DEAD PEOPLE'S REGRETS.
GOD DAMN IT, PERNELL, SHUT UP WITH THAT GHOST SHIT.

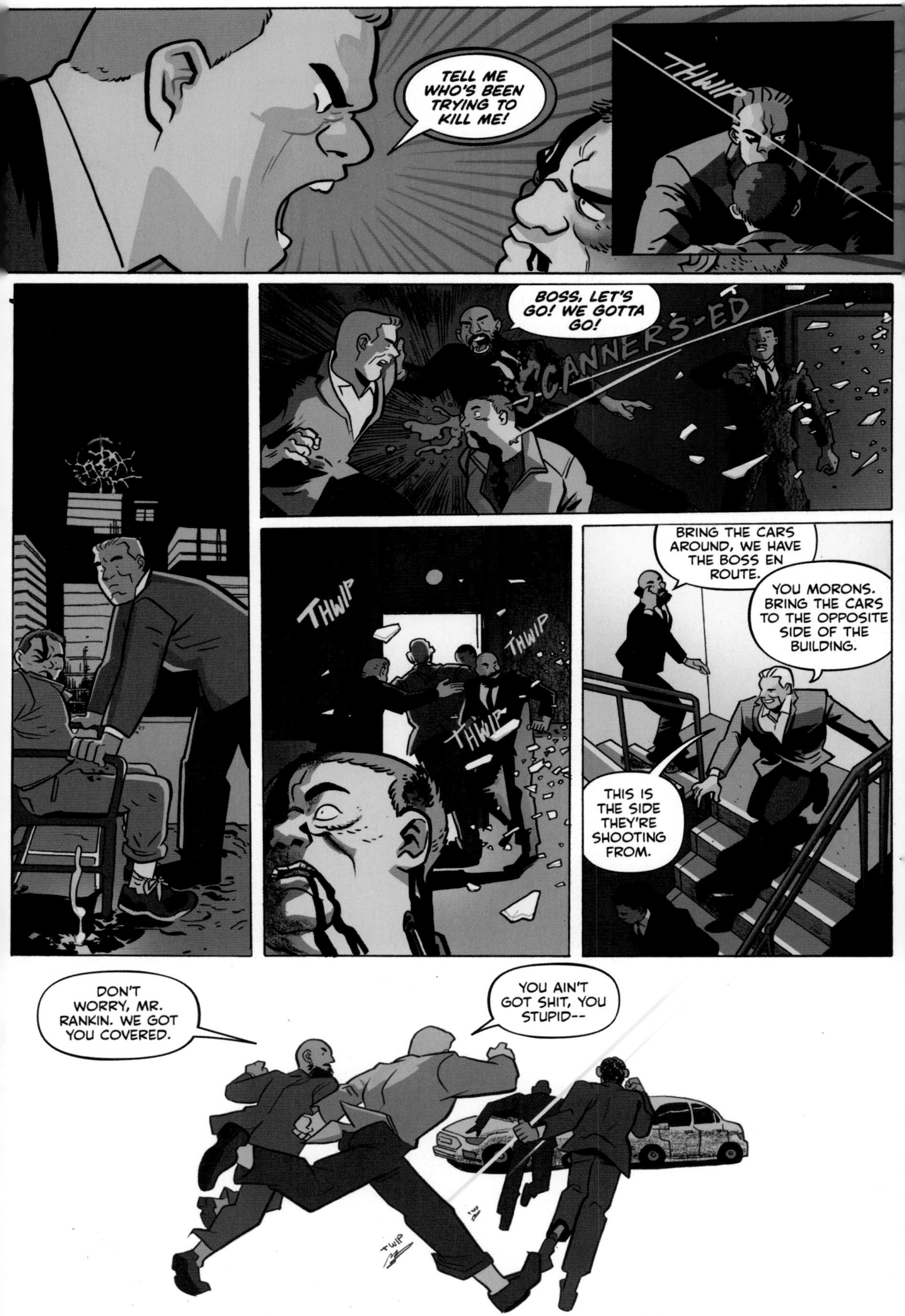

TELL ME WHO'S BEEN TRYING TO KILL ME!
THWIP
BOSS, LET'S GO! WE GOTTA GO!
SCANNERS-ED
THWIP
THWIP
THWIP
BRING THE CARS AROUND, WE HAVE THE BOSS EN ROUTE.
YOU MORONS. BRING THE CARS TO THE OPPOSITE SIDE OF THE BUILDING.
THIS IS THE SIDE THEY'RE SHOOTING FROM.
DON'T WORRY, MR. RANKIN. WE GOT YOU COVERED.
YOU AIN'T GOT SHIT, YOU STUPID--
TWIP

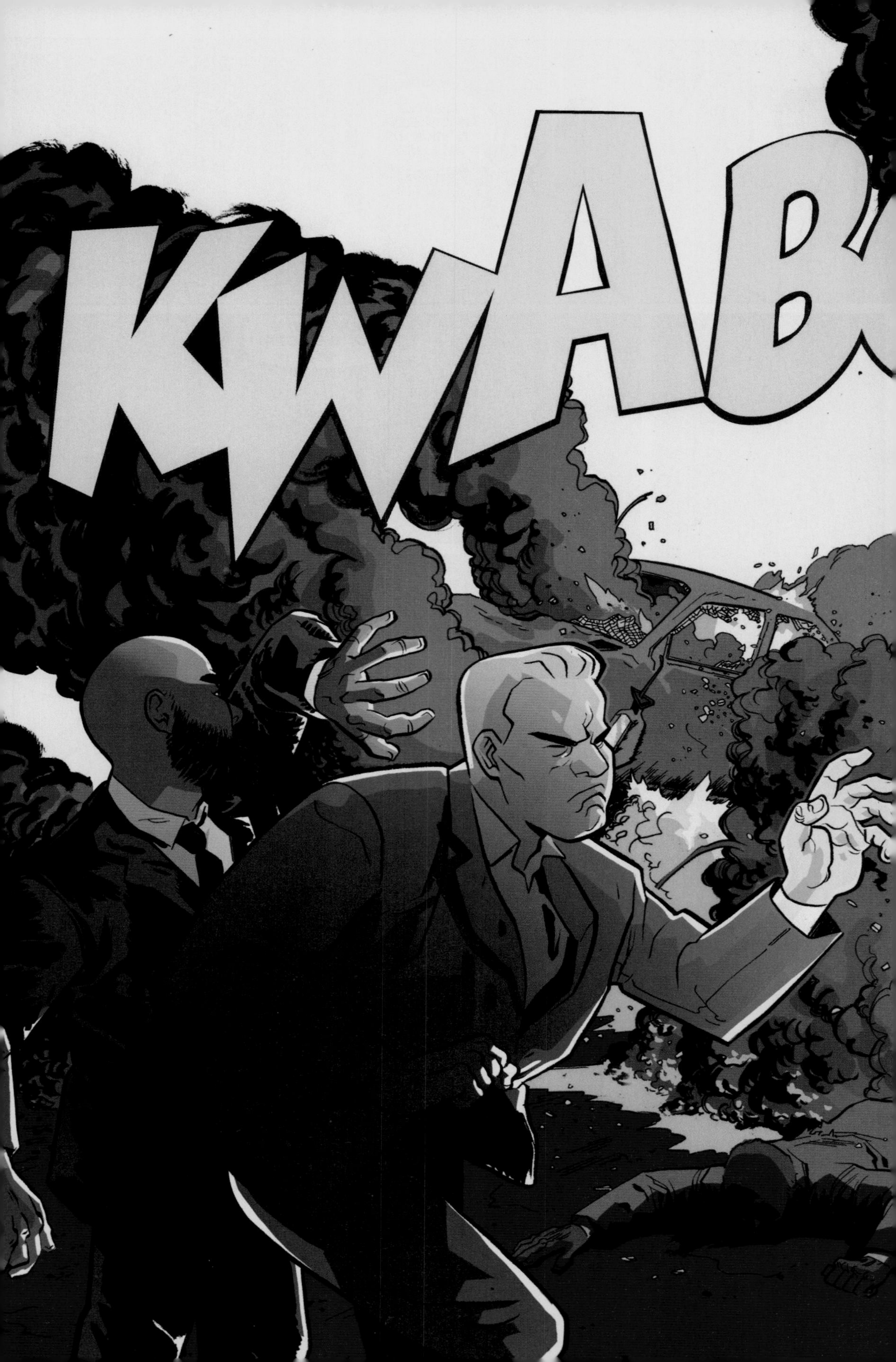
KWAB

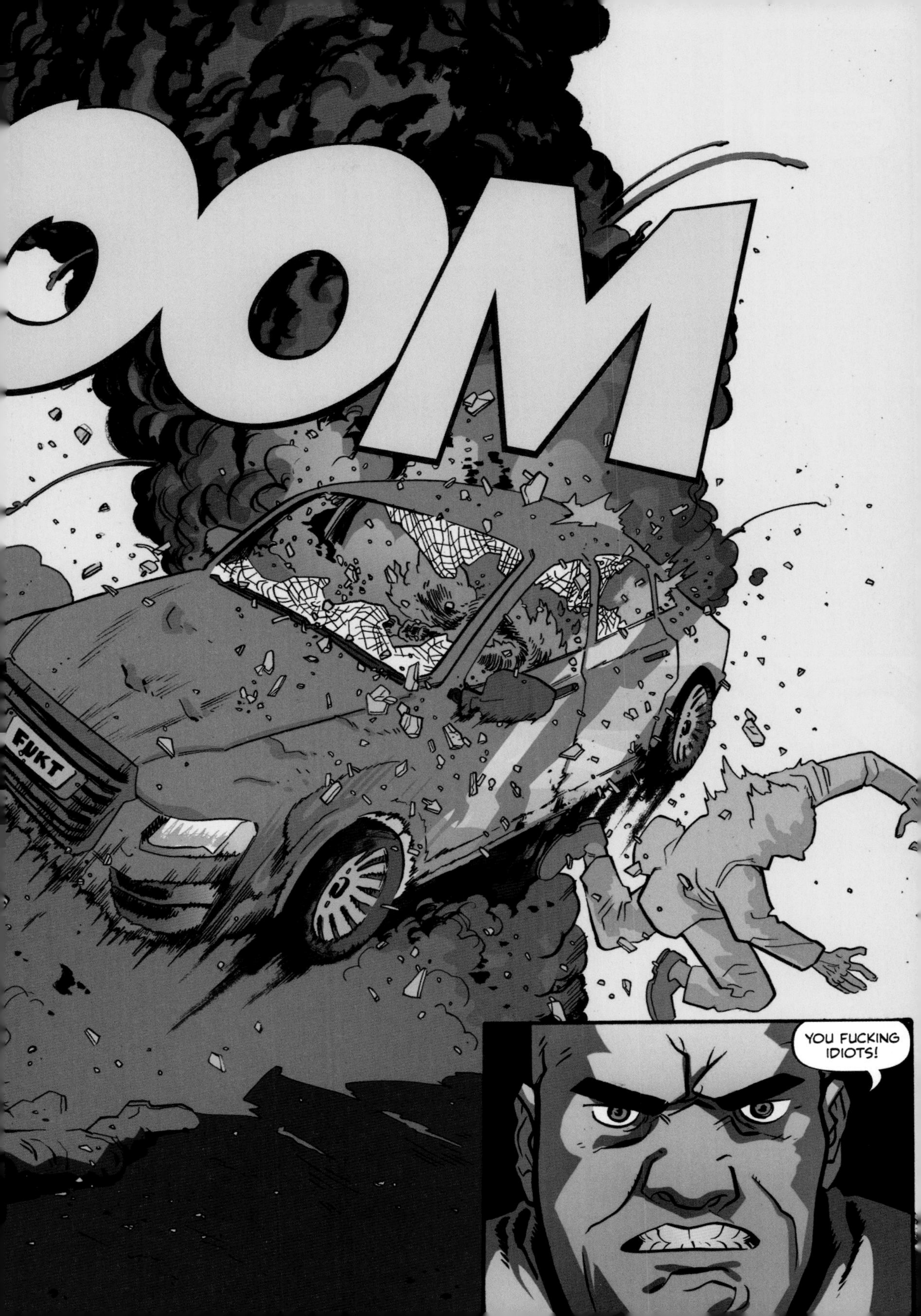
OOM
FUKT
YOU FUCKING IDIOTS!

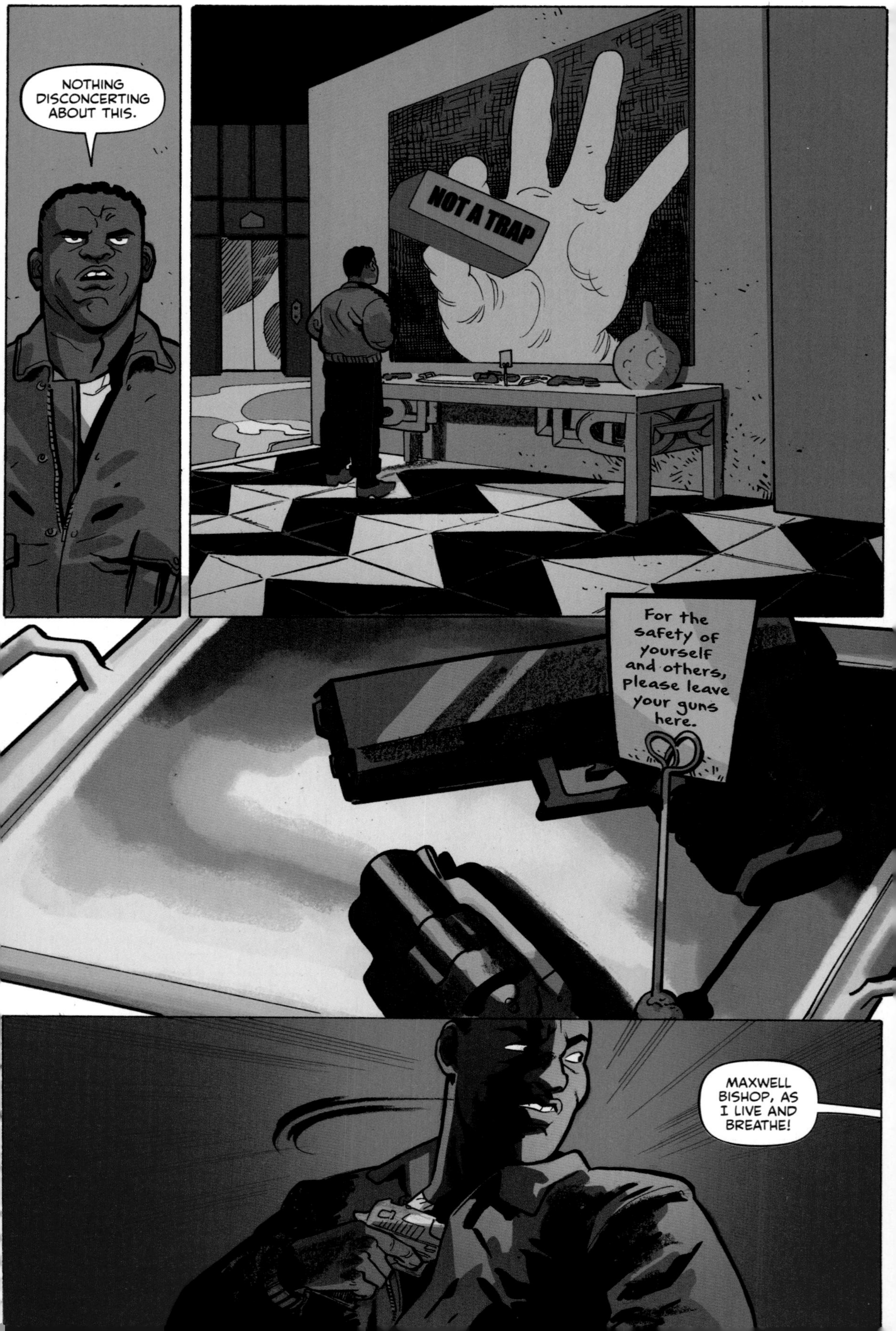
NOTHING DISCONCERTING ABOUT THIS.
NOT A TRAP
For the safety of yourself and others, please leave your guns here.
MAXWELL BISHOP, AS I LIVE AND BREATHE!

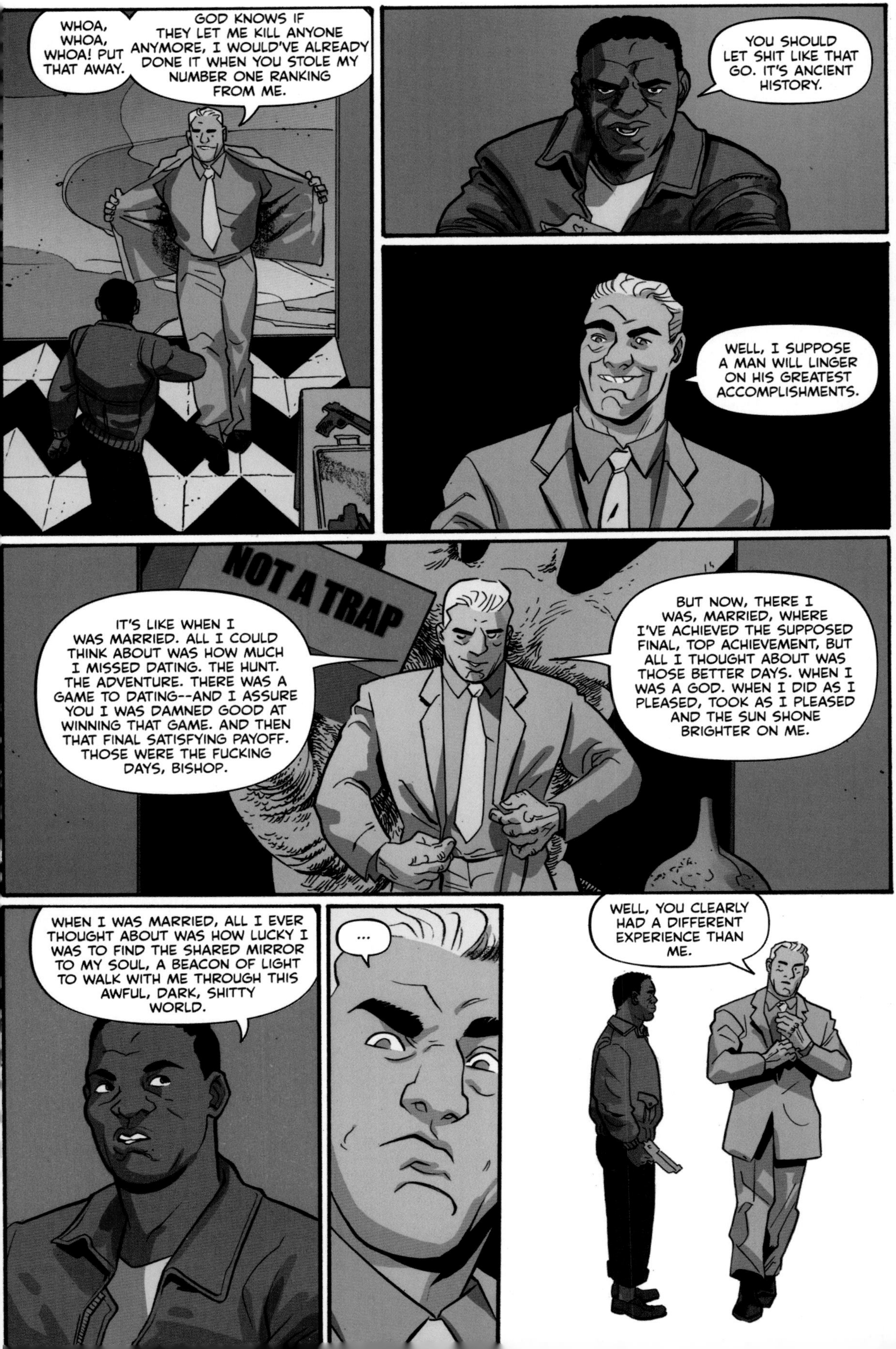
WHOA, WHOA, WHOA! PUT THAT AWAY.
GOD KNOWS IF THEY LET ME KILL ANYONE ANYMORE, I WOULD'VE ALREADY DONE IT WHEN YOU STOLE MY NUMBER ONE RANKING FROM ME.
YOU SHOULD LET SHIT LIKE THAT GO. IT'S ANCIENT HISTORY.
WELL, I SUPPOSE A MAN WILL LINGER ON HIS GREATEST ACCOMPLISHMENTS.
NOT A TRAP
IT'S LIKE WHEN I WAS MARRIED. ALL I COULD THINK ABOUT WAS HOW MUCH I MISSED DATING. THE HUNT. THE ADVENTURE. THERE WAS A GAME TO DATING--AND I ASSURE YOU I WAS DAMNED GOOD AT WINNING THAT GAME. AND THEN THAT FINAL SATISFYING PAYOFF. THOSE WERE THE FUCKING DAYS, BISHOP.
BUT NOW, THERE I WAS, MARRIED, WHERE I'VE ACHIEVED THE SUPPOSED FINAL, TOP ACHIEVEMENT, BUT ALL I THOUGHT ABOUT WAS THOSE BETTER DAYS. WHEN I WAS A GOD. WHEN I DID AS I PLEASED, TOOK AS I PLEASED AND THE SUN SHONE BRIGHTER ON ME.
WHEN I WAS MARRIED, ALL I EVER THOUGHT ABOUT WAS HOW LUCKY I WAS TO FIND THE SHARED MIRROR TO MY SOUL, A BEACON OF LIGHT TO WALK WITH ME THROUGH THIS AWFUL, DARK, SHITTY WORLD.
...
WELL, YOU CLEARLY HAD A DIFFERENT EXPERIENCE THAN ME.

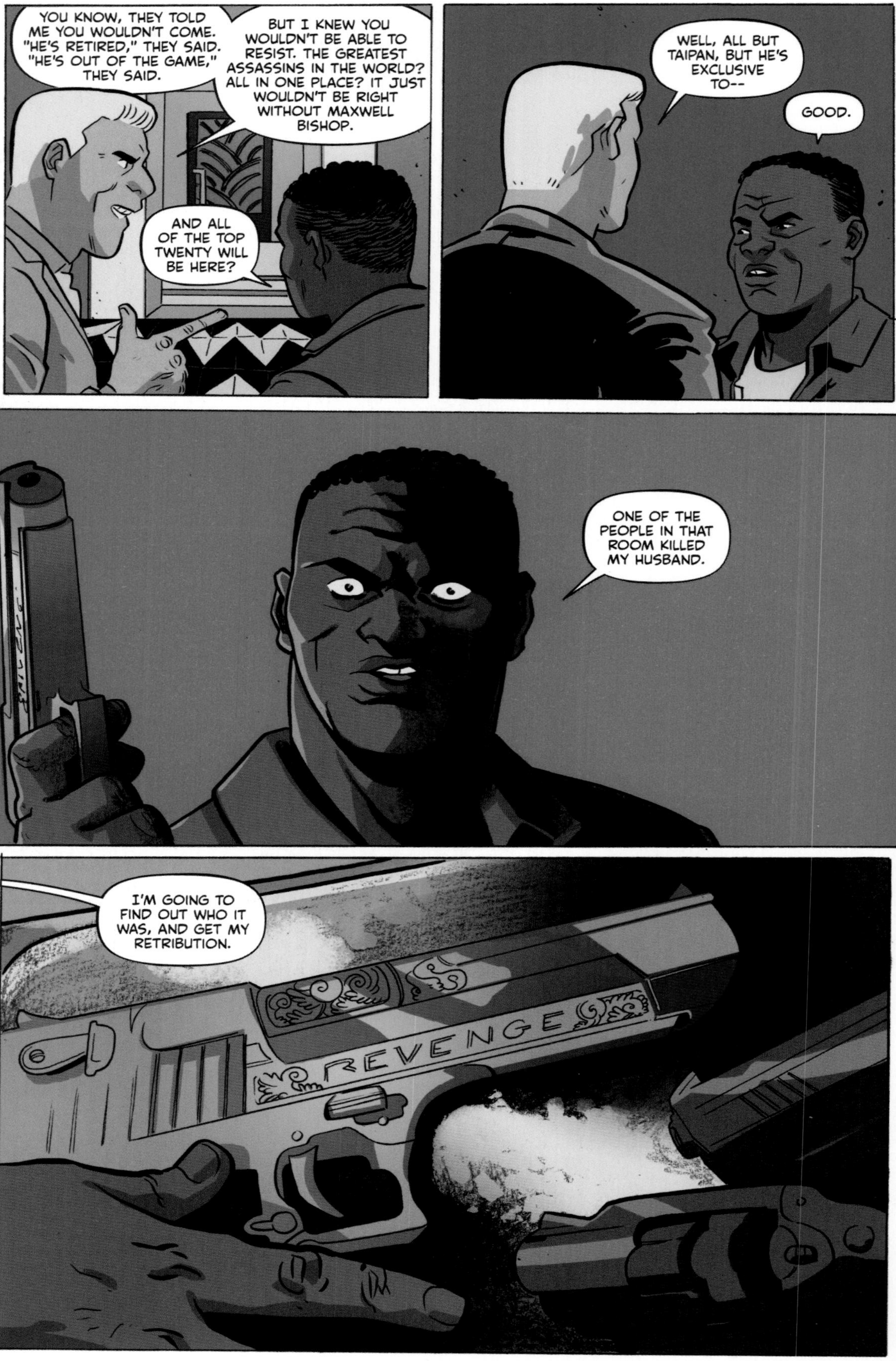
YOU KNOW, THEY TOLD ME YOU WOULDN'T COME. "HE'S RETIRED," THEY SAID. "HE'S OUT OF THE GAME," THEY SAID.
BUT I KNEW YOU WOULDN'T BE ABLE TO RESIST. THE GREATEST ASSASSINS IN THE WORLD? ALL IN ONE PLACE? IT JUST WOULDN'T BE RIGHT WITHOUT MAXWELL BISHOP.
AND ALL OF THE TOP TWENTY WILL BE HERE?
WELL, ALL BUT TAIPAN, BUT HE'S EXCLUSIVE TO--
GOOD.
ONE OF THE PEOPLE IN THAT ROOM KILLED MY HUSBAND.
I'M GOING TO FIND OUT WHO IT WAS, AND GET MY RETRIBUTION.
REVENGE

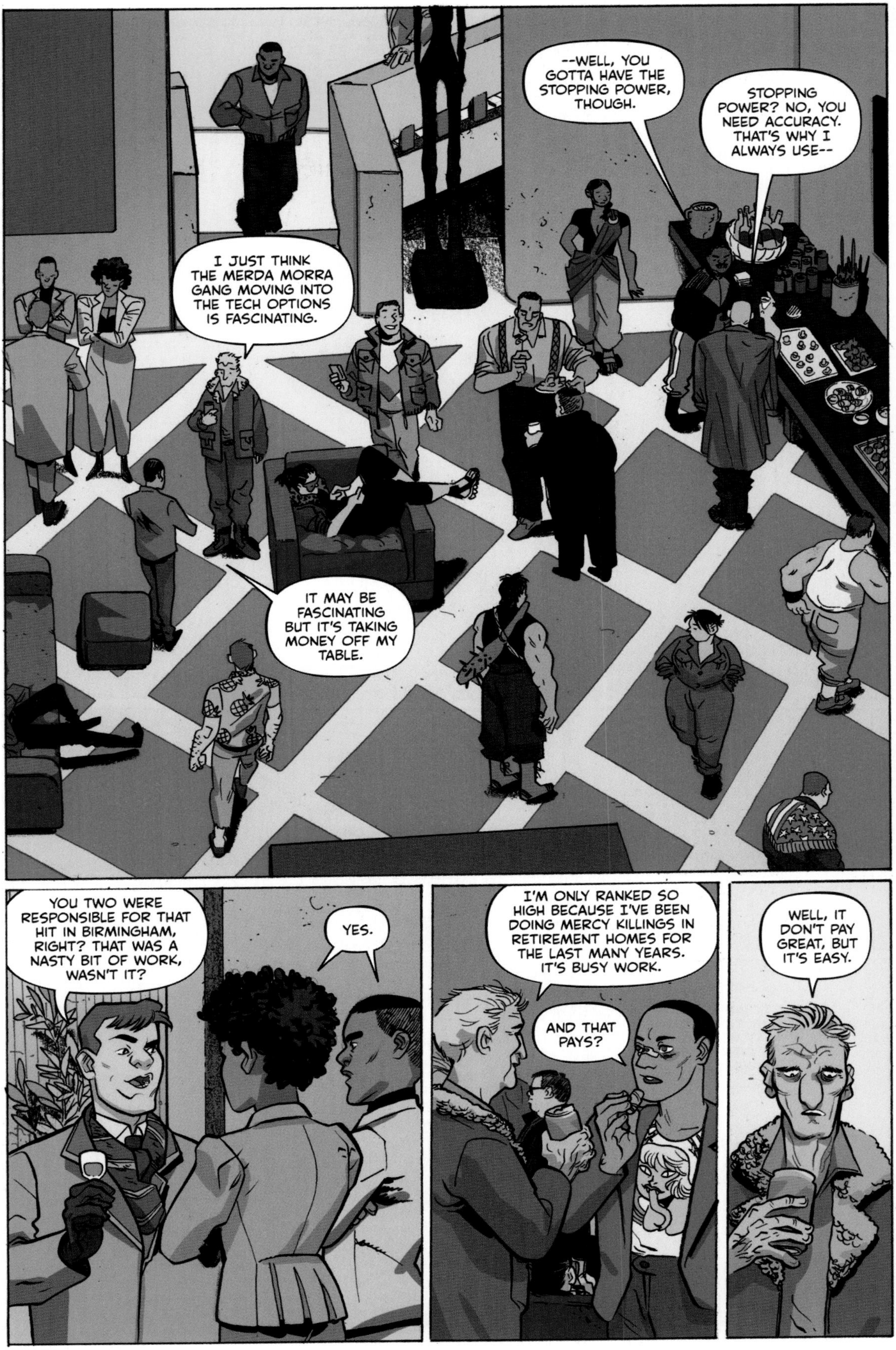
--WELL, YOU GOTTA HAVE THE STOPPING POWER, THOUGH.
STOPPING POWER? NO, YOU NEED ACCURACY. THAT'S WHY I ALWAYS USE--
I JUST THINK THE MERDA MORRA GANG MOVING INTO THE TECH OPTIONS IS FASCINATING.
IT MAY BE FASCINATING BUT IT'S TAKING MONEY OFF MY TABLE.
YOU TWO WERE RESPONSIBLE FOR THAT HIT IN BIRMINGHAM, RIGHT? THAT WAS A NASTY BIT OF WORK, WASN'T IT?
YES.
I'M ONLY RANKED SO HIGH BECAUSE I'VE BEEN DOING MERCY KILLINGS IN RETIREMENT HOMES FOR THE LAST MANY YEARS. IT'S BUSY WORK.
AND THAT PAYS?
WELL, IT DON'T PAY GREAT, BUT IT'S EASY.

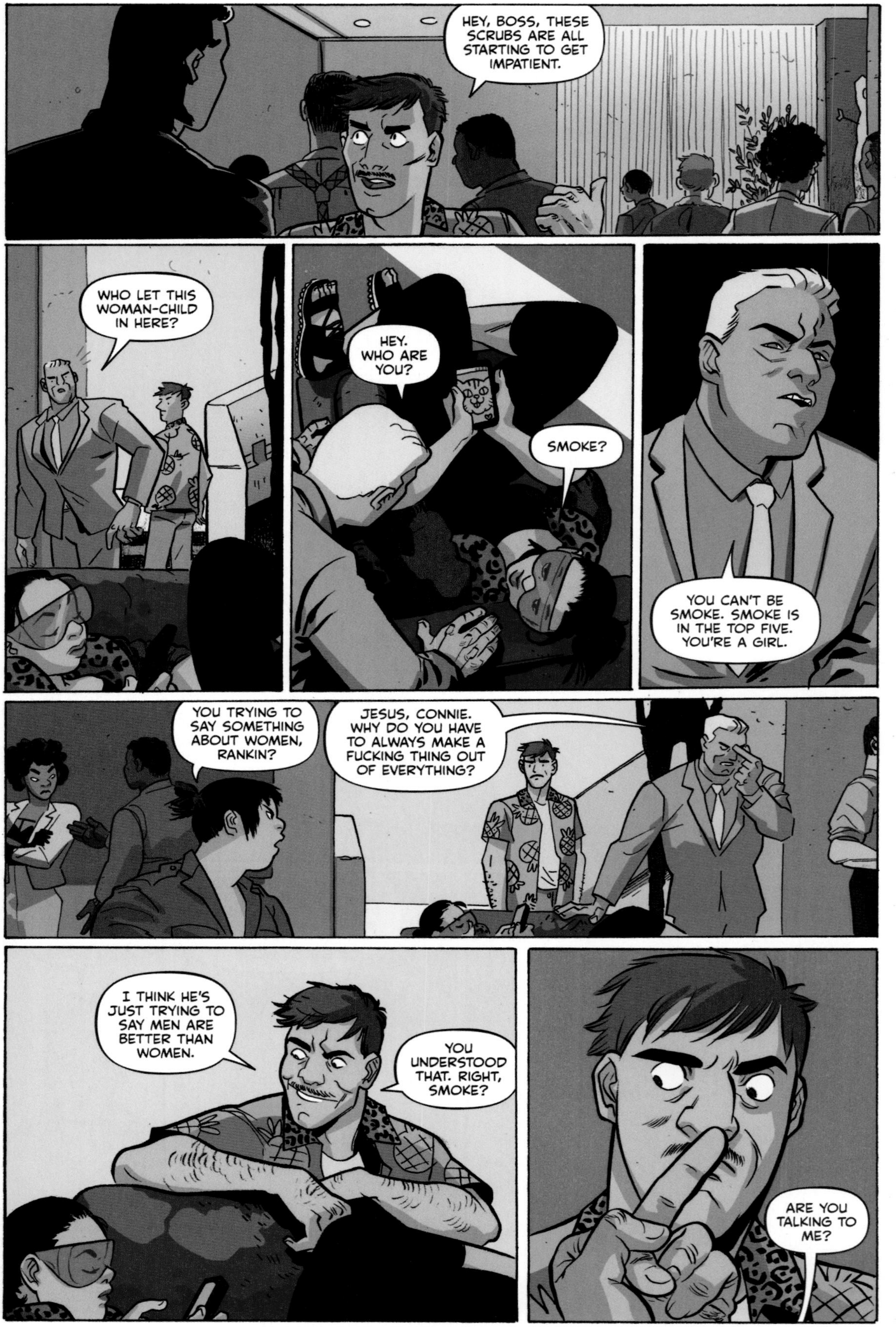
HEY, BOSS, THESE SCRUBS ARE ALL STARTING TO GET IMPATIENT.
WHO LET THIS WOMAN-CHILD IN HERE?
HEY. WHO ARE YOU?
SMOKE?
YOU CAN'T BE SMOKE. SMOKE IS IN THE TOP FIVE. YOU'RE A GIRL.
YOU TRYING TO SAY SOMETHING ABOUT WOMEN, RANKIN?
JESUS, CONNIE. WHY DO YOU HAVE TO ALWAYS MAKE A FUCKING THING OUT OF EVERYTHING?
I THINK HE'S JUST TRYING TO SAY MEN ARE BETTER THAN WOMEN.
YOU UNDERSTOOD THAT. RIGHT, SMOKE?
ARE YOU TALKING TO ME?

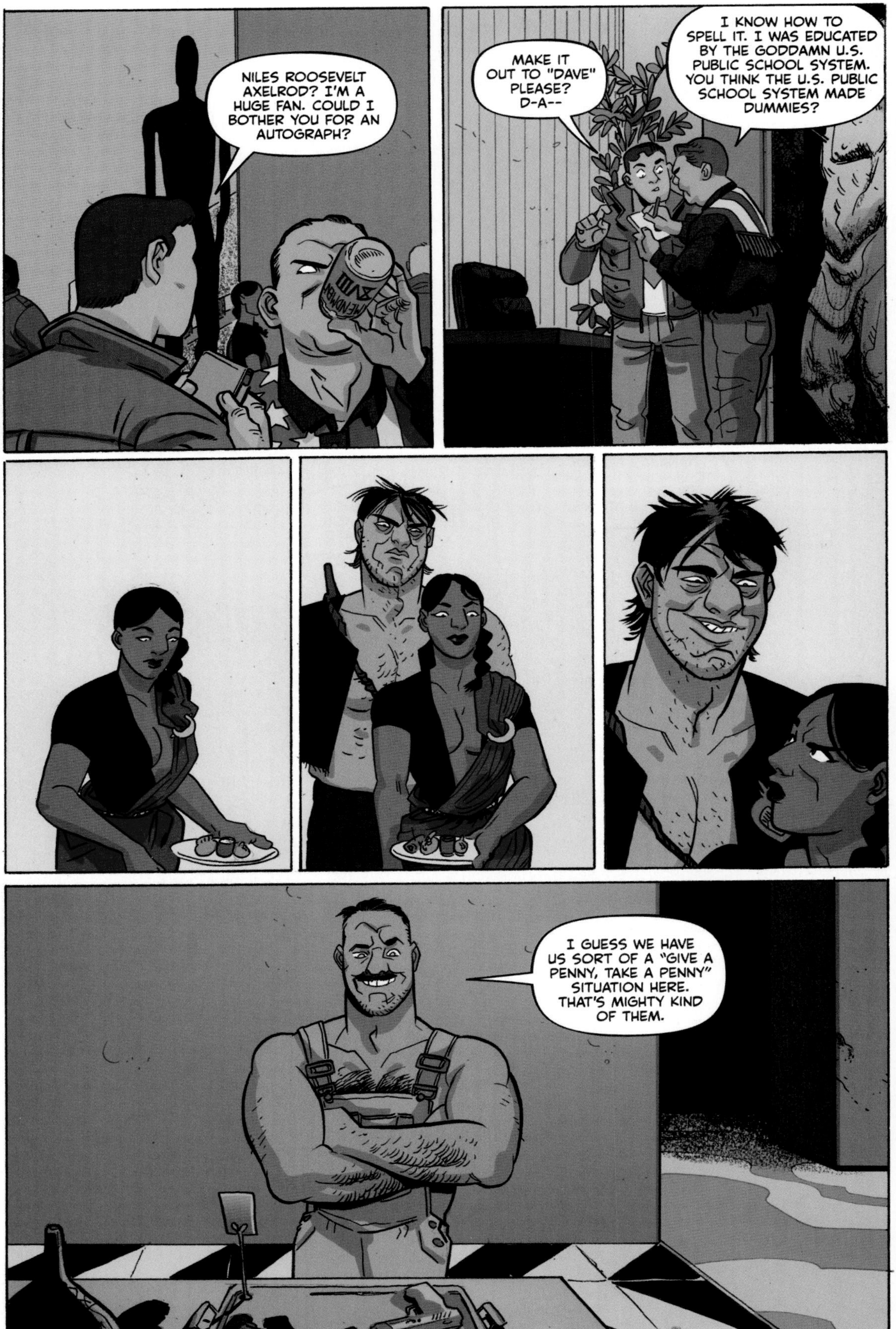
NILES ROOSEVELT AXELROD? I'M A HUGE FAN. COULD I BOTHER YOU FOR AN AUTOGRAPH?
MAKE IT OUT TO "DAVE" PLEASE? D-A--
I KNOW HOW TO SPELL IT. I WAS EDUCATED BY THE GODDAMN U.S. PUBLIC SCHOOL SYSTEM. YOU THINK THE U.S. PUBLIC SCHOOL SYSTEM MADE DUMMIES?
I GUESS WE HAVE US SORT OF A "GIVE A PENNY, TAKE A PENNY" SITUATION HERE. THAT'S MIGHTY KIND OF THEM.

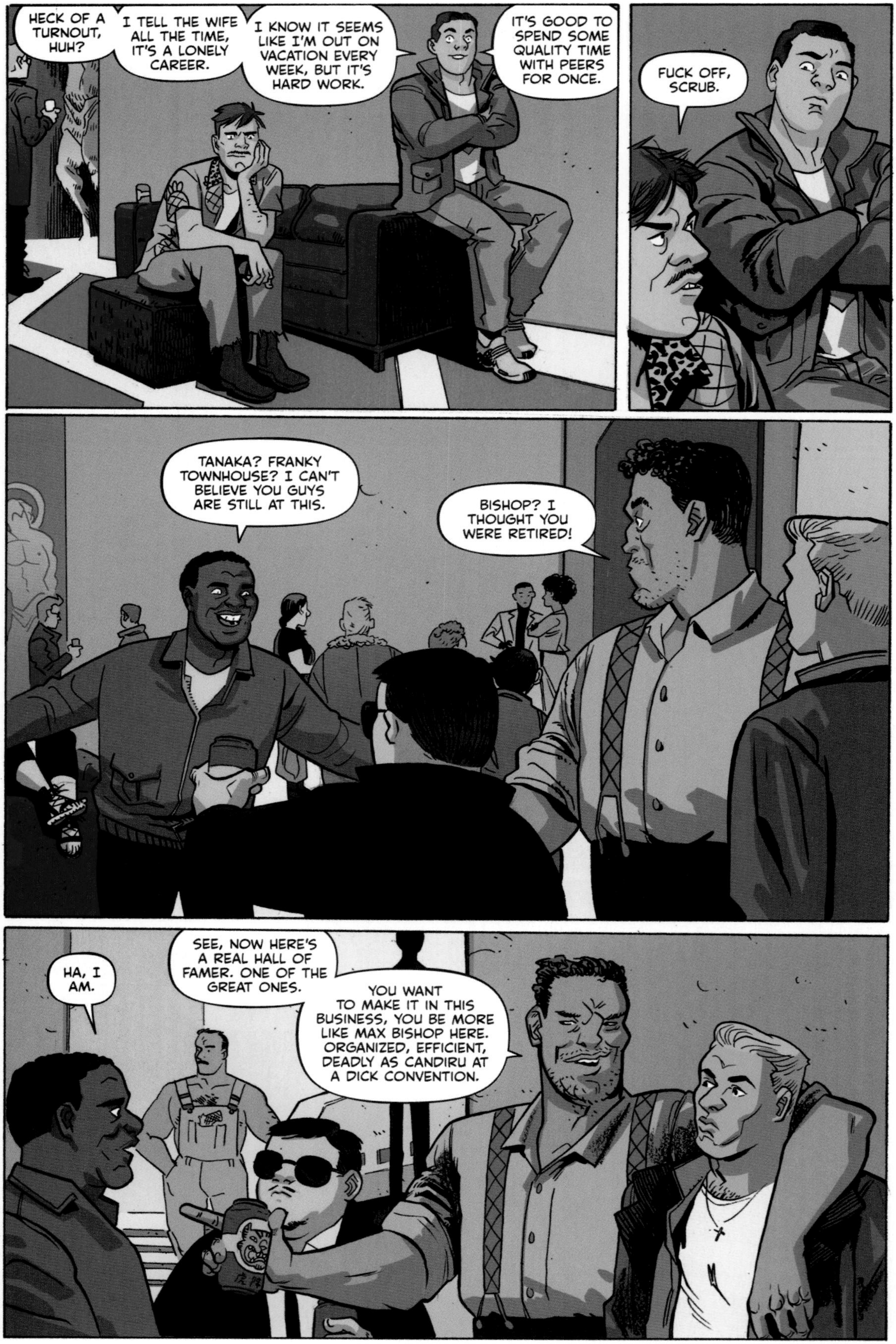
HECK OF A TURNOUT, HUH?
I TELL THE WIFE ALL THE TIME, IT'S A LONELY CAREER.
I KNOW IT SEEMS LIKE I'M OUT ON VACATION EVERY WEEK, BUT IT'S HARD WORK.
IT'S GOOD TO SPEND SOME QUALITY TIME WITH PEERS FOR ONCE.
FUCK OFF, SCRUB.
TANAKA? FRANKY TOWNHOUSE? I CAN'T BELIEVE YOU GUYS ARE STILL AT THIS.
BISHOP? I THOUGHT YOU WERE RETIRED!
HA, I AM.
SEE, NOW HERE'S A REAL HALL OF FAMER. ONE OF THE GREAT ONES.
YOU WANT TO MAKE IT IN THIS BUSINESS, YOU BE MORE LIKE MAX BISHOP HERE. ORGANIZED, EFFICIENT, DEADLY AS CANDIRU AT A DICK CONVENTION.

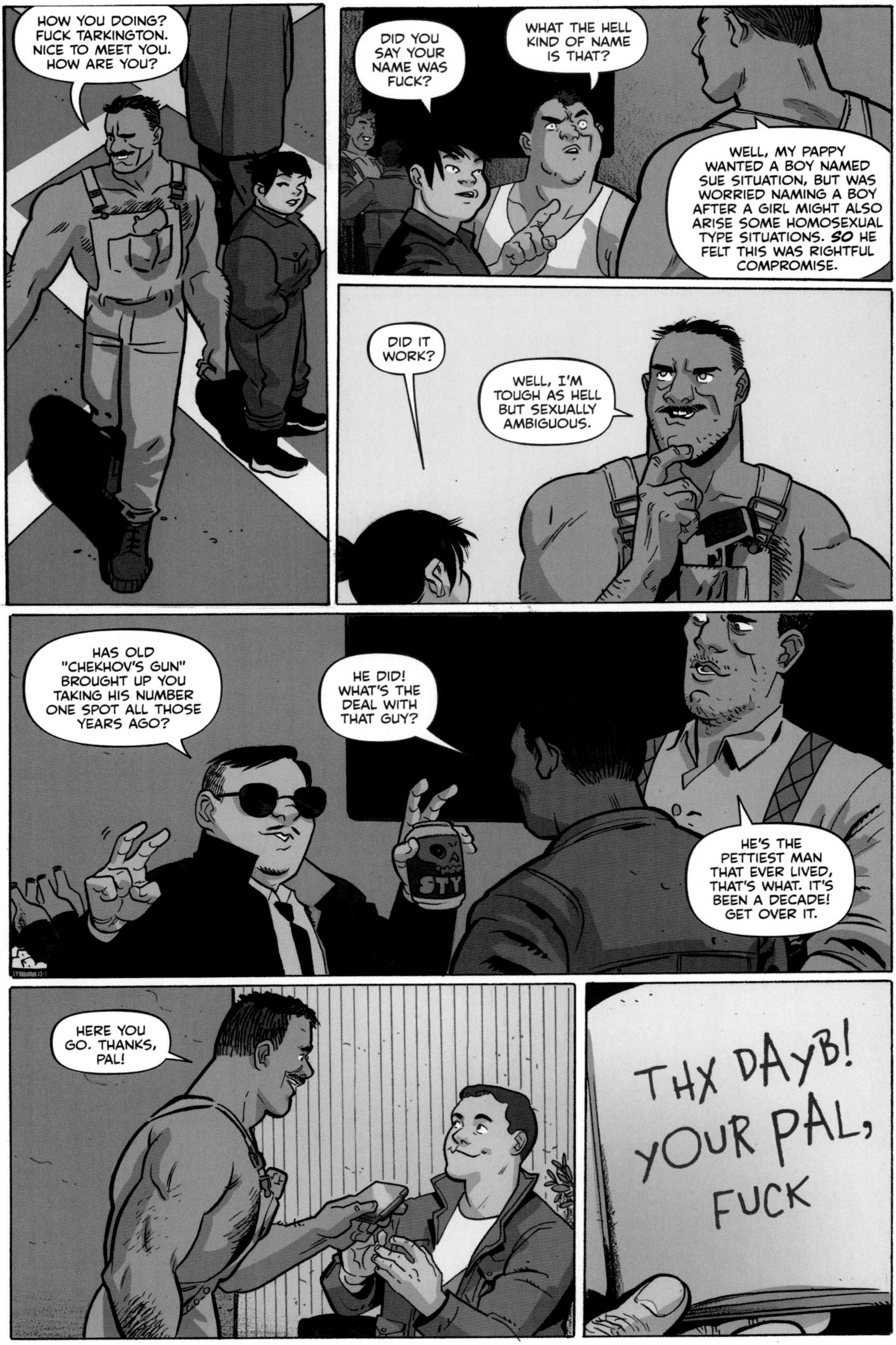
HOW YOU DOING? FUCK TARKINGTON. NICE TO MEET YOU. HOW ARE YOU?
DID YOU SAY YOUR NAME WAS FUCK?
WHAT THE HELL KIND OF NAME IS THAT?
WELL, MY PAPPY WANTED A BOY NAMED SUE SITUATION, BUT WAS WORRIED NAMING A BOY AFTER A GIRL MIGHT ALSO ARISE SOME HOMOSEXUAL TYPE SITUATIONS. SO HE FELT THIS WAS RIGHTFUL COMPROMISE.
DID IT WORK?
WELL, I'M TOUGH AS HELL BUT SEXUALLY AMBIGUOUS.
HAS OLD "CHEKHOV'S GUN" BROUGHT UP YOU TAKING HIS NUMBER ONE SPOT ALL THOSE YEARS AGO?
HE DID! WHAT'S THE DEAL WITH THAT GUY?
STY
HE'S THE PETTIEST MAN THAT EVER LIVED, THAT'S WHAT. IT'S BEEN A DECADE! GET OVER IT.
HERE YOU GO. THANKS, PAL!
THX DAYB! YOUR PAL, FUCK

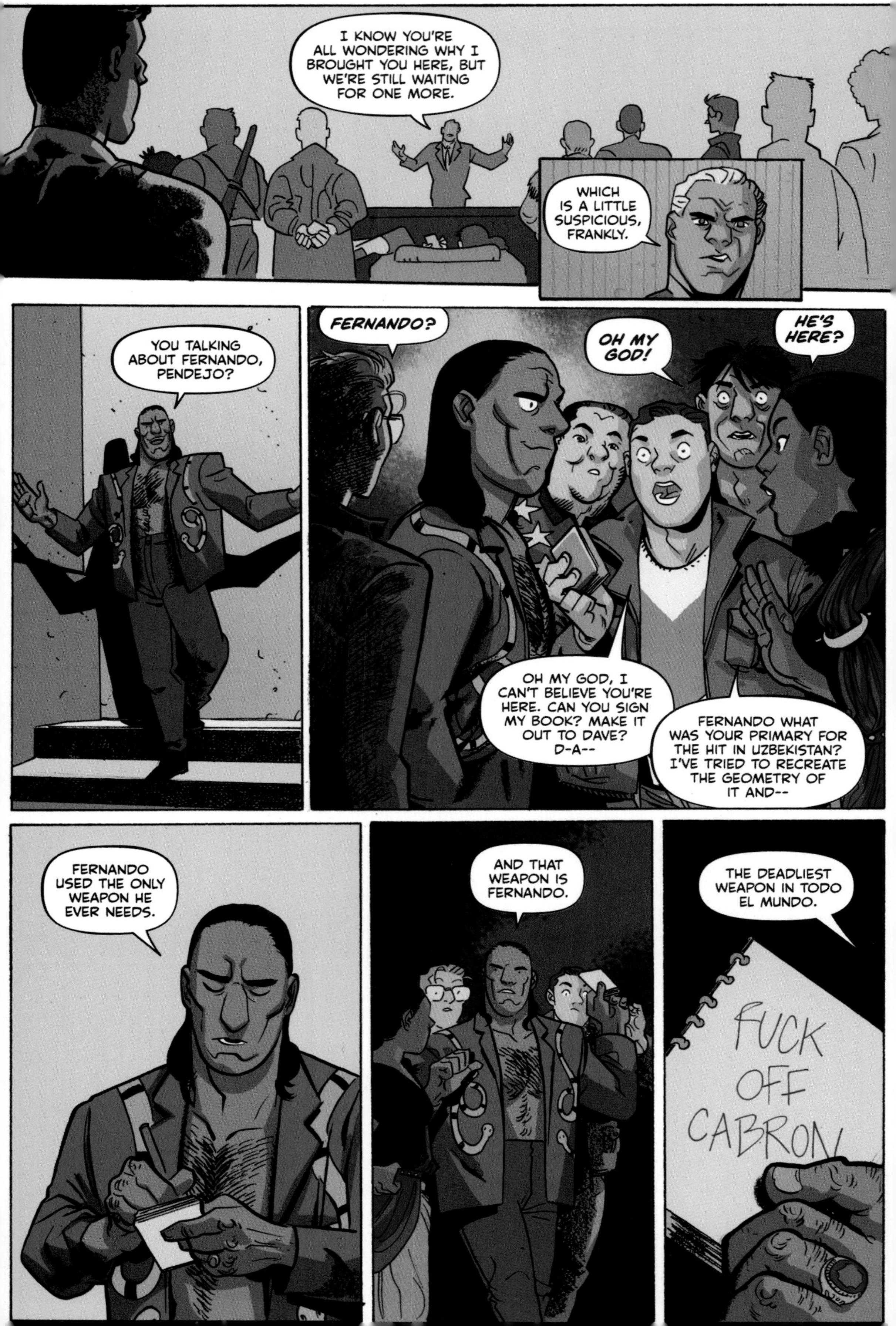
I KNOW YOU'RE ALL WONDERING WHY I BROUGHT YOU HERE, BUT WE'RE STILL WAITING FOR ONE MORE.
WHICH IS A LITTLE SUSPICIOUS, FRANKLY.
YOU TALKING ABOUT FERNANDO, PENDEJO?
FERNANDO?
OH MY GOD!
HE'S HERE?
OH MY GOD, I CAN'T BELIEVE YOU'RE HERE. CAN YOU SIGN MY BOOK? MAKE IT OUT TO DAVE? D-A--
FERNANDO WHAT WAS YOUR PRIMARY FOR THE HIT IN UZBEKISTAN? I'VE TRIED TO RECREATE THE GEOMETRY OF IT AND--
FERNANDO USED THE ONLY WEAPON HE EVER NEEDS.
AND THAT WEAPON IS FERNANDO.
THE DEADLIEST WEAPON IN TODO EL MUNDO.
FUCK OFF CABRON

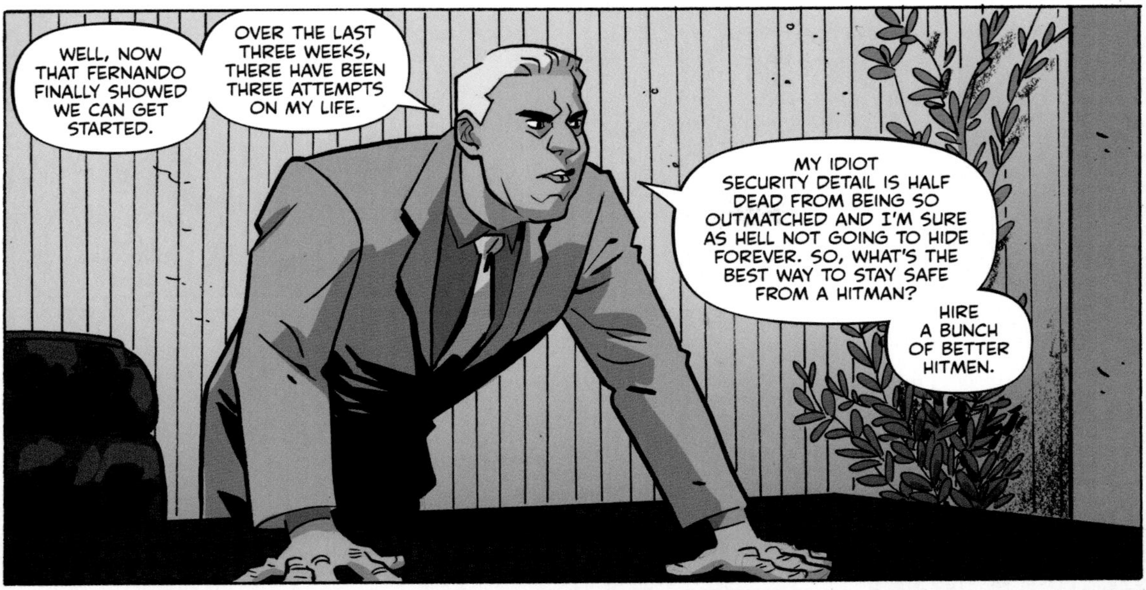
WELL, NOW THAT FERNANDO FINALLY SHOWED WE CAN GET STARTED.
OVER THE LAST THREE WEEKS, THERE HAVE BEEN THREE ATTEMPTS ON MY LIFE.
MY IDIOT SECURITY DETAIL IS HALF DEAD FROM BEING SO OUTMATCHED AND I'M SURE AS HELL NOT GOING TO HIDE FOREVER. SO, WHAT'S THE BEST WAY TO STAY SAFE FROM A HITMAN?
HIRE A BUNCH OF BETTER HITMEN.
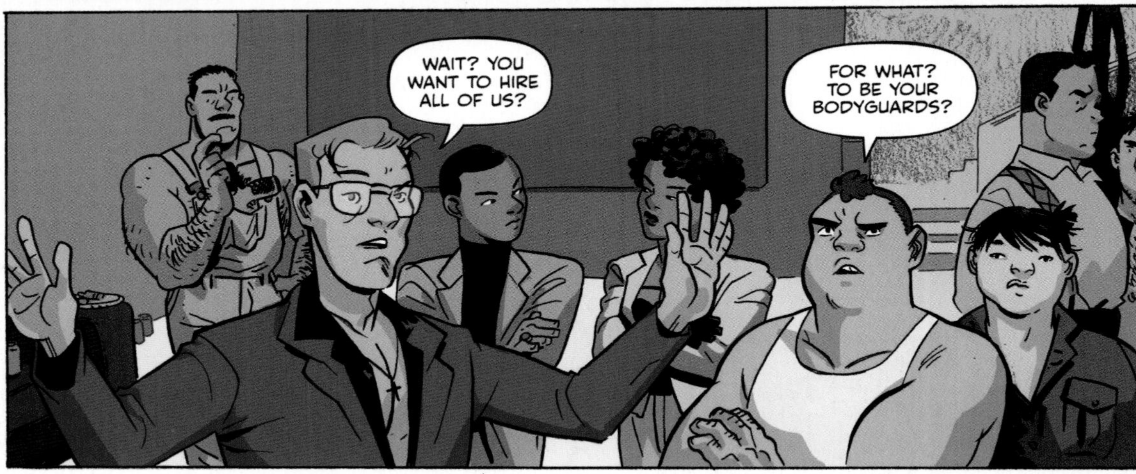
WAIT? YOU WANT TO HIRE ALL OF US?
FOR WHAT? TO BE YOUR BODYGUARDS?
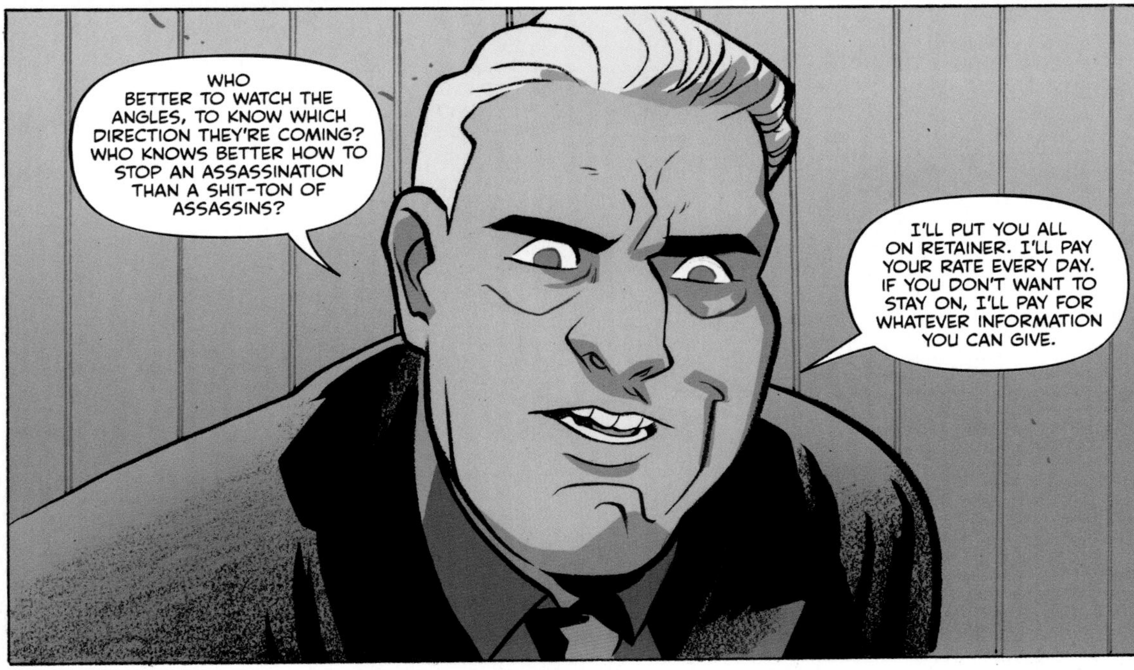
WHO BETTER TO WATCH THE ANGLES, TO KNOW WHICH DIRECTION THEY'RE COMING? WHO KNOWS BETTER HOW TO STOP AN ASSASSINATION THAN A SHIT-TON OF ASSASSINS?
I'LL PUT YOU ALL ON RETAINER. I'LL PAY YOUR RATE EVERY DAY. IF YOU DON'T WANT TO STAY ON, I'LL PAY FOR WHATEVER INFORMATION YOU CAN GIVE.

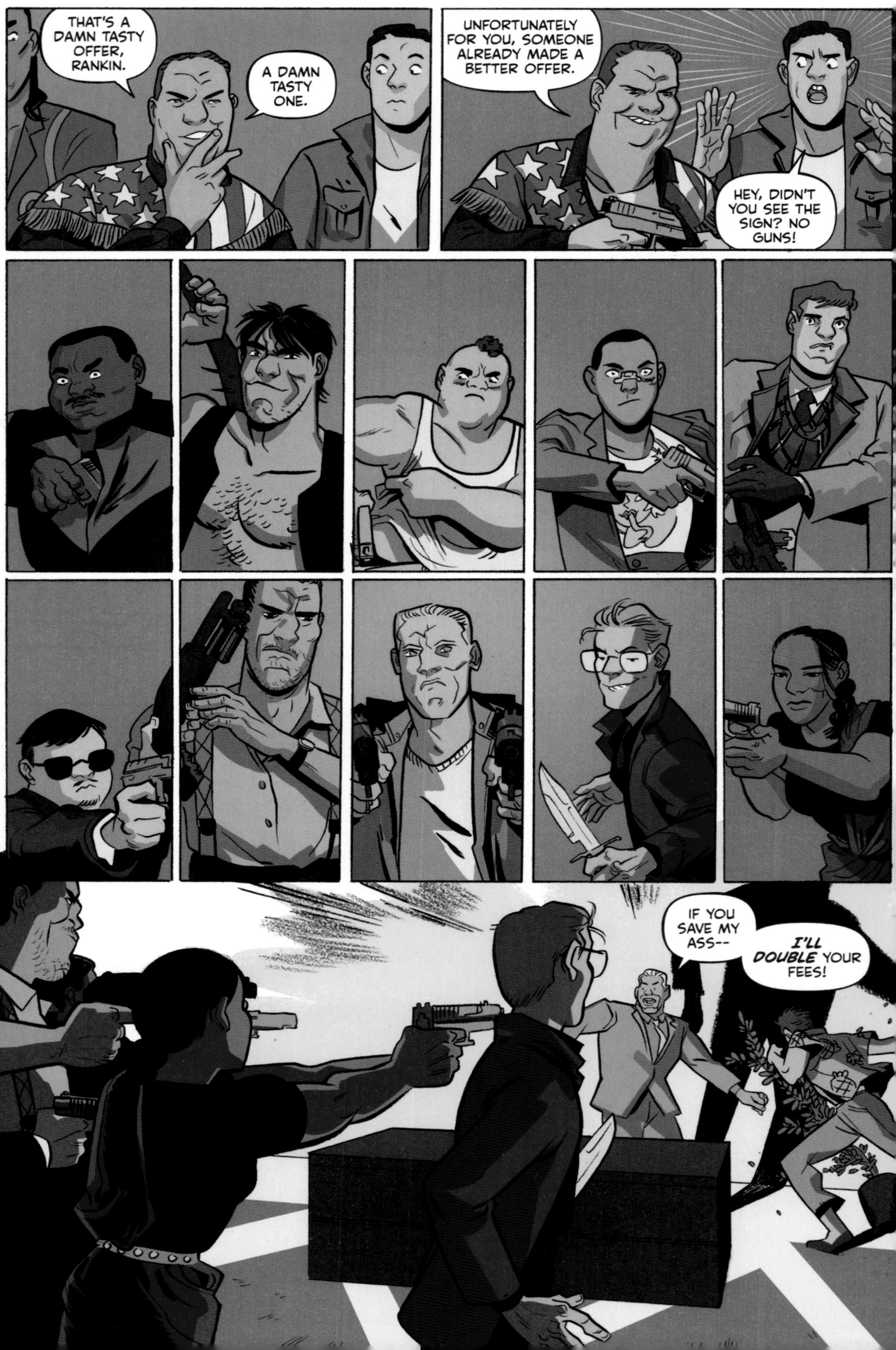
THAT'S A DAMN TASTY OFFER, RANKIN.
A DAMN TASTY ONE.
UNFORTUNATELY FOR YOU, SOMEONE ALREADY MADE A BETTER OFFER.
HEY, DIDN'T YOU SEE THE SIGN? NO GUNS!
IF YOU SAVE MY ASS--
I'LL DOUBLE YOUR FEES!

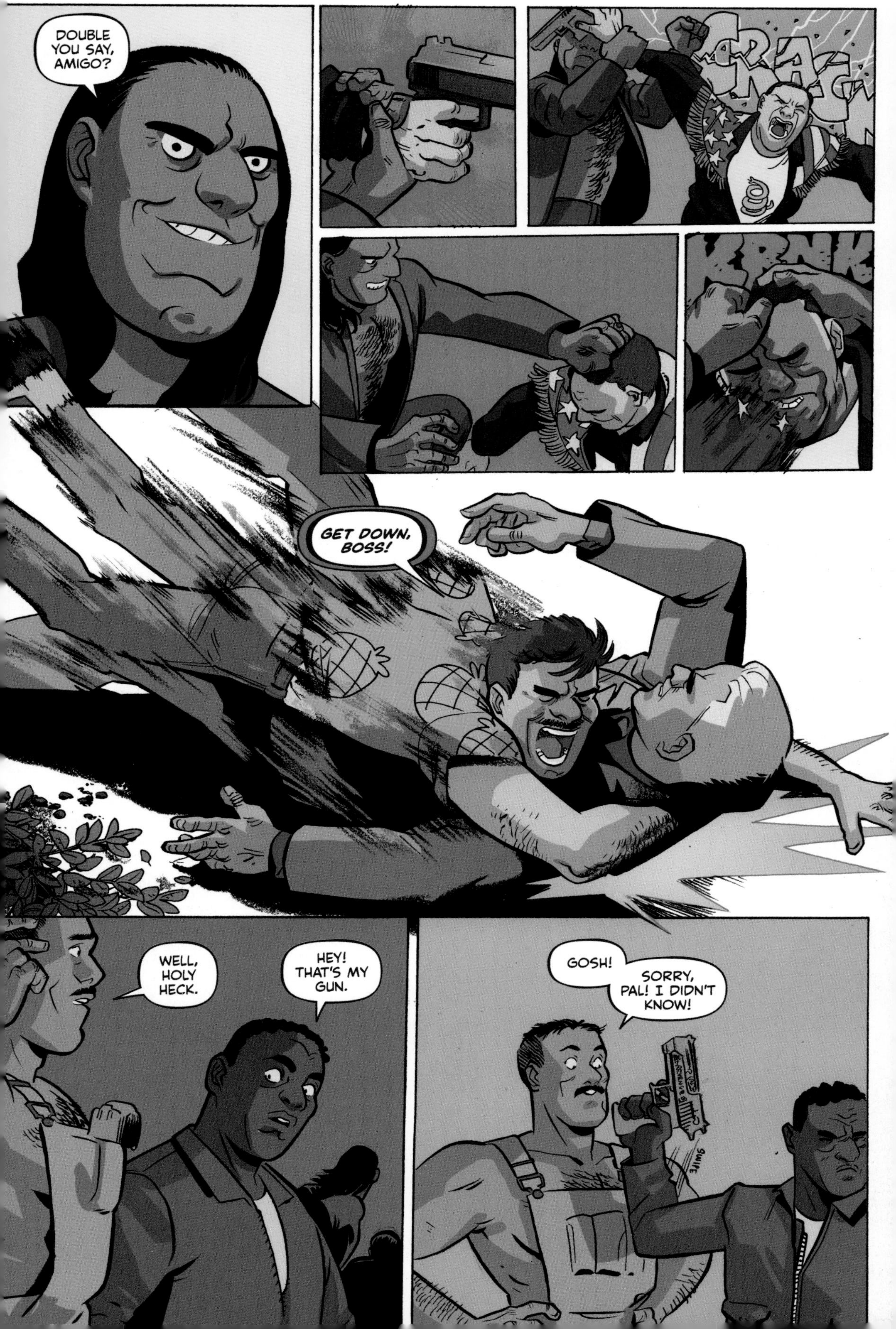
DOUBLE YOU SAY, AMIGO?
CRACK
KRNK
GET DOWN, BOSS!
WELL, HOLY HECK.
HEY! THAT'S MY GUN.
GOSH!
SORRY, PAL! I DIDN'T KNOW!

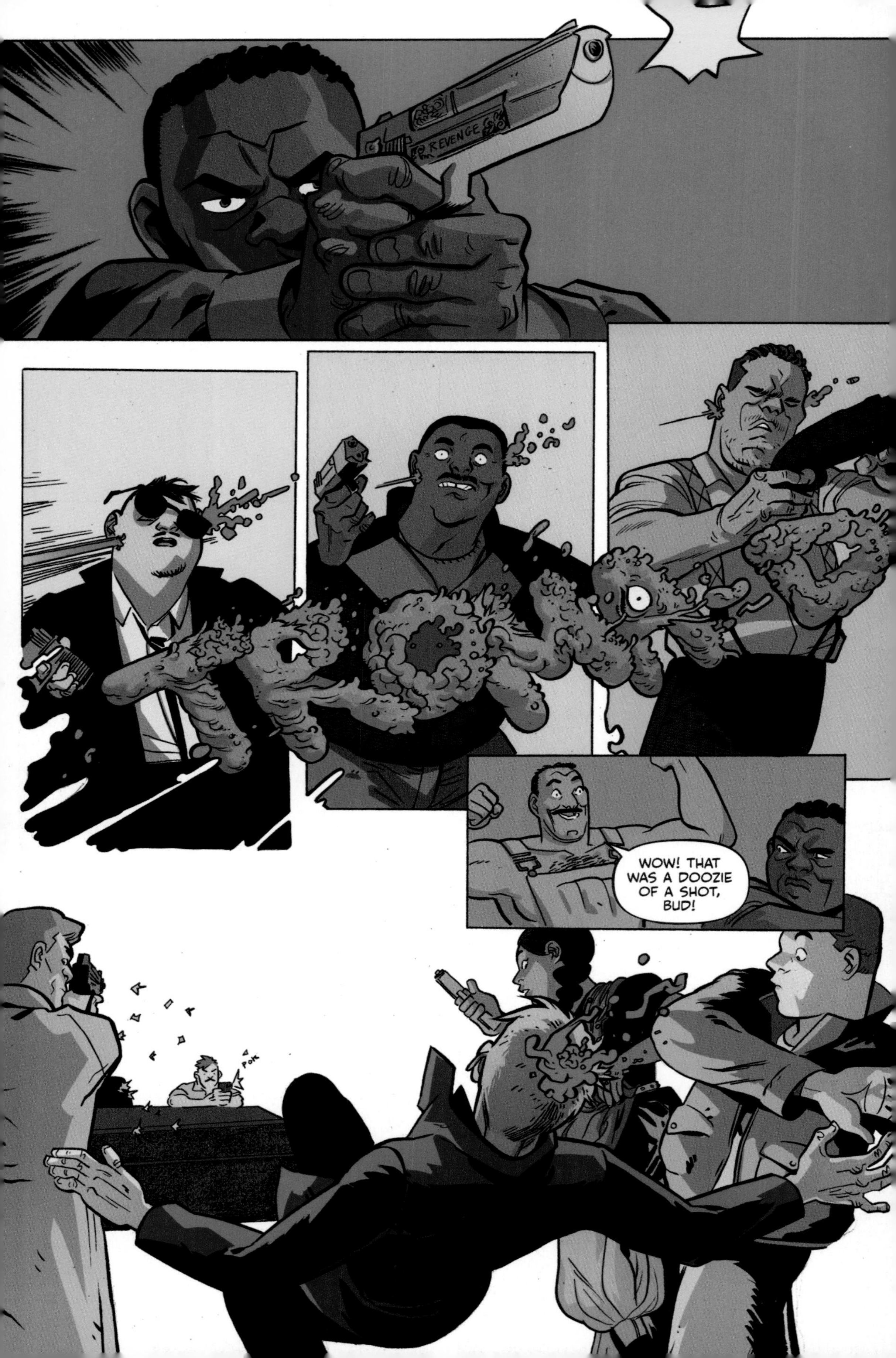
REVENGE
WOW! THAT WAS A DOOZIE OF A SHOT, BUD!
POK

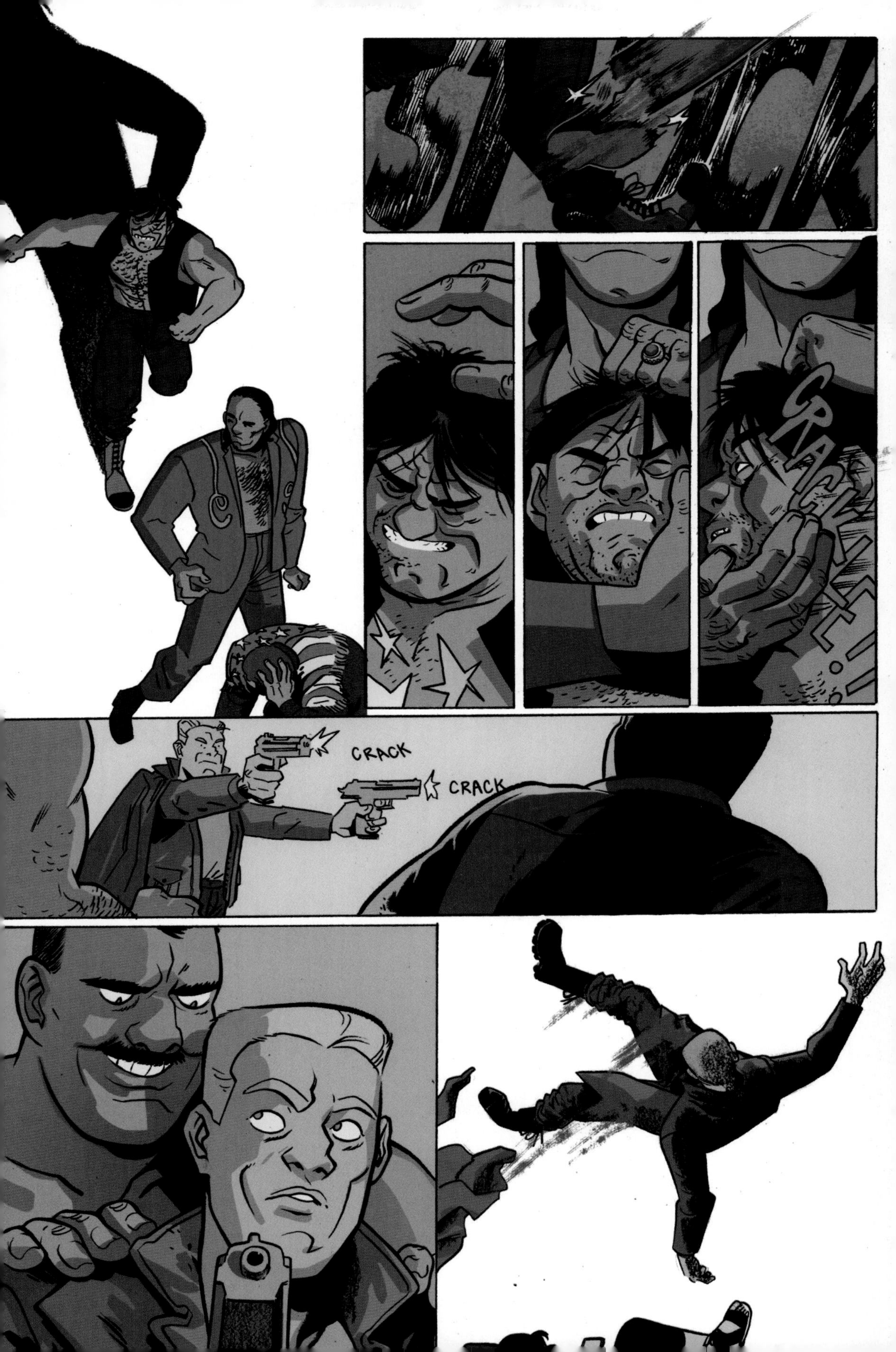
CRACKLL..!!
CRACK
CRACK

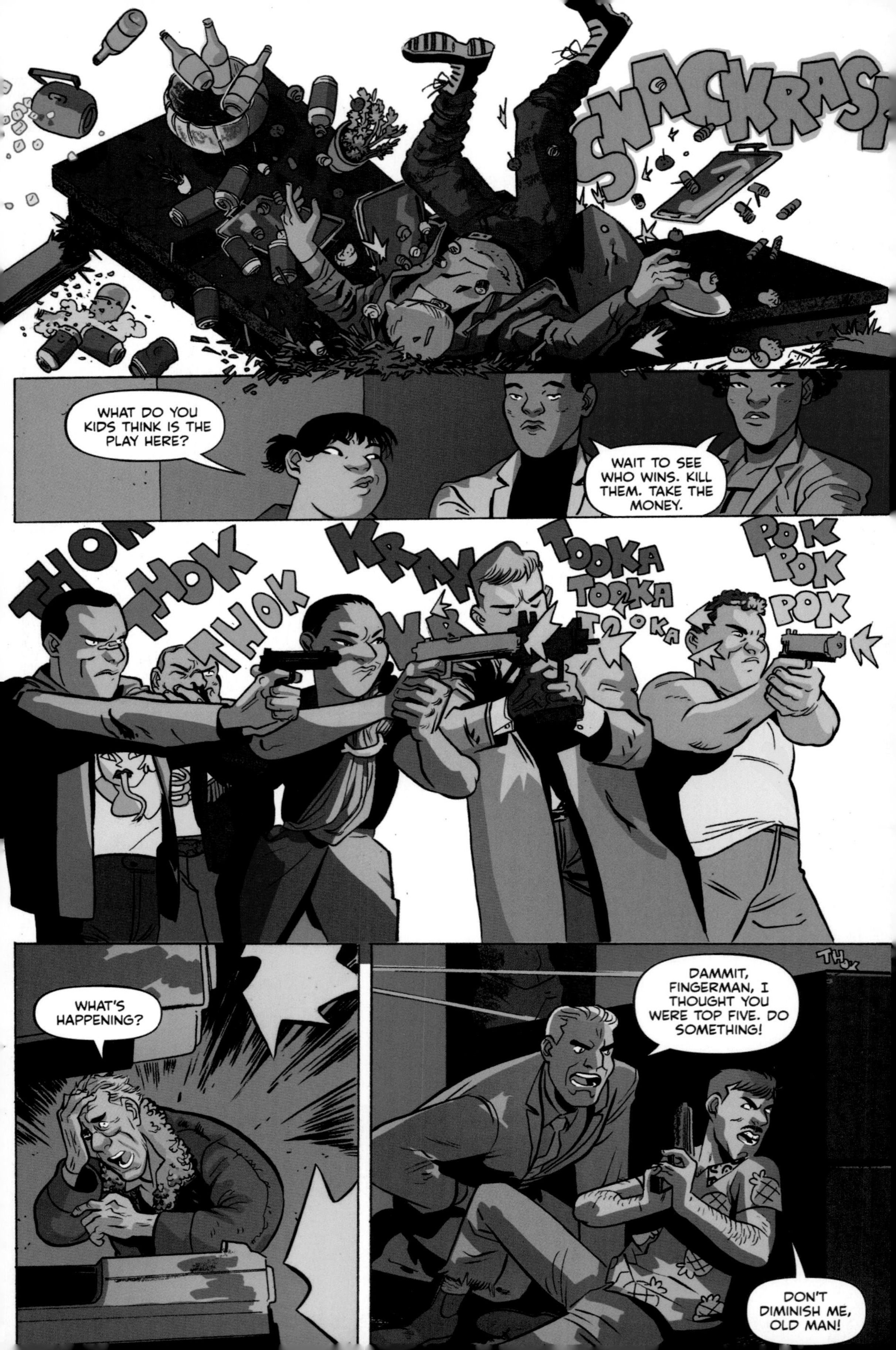
SMACKRASH
WHAT DO YOU KIDS THINK IS THE PLAY HERE?
WAIT TO SEE WHO WINS. KILL THEM. TAKE THE MONEY.
THOK THOK THOK
KRAY
TOOKA TOOKA TOOKA
POK POK POK
WHAT'S HAPPENING?
DAMMIT, FINGERMAN, I THOUGHT YOU WERE TOP FIVE. DO SOMETHING!
DON'T DIMINISH ME, OLD MAN!

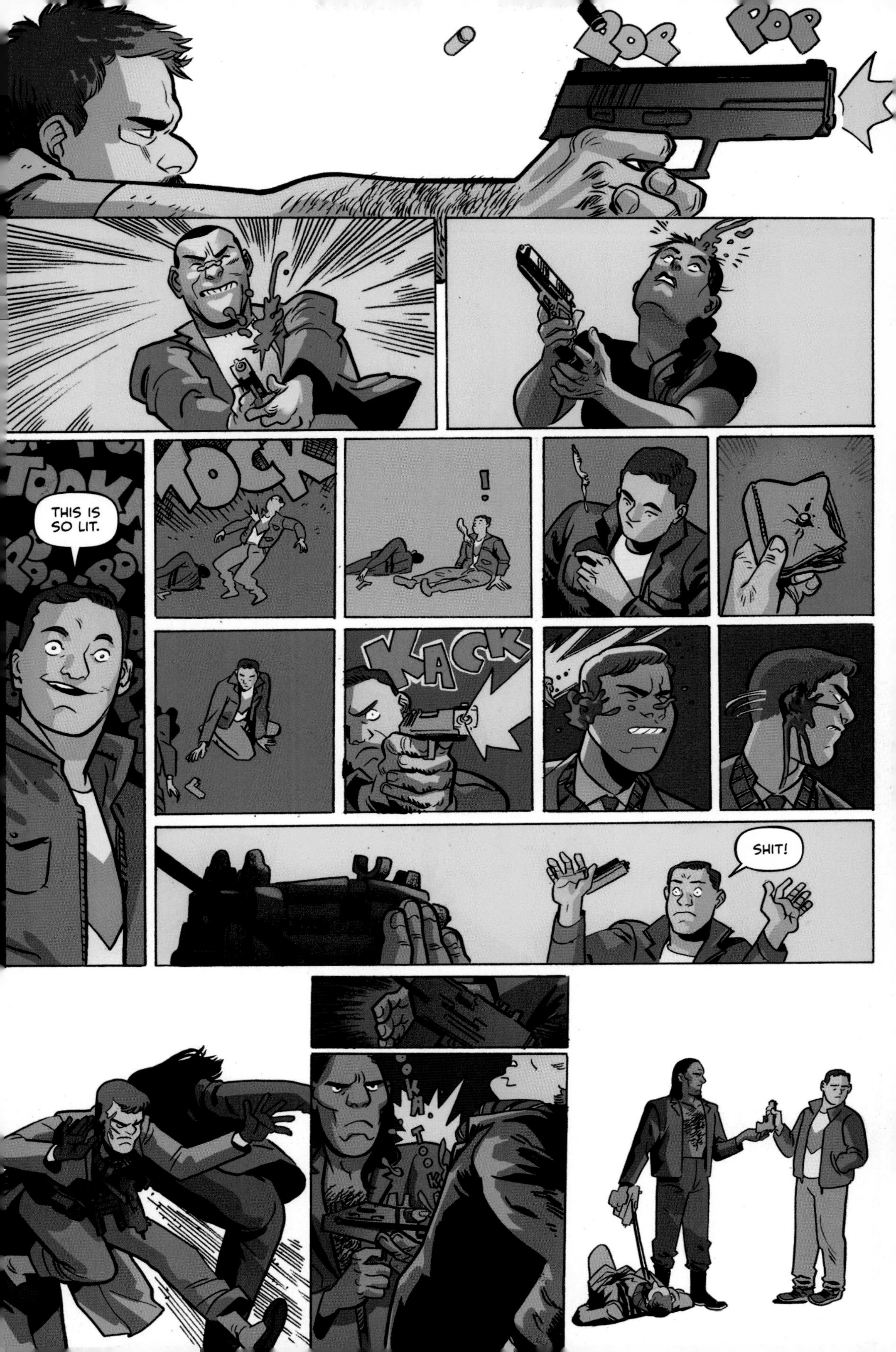
POP
POP
THIS IS SO LIT.
!
KACK
SHIT!

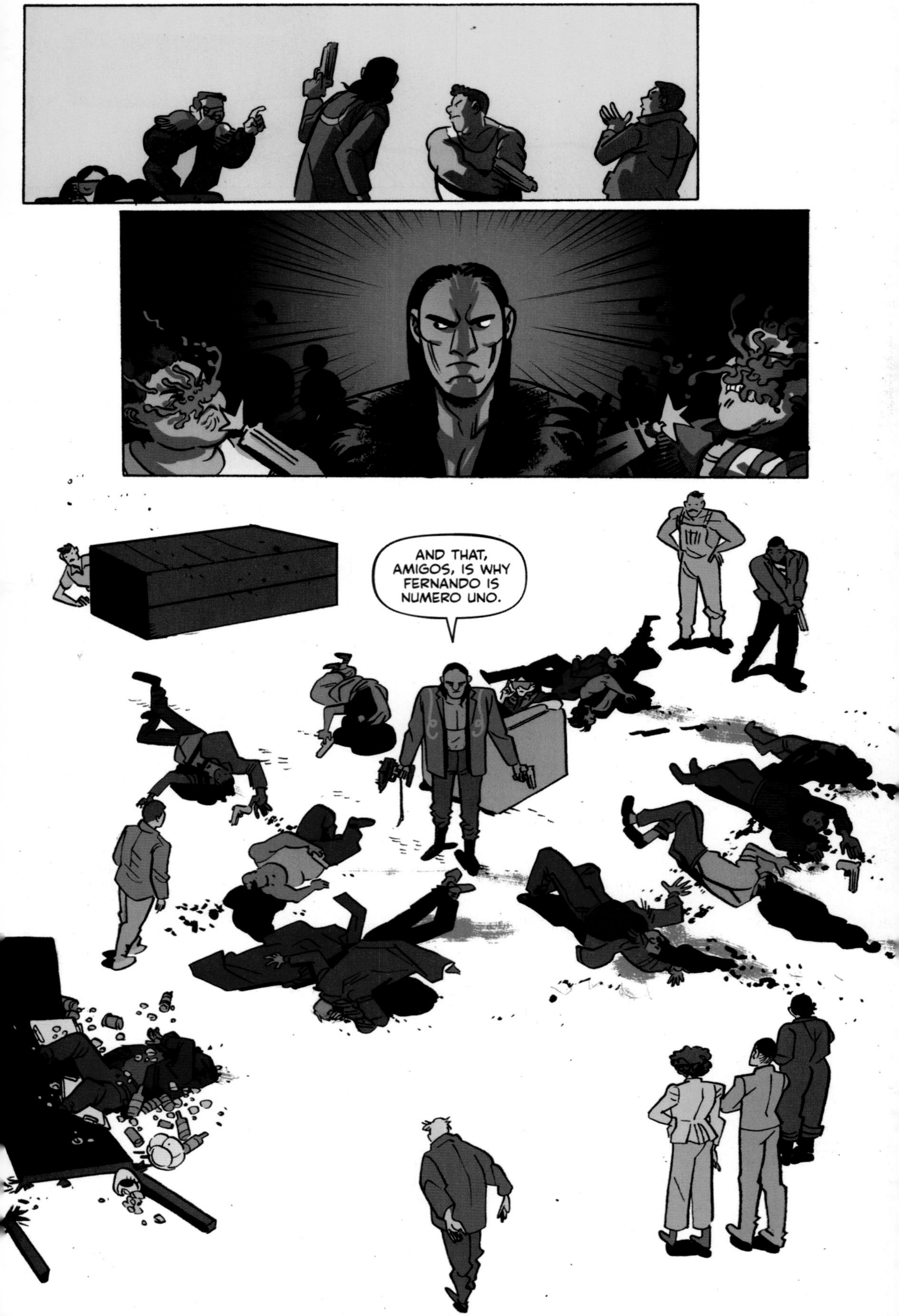
AND THAT, AMIGOS, IS WHY FERNANDO IS NUMERO UNO.

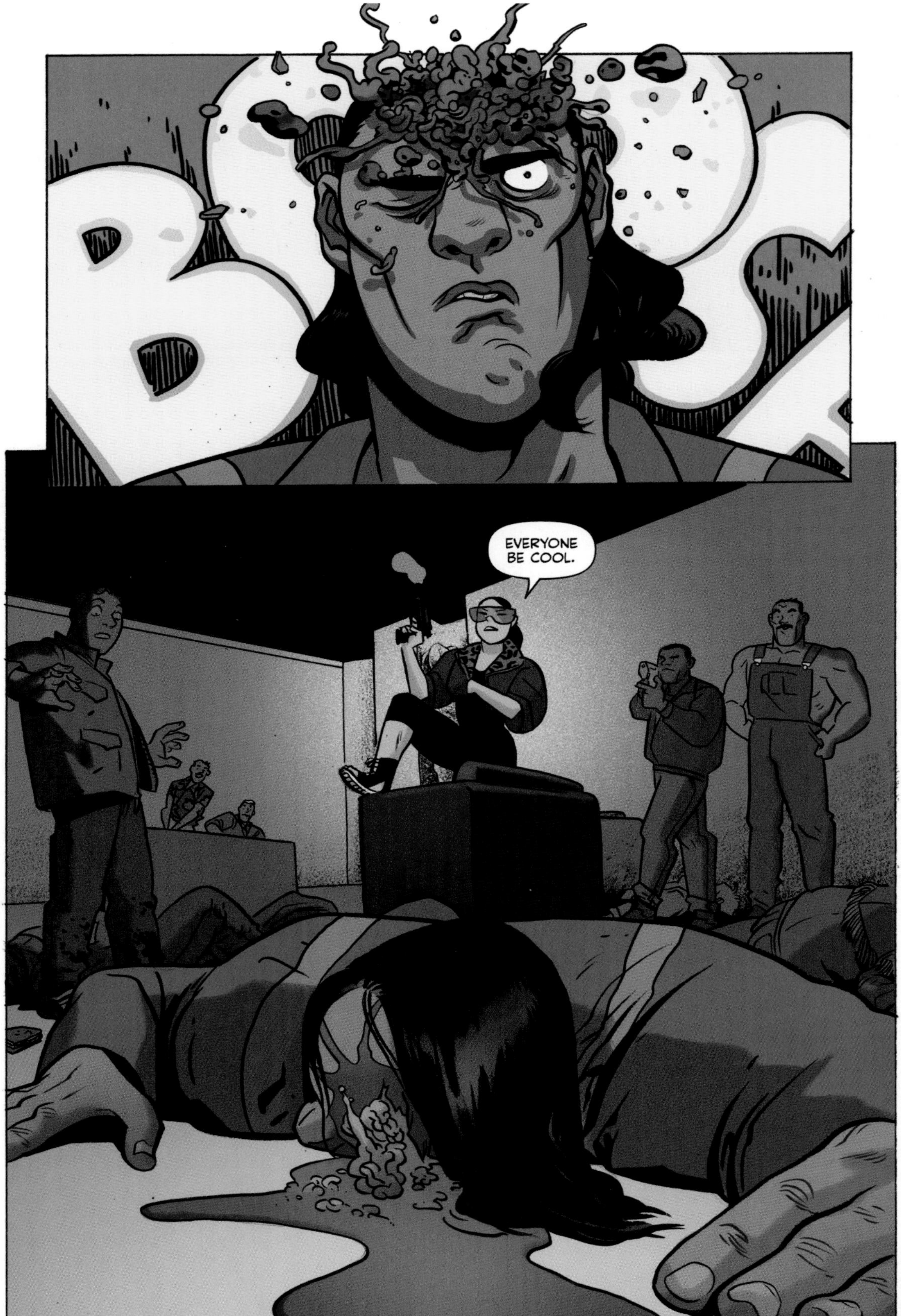
EVERYONE BE COOL.

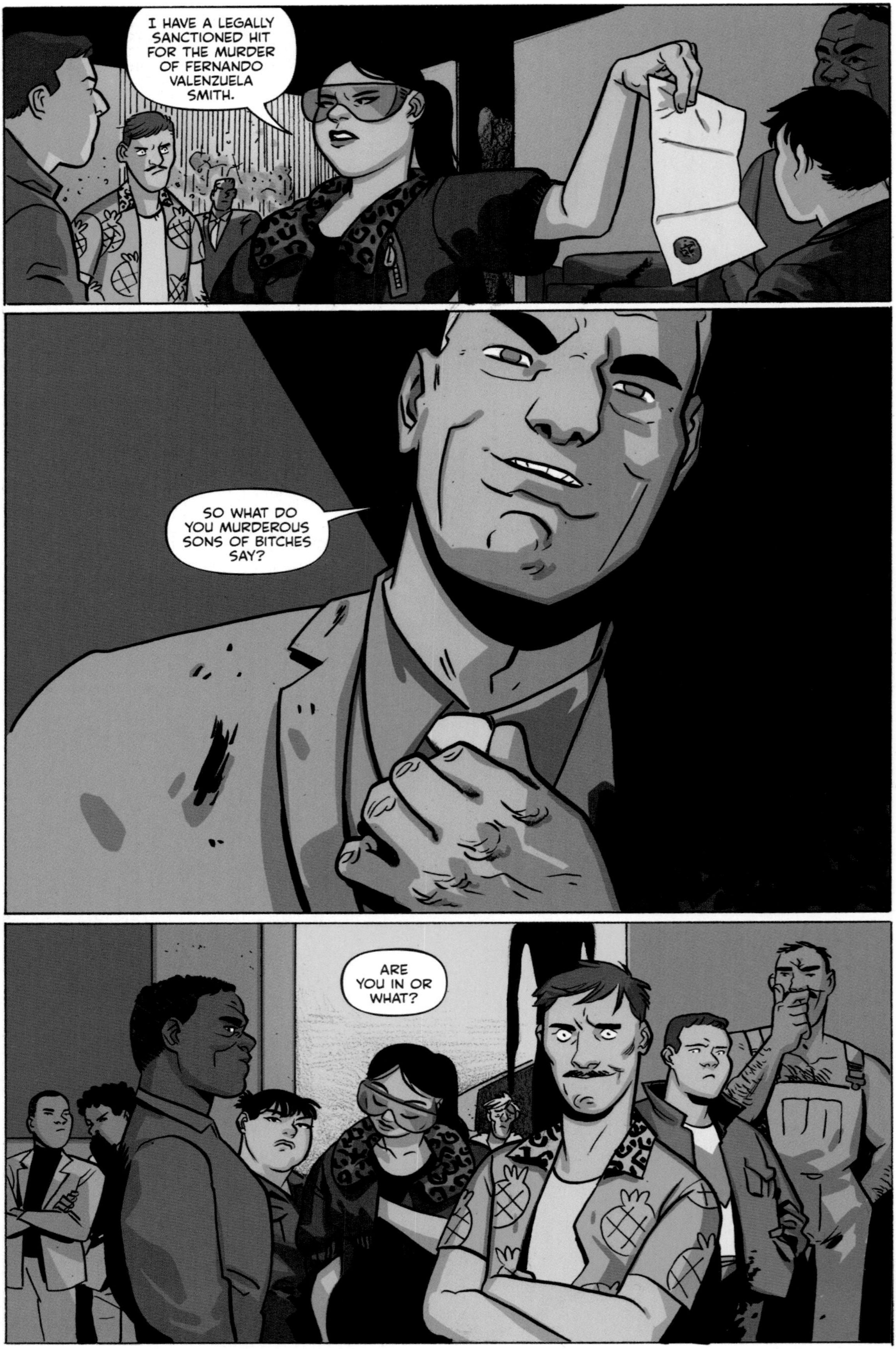
I HAVE A LEGALLY SANCTIONED HIT FOR THE MURDER OF FERNANDO VALENZUELA SMITH.
SO WHAT DO YOU MURDEROUS SONS OF BITCHES SAY?
ARE YOU IN OR WHAT?

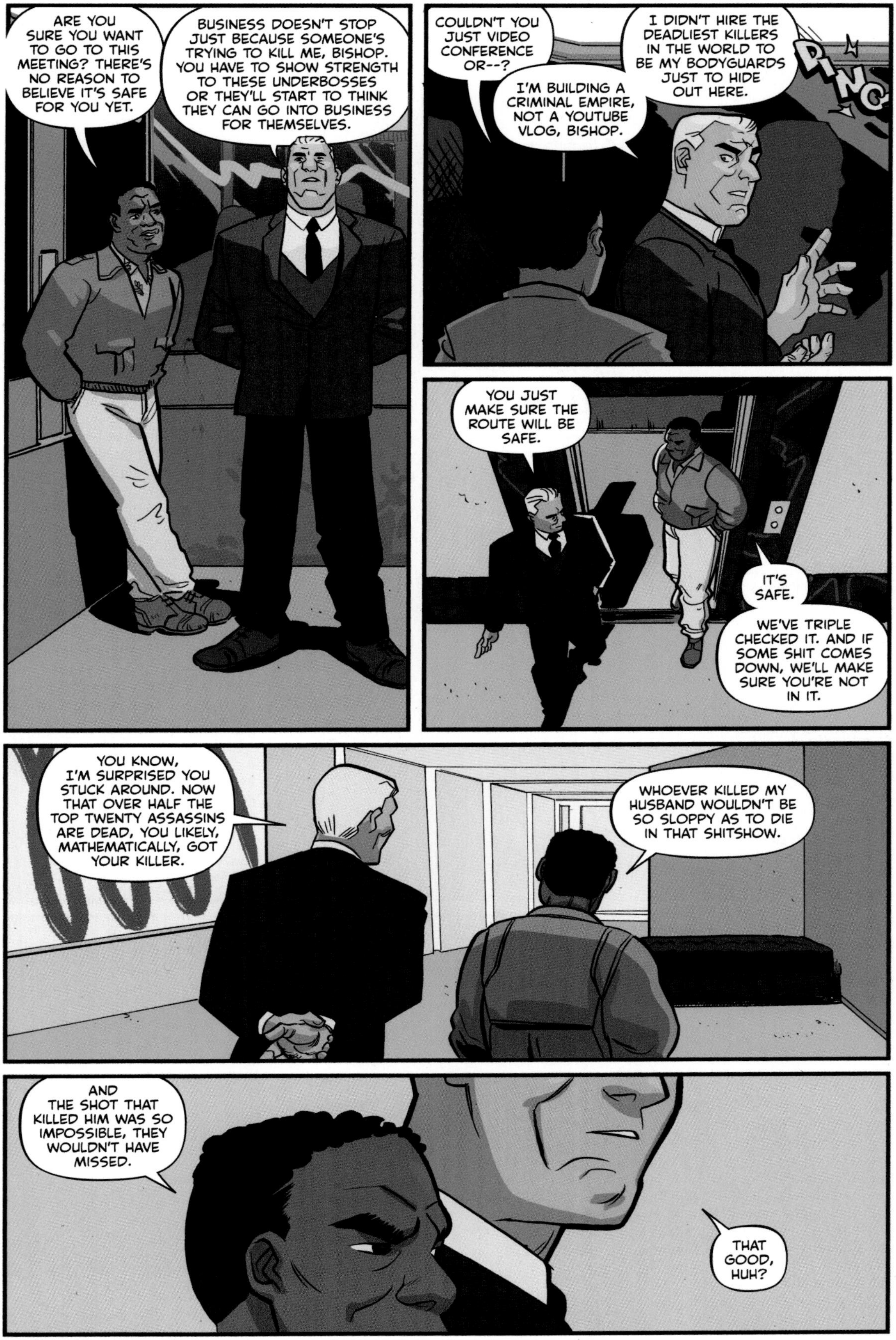
ARE YOU SURE YOU WANT TO GO TO THIS MEETING? THERE'S NO REASON TO BELIEVE IT'S SAFE FOR YOU YET.
BUSINESS DOESN'T STOP JUST BECAUSE SOMEONE'S TRYING TO KILL ME, BISHOP. YOU HAVE TO SHOW STRENGTH TO THESE UNDERBOSSES OR THEY'LL START TO THINK THEY CAN GO INTO BUSINESS FOR THEMSELVES.
COULDN'T YOU JUST VIDEO CONFERENCE OR--?
I'M BUILDING A CRIMINAL EMPIRE, NOT A YOUTUBE VLOG, BISHOP.
I DIDN'T HIRE THE DEADLIEST KILLERS IN THE WORLD TO BE MY BODYGUARDS JUST TO HIDE OUT HERE.
DING
YOU JUST MAKE SURE THE ROUTE WILL BE SAFE.
IT'S SAFE.
WE'VE TRIPLE CHECKED IT. AND IF SOME SHIT COMES DOWN, WE'LL MAKE SURE YOU'RE NOT IN IT.
YOU KNOW, I'M SURPRISED YOU STUCK AROUND. NOW THAT OVER HALF THE TOP TWENTY ASSASSINS ARE DEAD, YOU LIKELY, MATHEMATICALLY, GOT YOUR KILLER.
WHOEVER KILLED MY HUSBAND WOULDN'T BE SO SLOPPY AS TO DIE IN THAT SHITSHOW.
AND THE SHOT THAT KILLED HIM WAS SO IMPOSSIBLE, THEY WOULDN'T HAVE MISSED.
THAT GOOD, HUH?

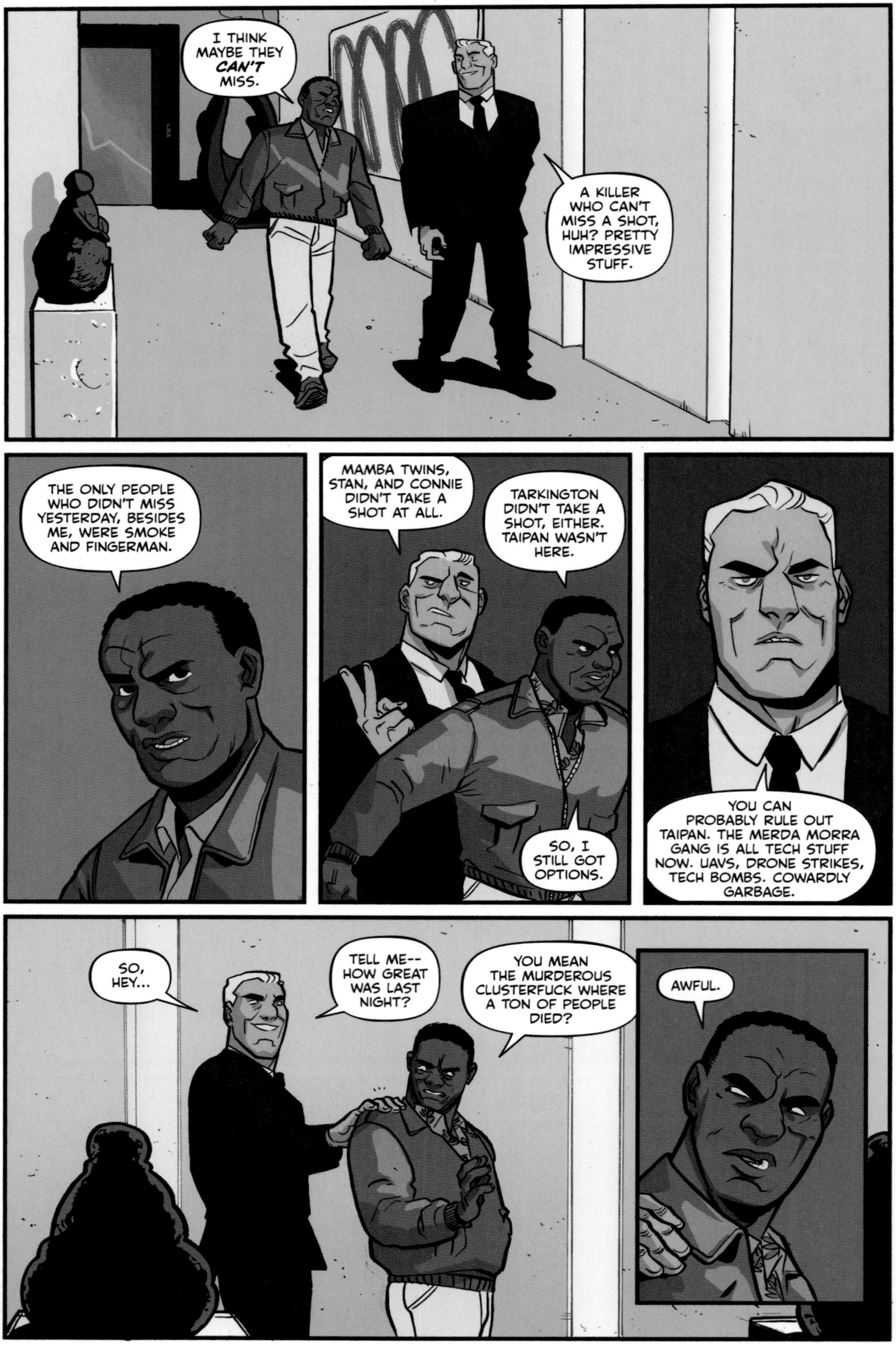
I THINK MAYBE THEY *CAN'T* MISS.
A KILLER WHO CAN'T MISS A SHOT, HUH? PRETTY IMPRESSIVE STUFF.
THE ONLY PEOPLE WHO DIDN'T MISS YESTERDAY, BESIDES ME, WERE SMOKE AND FINGERMAN.
MAMBA TWINS, STAN, AND CONNIE DIDN'T TAKE A SHOT AT ALL.
TARKINGTON DIDN'T TAKE A SHOT, EITHER. TAIPAN WASN'T HERE.
SO, I STILL GOT OPTIONS.
YOU CAN PROBABLY RULE OUT TAIPAN. THE MERDA MORRA GANG IS ALL TECH STUFF NOW. UAVS, DRONE STRIKES, TECH BOMBS. COWARDLY GARBAGE.
SO, HEY...
TELL ME-- HOW GREAT WAS LAST NIGHT?
YOU MEAN THE MURDEROUS CLUSTERFUCK WHERE A TON OF PEOPLE DIED?
AWFUL.

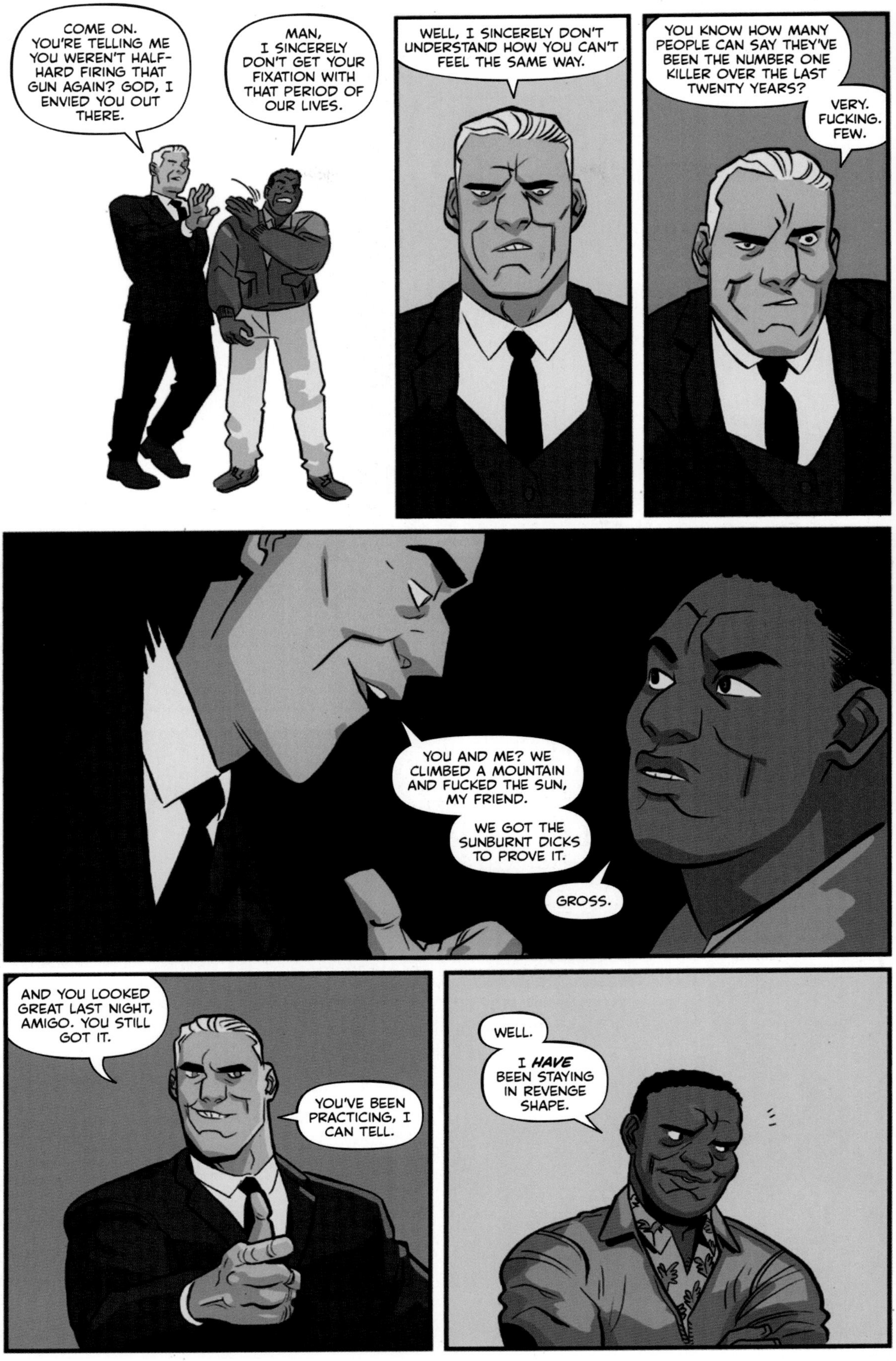
COME ON. YOU'RE TELLING ME YOU WEREN'T HALF-HARD FIRING THAT GUN AGAIN? GOD, I ENVIED YOU OUT THERE.
MAN, I SINCERELY DON'T GET YOUR FIXATION WITH THAT PERIOD OF OUR LIVES.
WELL, I SINCERELY DON'T UNDERSTAND HOW YOU CAN'T FEEL THE SAME WAY.
YOU KNOW HOW MANY PEOPLE CAN SAY THEY'VE BEEN THE NUMBER ONE KILLER OVER THE LAST TWENTY YEARS?
VERY. FUCKING. FEW.
YOU AND ME? WE CLIMBED A MOUNTAIN AND FUCKED THE SUN, MY FRIEND.
WE GOT THE SUNBURNT DICKS TO PROVE IT.
GROSS.
AND YOU LOOKED GREAT LAST NIGHT, AMIGO. YOU STILL GOT IT.
YOU'VE BEEN PRACTICING, I CAN TELL.
WELL.
I ***HAVE*** BEEN STAYING IN REVENGE SHAPE.

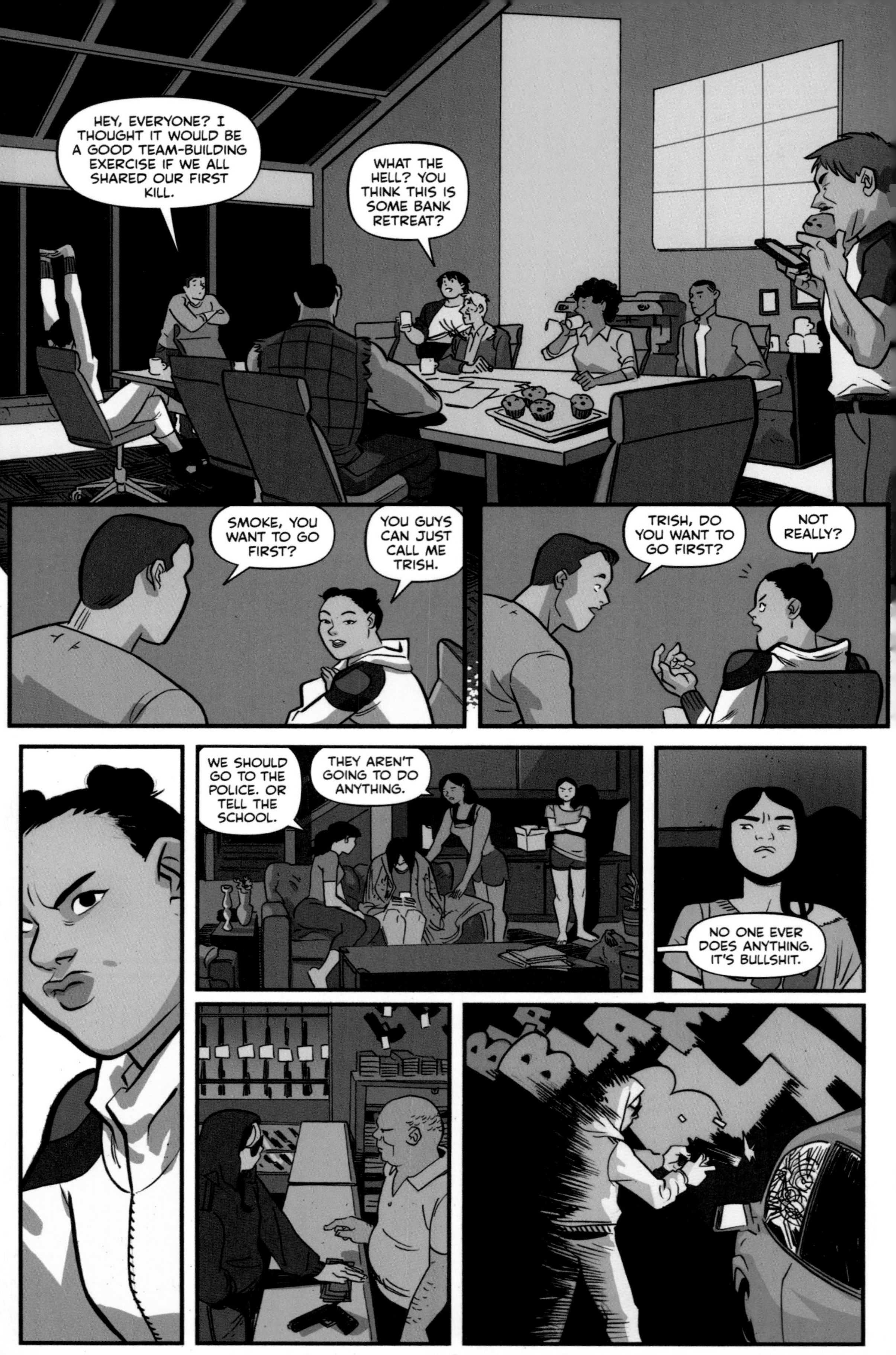

HEY, EVERYONE? I THOUGHT IT WOULD BE A GOOD TEAM-BUILDING EXERCISE IF WE ALL SHARED OUR FIRST KILL.
WHAT THE HELL? YOU THINK THIS IS SOME BANK RETREAT?
SMOKE, YOU WANT TO GO FIRST?
YOU GUYS CAN JUST CALL ME TRISH.
TRISH, DO YOU WANT TO GO FIRST?
NOT REALLY?
WE SHOULD GO TO THE POLICE. OR TELL THE SCHOOL.
THEY AREN'T GOING TO DO ANYTHING.
NO ONE EVER DOES ANYTHING. IT'S BULLSHIT.

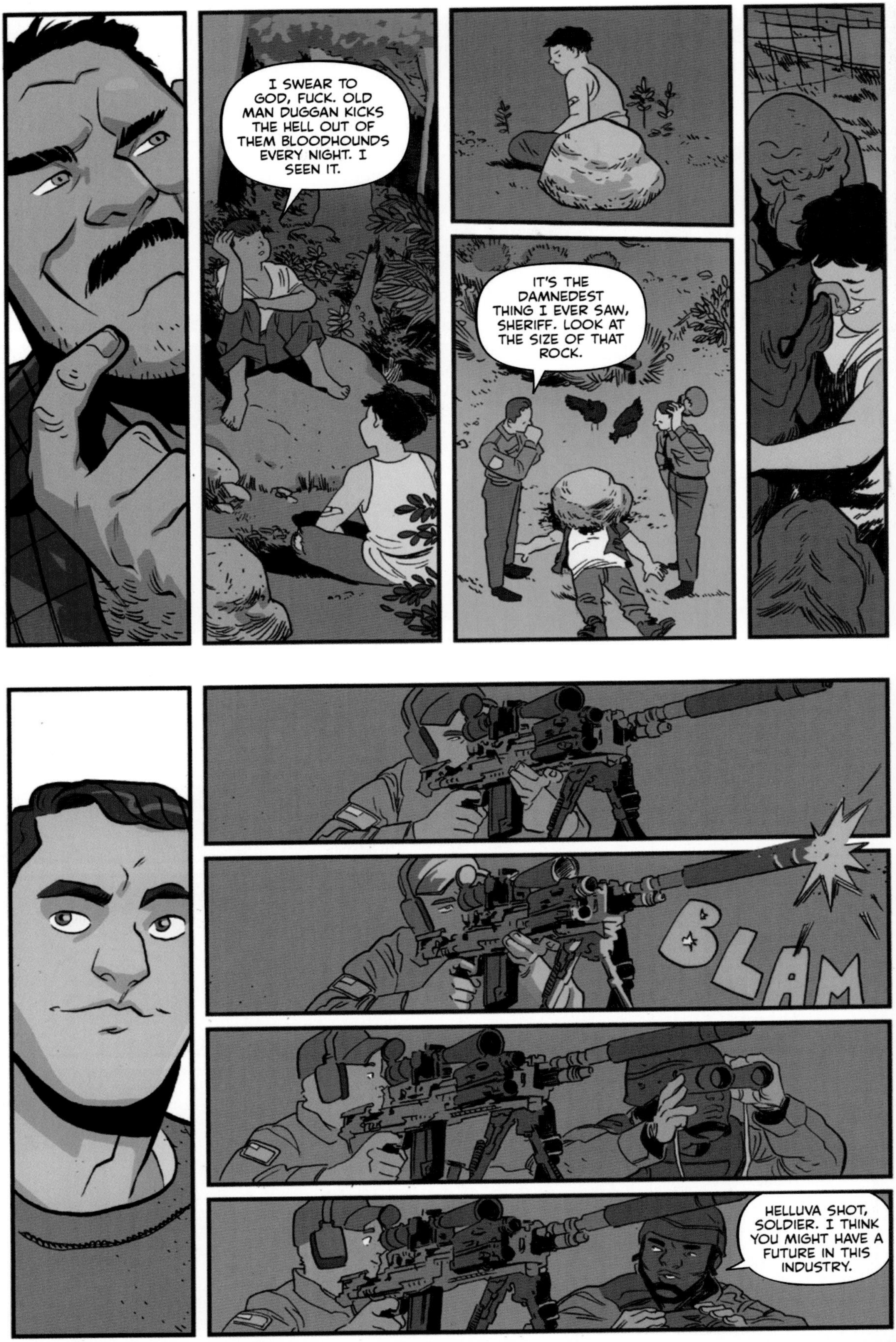
I SWEAR TO GOD, FUCK. OLD MAN DUGGAN KICKS THE HELL OUT OF THEM BLOODHOUNDS EVERY NIGHT. I SEEN IT.
IT'S THE DAMNEDEST THING I EVER SAW, SHERIFF. LOOK AT THE SIZE OF THAT ROCK.
BLAM
HELLUVA SHOT, SOLDIER. I THINK YOU MIGHT HAVE A FUTURE IN THIS INDUSTRY.

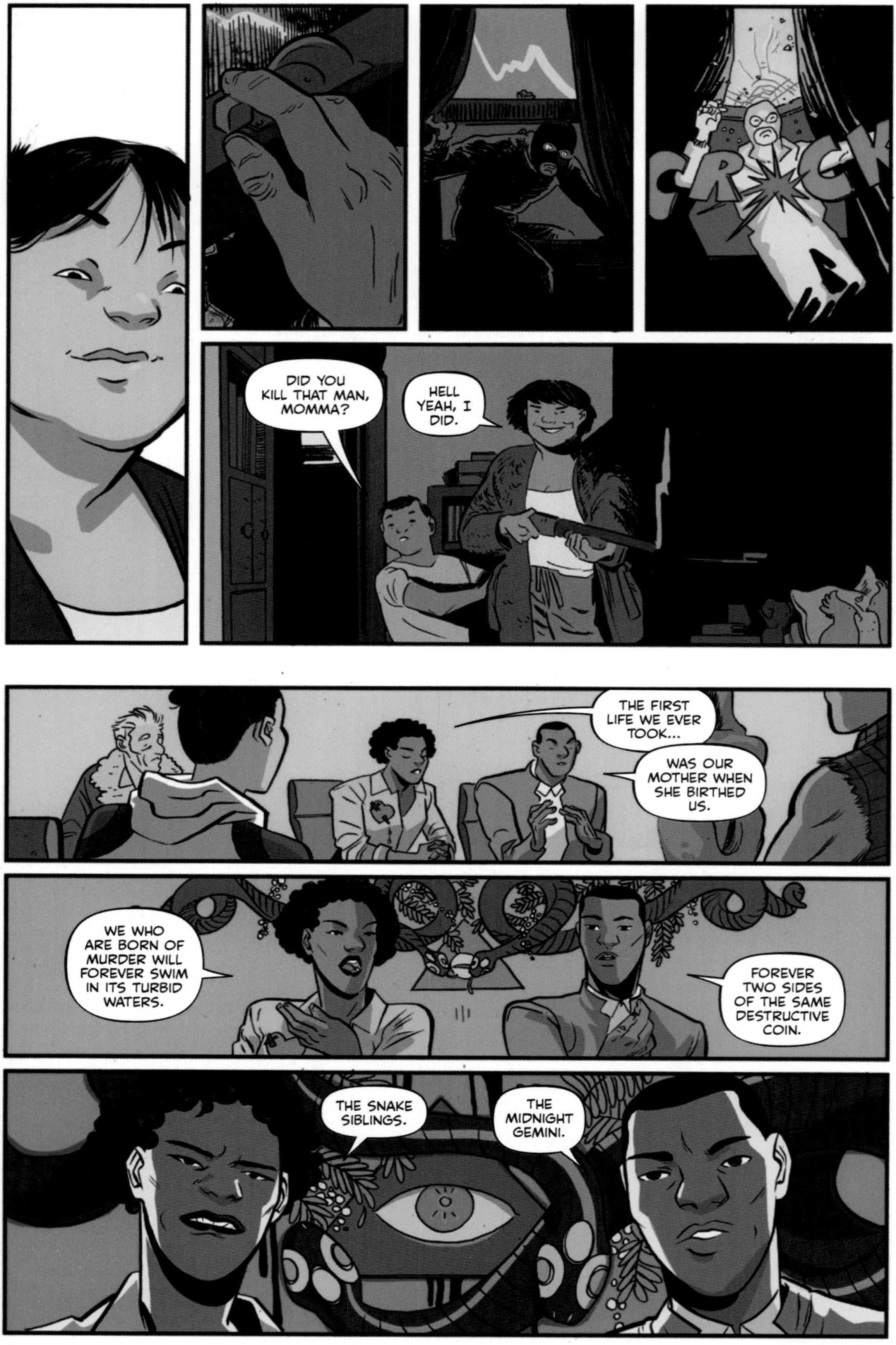
CRACK
DID YOU KILL THAT MAN, MOMMA?
HELL YEAH, I DID.
THE FIRST LIFE WE EVER TOOK...
WAS OUR MOTHER WHEN SHE BIRTHED US.
WE WHO ARE BORN OF MURDER WILL FOREVER SWIM IN ITS TURBID WATERS.
FOREVER TWO SIDES OF THE SAME DESTRUCTIVE COIN.
THE SNAKE SIBLINGS.
THE MIDNIGHT GEMINI.

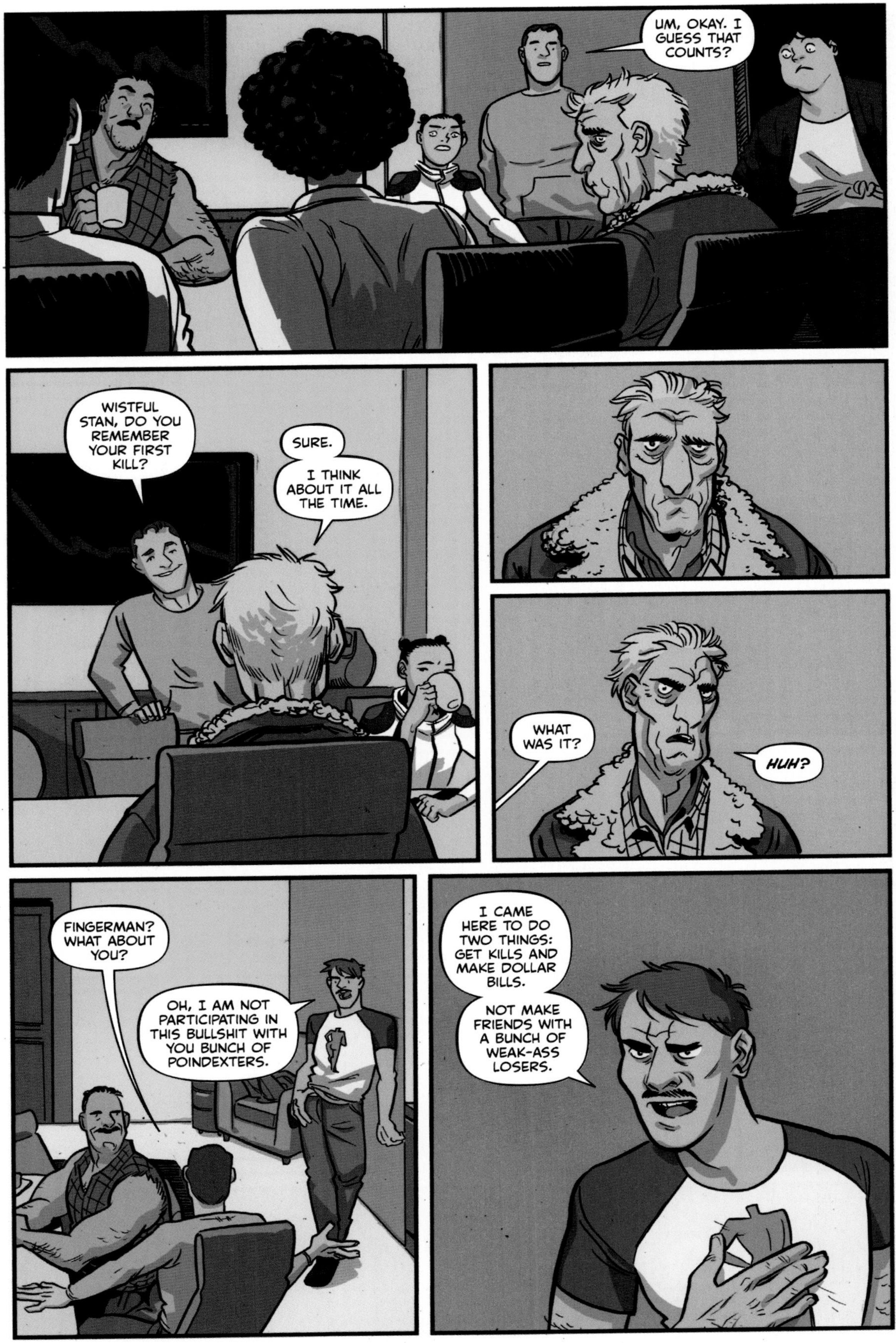
UM, OKAY. I GUESS THAT COUNTS?
WISTFUL STAN, DO YOU REMEMBER YOUR FIRST KILL?
SURE.
I THINK ABOUT IT ALL THE TIME.
WHAT WAS IT?
HUH?
FINGERMAN? WHAT ABOUT YOU?
OH, I AM NOT PARTICIPATING IN THIS BULLSHIT WITH YOU BUNCH OF POINDEXTERS.
I CAME HERE TO DO TWO THINGS: GET KILLS AND MAKE DOLLAR BILLS.
NOT MAKE FRIENDS WITH A BUNCH OF WEAK-ASS LOSERS.

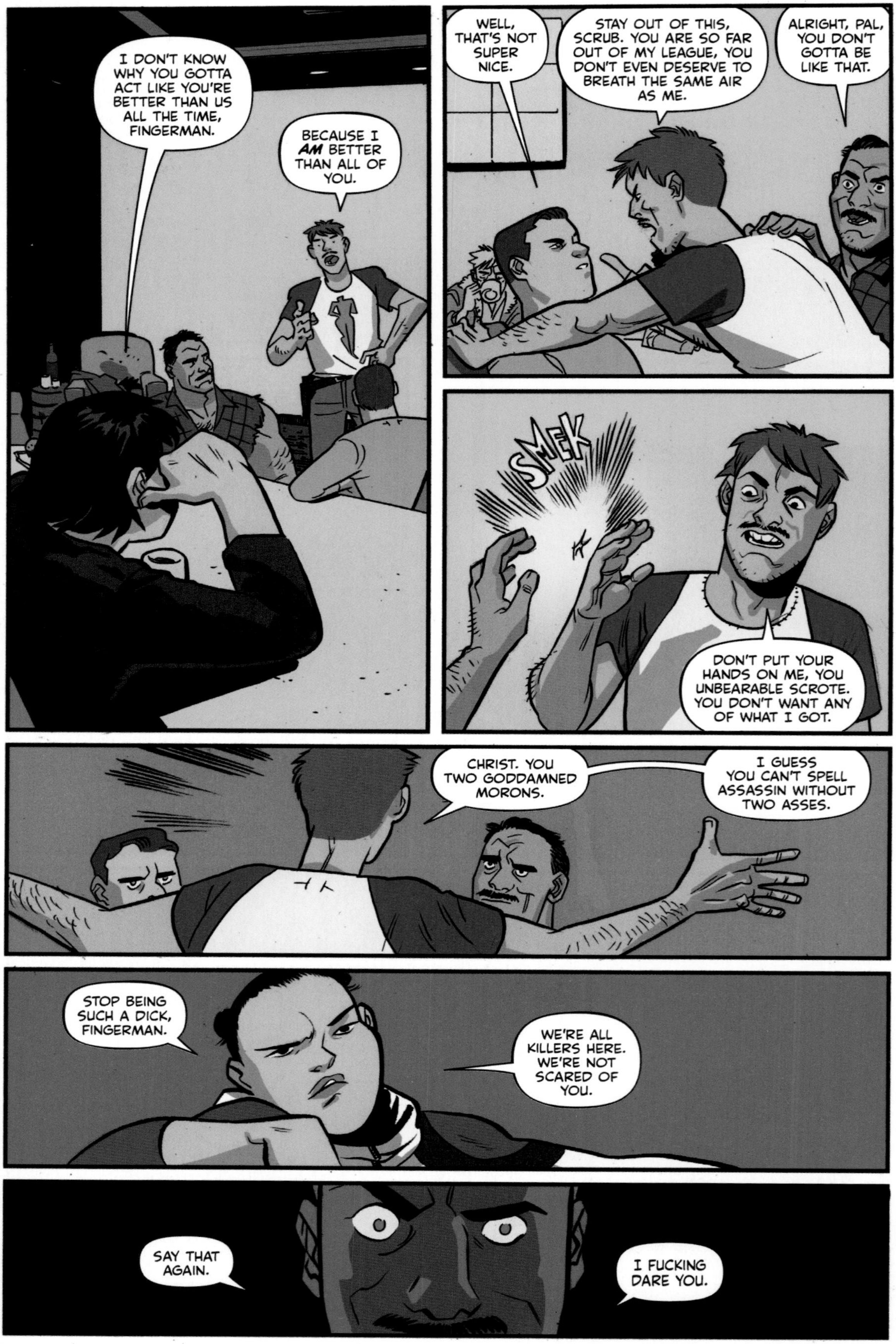
I DON'T KNOW WHY YOU GOTTA ACT LIKE YOU'RE BETTER THAN US ALL THE TIME, FINGERMAN.
BECAUSE I AM BETTER THAN ALL OF YOU.
WELL, THAT'S NOT SUPER NICE.
STAY OUT OF THIS, SCRUB. YOU ARE SO FAR OUT OF MY LEAGUE, YOU DON'T EVEN DESERVE TO BREATH THE SAME AIR AS ME.
ALRIGHT, PAL, YOU DON'T GOTTA BE LIKE THAT.
SMEK
DON'T PUT YOUR HANDS ON ME, YOU UNBEARABLE SCROTE. YOU DON'T WANT ANY OF WHAT I GOT.
CHRIST. YOU TWO GODDAMNED MORONS.
I GUESS YOU CAN'T SPELL ASSASSIN WITHOUT TWO ASSES.
STOP BEING SUCH A DICK, FINGERMAN.
WE'RE ALL KILLERS HERE. WE'RE NOT SCARED OF YOU.
SAY THAT AGAIN.
I FUCKING DARE YOU.

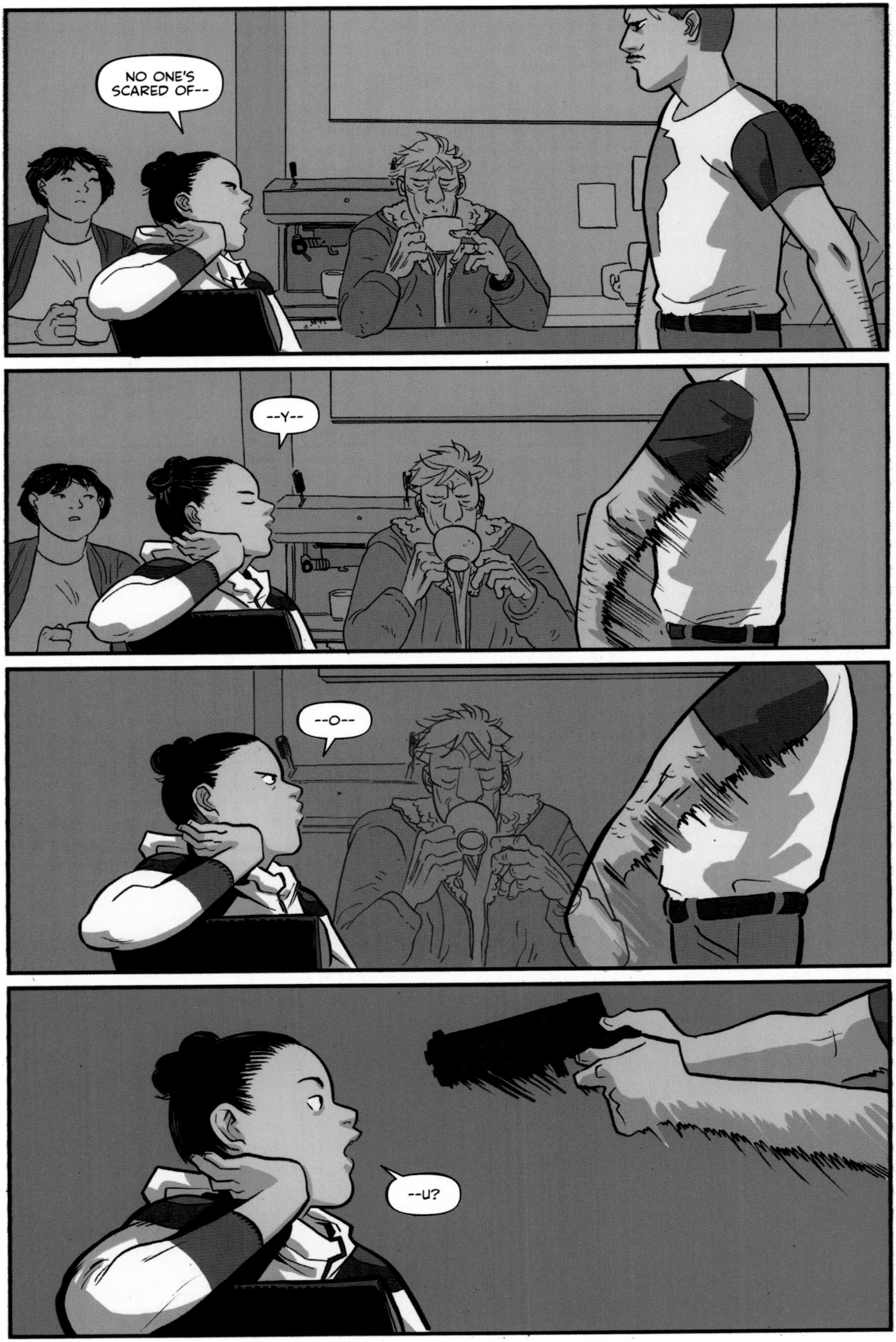
NO ONE'S SCARED OF--
--Y--
--O--
--U?

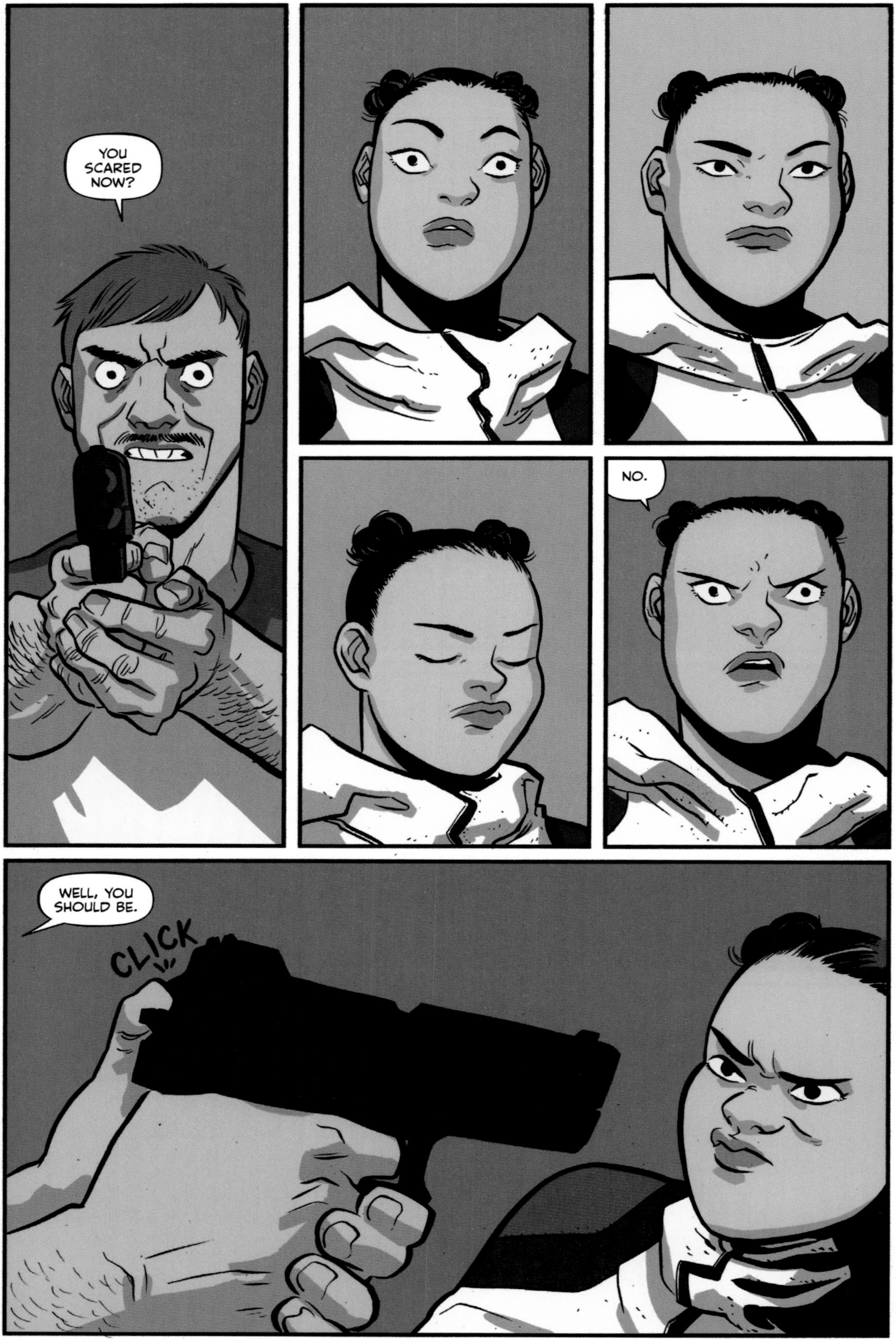
YOU SCARED NOW?
NO.
WELL, YOU SHOULD BE.
CLICK

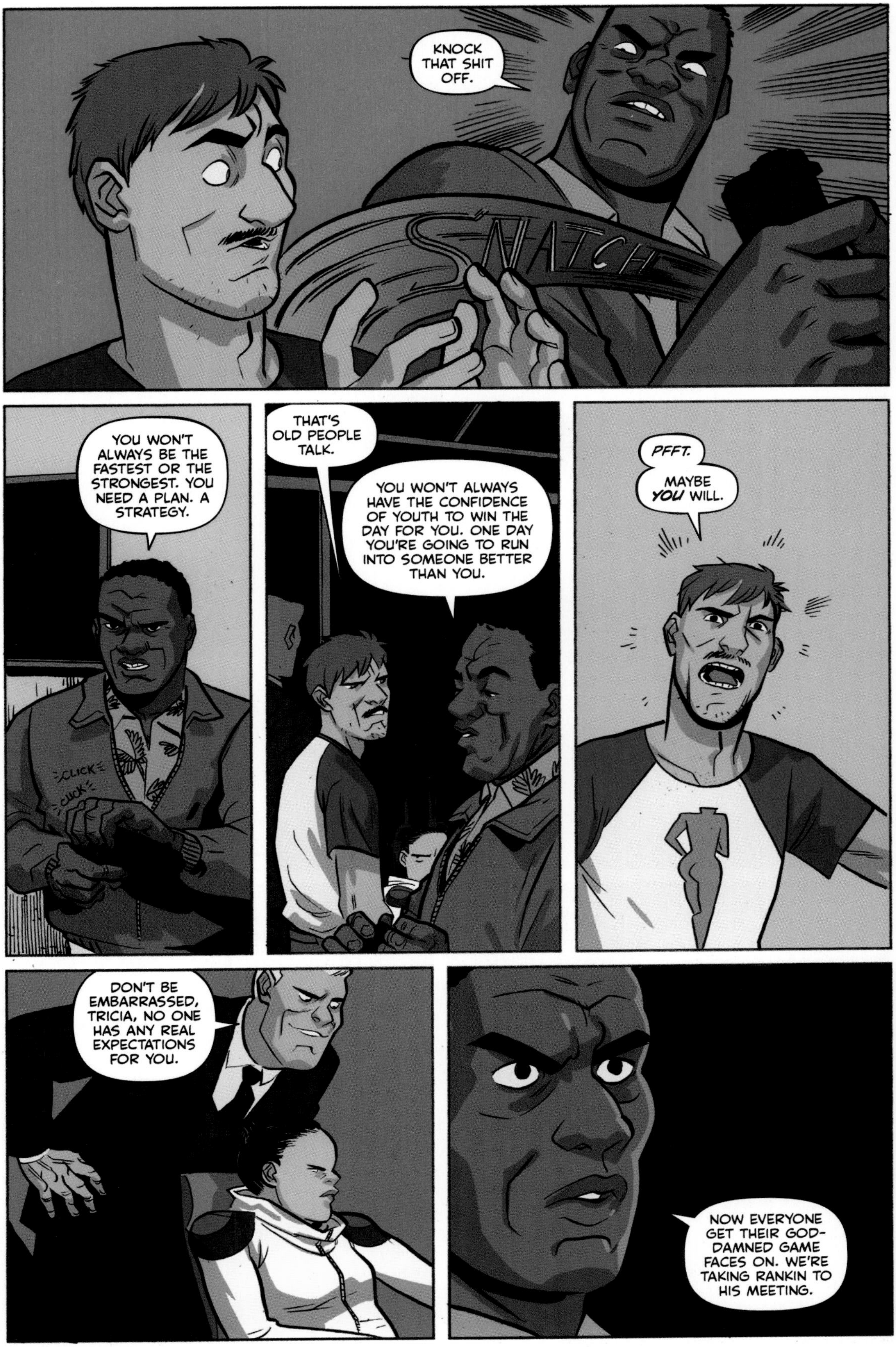
KNOCK THAT SHIT OFF.
SNATCH
YOU WON'T ALWAYS BE THE FASTEST OR THE STRONGEST. YOU NEED A PLAN. A STRATEGY.
CLICK
CLICK
THAT'S OLD PEOPLE TALK.
YOU WON'T ALWAYS HAVE THE CONFIDENCE OF YOUTH TO WIN THE DAY FOR YOU. ONE DAY YOU'RE GOING TO RUN INTO SOMEONE BETTER THAN YOU.
PFFT.
MAYBE YOU WILL.
DON'T BE EMBARRASSED, TRICIA, NO ONE HAS ANY REAL EXPECTATIONS FOR YOU.
NOW EVERYONE GET THEIR GOD-DAMNED GAME FACES ON. WE'RE TAKING RANKIN TO HIS MEETING.

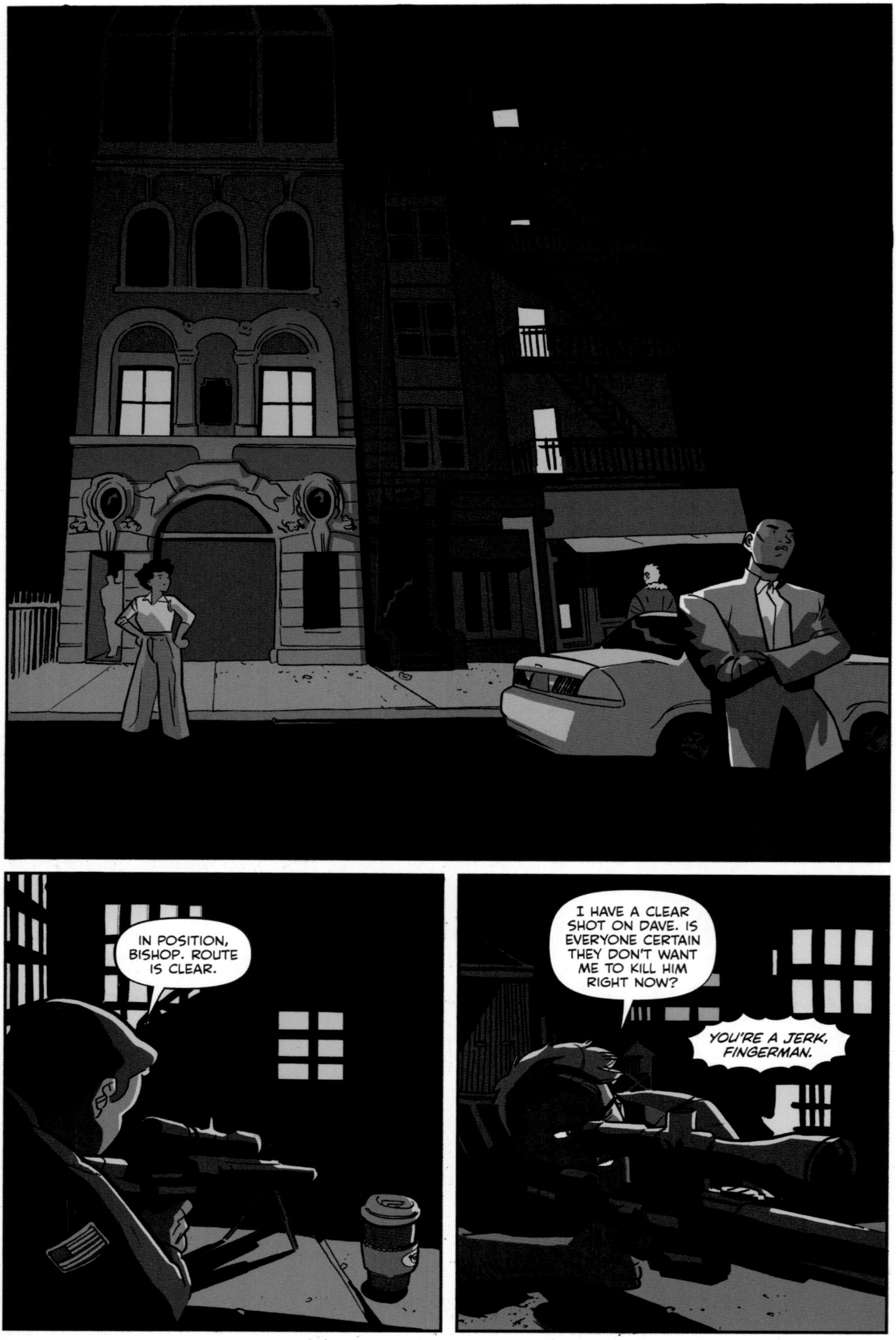
IN POSITION, BISHOP. ROUTE IS CLEAR.
I HAVE A CLEAR SHOT ON DAVE. IS EVERYONE CERTAIN THEY DON'T WANT ME TO KILL HIM RIGHT NOW?
YOU'RE A JERK, FINGERMAN.

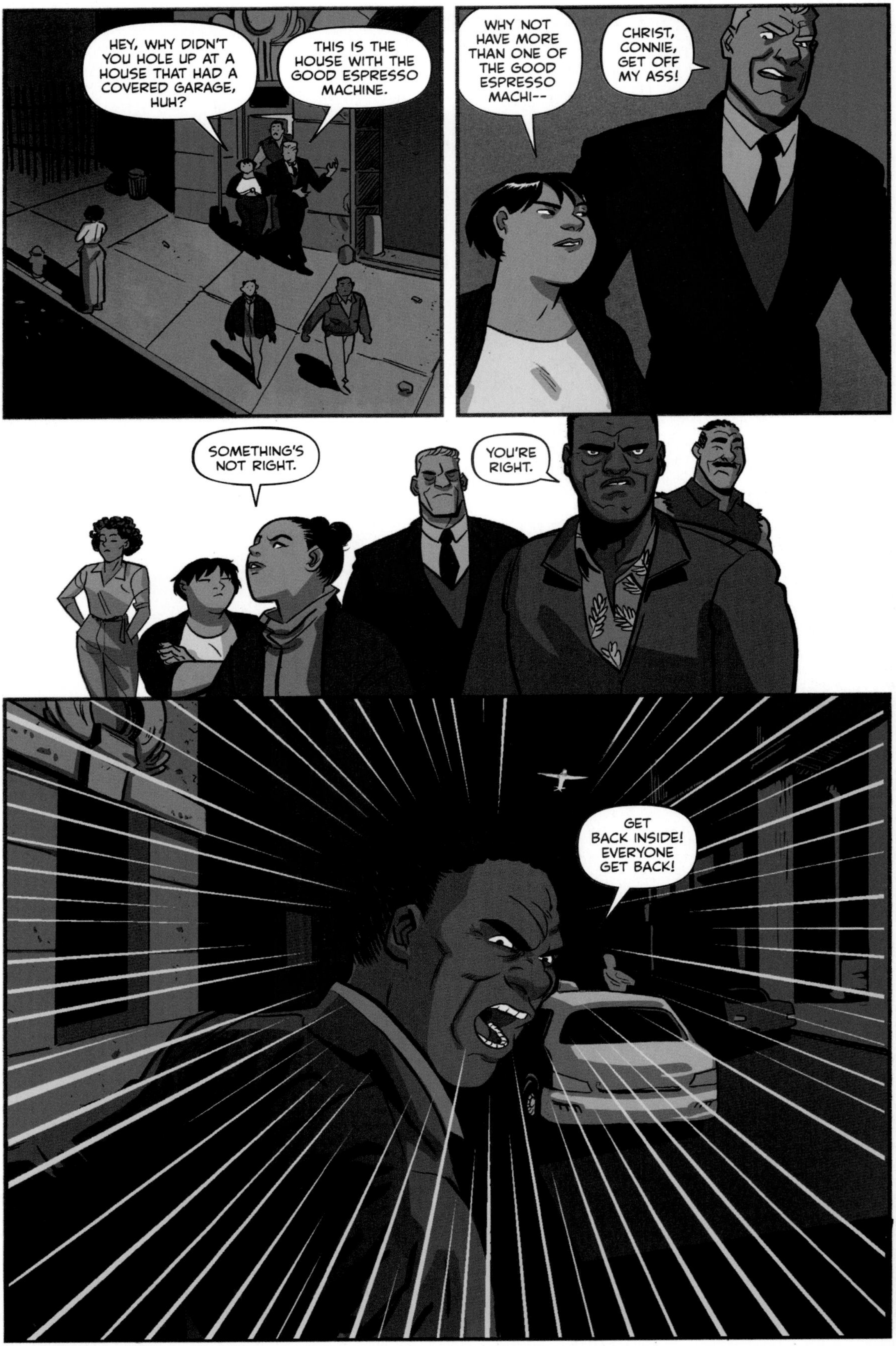
HEY, WHY DIDN'T YOU HOLE UP AT A HOUSE THAT HAD A COVERED GARAGE, HUH?
THIS IS THE HOUSE WITH THE GOOD ESPRESSO MACHINE.
WHY NOT HAVE MORE THAN ONE OF THE GOOD ESPRESSO MACHI--
CHRIST, CONNIE, GET OFF MY ASS!
SOMETHING'S NOT RIGHT.
YOU'RE RIGHT.
GET BACK INSIDE! EVERYONE GET BACK!

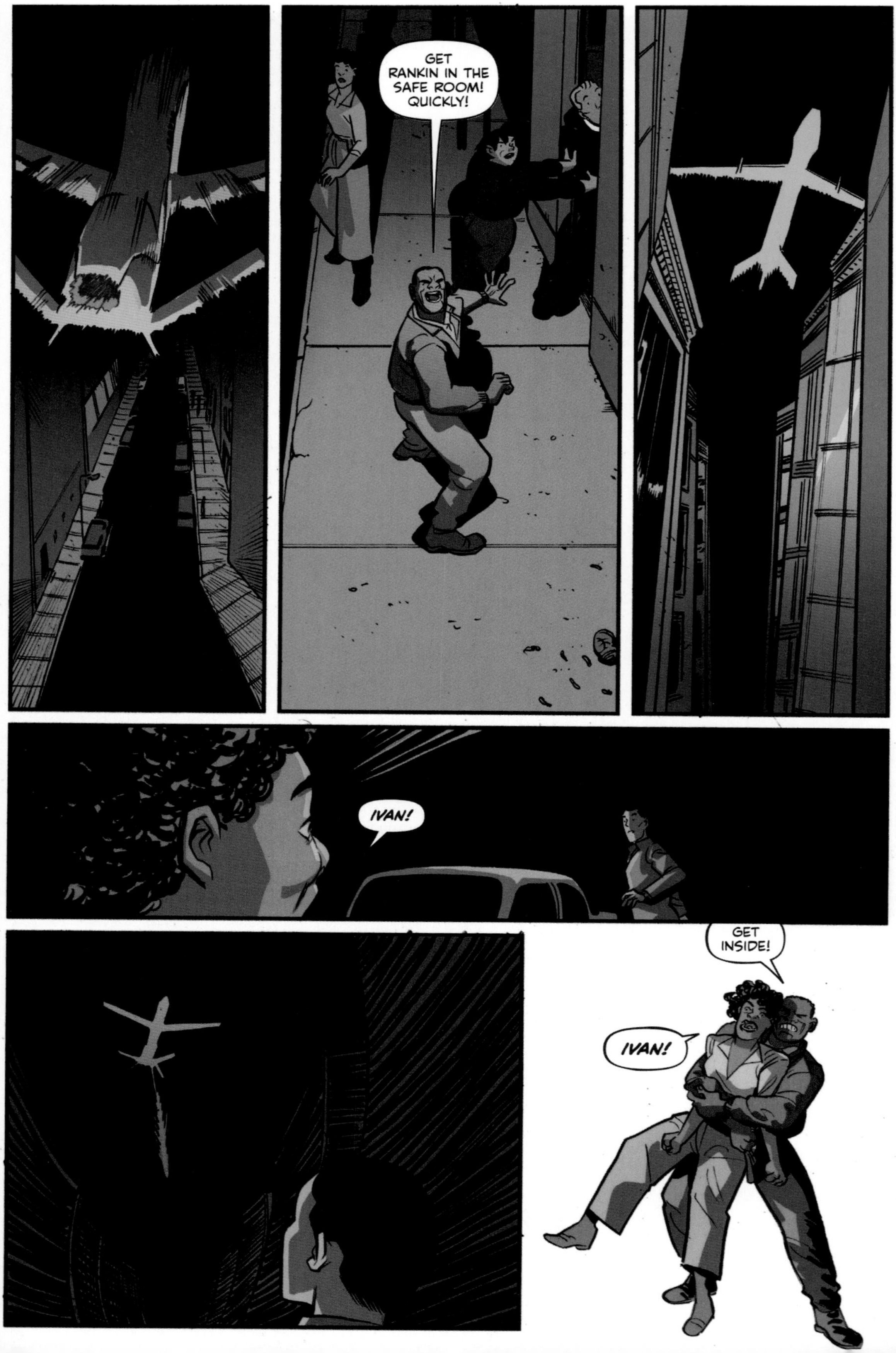
GET RANKIN IN THE SAFE ROOM! QUICKLY!
IVAN!
GET INSIDE!
IVAN!

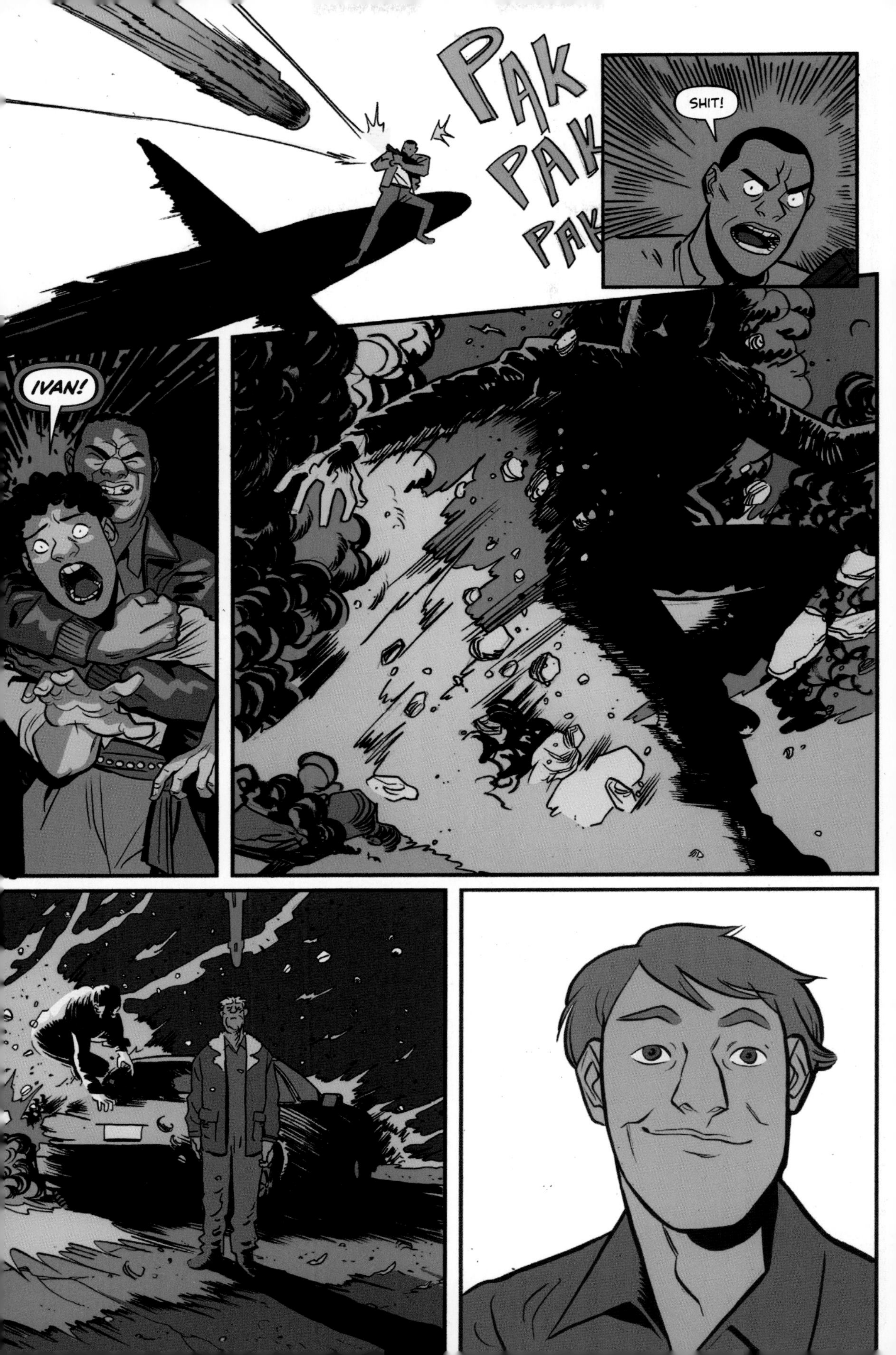
PAK
PAK
PAK
SHIT!
IVAN!

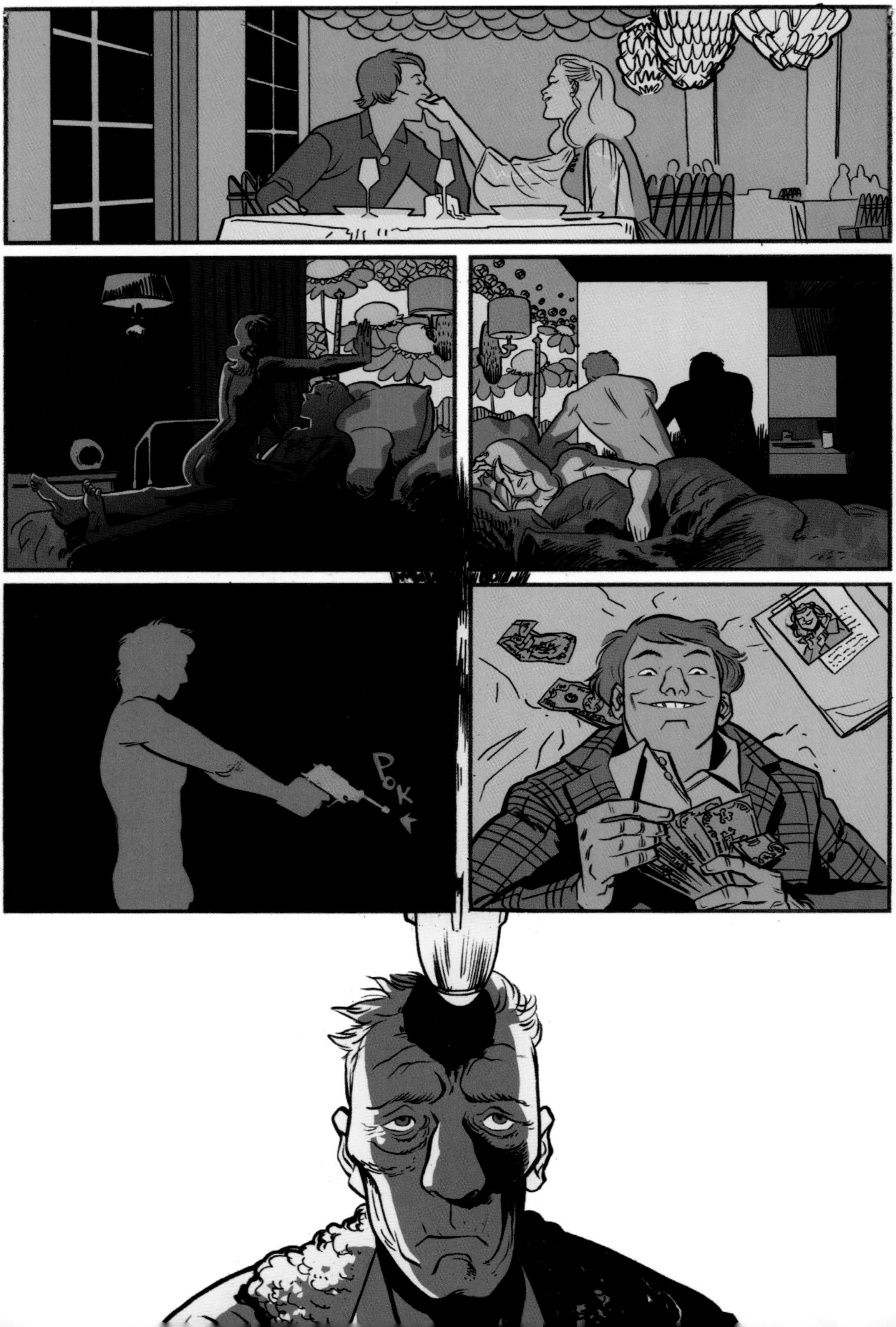
POK

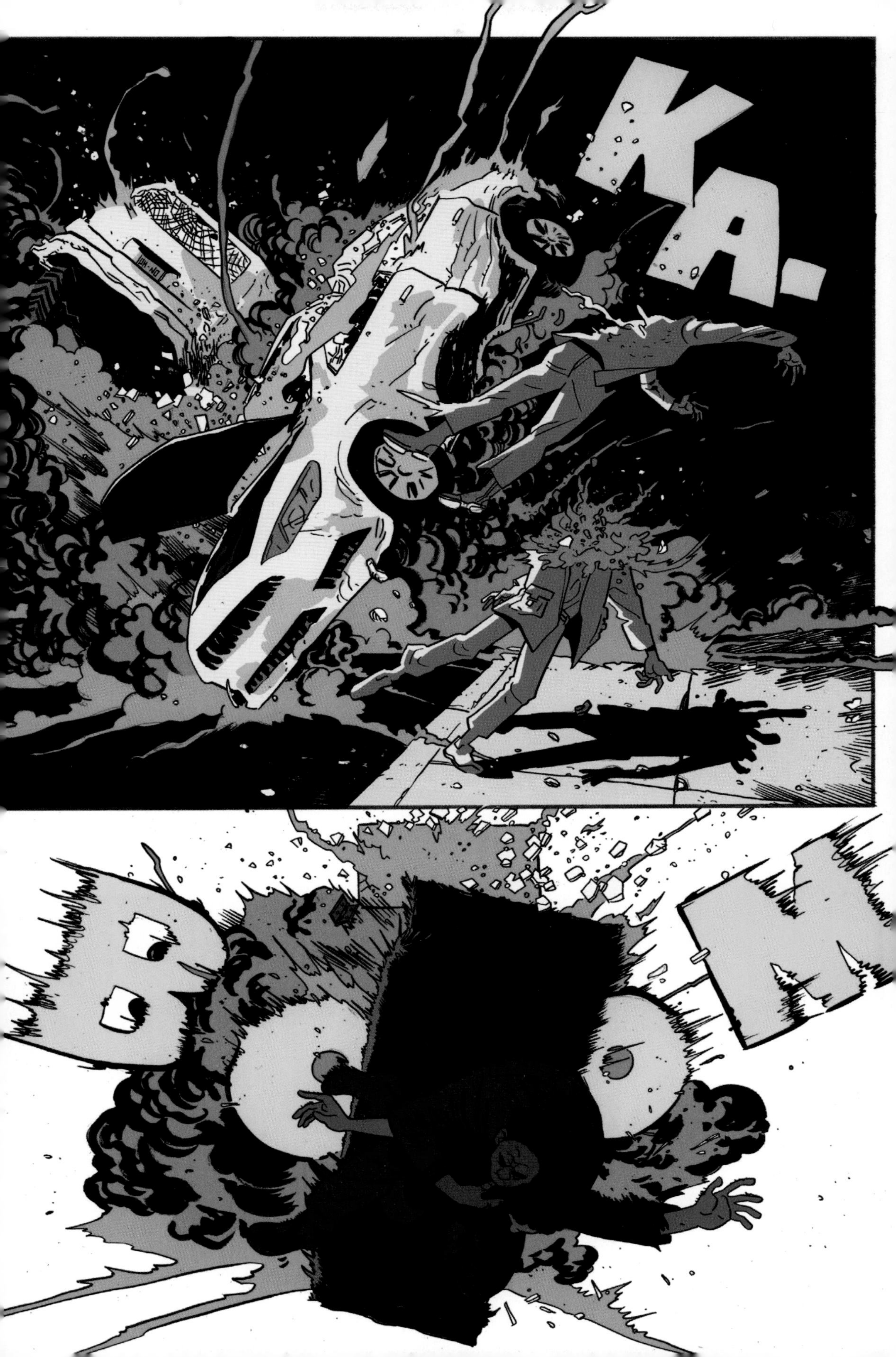
KA.
BOOM

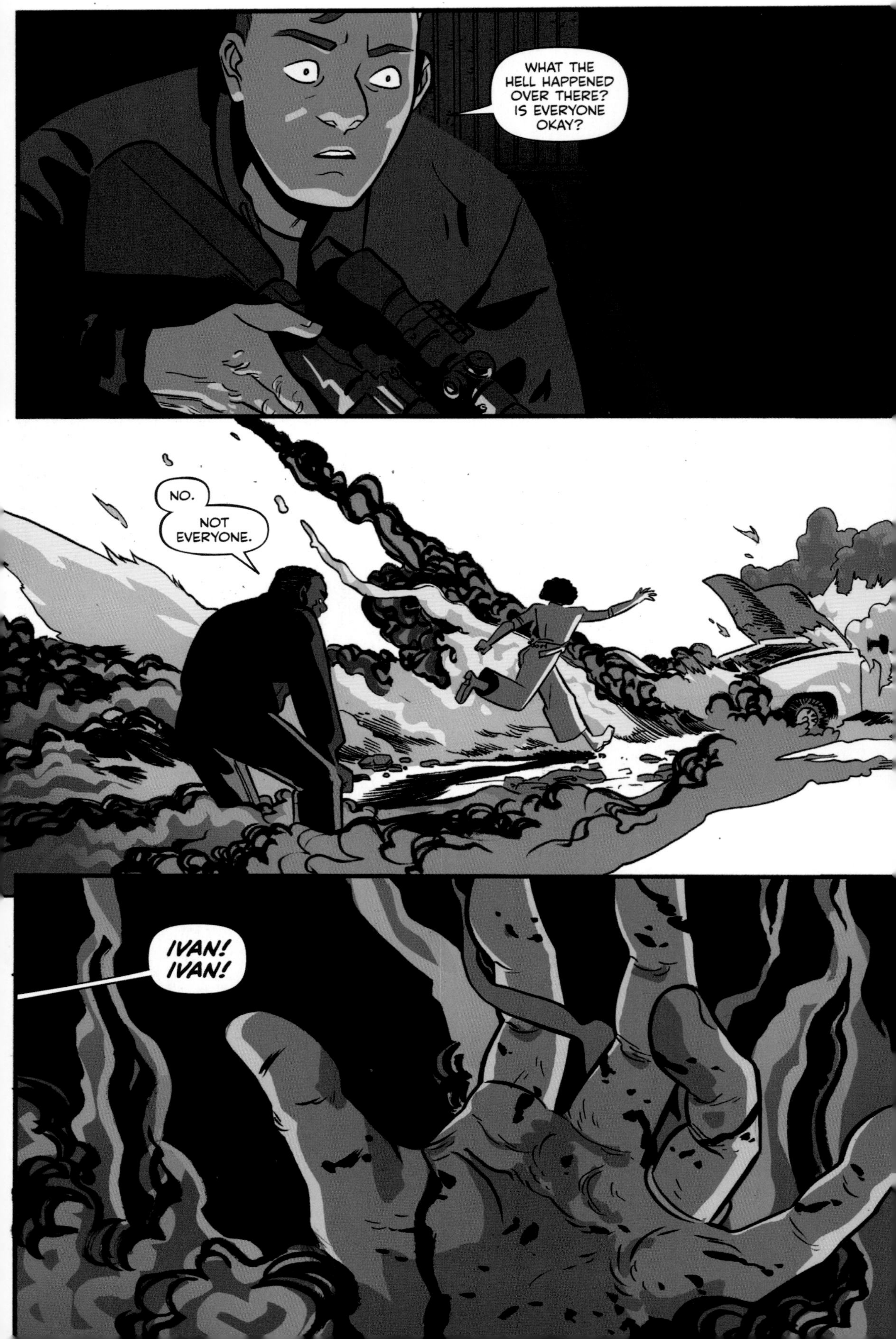
WHAT THE HELL HAPPENED OVER THERE? IS EVERYONE OKAY?
NO.
NOT EVERYONE.
IVAN! IVAN!

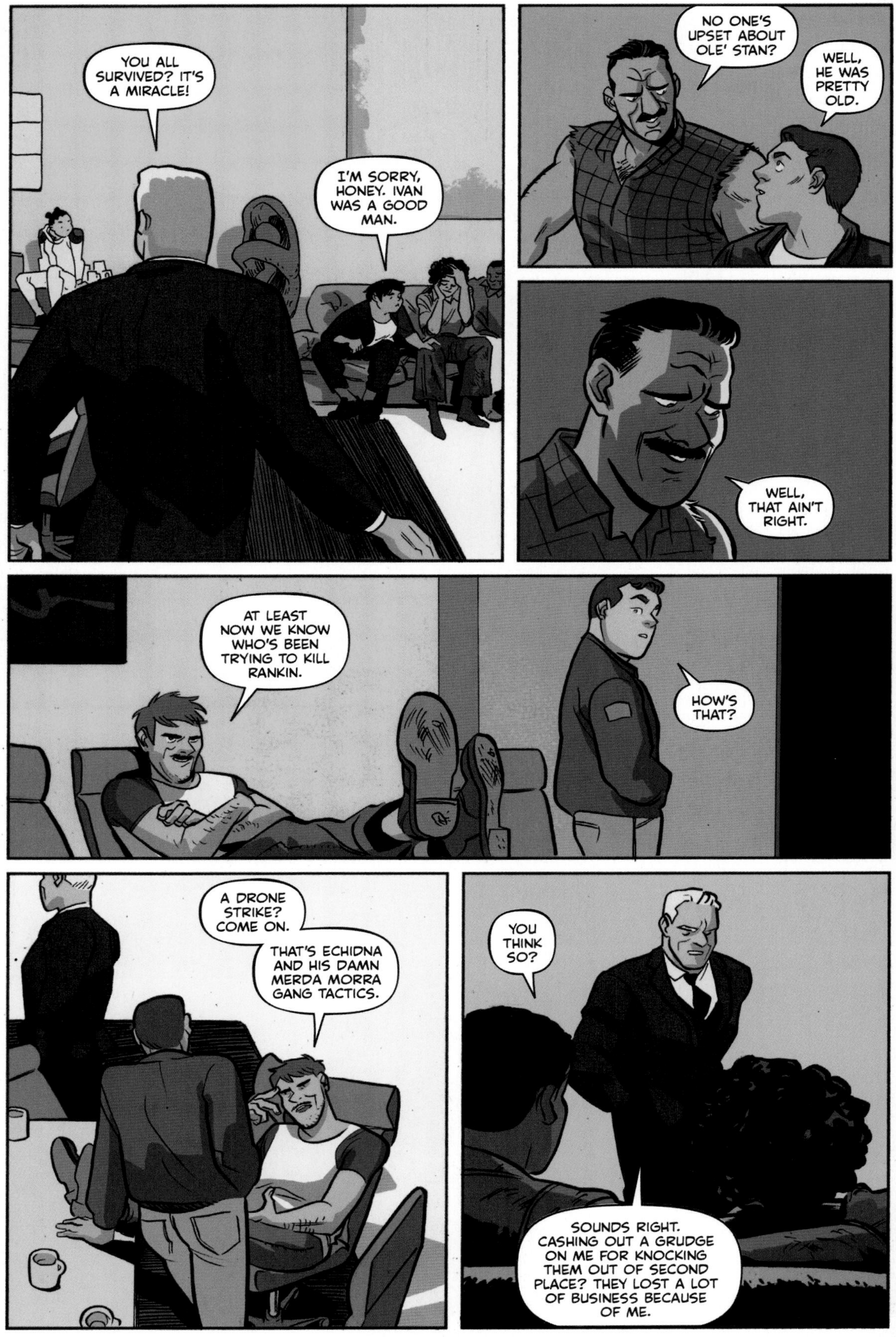
YOU ALL SURVIVED? IT'S A MIRACLE!
I'M SORRY, HONEY. IVAN WAS A GOOD MAN.
NO ONE'S UPSET ABOUT OLE' STAN?
WELL, HE WAS PRETTY OLD.
WELL, THAT AIN'T RIGHT.
AT LEAST NOW WE KNOW WHO'S BEEN TRYING TO KILL RANKIN.
HOW'S THAT?
A DRONE STRIKE? COME ON.
THAT'S ECHIDNA AND HIS DAMN MERDA MORRA GANG TACTICS.
YOU THINK SO?
SOUNDS RIGHT. CASHING OUT A GRUDGE ON ME FOR KNOCKING THEM OUT OF SECOND PLACE? THEY LOST A LOT OF BUSINESS BECAUSE OF ME.

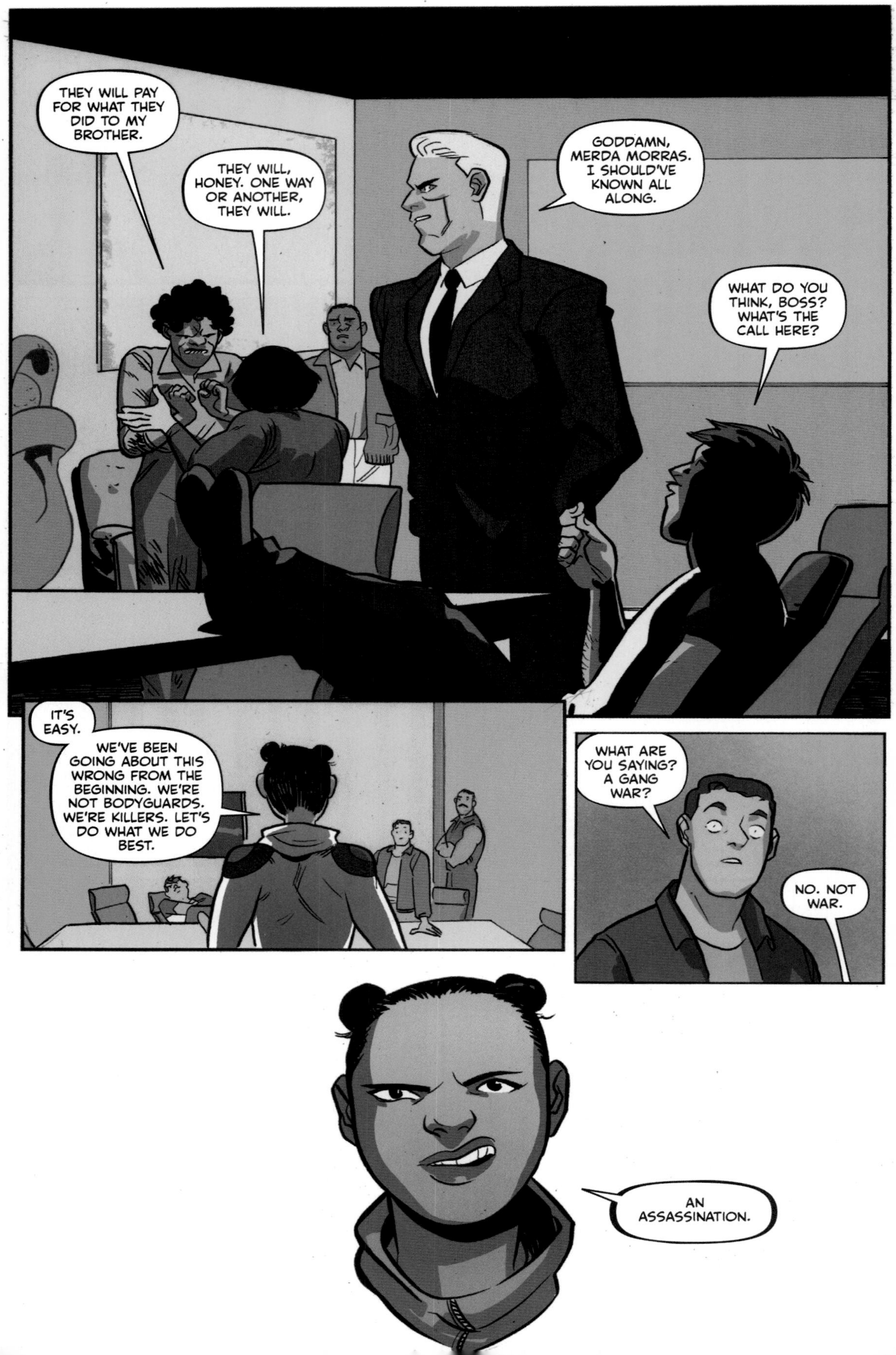
THEY WILL PAY FOR WHAT THEY DID TO MY BROTHER.
THEY WILL, HONEY. ONE WAY OR ANOTHER, THEY WILL.
GODDAMN, MERDA MORRAS. I SHOULD'VE KNOWN ALL ALONG.
WHAT DO YOU THINK, BOSS? WHAT'S THE CALL HERE?
IT'S EASY.
WE'VE BEEN GOING ABOUT THIS WRONG FROM THE BEGINNING. WE'RE NOT BODYGUARDS. WE'RE KILLERS. LET'S DO WHAT WE DO BEST.
WHAT ARE YOU SAYING? A GANG WAR?
NO. NOT WAR.
AN ASSASSINATION.

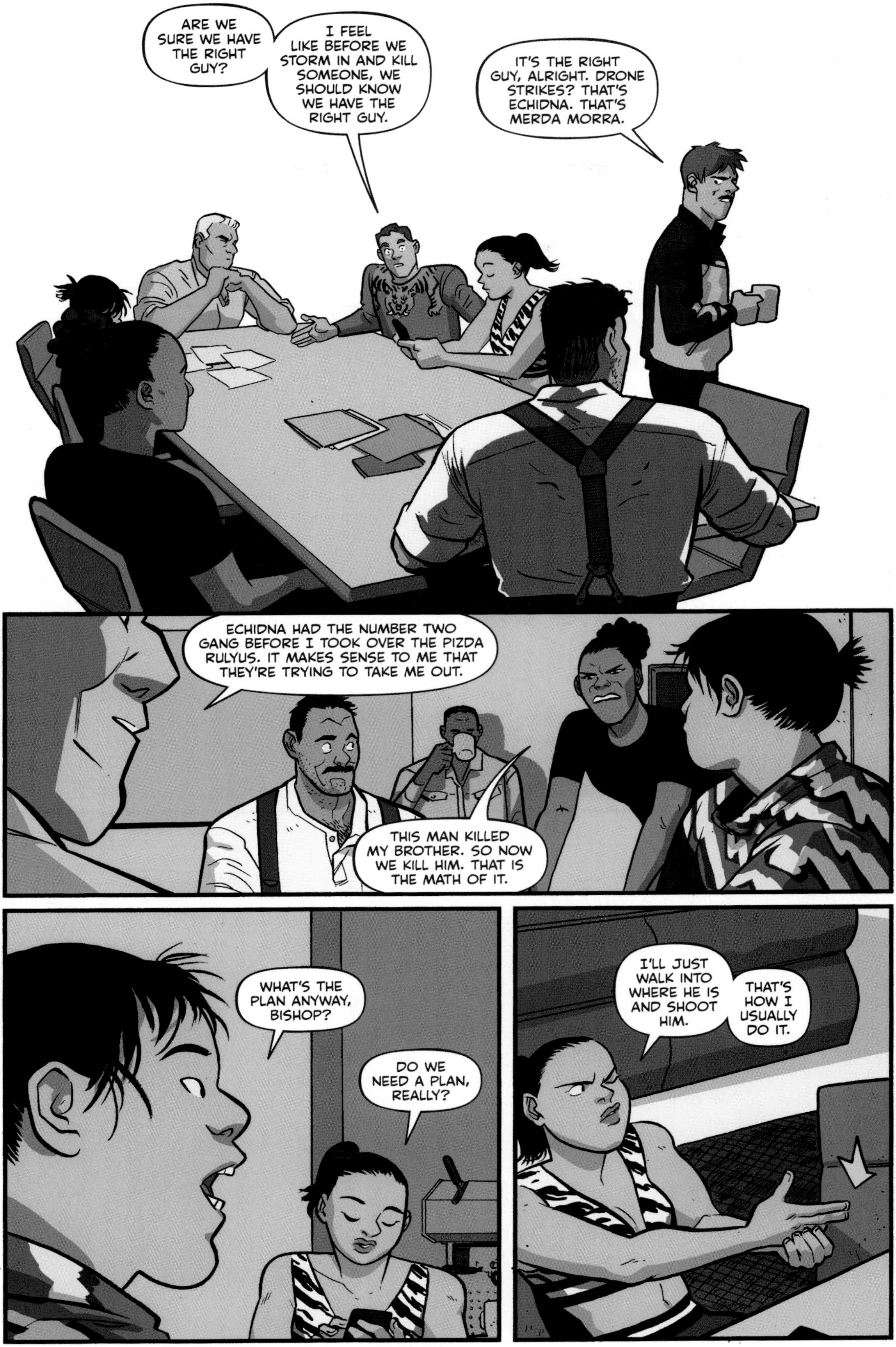
ARE WE SURE WE HAVE THE RIGHT GUY?
I FEEL LIKE BEFORE WE STORM IN AND KILL SOMEONE, WE SHOULD KNOW WE HAVE THE RIGHT GUY.
IT'S THE RIGHT GUY, ALRIGHT. DRONE STRIKES? THAT'S ECHIDNA. THAT'S MERDA MORRA.
ECHIDNA HAD THE NUMBER TWO GANG BEFORE I TOOK OVER THE PIZDA RULYUS. IT MAKES SENSE TO ME THAT THEY'RE TRYING TO TAKE ME OUT.
THIS MAN KILLED MY BROTHER. SO NOW WE KILL HIM. THAT IS THE MATH OF IT.
WHAT'S THE PLAN ANYWAY, BISHOP?
DO WE NEED A PLAN, REALLY?
I'LL JUST WALK INTO WHERE HE IS AND SHOOT HIM.
THAT'S HOW I USUALLY DO IT.

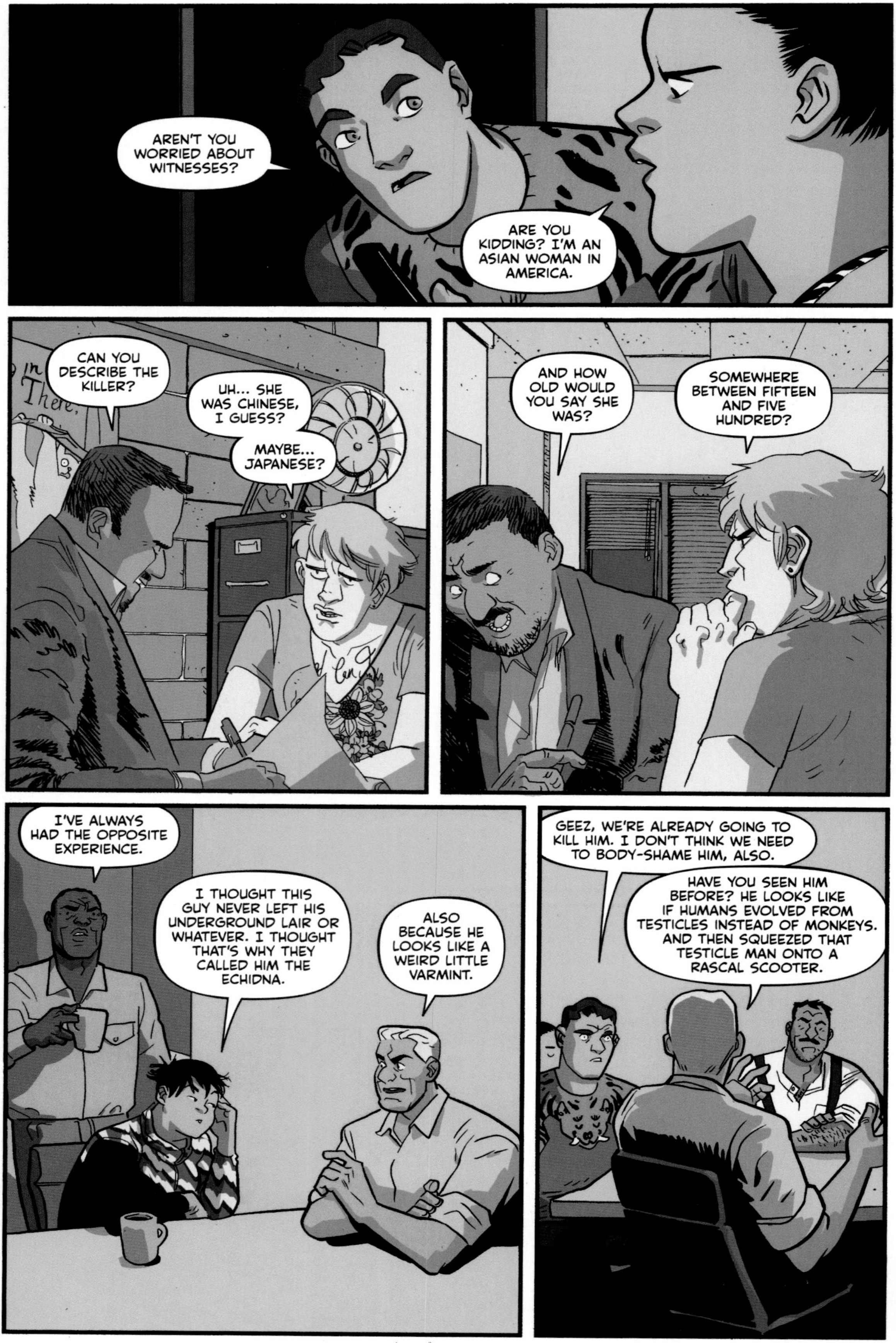
AREN'T YOU WORRIED ABOUT WITNESSES?
ARE YOU KIDDING? I'M AN ASIAN WOMAN IN AMERICA.
CAN YOU DESCRIBE THE KILLER?
UH... SHE WAS CHINESE, I GUESS?
MAYBE... JAPANESE?
AND HOW OLD WOULD YOU SAY SHE WAS?
SOMEWHERE BETWEEN FIFTEEN AND FIVE HUNDRED?
I'VE ALWAYS HAD THE OPPOSITE EXPERIENCE.
I THOUGHT THIS GUY NEVER LEFT HIS UNDERGROUND LAIR OR WHATEVER. I THOUGHT THAT'S WHY THEY CALLED HIM THE ECHIDNA.
ALSO BECAUSE HE LOOKS LIKE A WEIRD LITTLE VARMINT.
GEEZ, WE'RE ALREADY GOING TO KILL HIM. I DON'T THINK WE NEED TO BODY-SHAME HIM, ALSO.
HAVE YOU SEEN HIM BEFORE? HE LOOKS LIKE IF HUMANS EVOLVED FROM TESTICLES INSTEAD OF MONKEYS. AND THEN SQUEEZED THAT TESTICLE MAN ONTO A RASCAL SCOOTER.

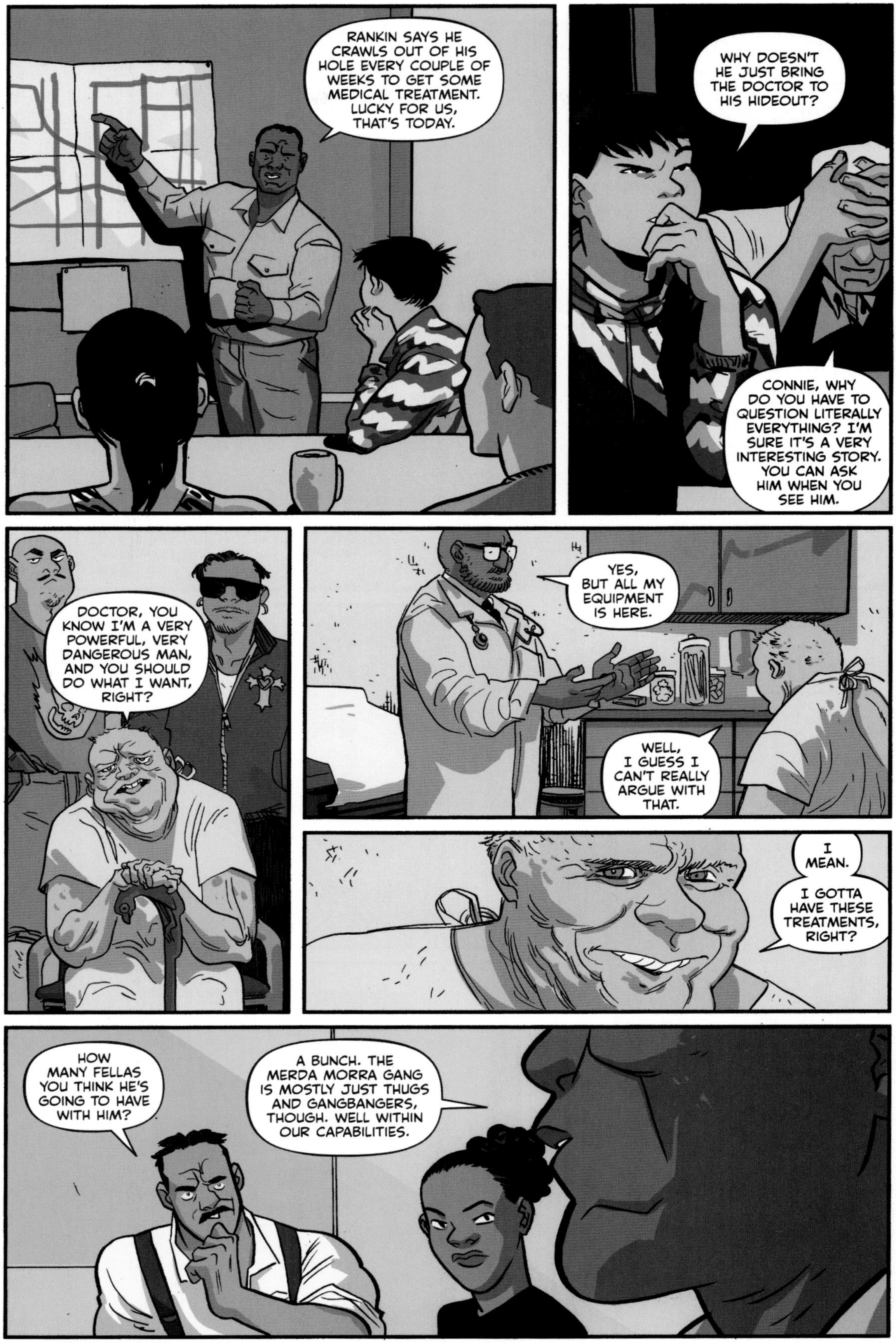
RANKIN SAYS HE CRAWLS OUT OF HIS HOLE EVERY COUPLE OF WEEKS TO GET SOME MEDICAL TREATMENT. LUCKY FOR US, THAT'S TODAY.
WHY DOESN'T HE JUST BRING THE DOCTOR TO HIS HIDEOUT?
CONNIE, WHY DO YOU HAVE TO QUESTION LITERALLY EVERYTHING? I'M SURE IT'S A VERY INTERESTING STORY. YOU CAN ASK HIM WHEN YOU SEE HIM.
DOCTOR, YOU KNOW I'M A VERY POWERFUL, VERY DANGEROUS MAN, AND YOU SHOULD DO WHAT I WANT, RIGHT?
YES, BUT ALL MY EQUIPMENT IS HERE.
WELL, I GUESS I CAN'T REALLY ARGUE WITH THAT.
I MEAN.
I GOTTA HAVE THESE TREATMENTS, RIGHT?
HOW MANY FELLAS YOU THINK HE'S GOING TO HAVE WITH HIM?
A BUNCH. THE MERDA MORRA GANG IS MOSTLY JUST THUGS AND GANGBANGERS, THOUGH. WELL WITHIN OUR CAPABILITIES.

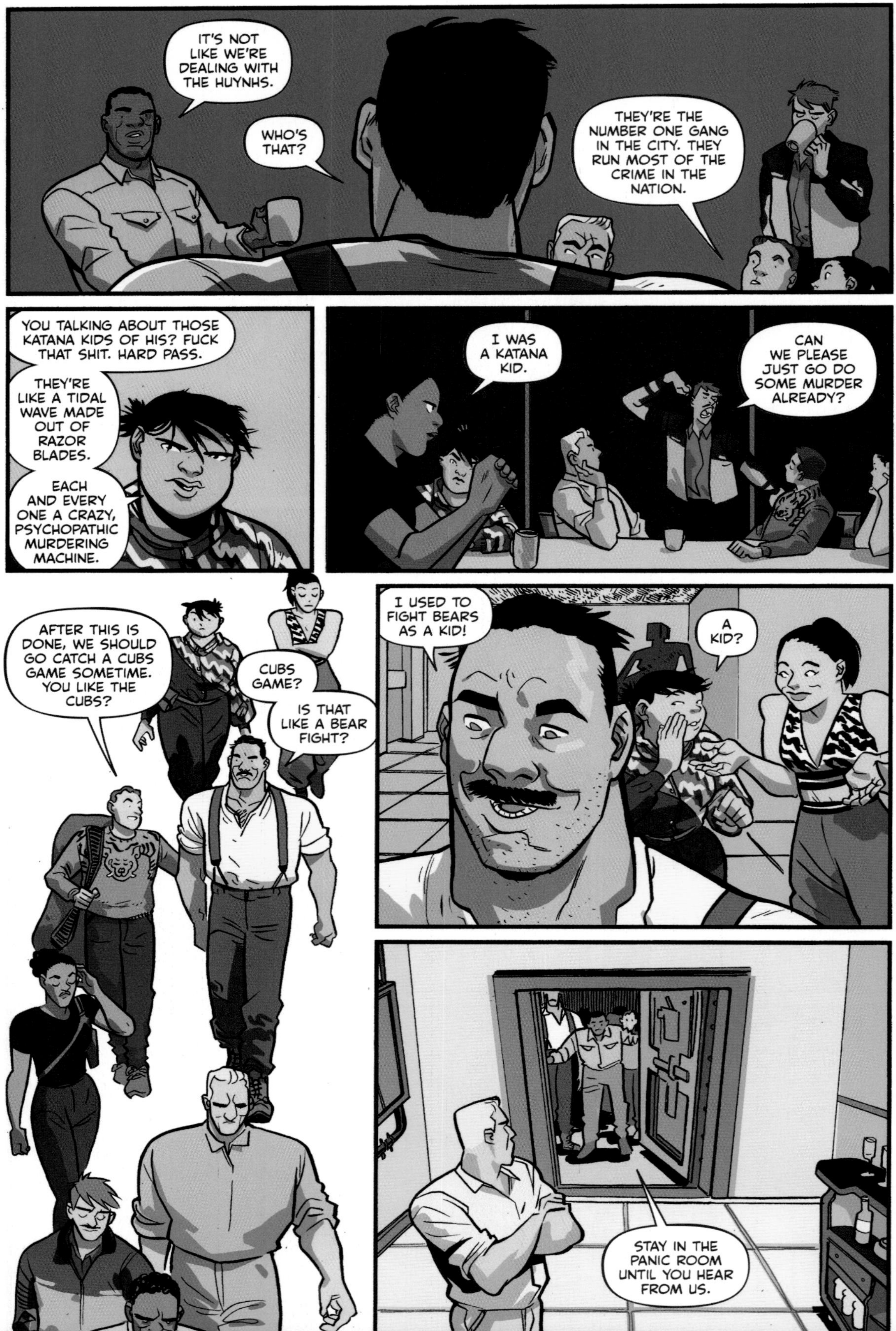
IT'S NOT LIKE WE'RE DEALING WITH THE HUYNHS.
WHO'S THAT?
THEY'RE THE NUMBER ONE GANG IN THE CITY. THEY RUN MOST OF THE CRIME IN THE NATION.
YOU TALKING ABOUT THOSE KATANA KIDS OF HIS? FUCK THAT SHIT. HARD PASS.
THEY'RE LIKE A TIDAL WAVE MADE OUT OF RAZOR BLADES.
EACH AND EVERY ONE A CRAZY, PSYCHOPATHIC MURDERING MACHINE.
I WAS A KATANA KID.
CAN WE PLEASE JUST GO DO SOME MURDER ALREADY?
AFTER THIS IS DONE, WE SHOULD GO CATCH A CUBS GAME SOMETIME. YOU LIKE THE CUBS?
CUBS GAME?
IS THAT LIKE A BEAR FIGHT?
I USED TO FIGHT BEARS AS A KID!
A KID?
STAY IN THE PANIC ROOM UNTIL YOU HEAR FROM US.

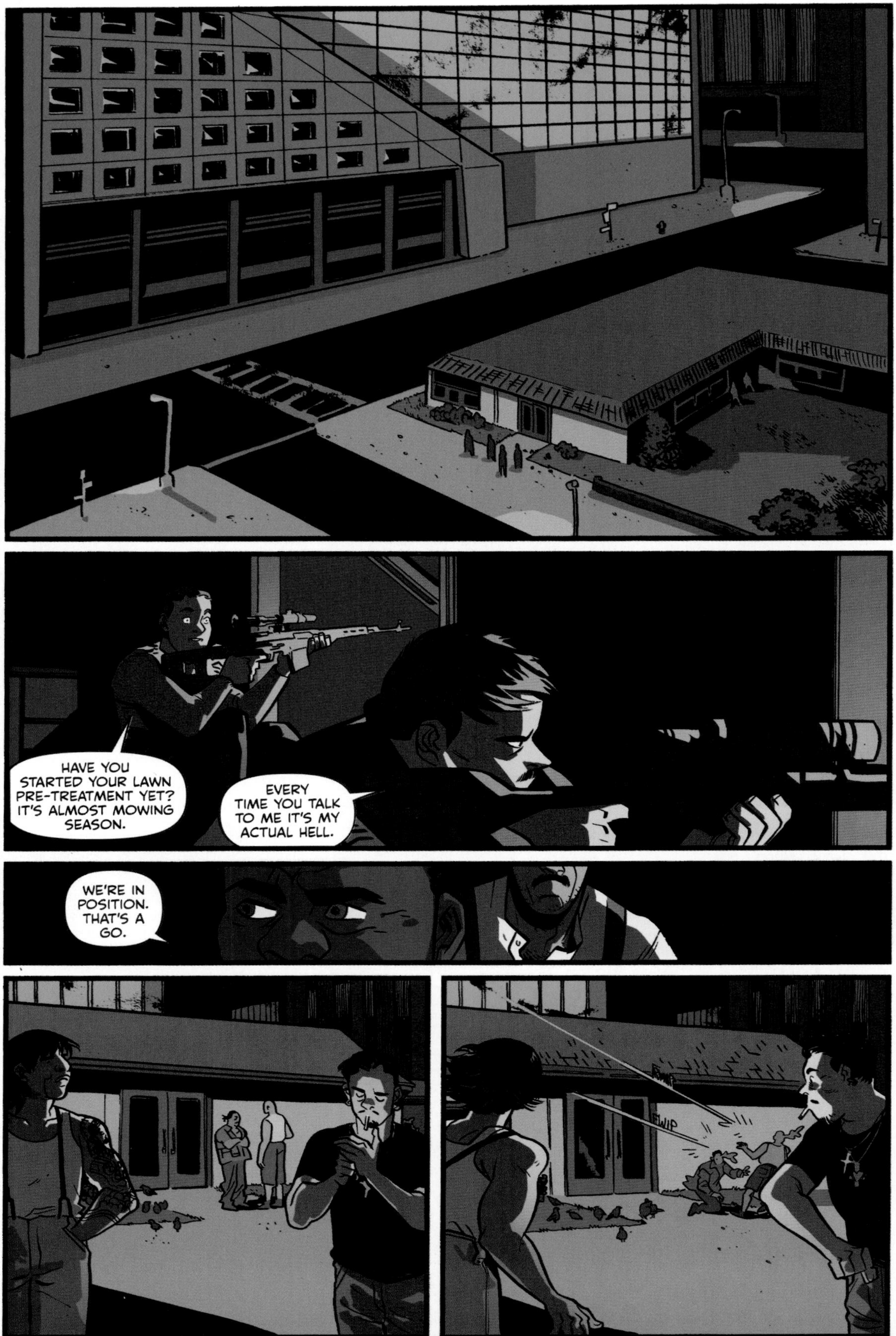
HAVE YOU STARTED YOUR LAWN PRE-TREATMENT YET? IT'S ALMOST MOWING SEASON.
EVERY TIME YOU TALK TO ME IT'S MY ACTUAL HELL.
WE'RE IN POSITION. THAT'S A GO.
FWIP

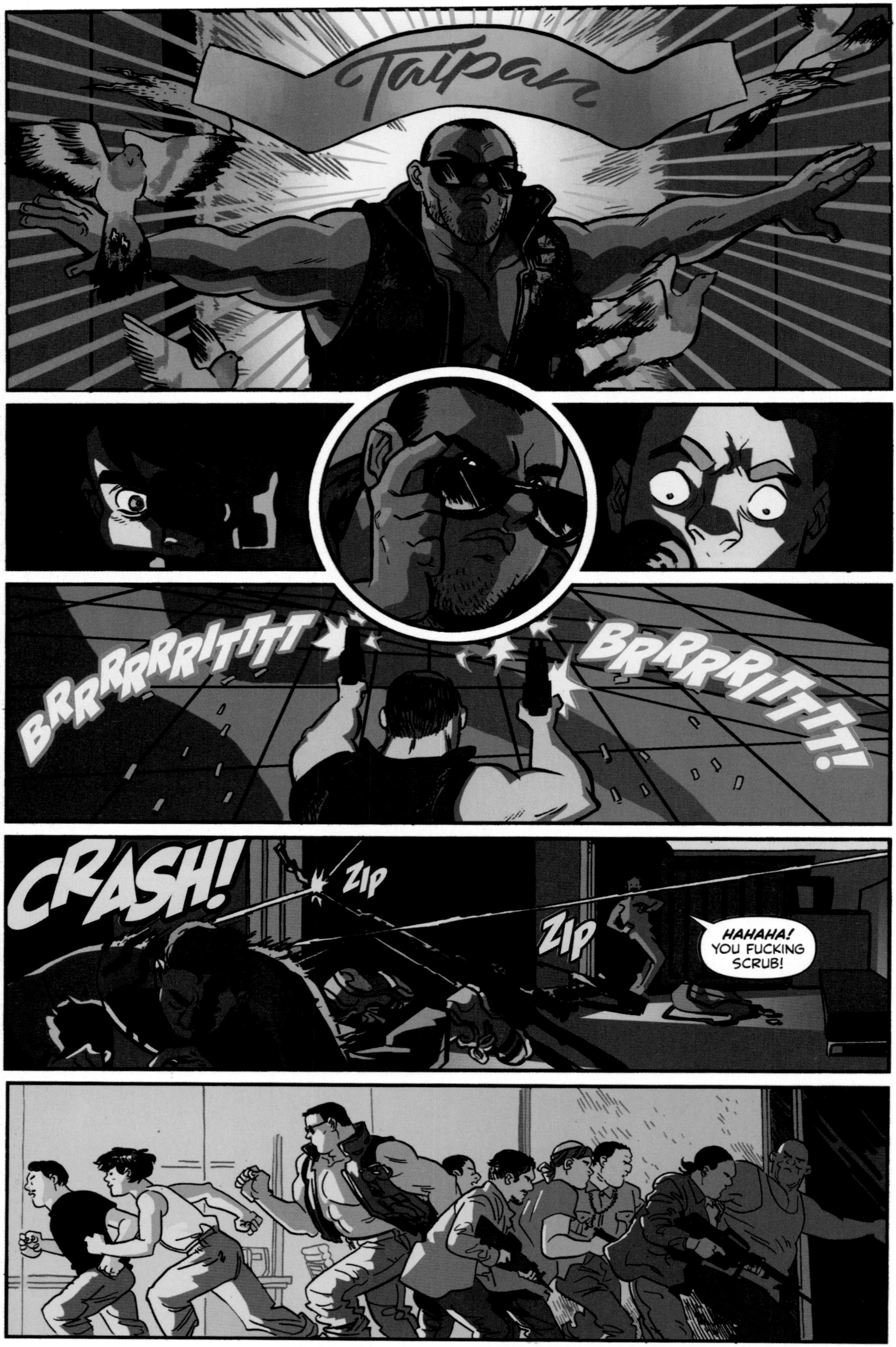

Taipan
BRRRRRRITTTT
BRRRRITTTT!
CRASH!
ZIP
ZIP
HAHAHA! YOU FUCKING SCRUB!

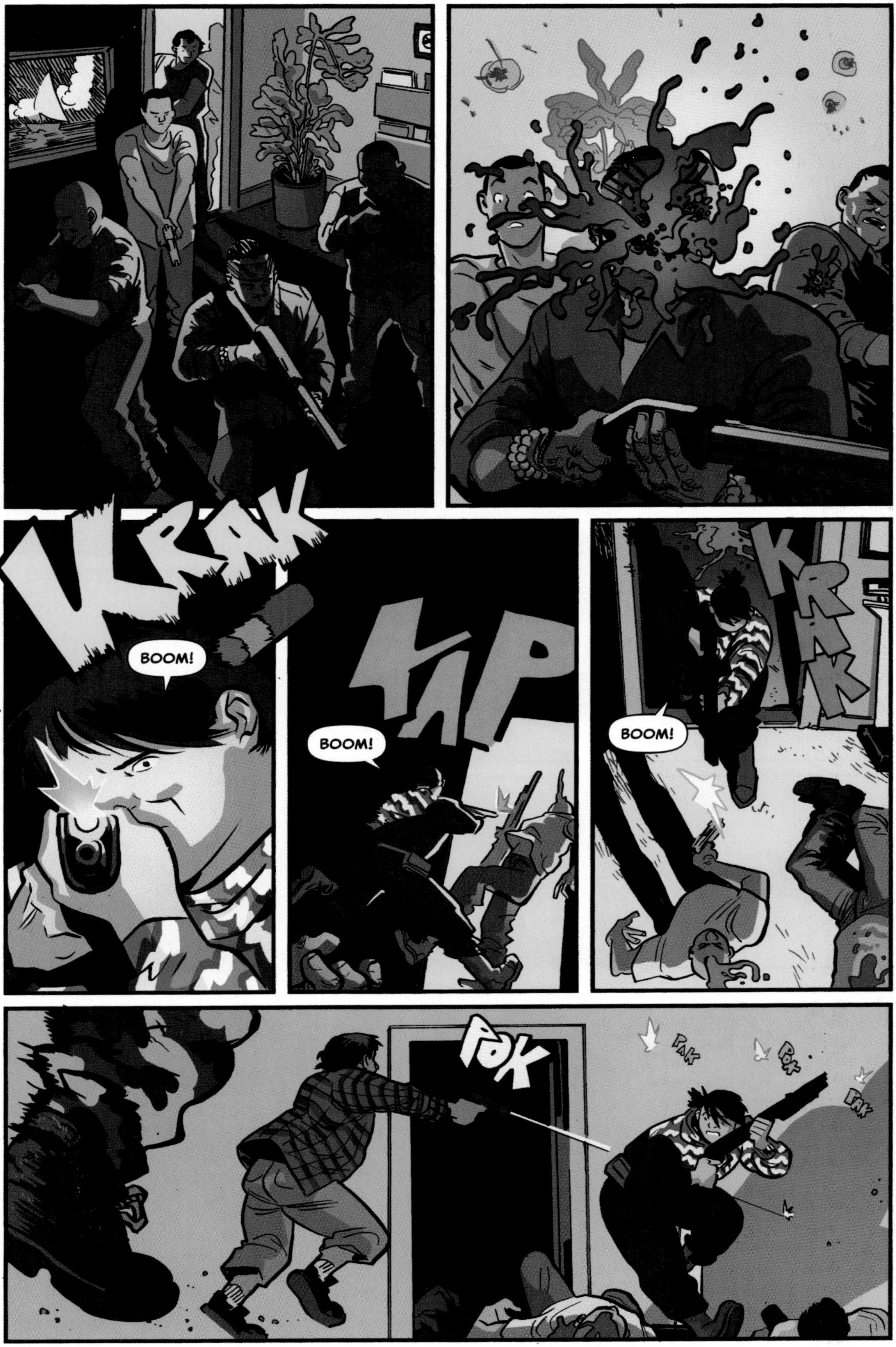
KRAK
BOOM!
BOOM!
KRAK
BOOM!
POK
PAK
POK
PAK

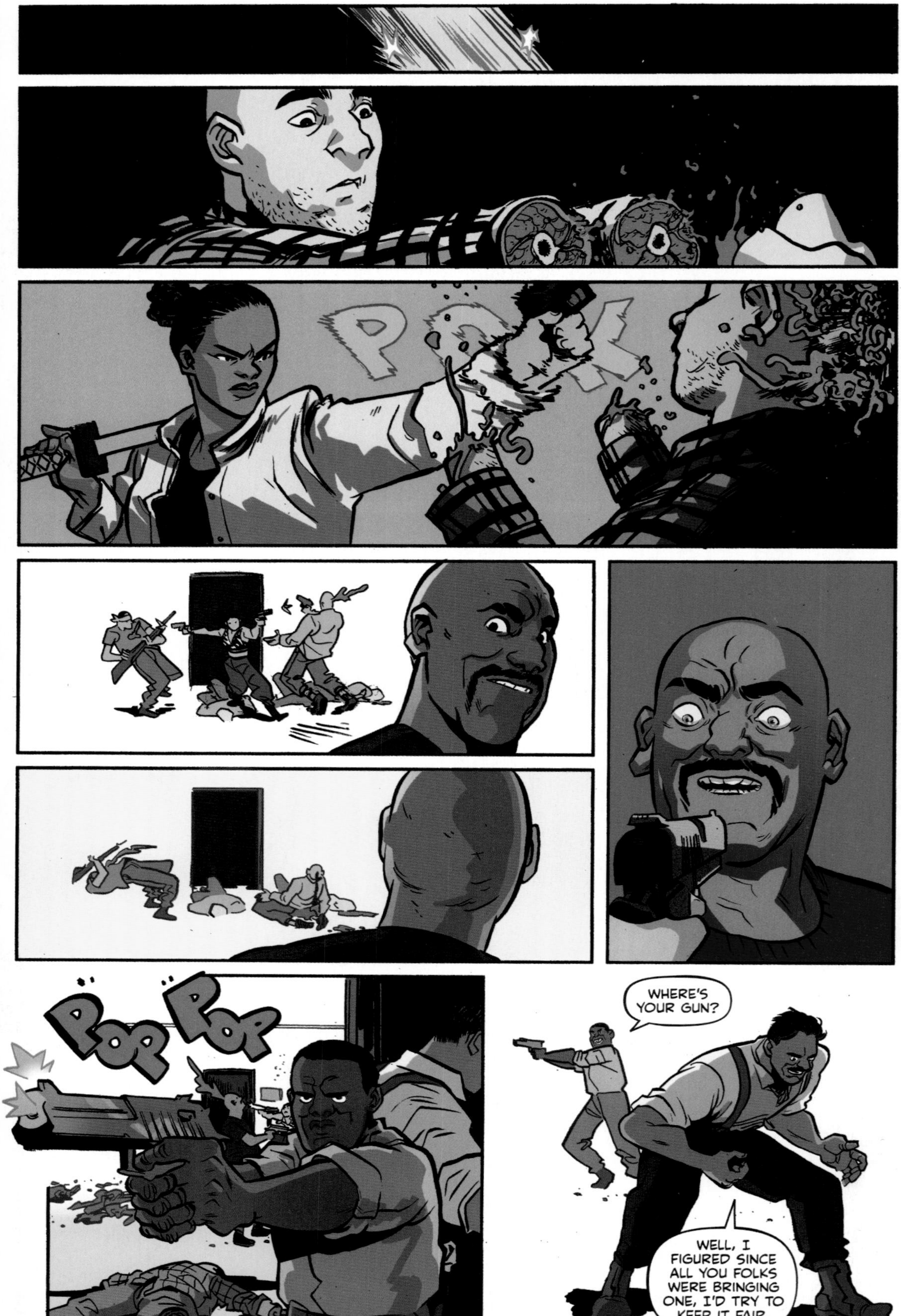
POP POP
WHERE'S YOUR GUN?
WELL, I FIGURED SINCE ALL YOU FOLKS WERE BRINGING ONE, I'D TRY TO KEEP IT FAIR.

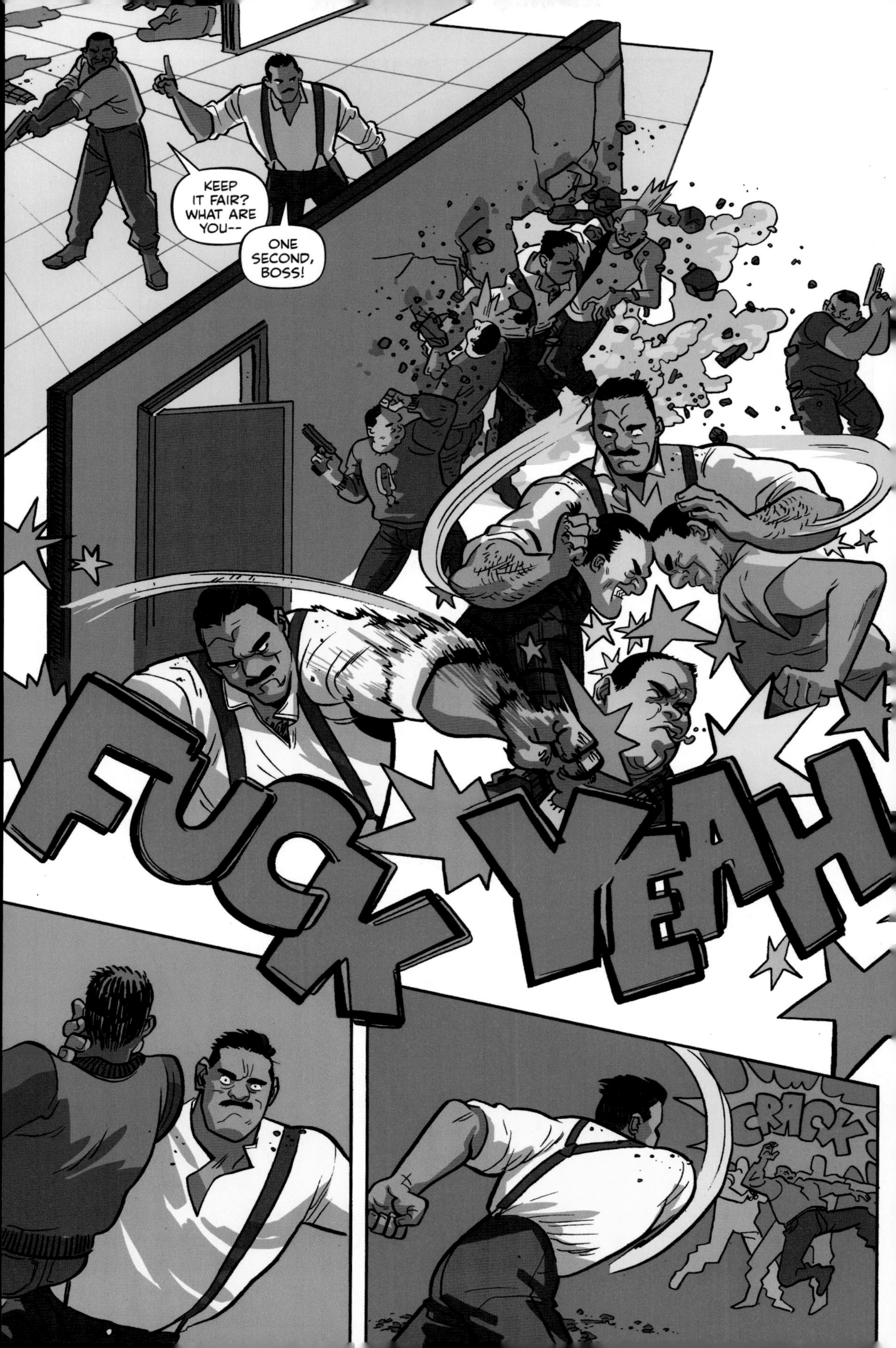

KEEP IT FAIR? WHAT ARE YOU--
ONE SECOND, BOSS!
FUCK YEAH
CRACK

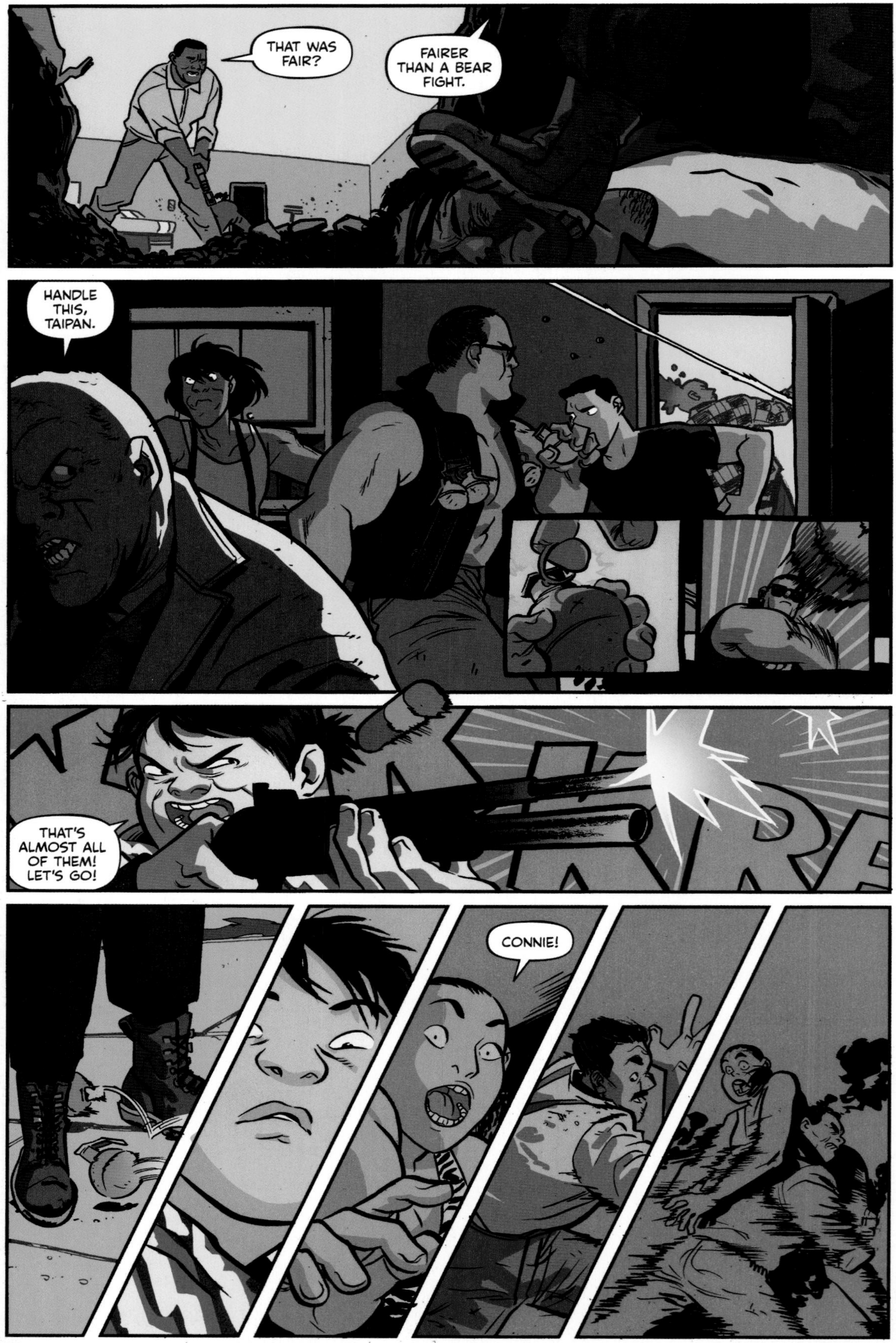

THAT WAS FAIR?
FAIRER THAN A BEAR FIGHT.
HANDLE THIS, TAIPAN.
THAT'S ALMOST ALL OF THEM! LET'S GO!
CONNIE!

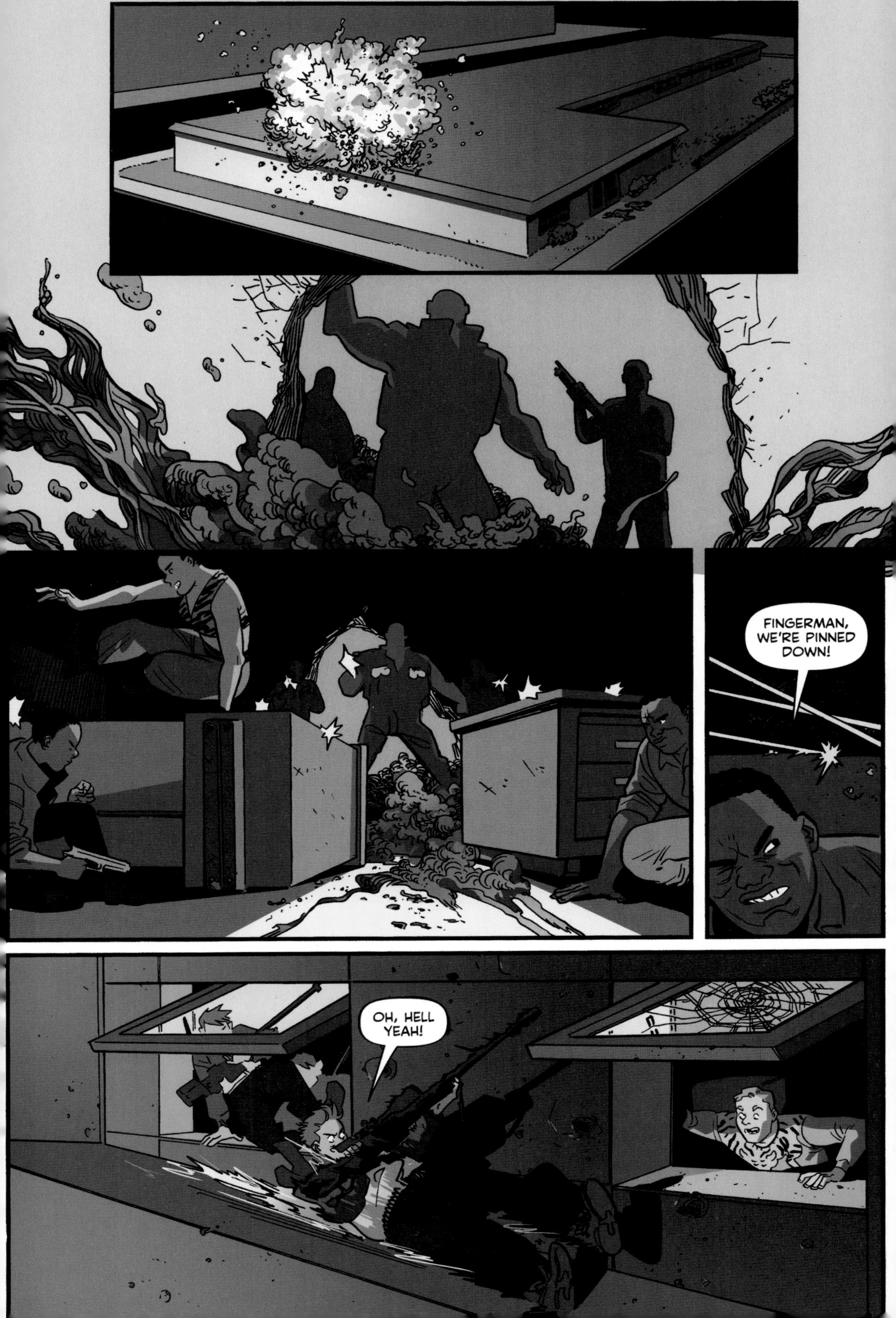
FINGERMAN, WE'RE PINNED DOWN!
OH, HELL YEAH!

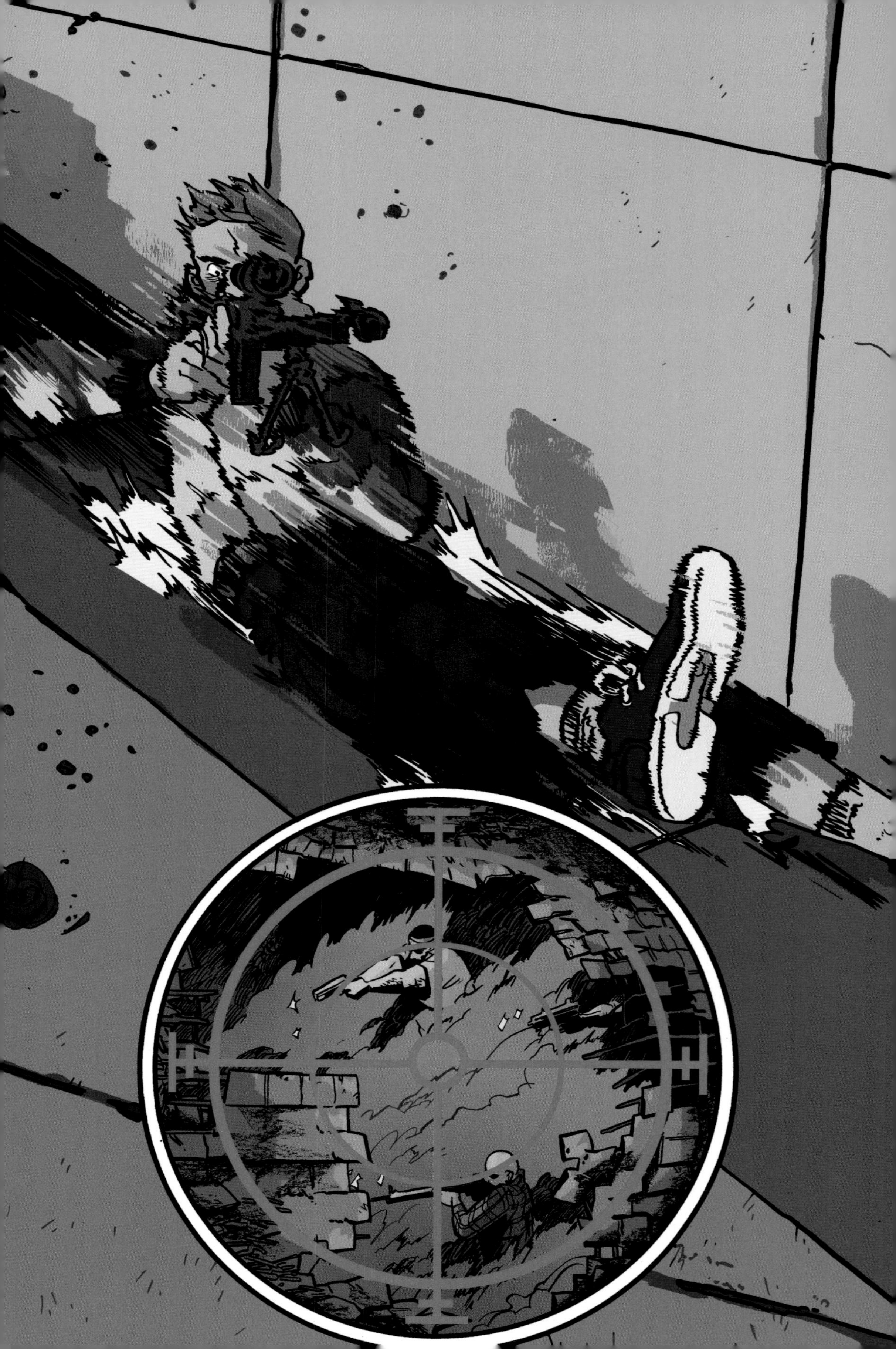

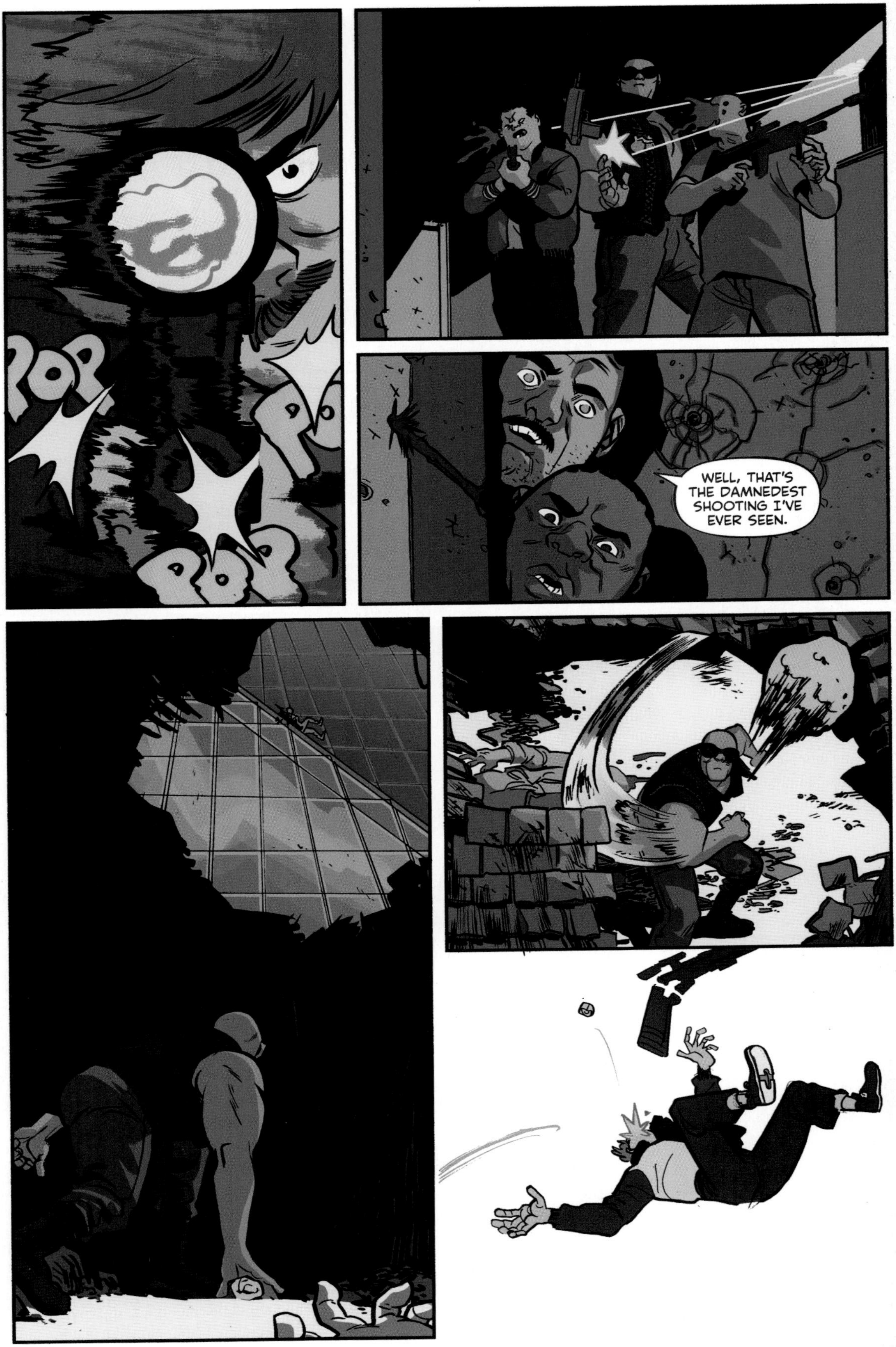
POP
POP
POP
WELL, THAT'S THE DAMNEDEST SHOOTING I'VE EVER SEEN.

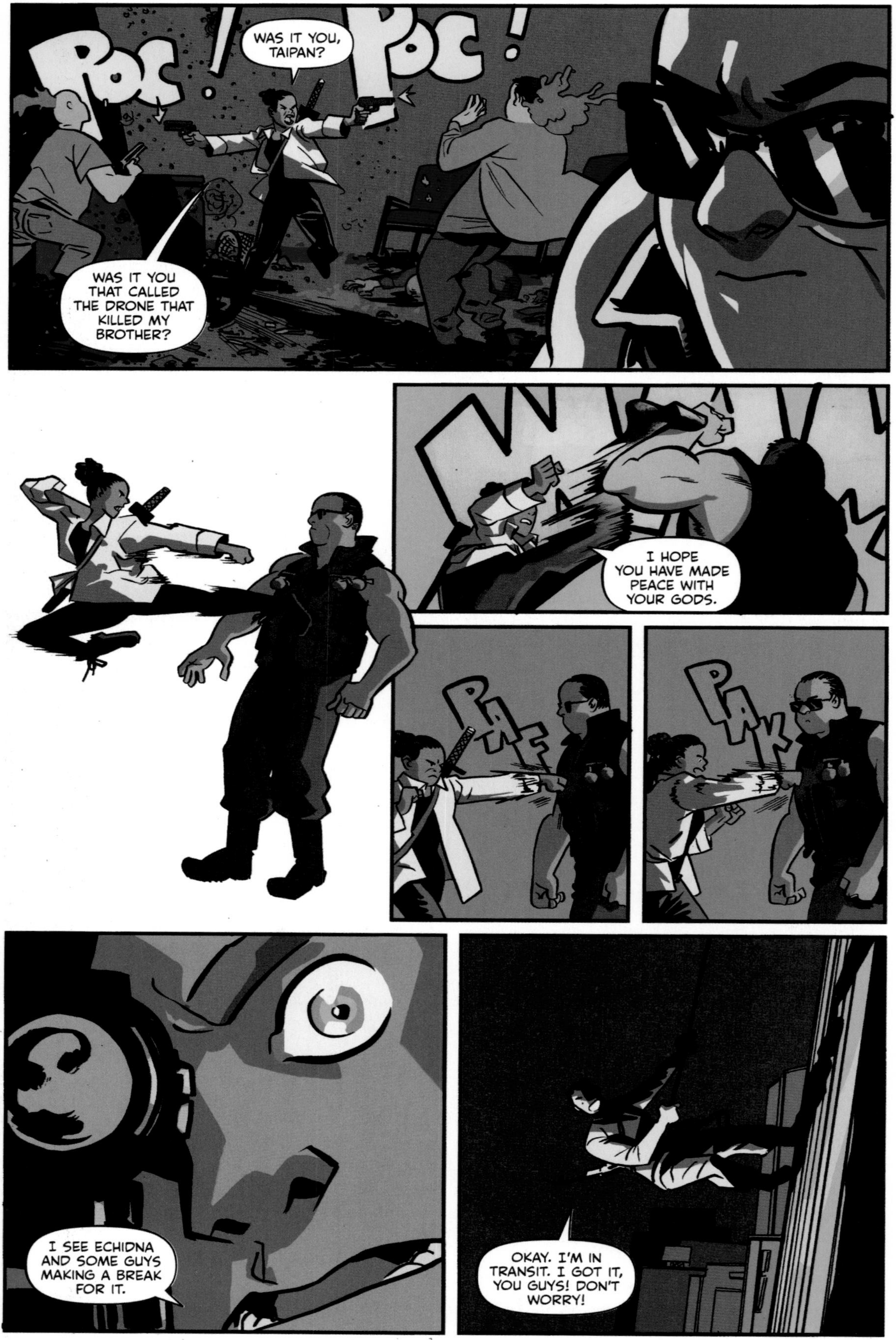
POC!
WAS IT YOU, TAIPAN?
POC!
WAS IT YOU THAT CALLED THE DRONE THAT KILLED MY BROTHER?
I HOPE YOU HAVE MADE PEACE WITH YOUR GODS.
PAF
PAK
I SEE ECHIDNA AND SOME GUYS MAKING A BREAK FOR IT.
OKAY. I'M IN TRANSIT. I GOT IT, YOU GUYS! DON'T WORRY!

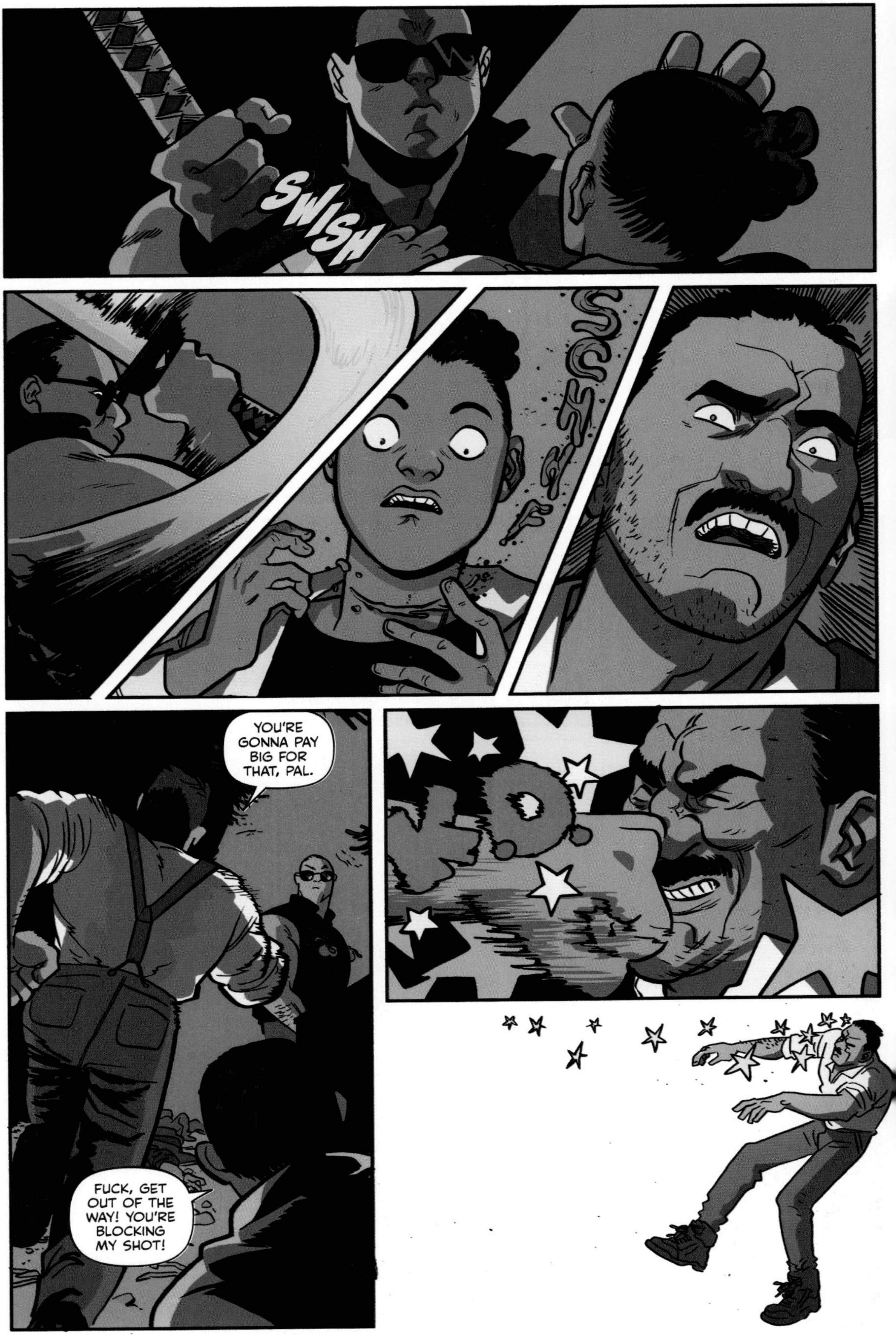
SWISH
YOU'RE GONNA PAY BIG FOR THAT, PAL.
FUCK, GET OUT OF THE WAY! YOU'RE BLOCKING MY SHOT!

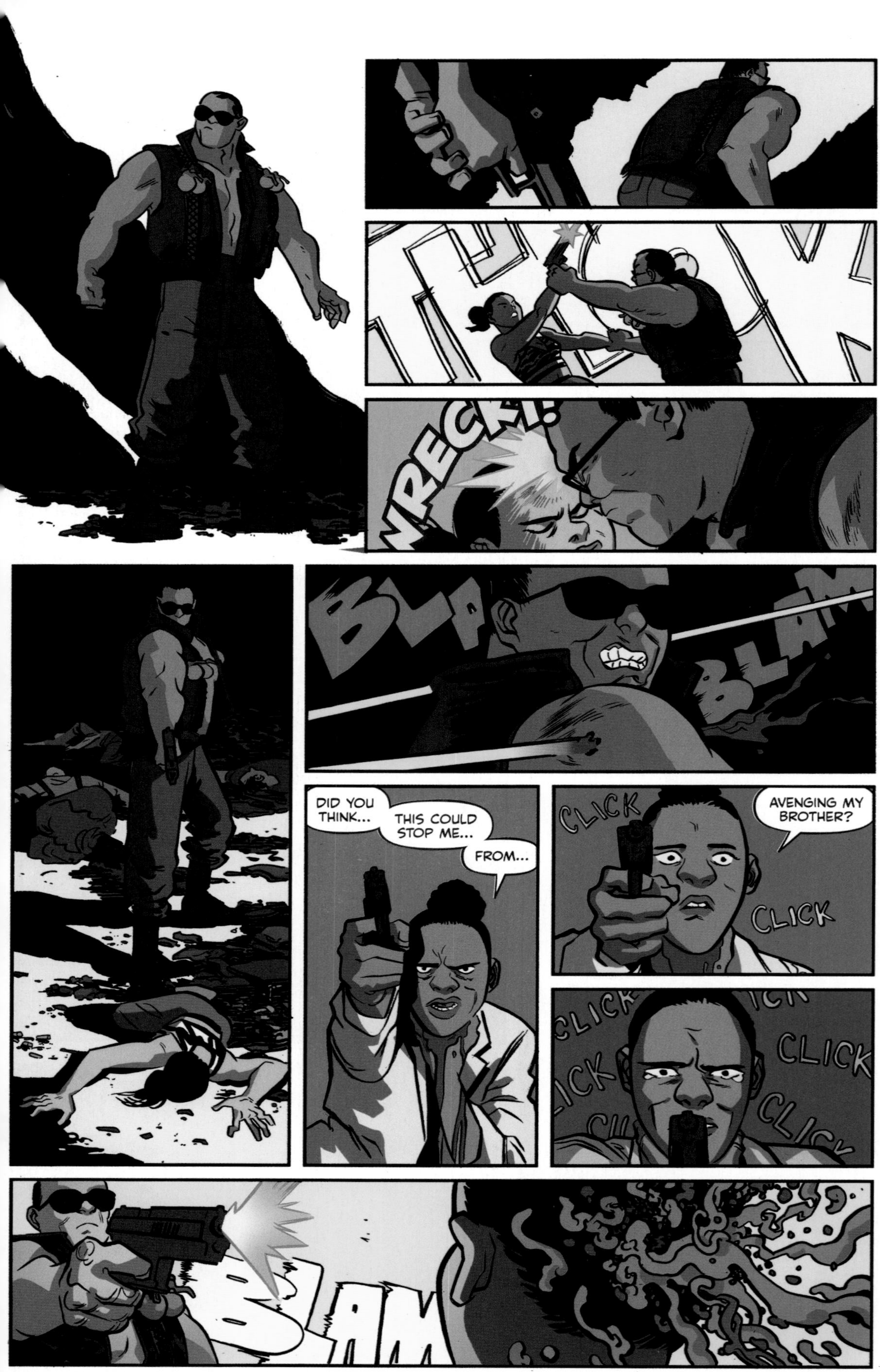

KRECK!
BLAM
BLAM
DID YOU THINK...
THIS COULD STOP ME...
FROM...
CLICK
AVENGING MY BROTHER?
CLICK
CLICK
CLICK
CLICK

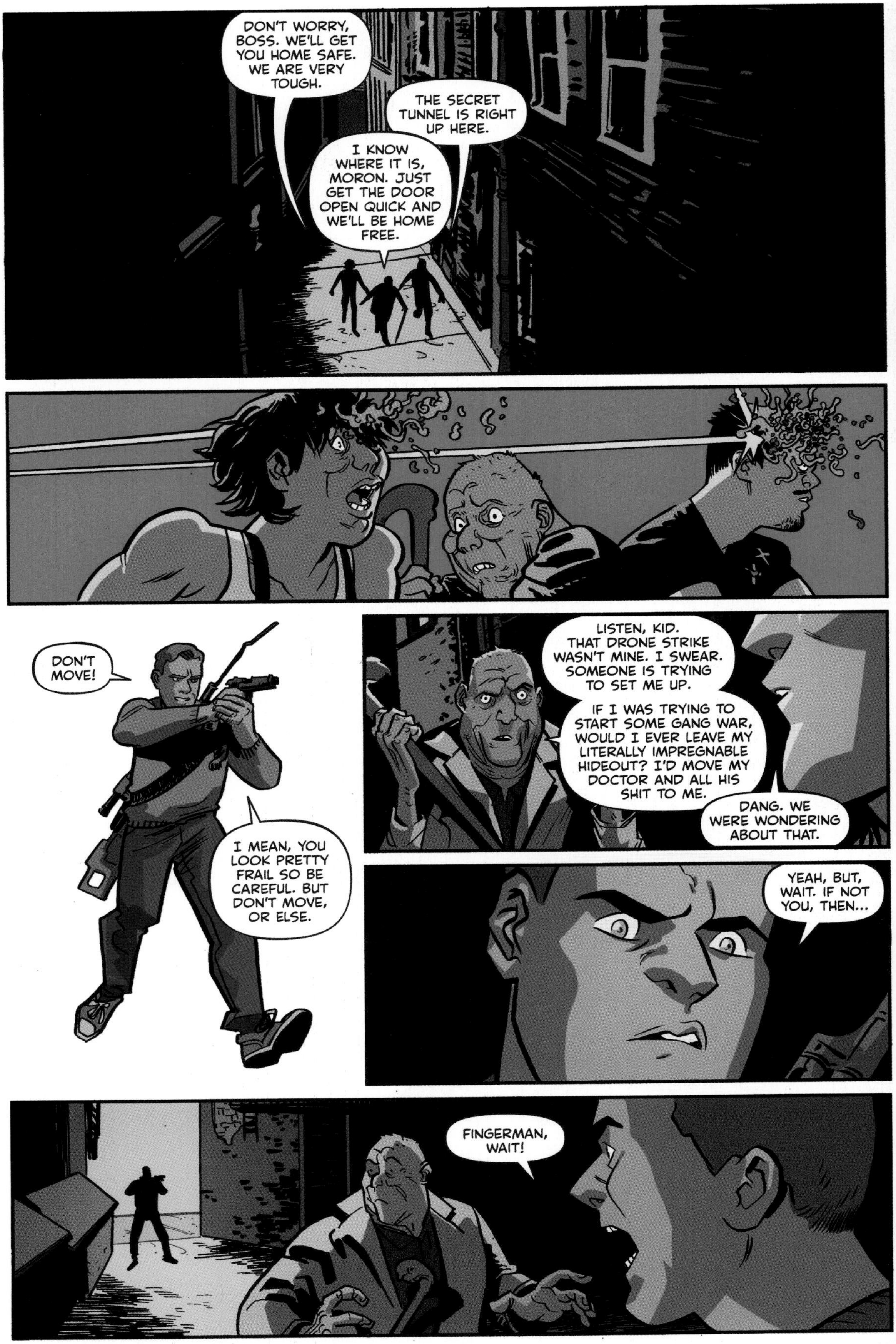

DON'T WORRY, BOSS. WE'LL GET YOU HOME SAFE. WE ARE VERY TOUGH.
THE SECRET TUNNEL IS RIGHT UP HERE.
I KNOW WHERE IT IS, MORON. JUST GET THE DOOR OPEN QUICK AND WE'LL BE HOME FREE.
DON'T MOVE!
I MEAN, YOU LOOK PRETTY FRAIL SO BE CAREFUL. BUT DON'T MOVE, OR ELSE.
LISTEN, KID. THAT DRONE STRIKE WASN'T MINE. I SWEAR. SOMEONE IS TRYING TO SET ME UP.
IF I WAS TRYING TO START SOME GANG WAR, WOULD I EVER LEAVE MY LITERALLY IMPREGNABLE HIDEOUT? I'D MOVE MY DOCTOR AND ALL HIS SHIT TO ME.
DANG. WE WERE WONDERING ABOUT THAT.
YEAH, BUT, WAIT. IF NOT YOU, THEN...
FINGERMAN, WAIT!

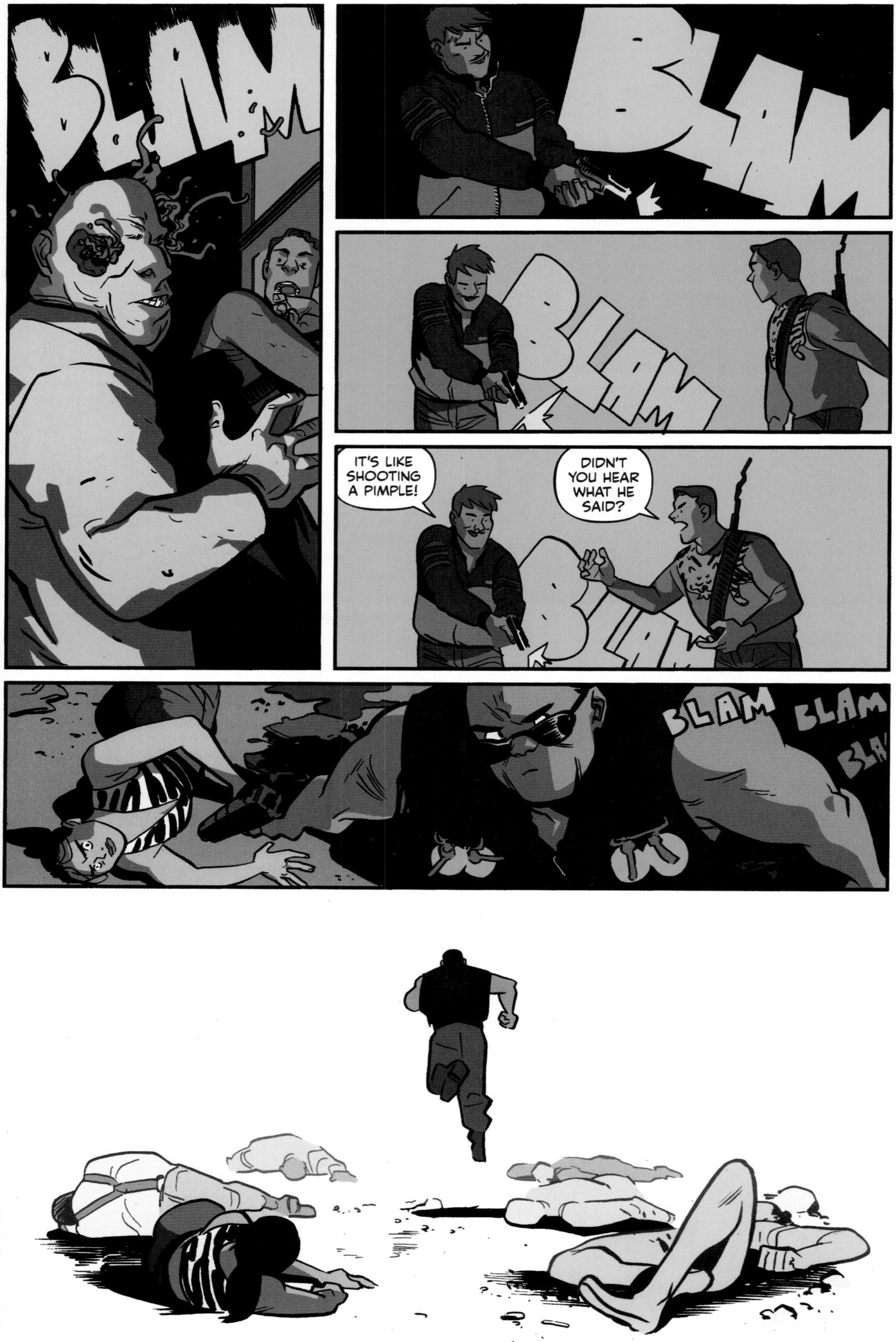
BLAM
BLAM
BLAM
IT'S LIKE SHOOTING A PIMPLE!
DIDN'T YOU HEAR WHAT HE SAID?
BLAM
BLAM
BLAM

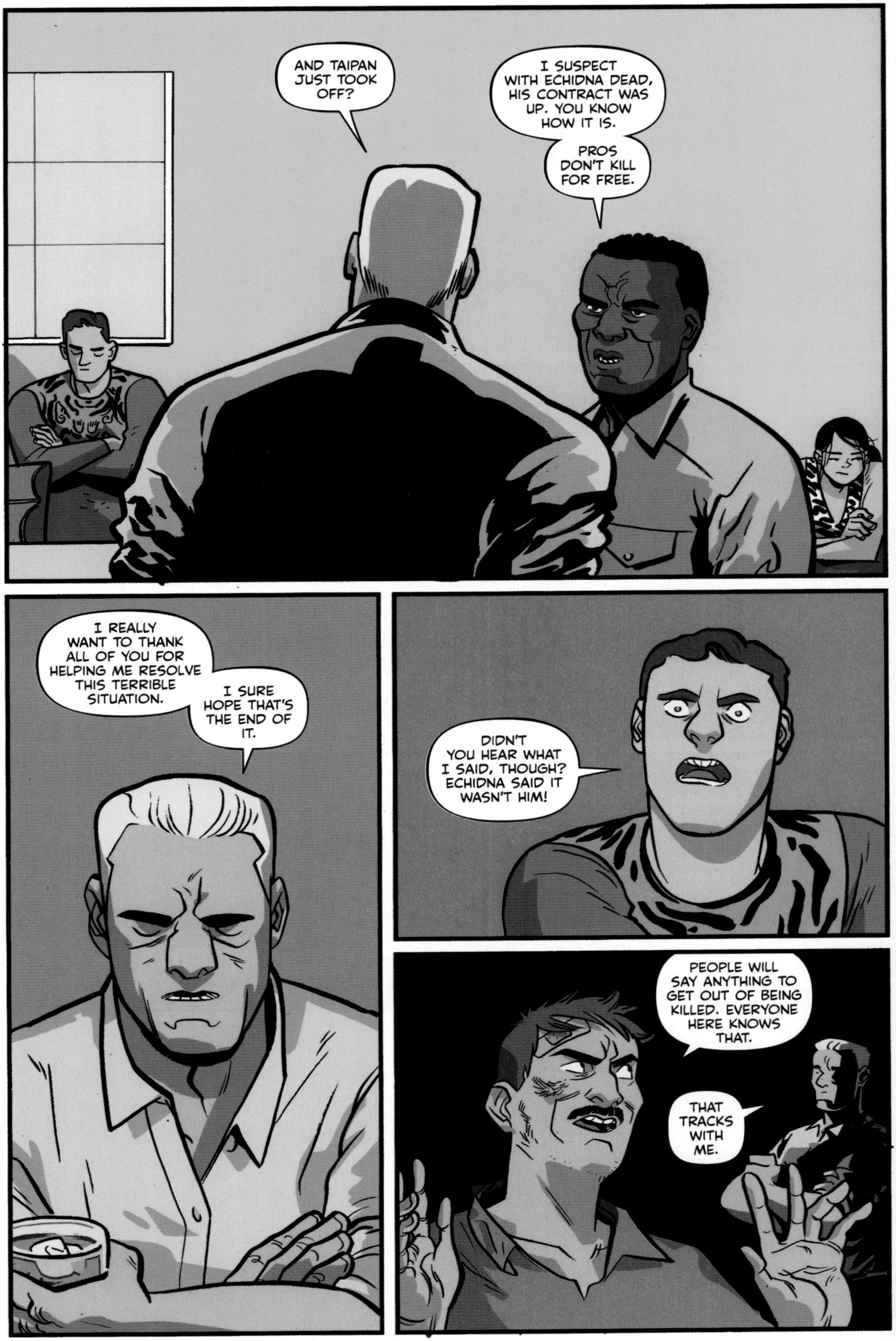
AND TAIPAN JUST TOOK OFF?
I SUSPECT WITH ECHIDNA DEAD, HIS CONTRACT WAS UP. YOU KNOW HOW IT IS.
PROS DON'T KILL FOR FREE.
I REALLY WANT TO THANK ALL OF YOU FOR HELPING ME RESOLVE THIS TERRIBLE SITUATION.
I SURE HOPE THAT'S THE END OF IT.
DIDN'T YOU HEAR WHAT I SAID, THOUGH? ECHIDNA SAID IT WASN'T HIM!
PEOPLE WILL SAY ANYTHING TO GET OUT OF BEING KILLED. EVERYONE HERE KNOWS THAT.
THAT TRACKS WITH ME.

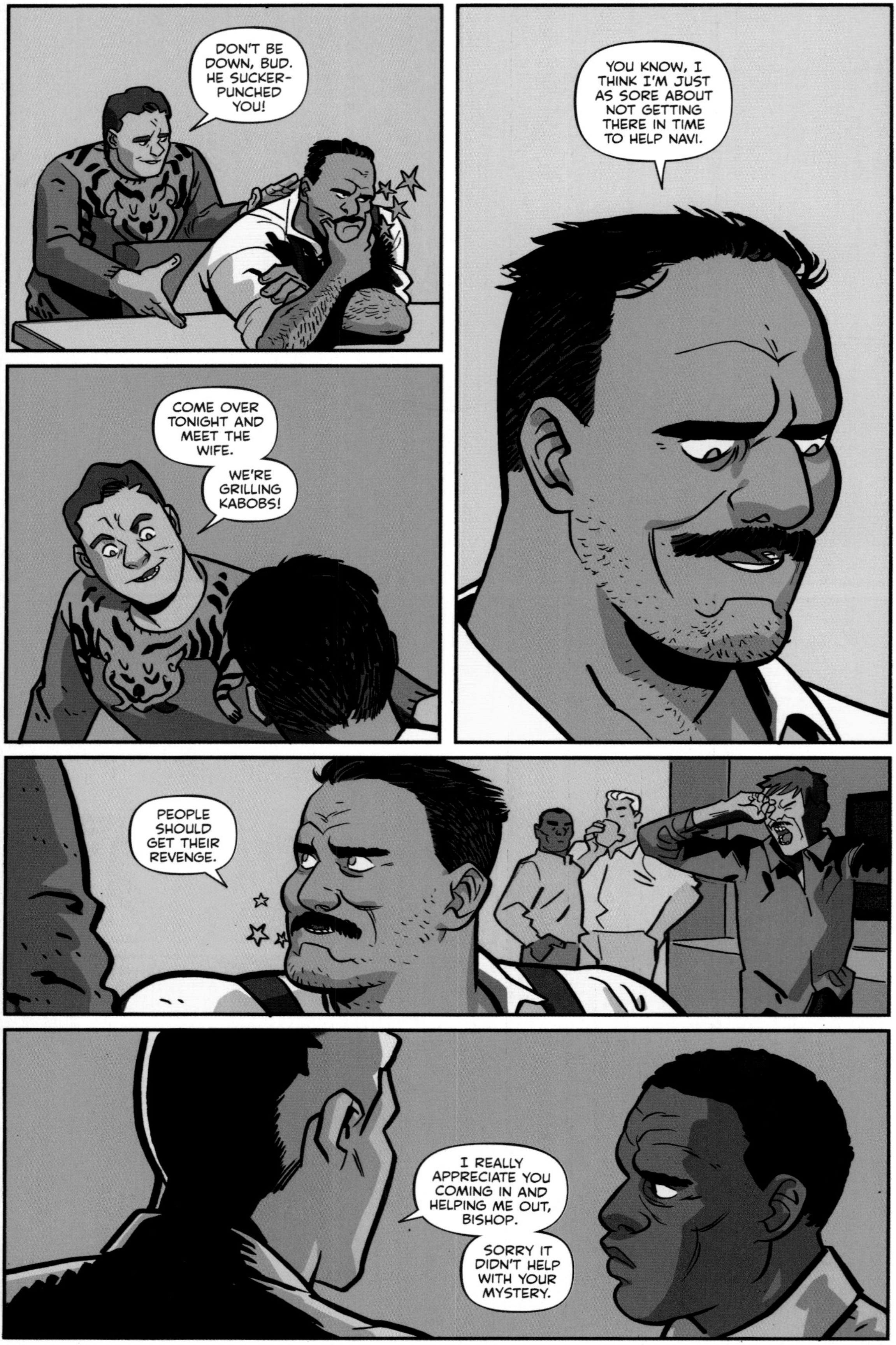
DON'T BE DOWN, BUD. HE SUCKER-PUNCHED YOU!
YOU KNOW, I THINK I'M JUST AS SORE ABOUT NOT GETTING THERE IN TIME TO HELP NAVI.
COME OVER TONIGHT AND MEET THE WIFE.
WE'RE GRILLING KABOBS!
PEOPLE SHOULD GET THEIR REVENGE.
I REALLY APPRECIATE YOU COMING IN AND HELPING ME OUT, BISHOP.
SORRY IT DIDN'T HELP WITH YOUR MYSTERY.

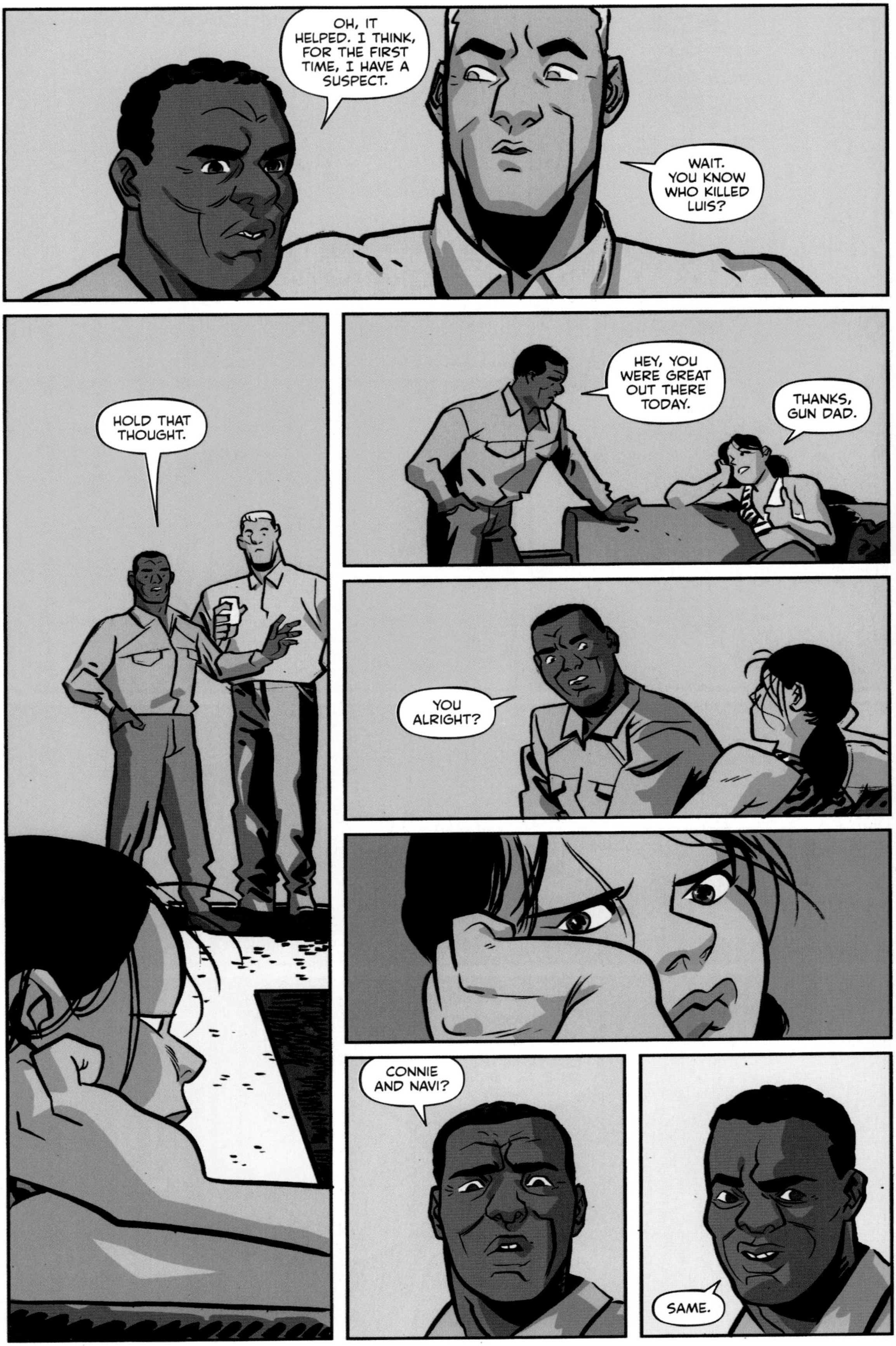
OH, IT HELPED. I THINK, FOR THE FIRST TIME, I HAVE A SUSPECT.
WAIT. YOU KNOW WHO KILLED LUIS?
HOLD THAT THOUGHT.
HEY, YOU WERE GREAT OUT THERE TODAY.
THANKS, GUN DAD.
YOU ALRIGHT?
CONNIE AND NAVI?
SAME.

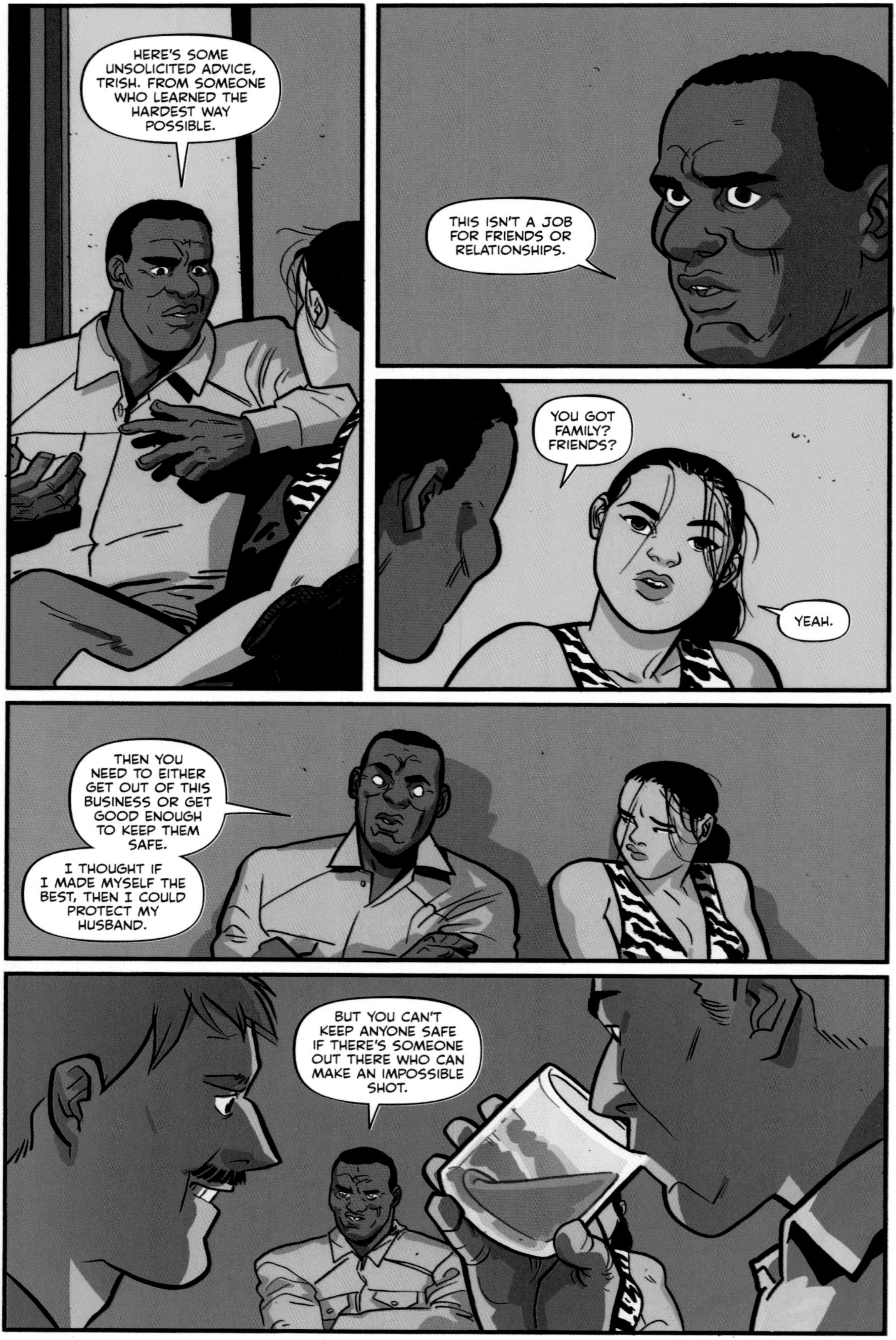
HERE'S SOME UNSOLICITED ADVICE, TRISH. FROM SOMEONE WHO LEARNED THE HARDEST WAY POSSIBLE.
THIS ISN'T A JOB FOR FRIENDS OR RELATIONSHIPS.
YOU GOT FAMILY? FRIENDS?
YEAH.
THEN YOU NEED TO EITHER GET OUT OF THIS BUSINESS OR GET GOOD ENOUGH TO KEEP THEM SAFE.
I THOUGHT IF I MADE MYSELF THE BEST, THEN I COULD PROTECT MY HUSBAND.
BUT YOU CAN'T KEEP ANYONE SAFE IF THERE'S SOMEONE OUT THERE WHO CAN MAKE AN IMPOSSIBLE SHOT.

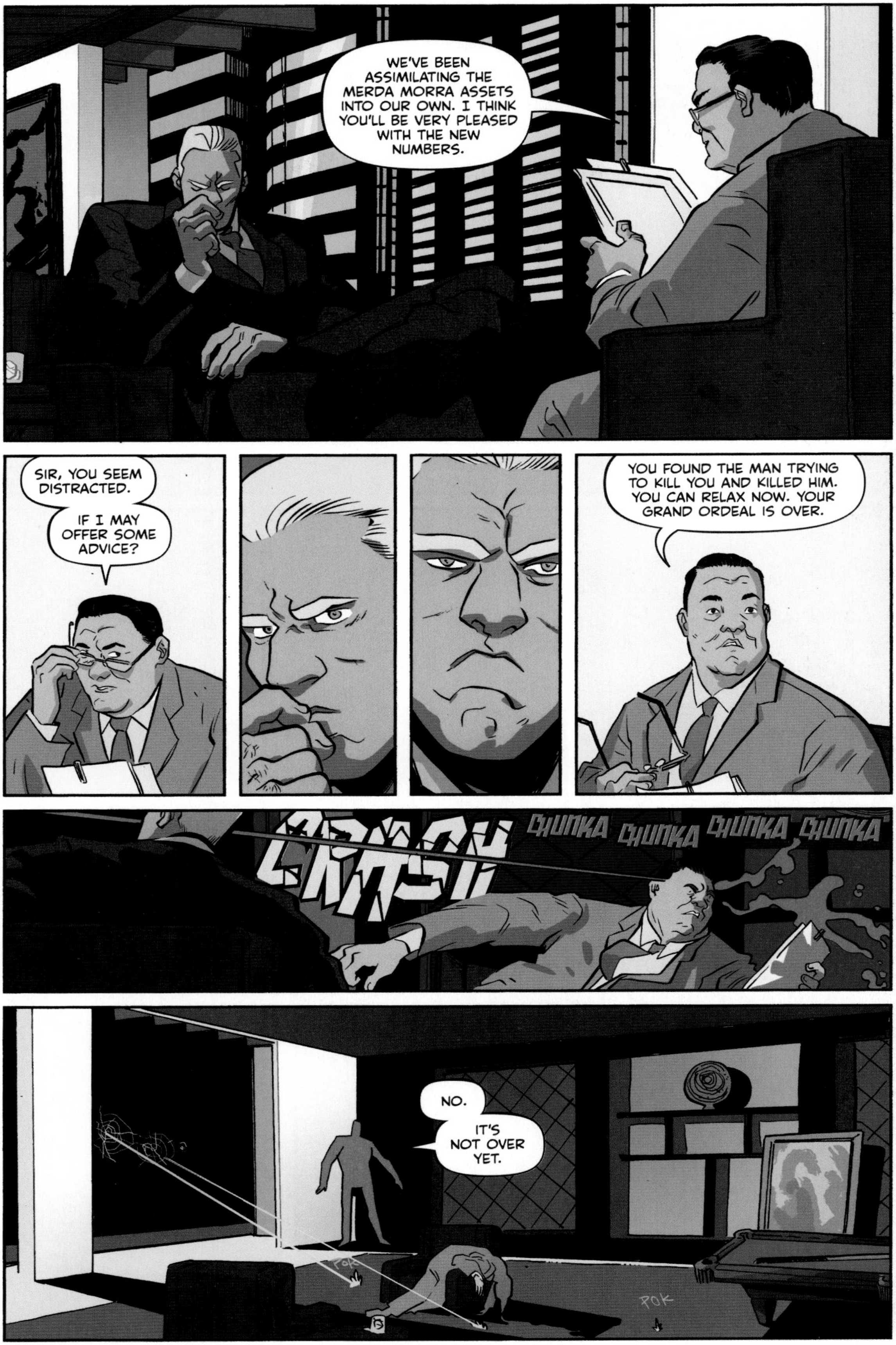

WE'VE BEEN ASSIMILATING THE MERDA MORRA ASSETS INTO OUR OWN. I THINK YOU'LL BE VERY PLEASED WITH THE NEW NUMBERS.
SIR, YOU SEEM DISTRACTED.
IF I MAY OFFER SOME ADVICE?
YOU FOUND THE MAN TRYING TO KILL YOU AND KILLED HIM. YOU CAN RELAX NOW. YOUR GRAND ORDEAL IS OVER.
CRASH
CHUNKA CHUNKA CHUNKA CHUNKA
NO.
IT'S NOT OVER YET.
POK
POK

ARE YOU HAVING THAT DREAM AGAIN?

EVERY NIGHT.

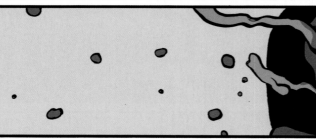

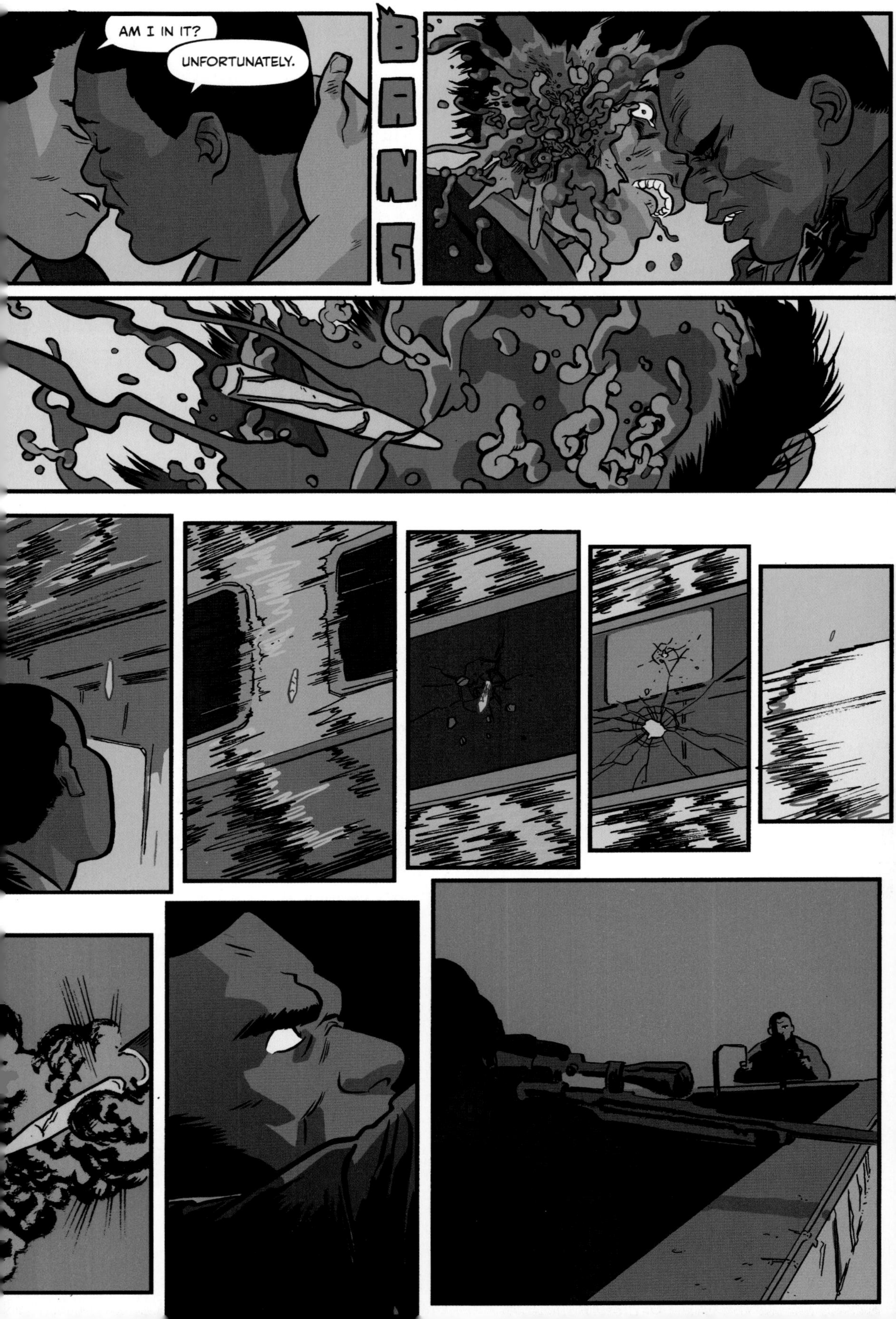
AM I IN IT?
UNFORTUNATELY.
BANG

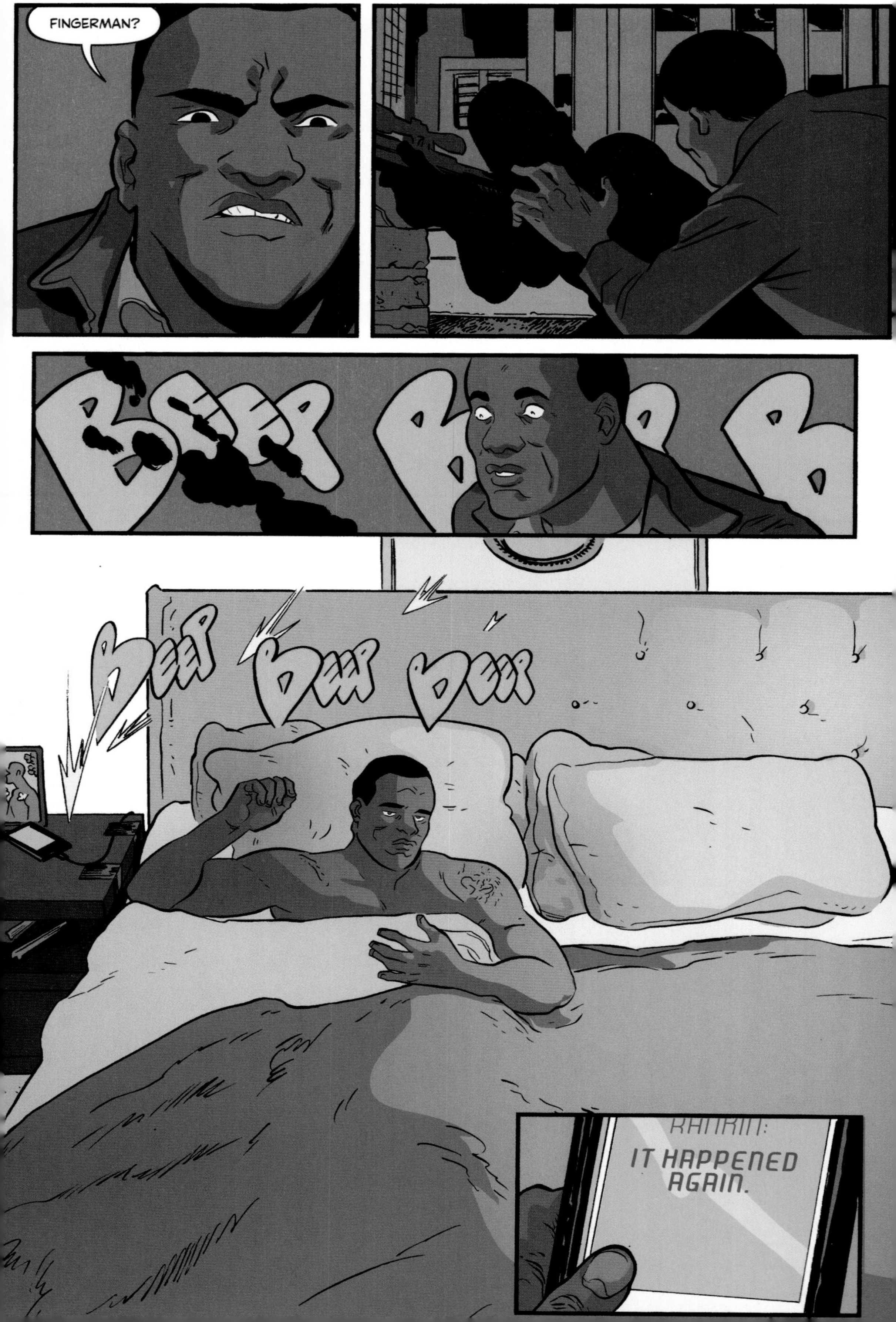
FINGERMAN?
BEEP
BEEP BEEP BEEP
IT HAPPENED AGAIN.

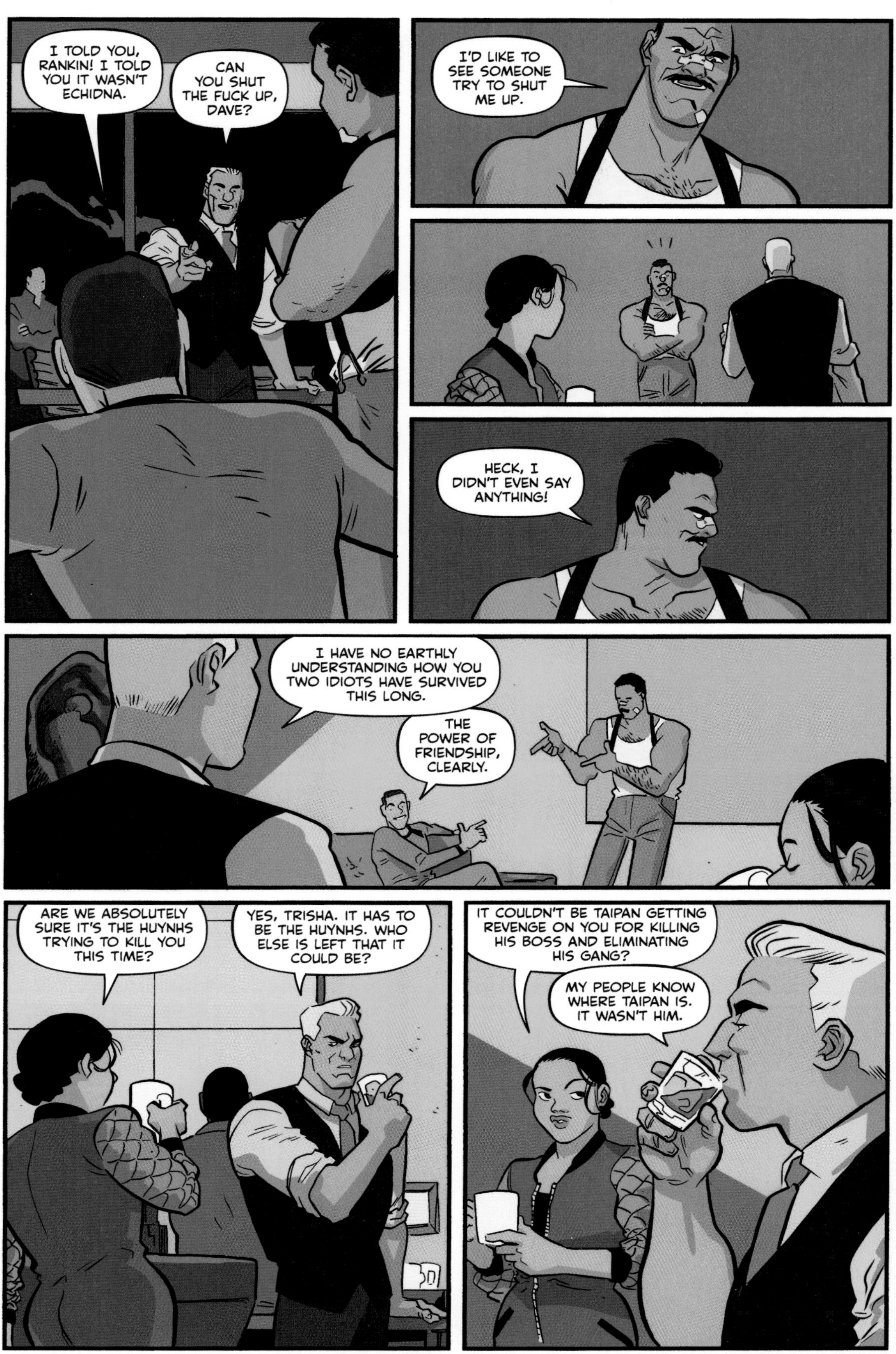

I TOLD YOU, RANKIN! I TOLD YOU IT WASN'T ECHIDNA.
CAN YOU SHUT THE FUCK UP, DAVE?
I'D LIKE TO SEE SOMEONE TRY TO SHUT ME UP.
HECK, I DIDN'T EVEN SAY ANYTHING!
I HAVE NO EARTHLY UNDERSTANDING HOW YOU TWO IDIOTS HAVE SURVIVED THIS LONG.
THE POWER OF FRIENDSHIP, CLEARLY.
ARE WE ABSOLUTELY SURE IT'S THE HUYNHS TRYING TO KILL YOU THIS TIME?
YES, TRISHA. IT HAS TO BE THE HUYNHS. WHO ELSE IS LEFT THAT IT COULD BE?
IT COULDN'T BE TAIPAN GETTING REVENGE ON YOU FOR KILLING HIS BOSS AND ELIMINATING HIS GANG?
MY PEOPLE KNOW WHERE TAIPAN IS. IT WASN'T HIM.

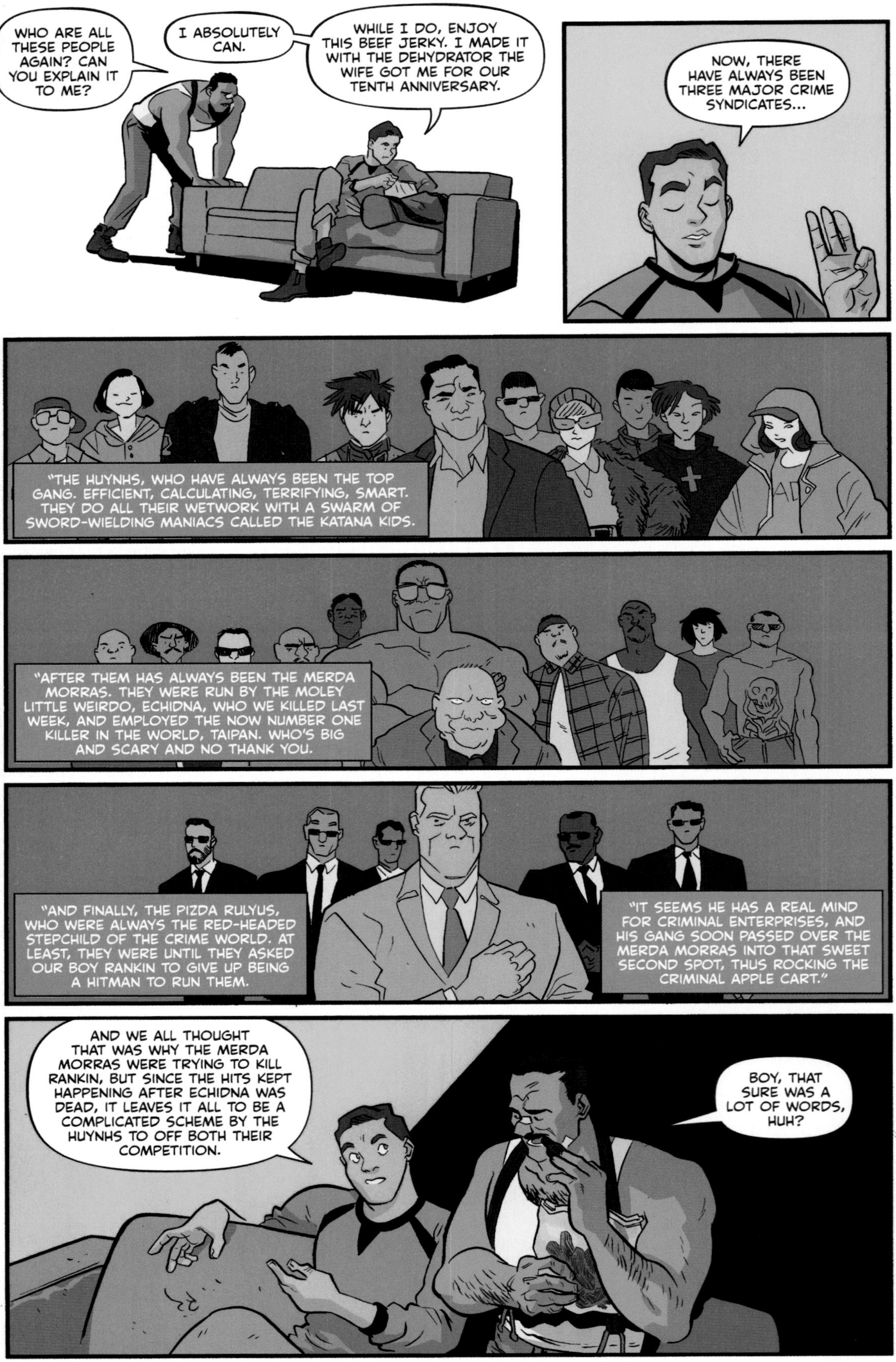

WHO ARE ALL THESE PEOPLE AGAIN? CAN YOU EXPLAIN IT TO ME?
I ABSOLUTELY CAN.
WHILE I DO, ENJOY THIS BEEF JERKY. I MADE IT WITH THE DEHYDRATOR THE WIFE GOT ME FOR OUR TENTH ANNIVERSARY.
NOW, THERE HAVE ALWAYS BEEN THREE MAJOR CRIME SYNDICATES...
"THE HUYNHS, WHO HAVE ALWAYS BEEN THE TOP GANG. EFFICIENT, CALCULATING, TERRIFYING, SMART. THEY DO ALL THEIR WETWORK WITH A SWARM OF SWORD-WIELDING MANIACS CALLED THE KATANA KIDS.
"AFTER THEM HAS ALWAYS BEEN THE MERDA MORRAS. THEY WERE RUN BY THE MOLEY LITTLE WEIRDO, ECHIDNA, WHO WE KILLED LAST WEEK, AND EMPLOYED THE NOW NUMBER ONE KILLER IN THE WORLD, TAIPAN. WHO'S BIG AND SCARY AND NO THANK YOU.
"AND FINALLY, THE PIZDA RULYUS, WHO WERE ALWAYS THE RED-HEADED STEPCHILD OF THE CRIME WORLD. AT LEAST, THEY WERE UNTIL THEY ASKED OUR BOY RANKIN TO GIVE UP BEING A HITMAN TO RUN THEM.
"IT SEEMS HE HAS A REAL MIND FOR CRIMINAL ENTERPRISES, AND HIS GANG SOON PASSED OVER THE MERDA MORRAS INTO THAT SWEET SECOND SPOT, THUS ROCKING THE CRIMINAL APPLE CART."
AND WE ALL THOUGHT THAT WAS WHY THE MERDA MORRAS WERE TRYING TO KILL RANKIN, BUT SINCE THE HITS KEPT HAPPENING AFTER ECHIDNA WAS DEAD, IT LEAVES IT ALL TO BE A COMPLICATED SCHEME BY THE HUYNHS TO OFF BOTH THEIR COMPETITION.
BOY, THAT SURE WAS A LOT OF WORDS, HUH?

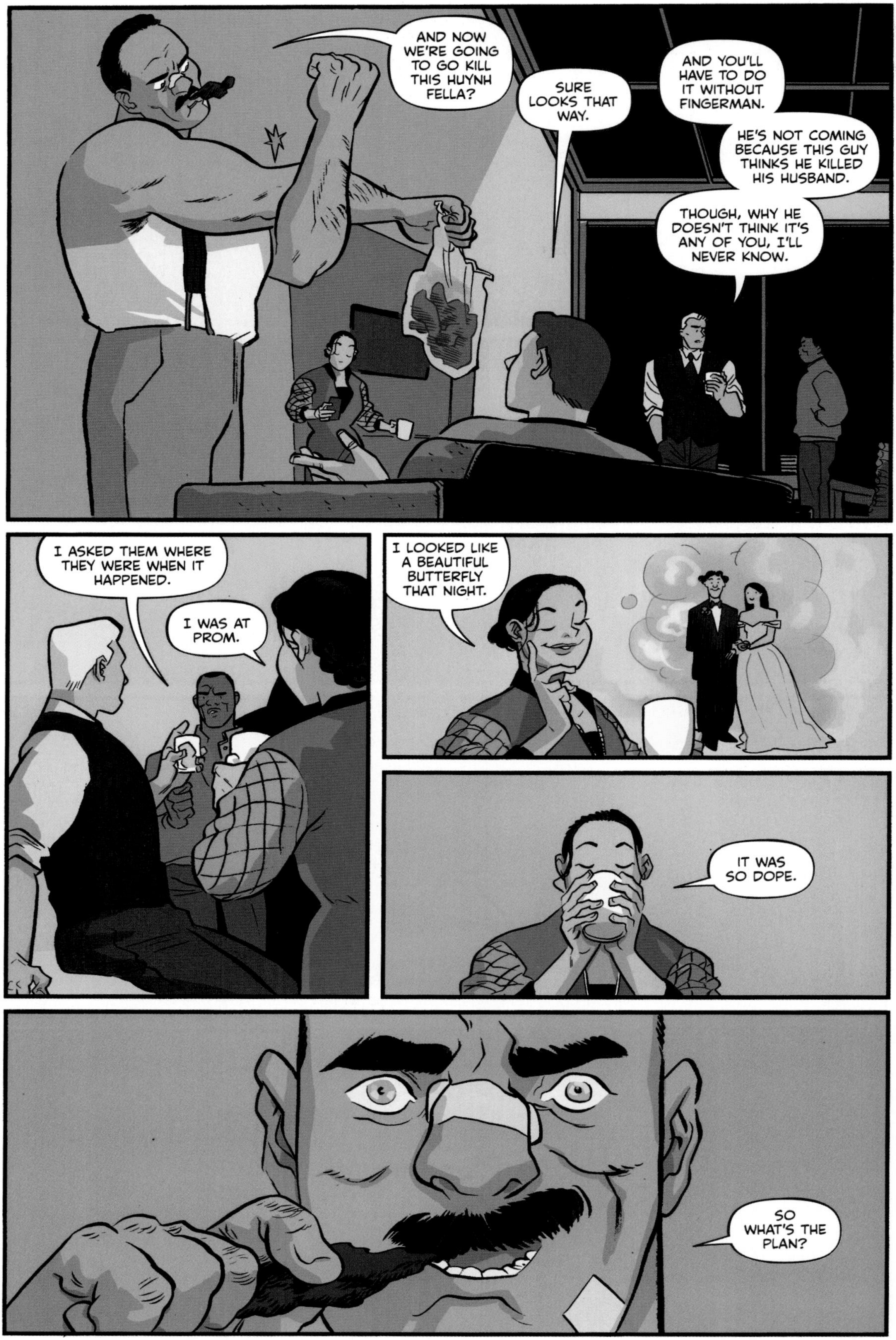
AND NOW WE'RE GOING TO GO KILL THIS HUYNH FELLA?
SURE LOOKS THAT WAY.
AND YOU'LL HAVE TO DO IT WITHOUT FINGERMAN.
HE'S NOT COMING BECAUSE THIS GUY THINKS HE KILLED HIS HUSBAND.
THOUGH, WHY HE DOESN'T THINK IT'S ANY OF YOU, I'LL NEVER KNOW.
I ASKED THEM WHERE THEY WERE WHEN IT HAPPENED.
I WAS AT PROM.
I LOOKED LIKE A BEAUTIFUL BUTTERFLY THAT NIGHT.
IT WAS SO DOPE.
SO WHAT'S THE PLAN?

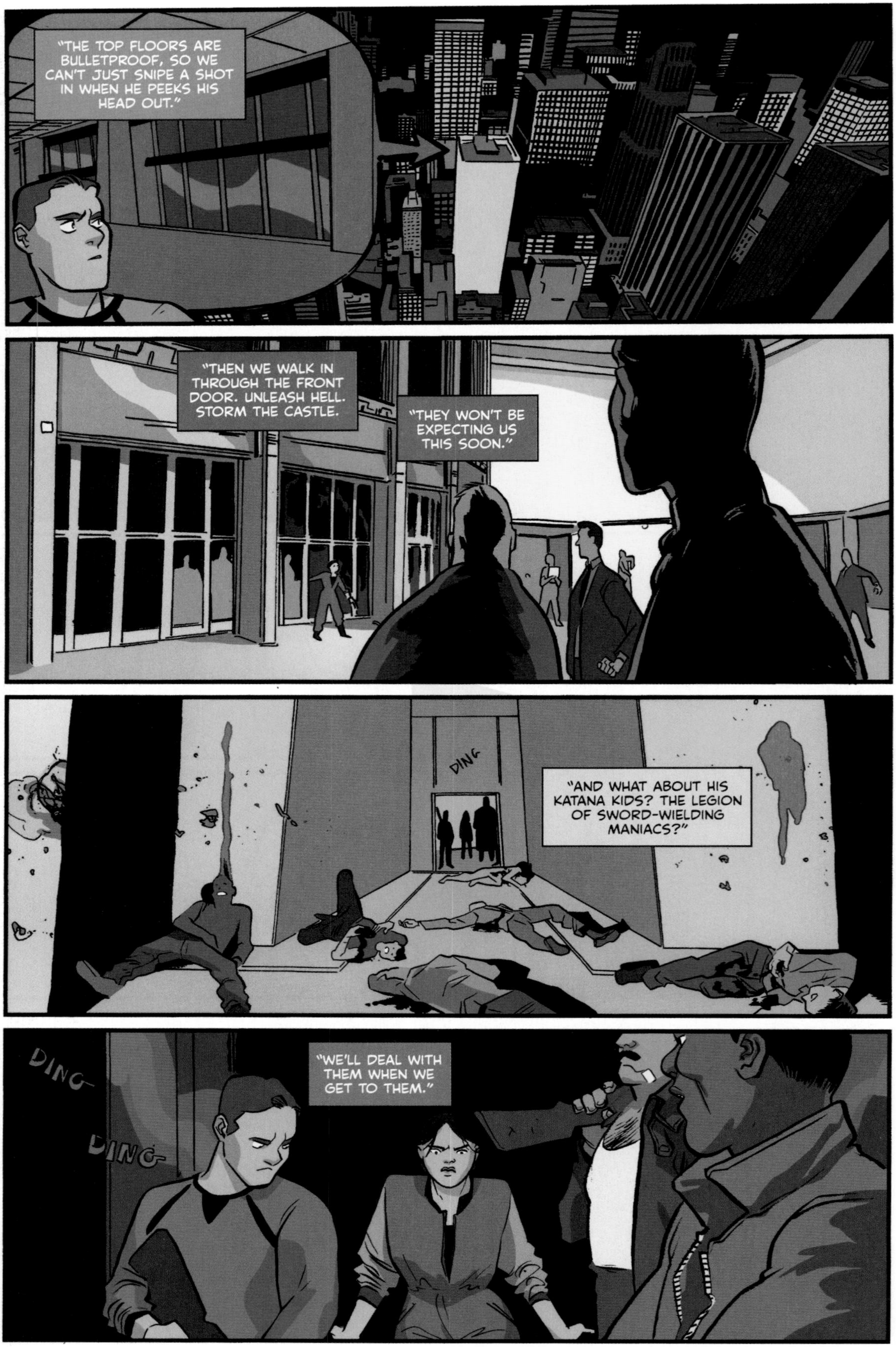
"THE TOP FLOORS ARE BULLETPROOF, SO WE CAN'T JUST SNIPE A SHOT IN WHEN HE PEEKS HIS HEAD OUT."
"THEN WE WALK IN THROUGH THE FRONT DOOR. UNLEASH HELL. STORM THE CASTLE.
"THEY WON'T BE EXPECTING US THIS SOON."
DING
"AND WHAT ABOUT HIS KATANA KIDS? THE LEGION OF SWORD-WIELDING MANIACS?"
DING-
DING-
"WE'LL DEAL WITH THEM WHEN WE GET TO THEM."

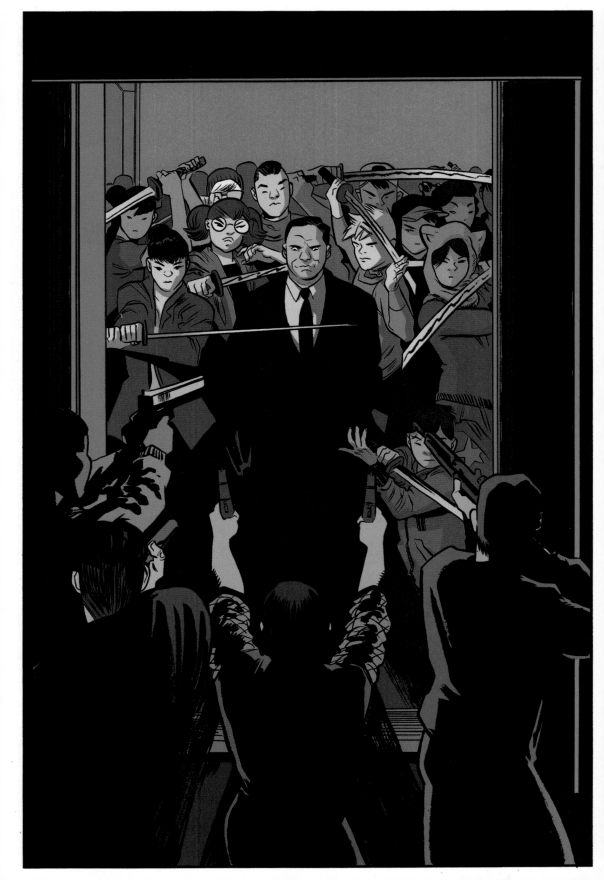

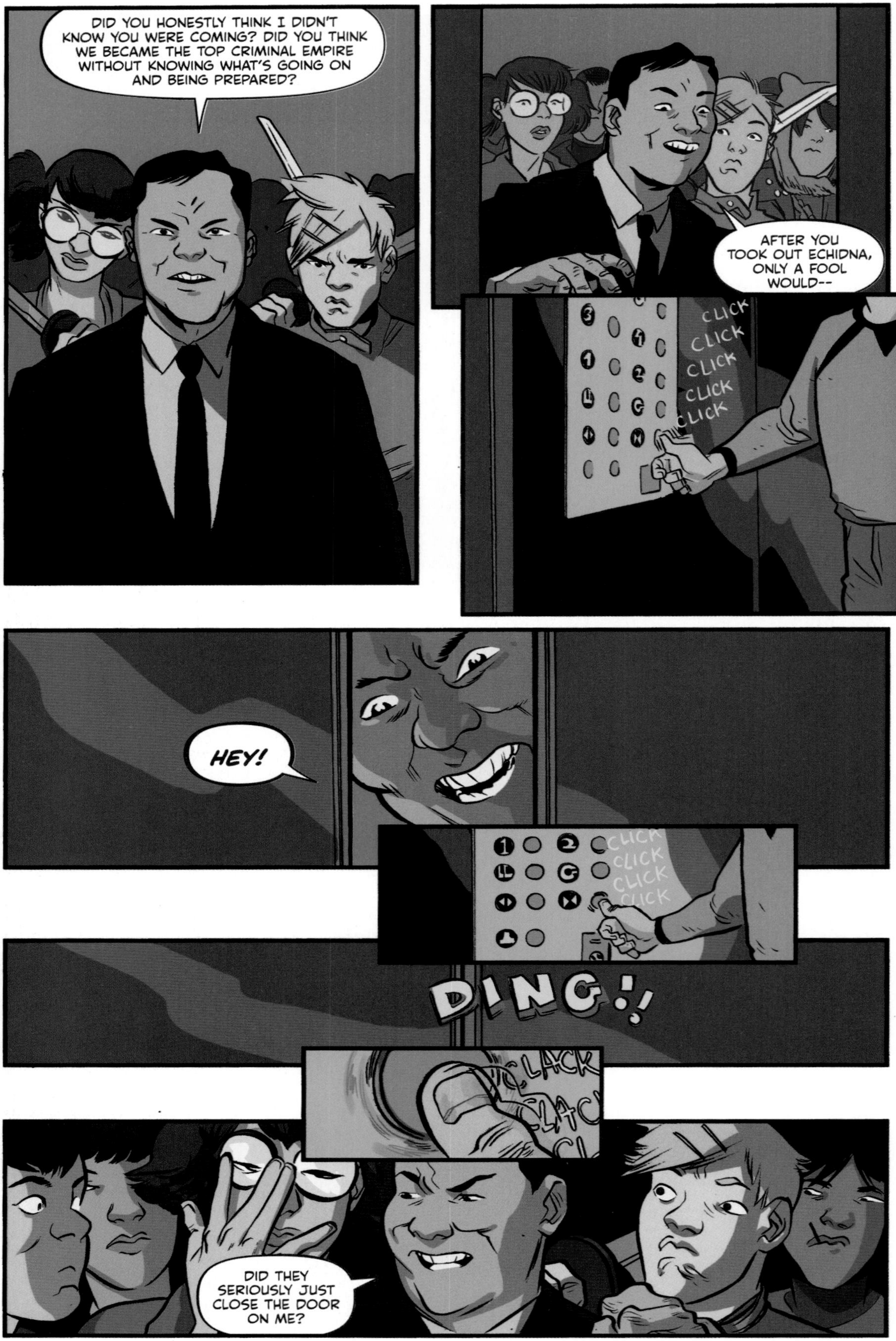
DID YOU HONESTLY THINK I DIDN'T KNOW YOU WERE COMING? DID YOU THINK WE BECAME THE TOP CRIMINAL EMPIRE WITHOUT KNOWING WHAT'S GOING ON AND BEING PREPARED?
AFTER YOU TOOK OUT ECHIDNA, ONLY A FOOL WOULD--
CLICK CLICK CLICK CLICK CLICK
HEY!
CLICK CLICK CLICK CLICK
DING!!
CLACK CLACK
DID THEY SERIOUSLY JUST CLOSE THE DOOR ON ME?

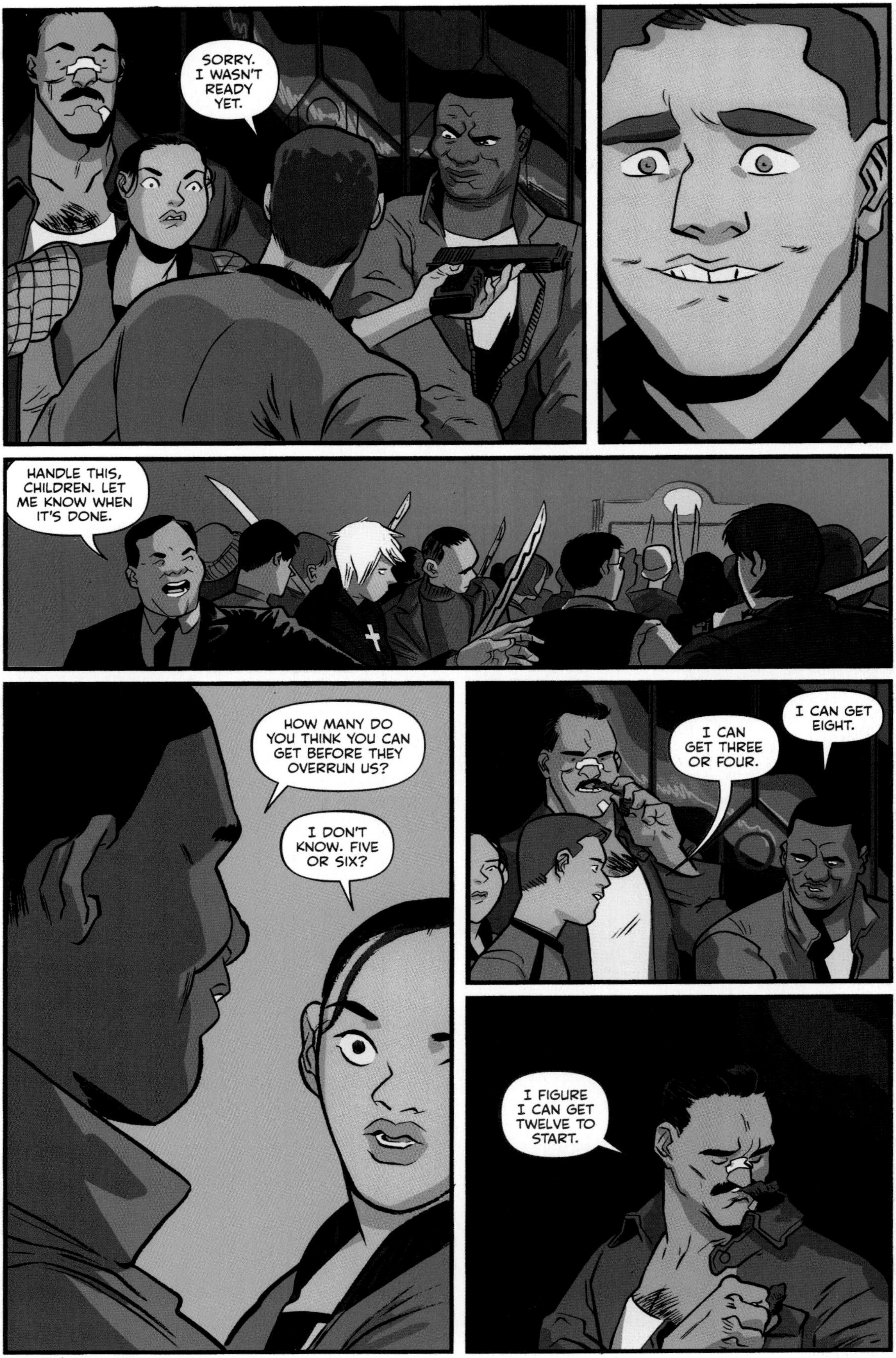
SORRY. I WASN'T READY YET.
HANDLE THIS, CHILDREN. LET ME KNOW WHEN IT'S DONE.
HOW MANY DO YOU THINK YOU CAN GET BEFORE THEY OVERRUN US?
I DON'T KNOW. FIVE OR SIX?
I CAN GET THREE OR FOUR.
I CAN GET EIGHT.
I FIGURE I CAN GET TWELVE TO START.

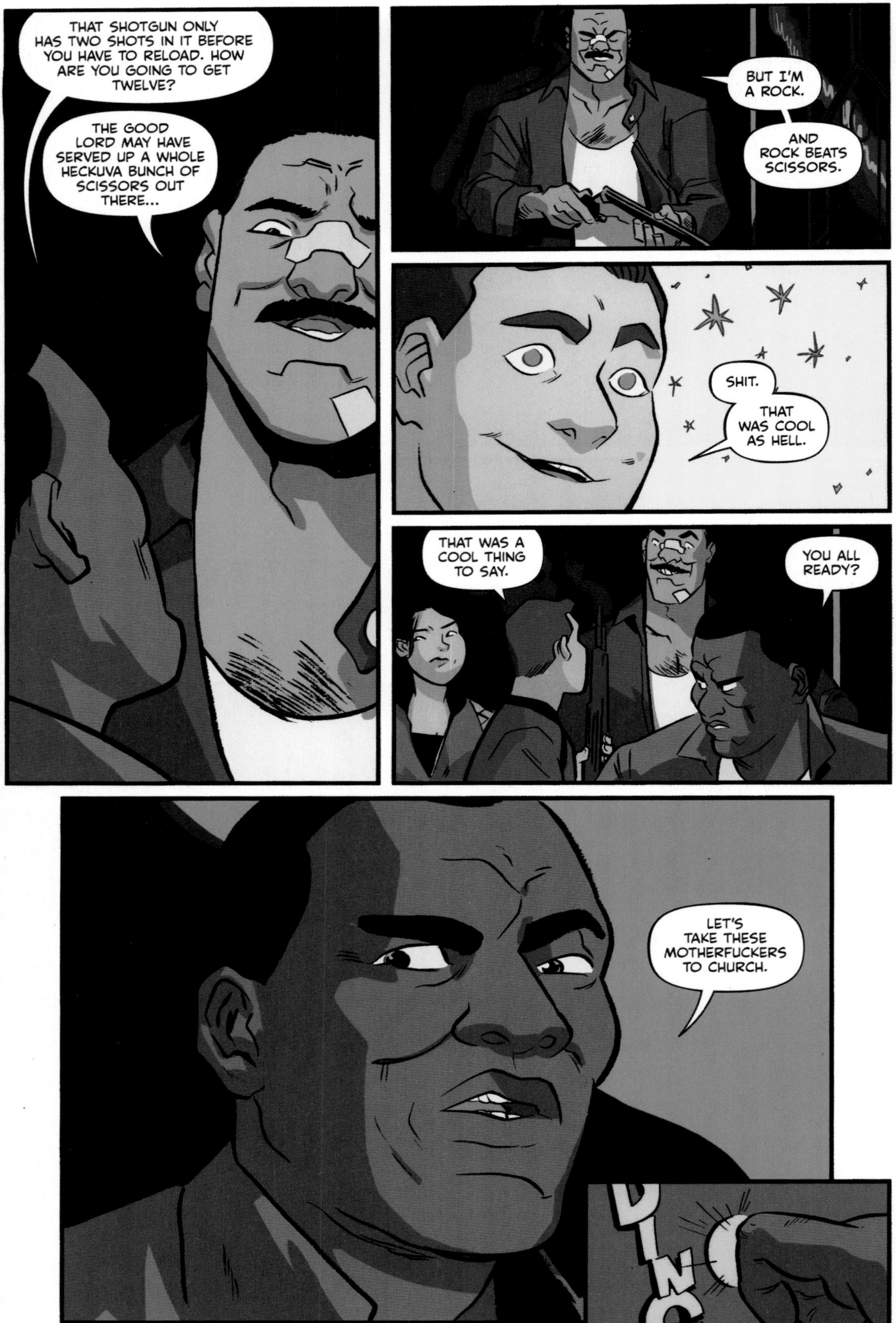
THAT SHOTGUN ONLY HAS TWO SHOTS IN IT BEFORE YOU HAVE TO RELOAD. HOW ARE YOU GOING TO GET TWELVE?
THE GOOD LORD MAY HAVE SERVED UP A WHOLE HECKUVA BUNCH OF SCISSORS OUT THERE...
BUT I'M A ROCK.
AND ROCK BEATS SCISSORS.
SHIT.
THAT WAS COOL AS HELL.
THAT WAS A COOL THING TO SAY.
YOU ALL READY?
LET'S TAKE THESE MOTHERFUCKERS TO CHURCH.
DING

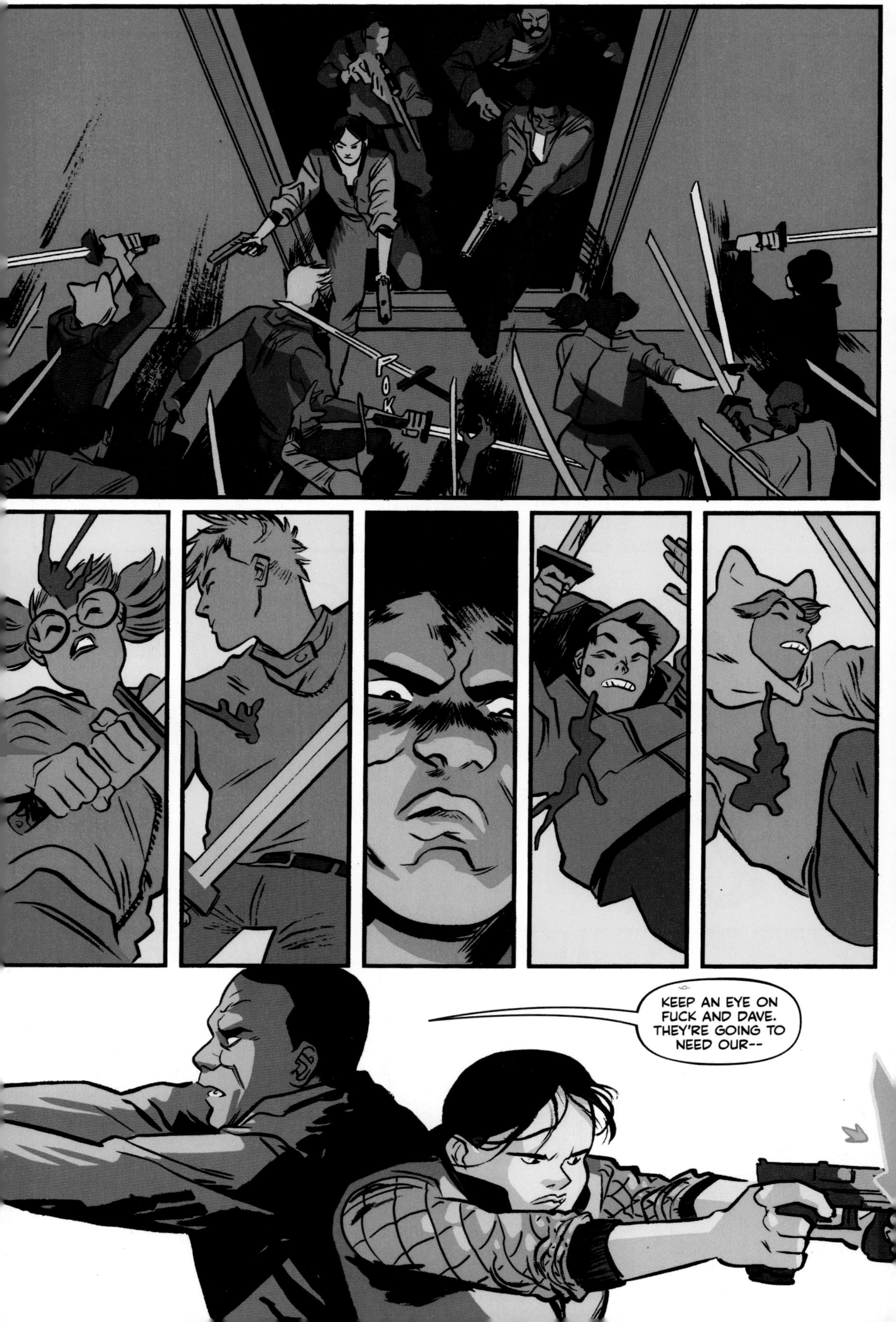
POK
KEEP AN EYE ON FUCK AND DAVE. THEY'RE GOING TO NEED OUR--

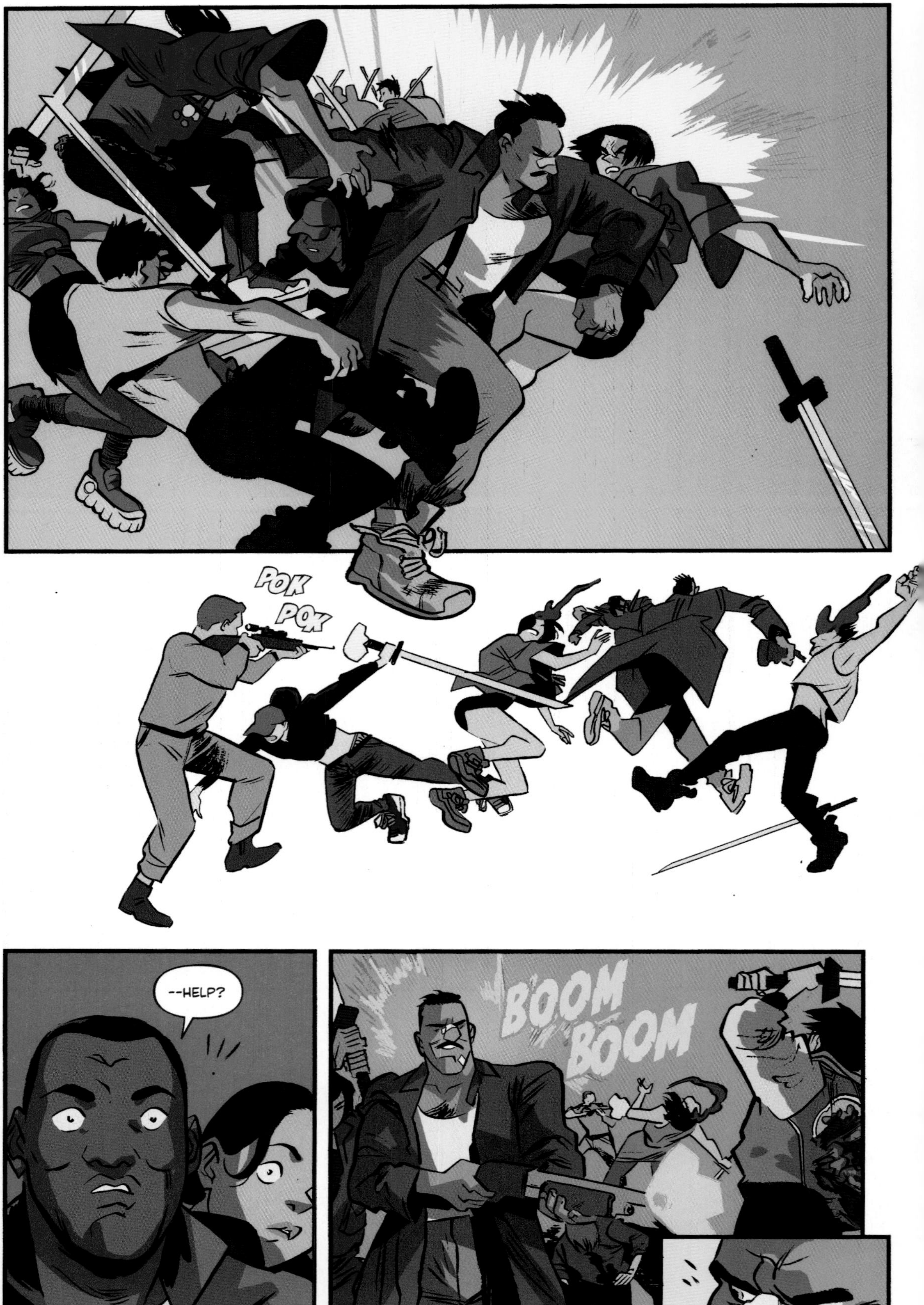
POK
POK
--HELP?
BOOM
BOOM

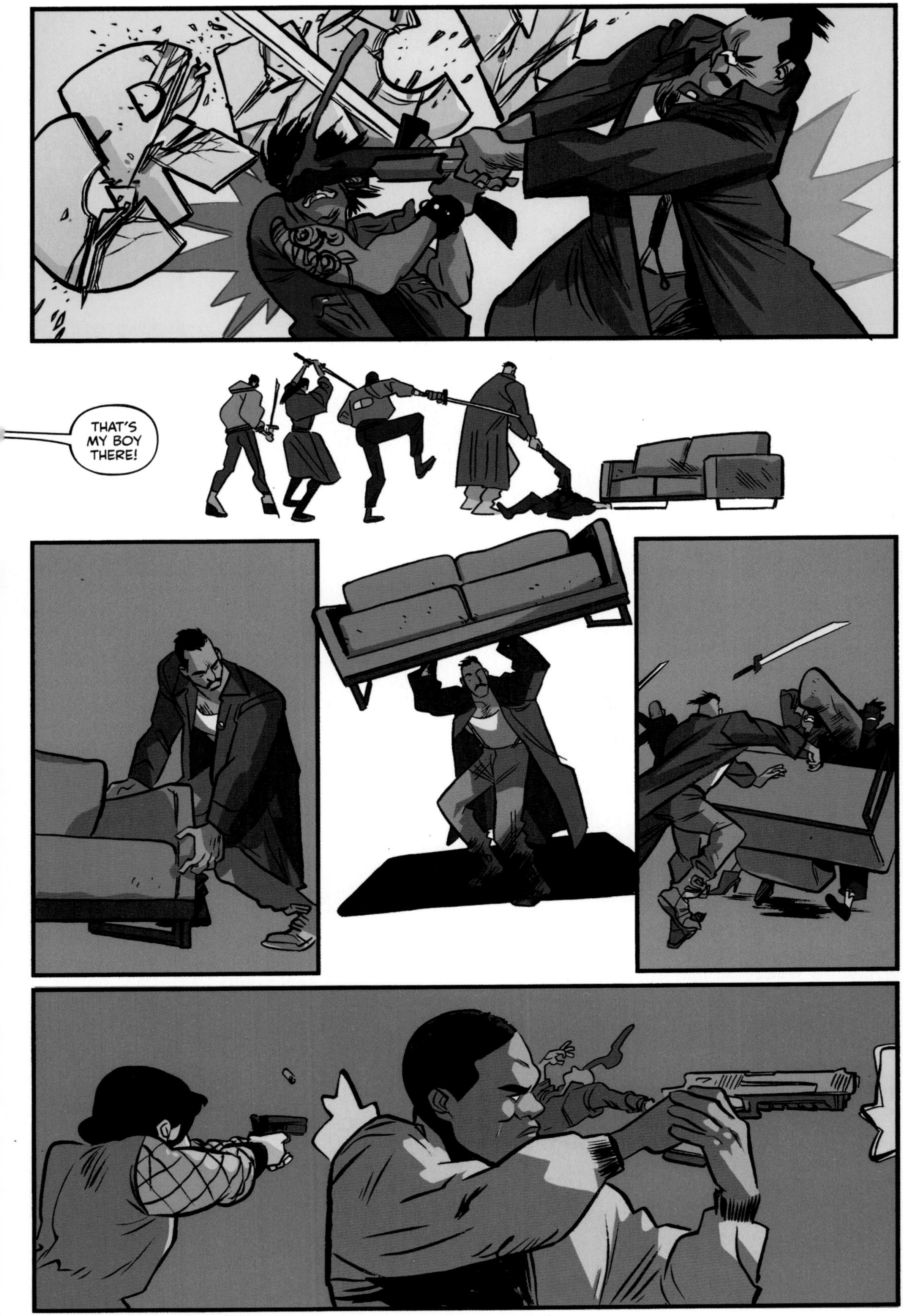
THAT'S MY BOY THERE!

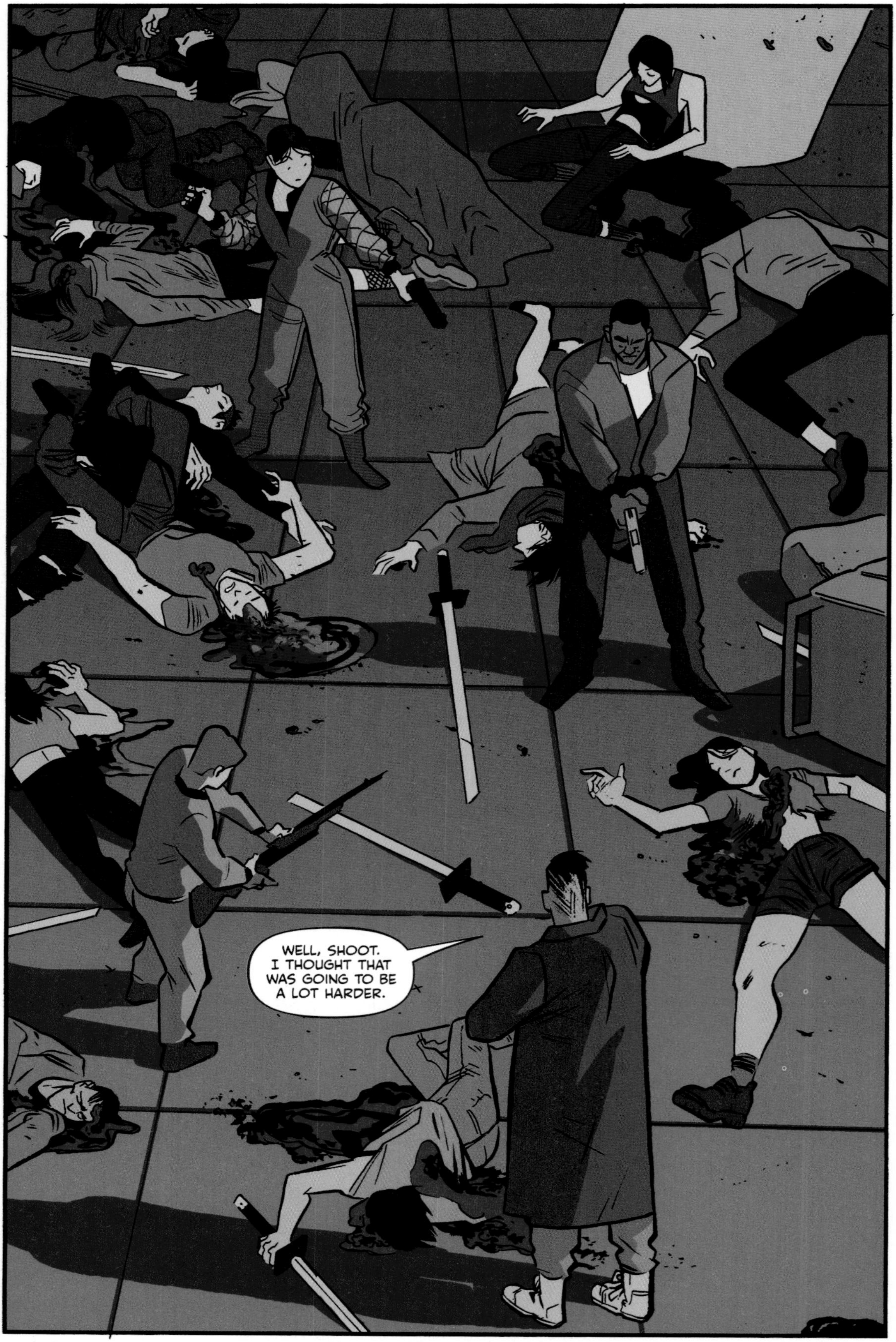
WELL, SHOOT. I THOUGHT THAT WAS GOING TO BE A LOT HARDER.

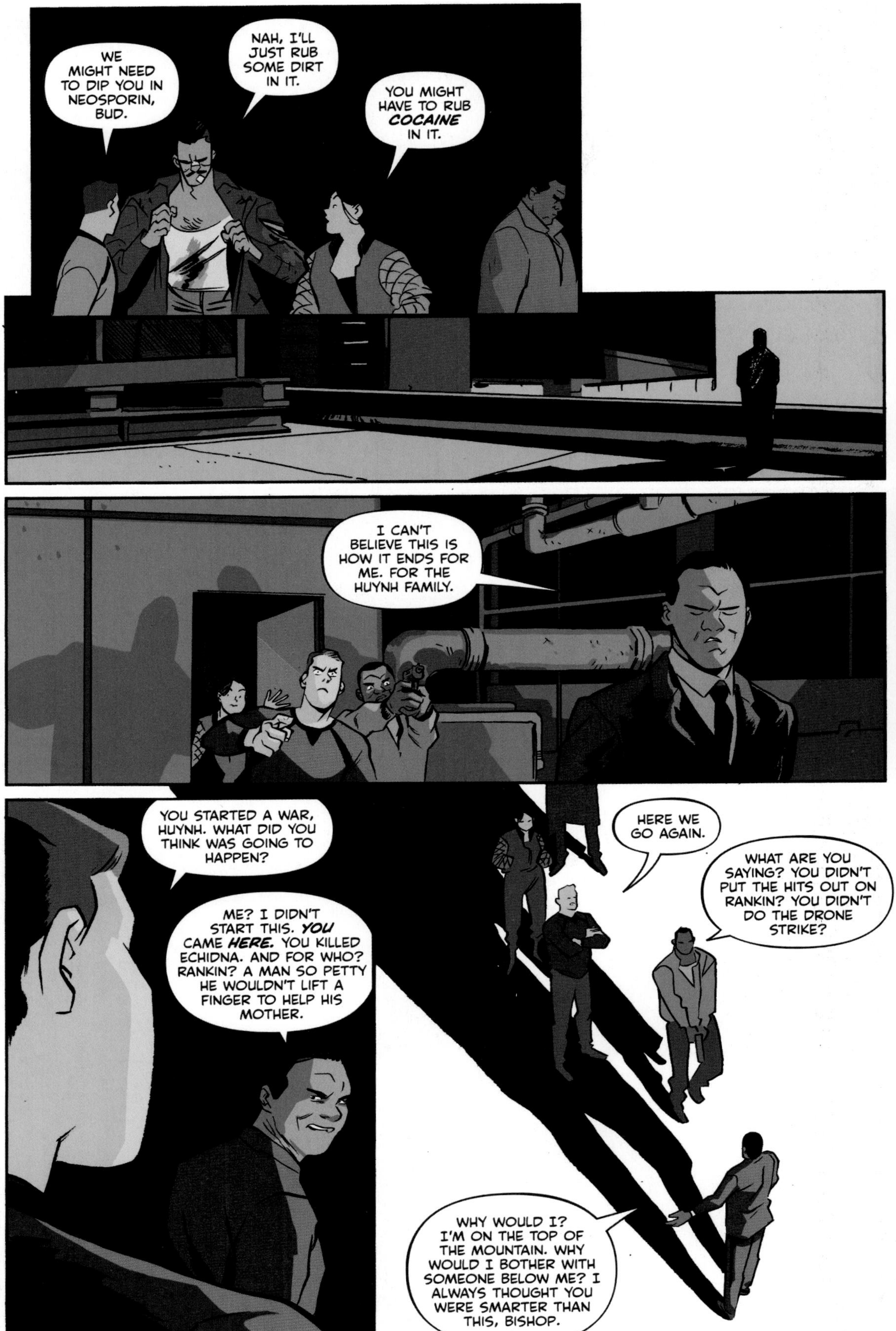
WE MIGHT NEED TO DIP YOU IN NEOSPORIN, BUD.
NAH, I'LL JUST RUB SOME DIRT IN IT.
YOU MIGHT HAVE TO RUB *COCAINE* IN IT.
I CAN'T BELIEVE THIS IS HOW IT ENDS FOR ME. FOR THE HUYNH FAMILY.
YOU STARTED A WAR, HUYNH. WHAT DID YOU THINK WAS GOING TO HAPPEN?
HERE WE GO AGAIN.
ME? I DIDN'T START THIS. *YOU* CAME *HERE.* YOU KILLED ECHIDNA. AND FOR WHO? RANKIN? A MAN SO PETTY HE WOULDN'T LIFT A FINGER TO HELP HIS MOTHER.
WHAT ARE YOU SAYING? YOU DIDN'T PUT THE HITS OUT ON RANKIN? YOU DIDN'T DO THE DRONE STRIKE?
WHY WOULD I? I'M ON THE TOP OF THE MOUNTAIN. WHY WOULD I BOTHER WITH SOMEONE BELOW ME? I ALWAYS THOUGHT YOU WERE SMARTER THAN THIS, BISHOP.

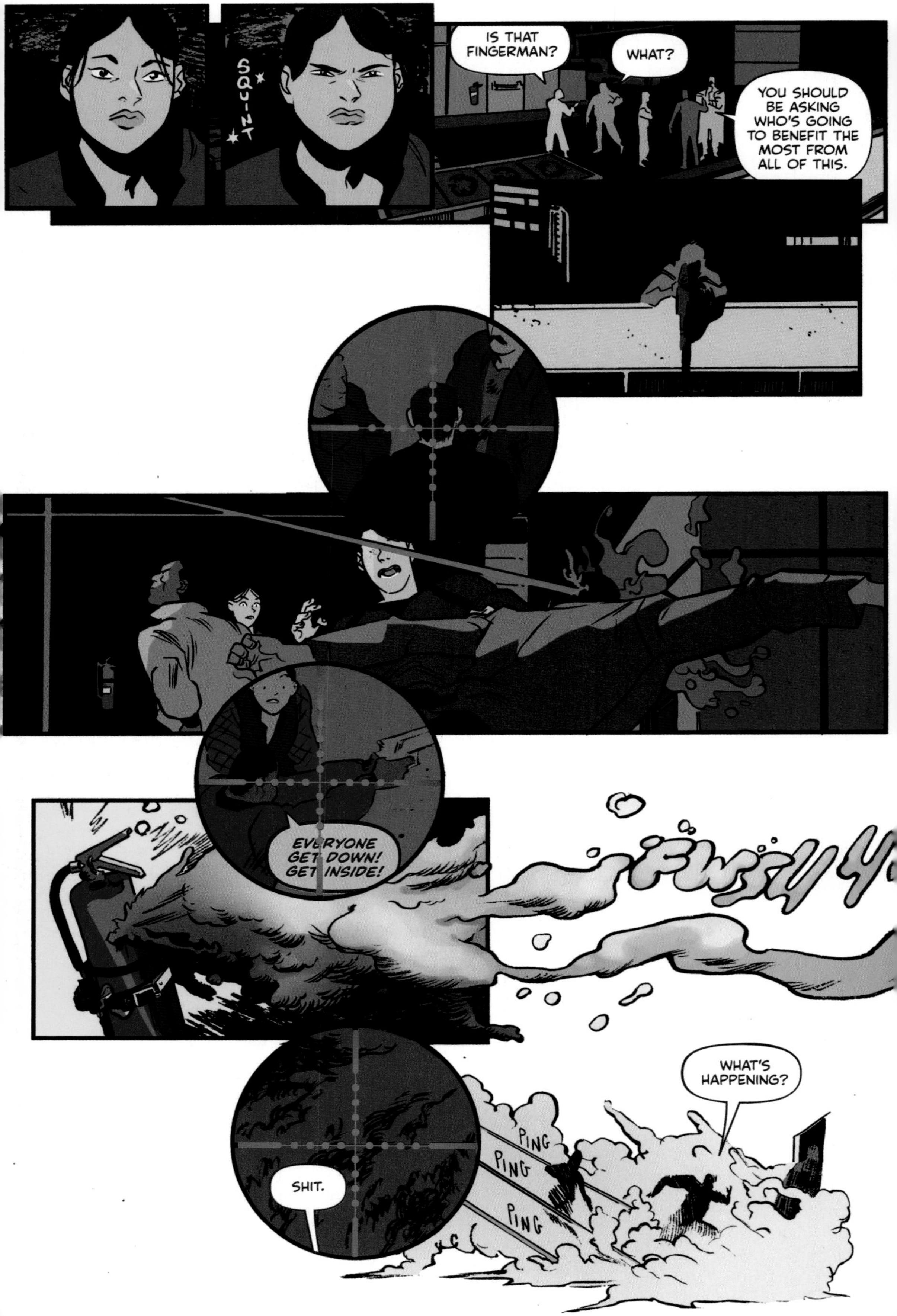

SQUINT
IS THAT FINGERMAN?
WHAT?
YOU SHOULD BE ASKING WHO'S GOING TO BENEFIT THE MOST FROM ALL OF THIS.
EVERYONE GET DOWN! GET INSIDE!
FWSSHH
WHAT'S HAPPENING?
PING
PING
PING
SHIT.

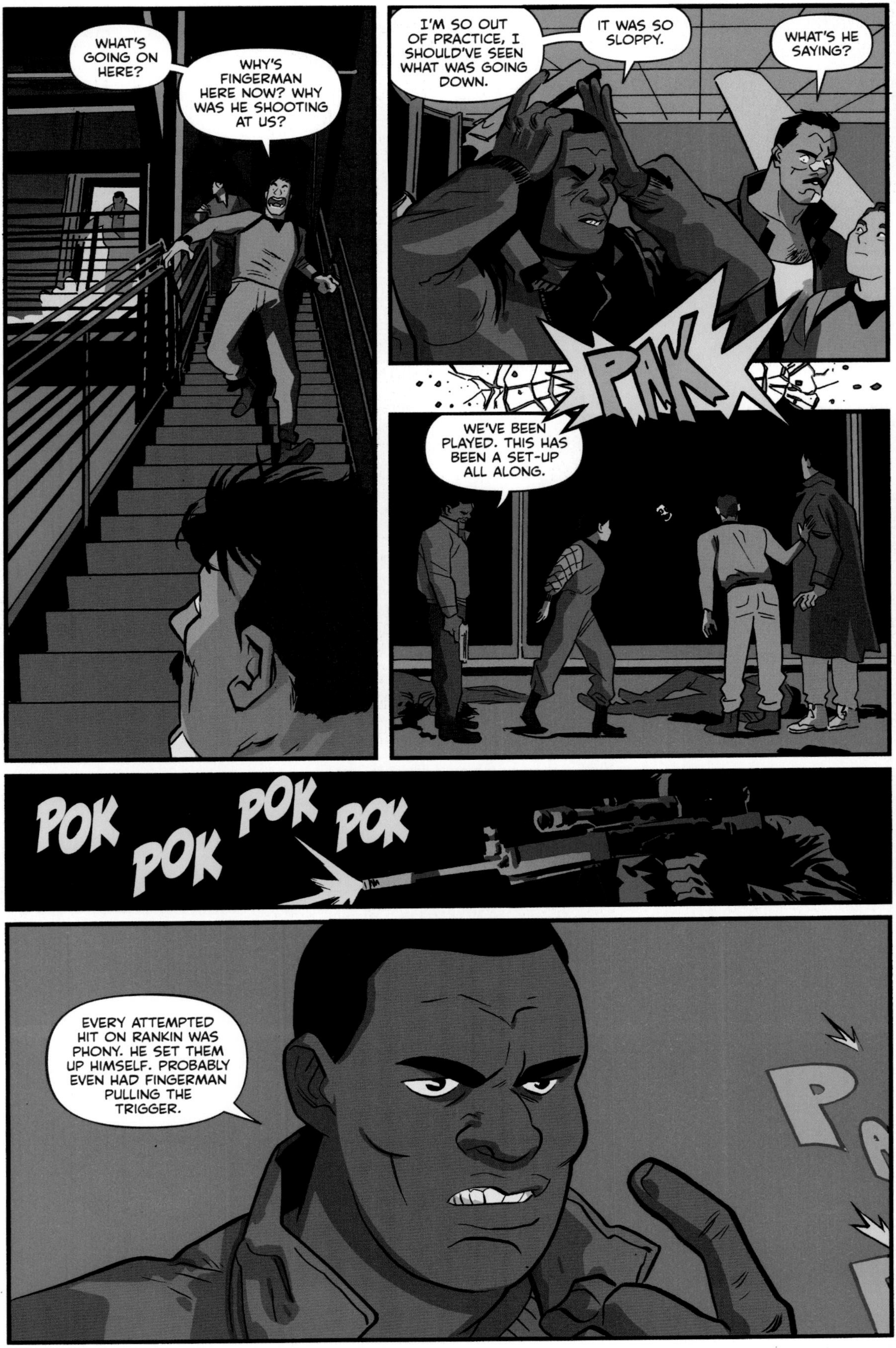
WHAT'S GOING ON HERE?
WHY'S FINGERMAN HERE NOW? WHY WAS HE SHOOTING AT US?
I'M SO OUT OF PRACTICE, I SHOULD'VE SEEN WHAT WAS GOING DOWN.
IT WAS SO SLOPPY.
WHAT'S HE SAYING?
PAK
WE'VE BEEN PLAYED. THIS HAS BEEN A SET-UP ALL ALONG.
POK
POK
POK
POK
EVERY ATTEMPTED HIT ON RANKIN WAS PHONY. HE SET THEM UP HIMSELF. PROBABLY EVEN HAD FINGERMAN PULLING THE TRIGGER.

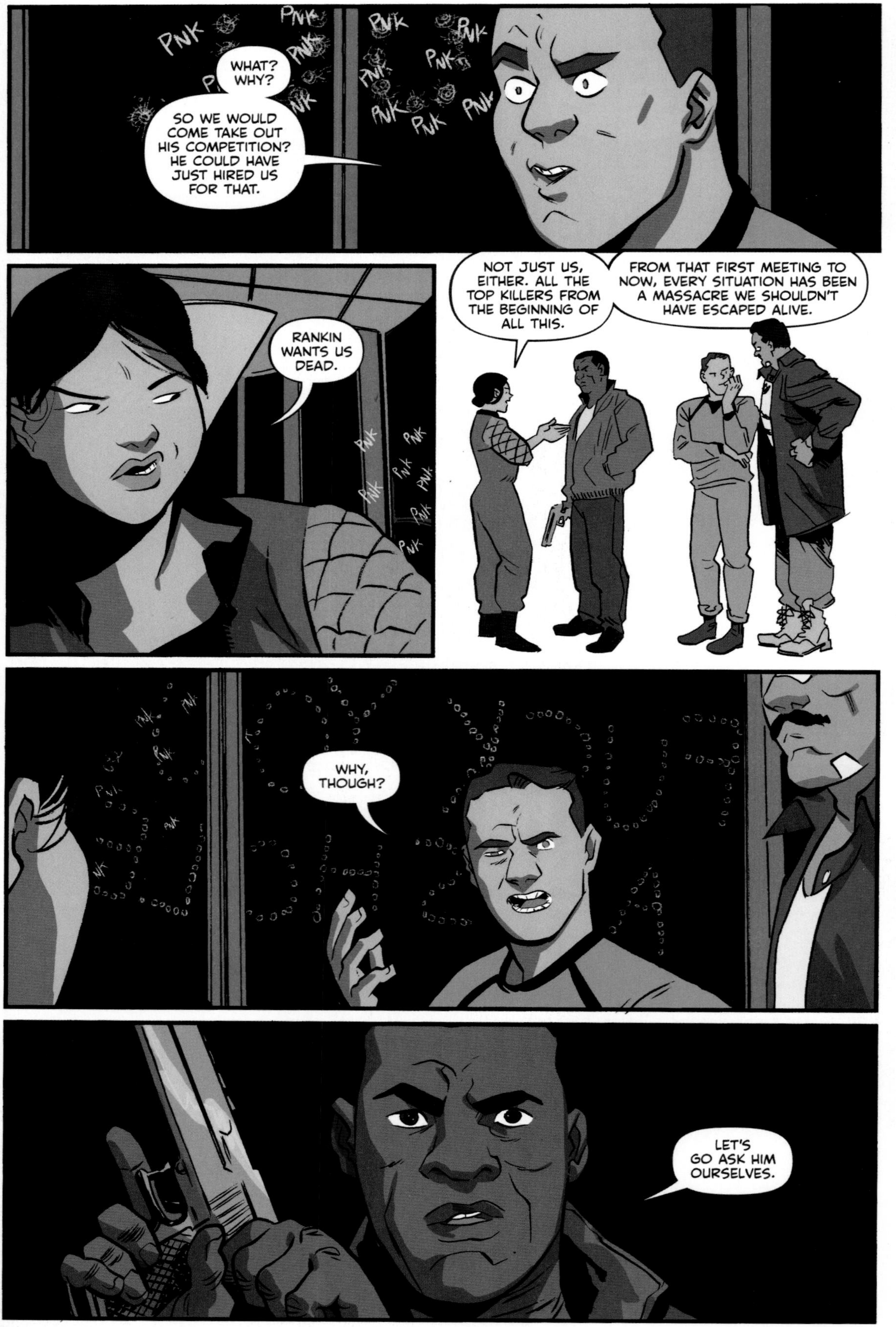
PNK
WHAT? WHY?
SO WE WOULD COME TAKE OUT HIS COMPETITION? HE COULD HAVE JUST HIRED US FOR THAT.
RANKIN WANTS US DEAD.
NOT JUST US, EITHER. ALL THE TOP KILLERS FROM THE BEGINNING OF ALL THIS.
FROM THAT FIRST MEETING TO NOW, EVERY SITUATION HAS BEEN A MASSACRE WE SHOULDN'T HAVE ESCAPED ALIVE.
WHY, THOUGH?
LET'S GO ASK HIM OURSELVES.

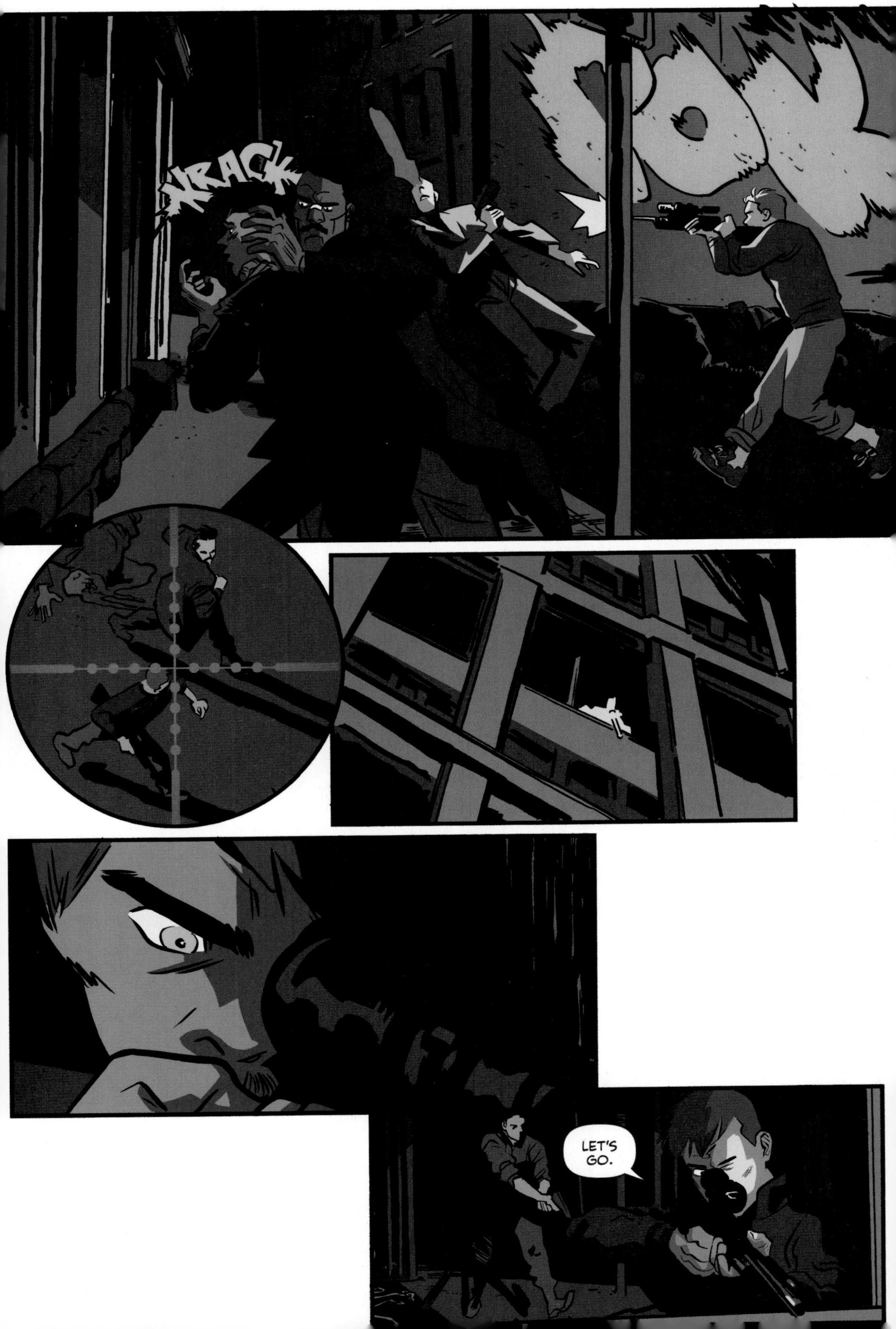
KRACK
LET'S GO.

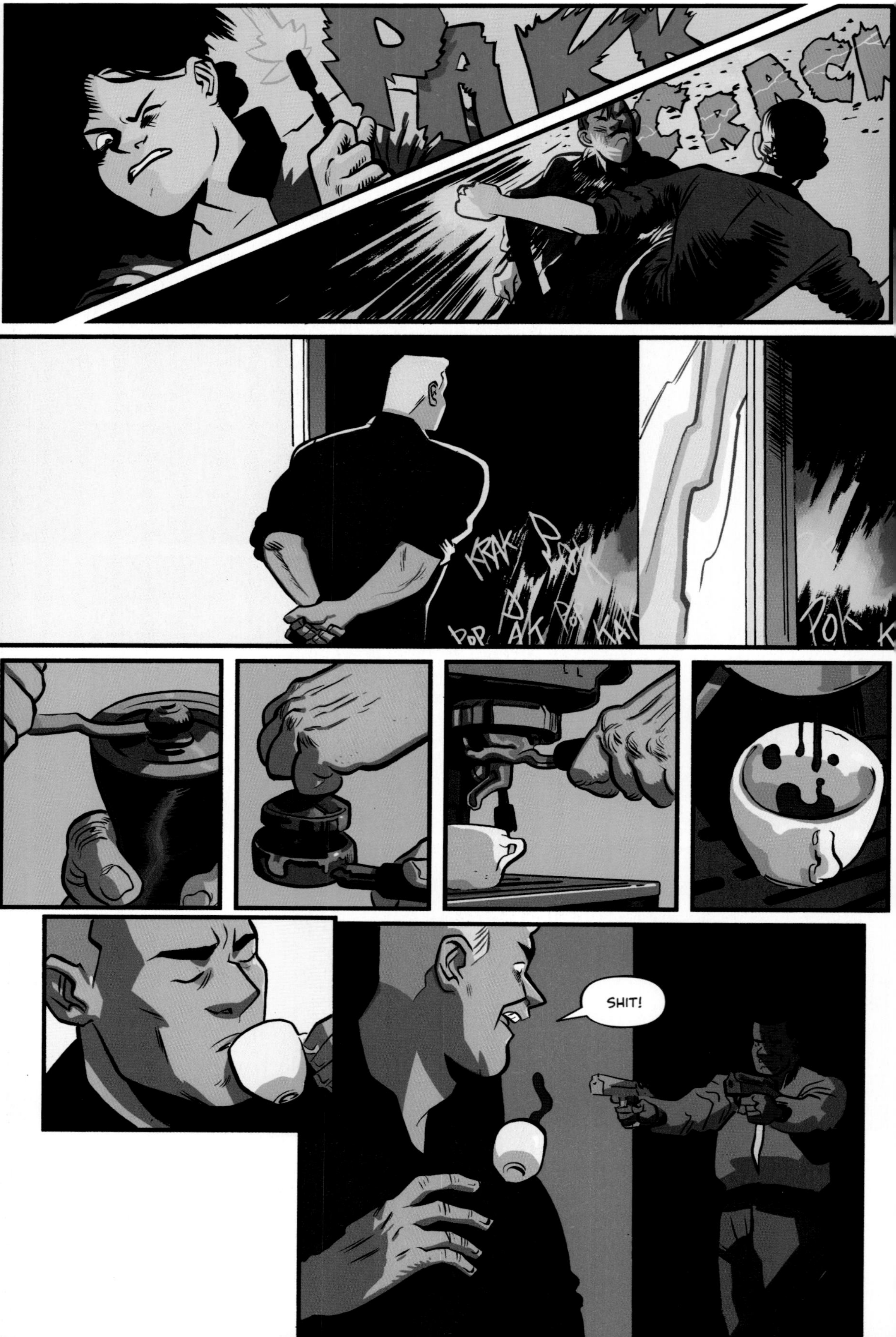

CRACK
KRAK
POP
PAK
POP
KAK
POK
SHIT!

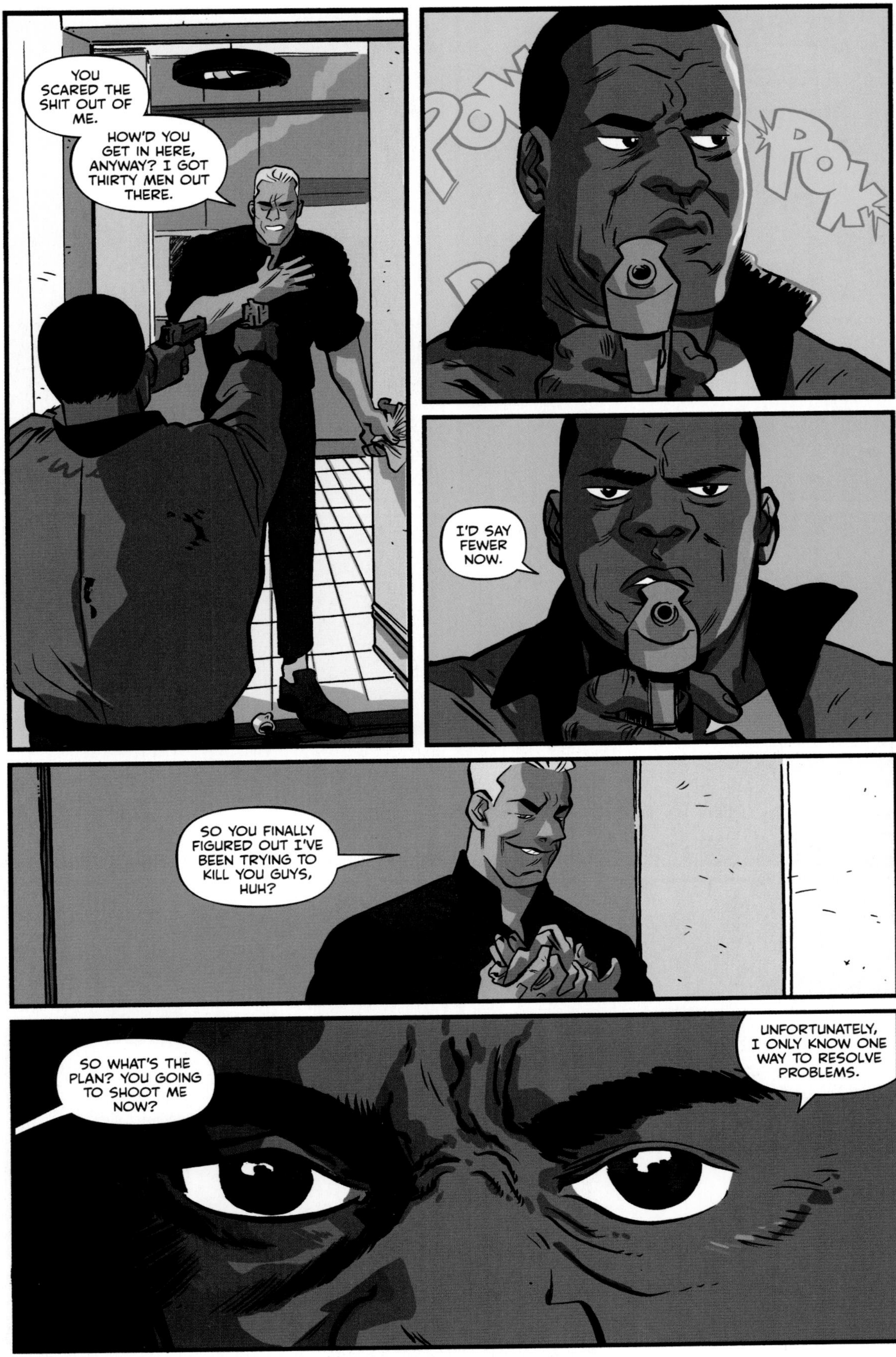
YOU SCARED THE SHIT OUT OF ME.
HOW'D YOU GET IN HERE, ANYWAY? I GOT THIRTY MEN OUT THERE.
POW
POW
I'D SAY FEWER NOW.
SO YOU FINALLY FIGURED OUT I'VE BEEN TRYING TO KILL YOU GUYS, HUH?
SO WHAT'S THE PLAN? YOU GOING TO SHOOT ME NOW?
UNFORTUNATELY, I ONLY KNOW ONE WAY TO RESOLVE PROBLEMS.

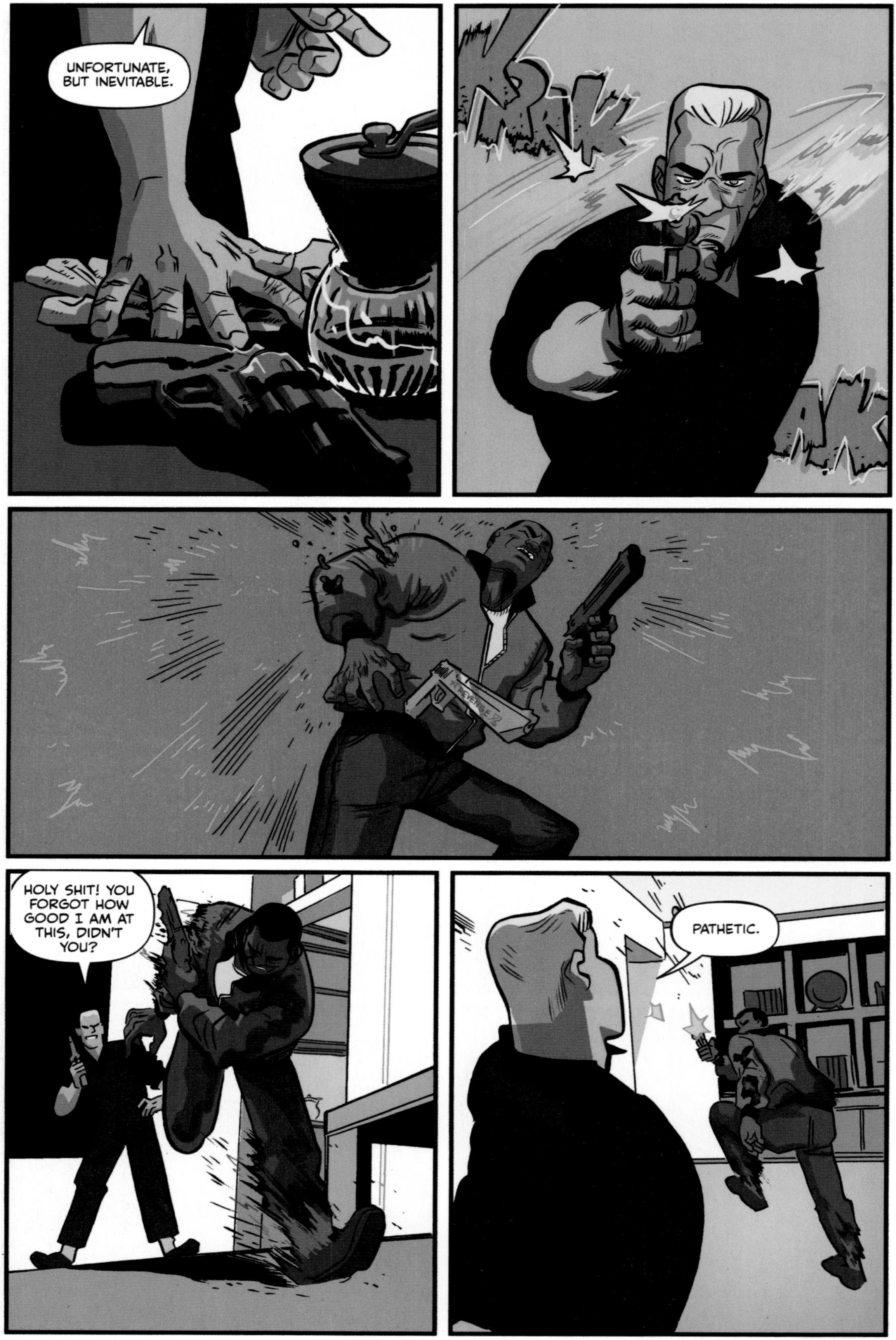
UNFORTUNATE, BUT INEVITABLE.
HOLY SHIT! YOU FORGOT HOW GOOD I AM AT THIS, DIDN'T YOU?
PATHETIC.

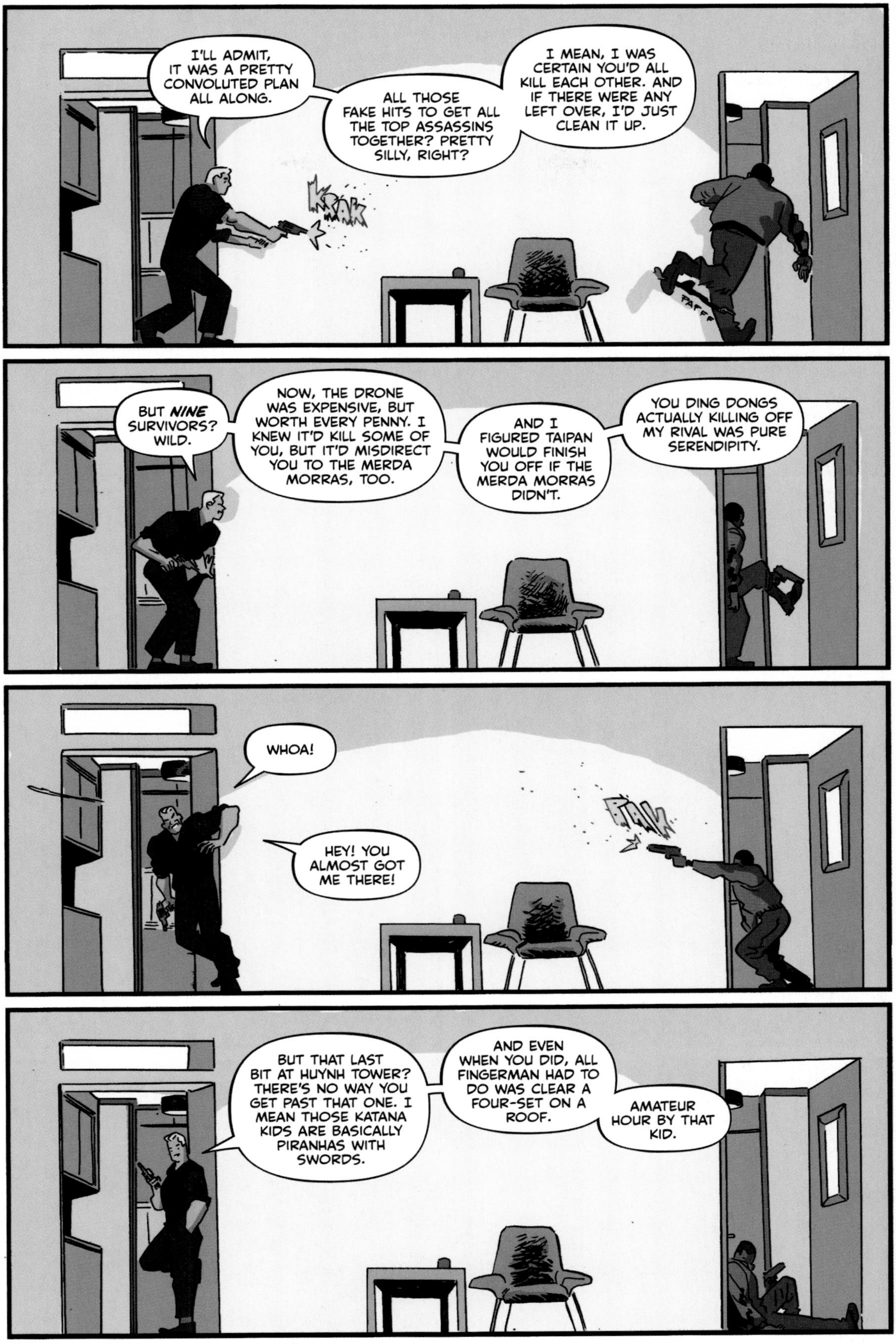
I'LL ADMIT, IT WAS A PRETTY CONVOLUTED PLAN ALL ALONG.
ALL THOSE FAKE HITS TO GET ALL THE TOP ASSASSINS TOGETHER? PRETTY SILLY, RIGHT?
I MEAN, I WAS CERTAIN YOU'D ALL KILL EACH OTHER. AND IF THERE WERE ANY LEFT OVER, I'D JUST CLEAN IT UP.
BUT *NINE* SURVIVORS? WILD.
NOW, THE DRONE WAS EXPENSIVE, BUT WORTH EVERY PENNY. I KNEW IT'D KILL SOME OF YOU, BUT IT'D MISDIRECT YOU TO THE MERDA MORRAS, TOO.
AND I FIGURED TAIPAN WOULD FINISH YOU OFF IF THE MERDA MORRAS DIDN'T.
YOU DING DONGS ACTUALLY KILLING OFF MY RIVAL WAS PURE SERENDIPITY.
WHOA!
HEY! YOU ALMOST GOT ME THERE!
BUT THAT LAST BIT AT HUYNH TOWER? THERE'S NO WAY YOU GET PAST THAT ONE. I MEAN THOSE KATANA KIDS ARE BASICALLY PIRANHAS WITH SWORDS.
AND EVEN WHEN YOU DID, ALL FINGERMAN HAD TO DO WAS CLEAR A FOUR-SET ON A ROOF.
AMATEUR HOUR BY THAT KID.

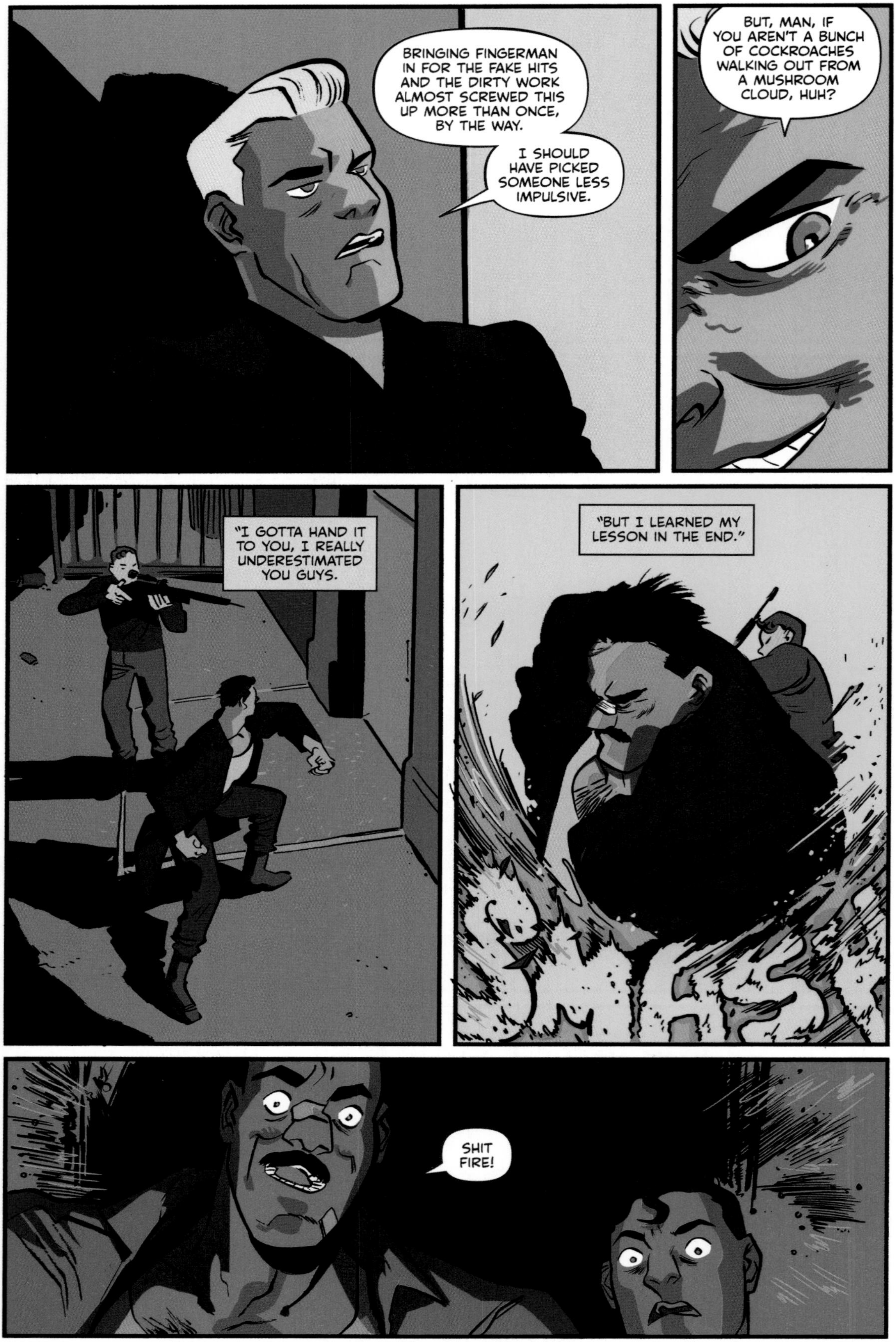
BRINGING FINGERMAN IN FOR THE FAKE HITS AND THE DIRTY WORK ALMOST SCREWED THIS UP MORE THAN ONCE, BY THE WAY.
I SHOULD HAVE PICKED SOMEONE LESS IMPULSIVE.
BUT, MAN, IF YOU AREN'T A BUNCH OF COCKROACHES WALKING OUT FROM A MUSHROOM CLOUD, HUH?
"I GOTTA HAND IT TO YOU, I REALLY UNDERESTIMATED YOU GUYS.
"BUT I LEARNED MY LESSON IN THE END."
SHIT FIRE!

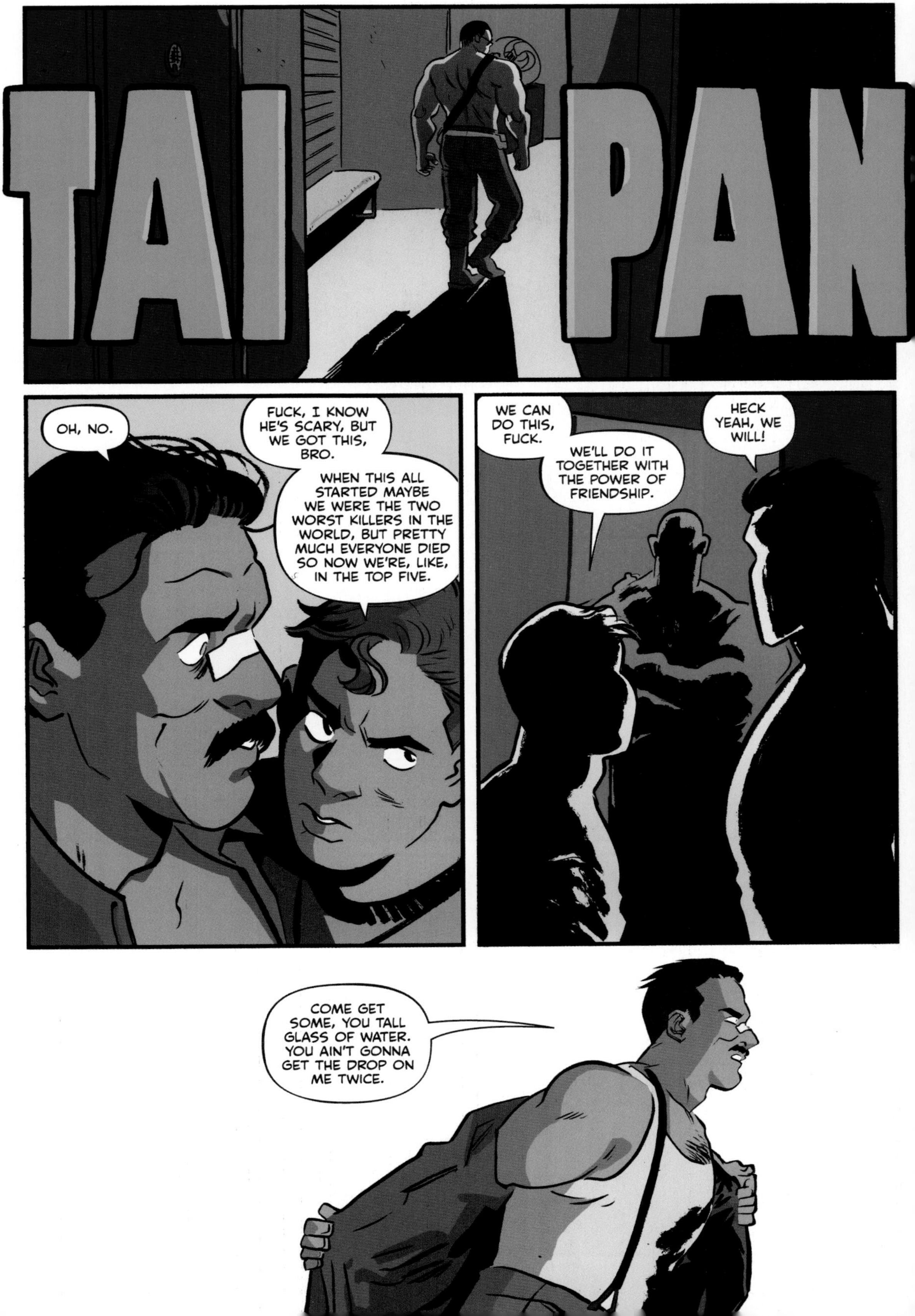
TAI PAN
OH, NO.
FUCK, I KNOW HE'S SCARY, BUT WE GOT THIS, BRO.
WHEN THIS ALL STARTED MAYBE WE WERE THE TWO WORST KILLERS IN THE WORLD, BUT PRETTY MUCH EVERYONE DIED SO NOW WE'RE, LIKE, IN THE TOP FIVE.
WE CAN DO THIS, FUCK.
WE'LL DO IT TOGETHER WITH THE POWER OF FRIENDSHIP.
HECK YEAH, WE WILL!
COME GET SOME, YOU TALL GLASS OF WATER. YOU AIN'T GONNA GET THE DROP ON ME TWICE.

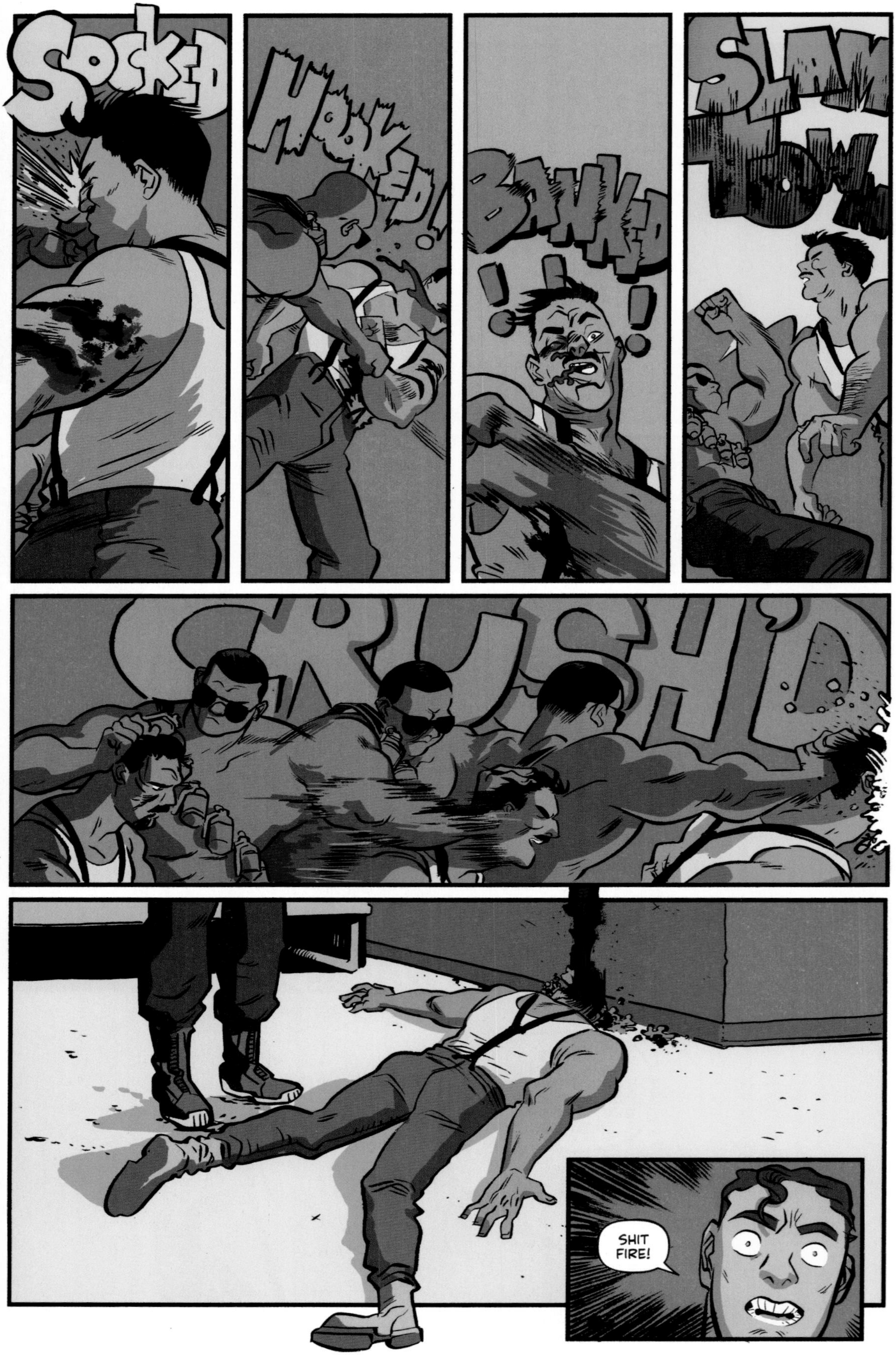
SOCKED
HOOKED!!
BANKED!!!
SLAM BLAM
CRUSH'D!
SHIT FIRE!

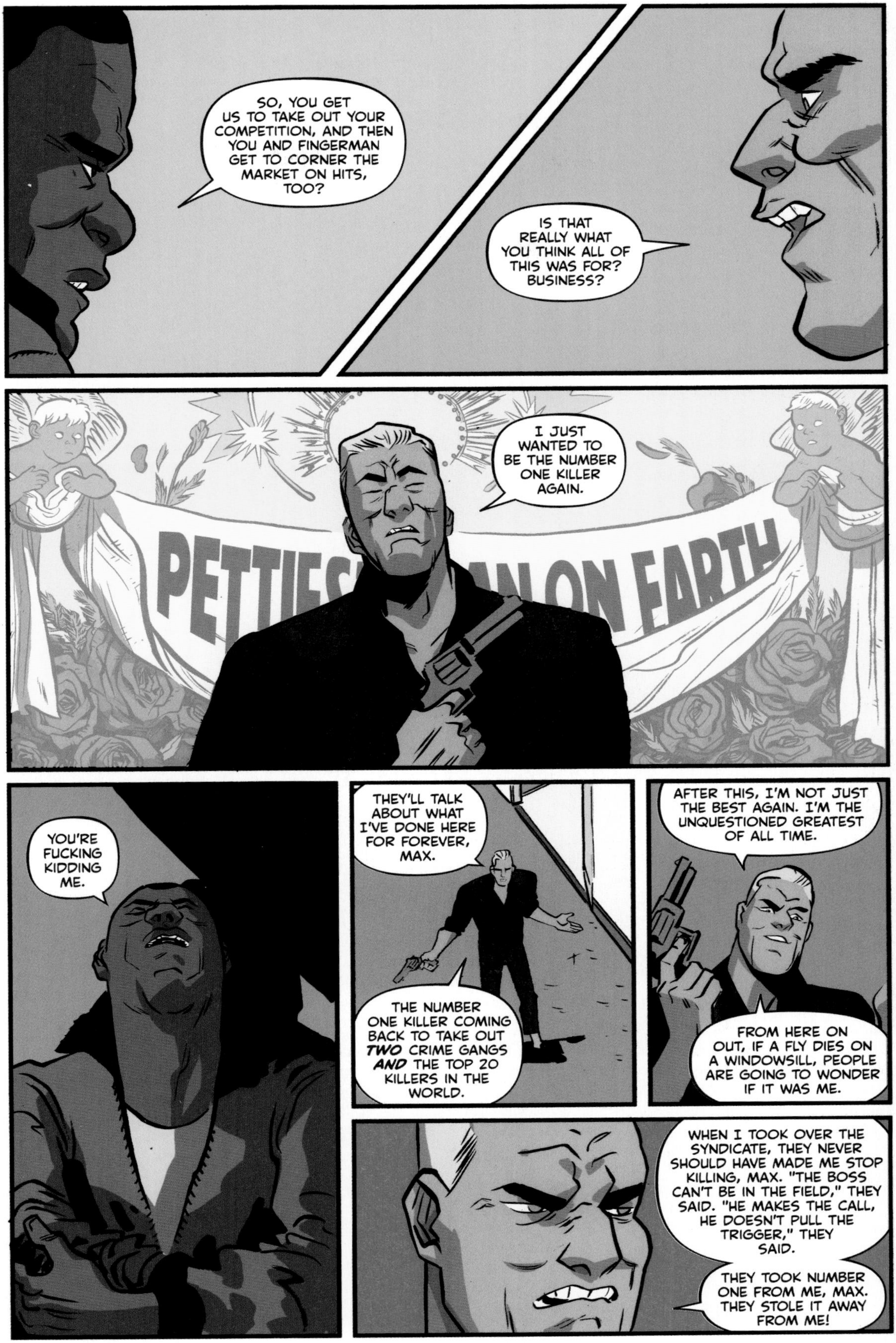
SO, YOU GET US TO TAKE OUT YOUR COMPETITION, AND THEN YOU AND FINGERMAN GET TO CORNER THE MARKET ON HITS, TOO?
IS THAT REALLY WHAT YOU THINK ALL OF THIS WAS FOR? BUSINESS?
I JUST WANTED TO BE THE NUMBER ONE KILLER AGAIN.
YOU'RE FUCKING KIDDING ME.
THEY'LL TALK ABOUT WHAT I'VE DONE HERE FOR FOREVER, MAX.
THE NUMBER ONE KILLER COMING BACK TO TAKE OUT *TWO* CRIME GANGS *AND* THE TOP 20 KILLERS IN THE WORLD.
AFTER THIS, I'M NOT JUST THE BEST AGAIN. I'M THE UNQUESTIONED GREATEST OF ALL TIME.
FROM HERE ON OUT, IF A FLY DIES ON A WINDOWSILL, PEOPLE ARE GOING TO WONDER IF IT WAS ME.
WHEN I TOOK OVER THE SYNDICATE, THEY NEVER SHOULD HAVE MADE ME STOP KILLING, MAX. "THE BOSS CAN'T BE IN THE FIELD," THEY SAID. "HE MAKES THE CALL, HE DOESN'T PULL THE TRIGGER," THEY SAID.
THEY TOOK NUMBER ONE FROM ME, MAX. THEY STOLE IT AWAY FROM ME!

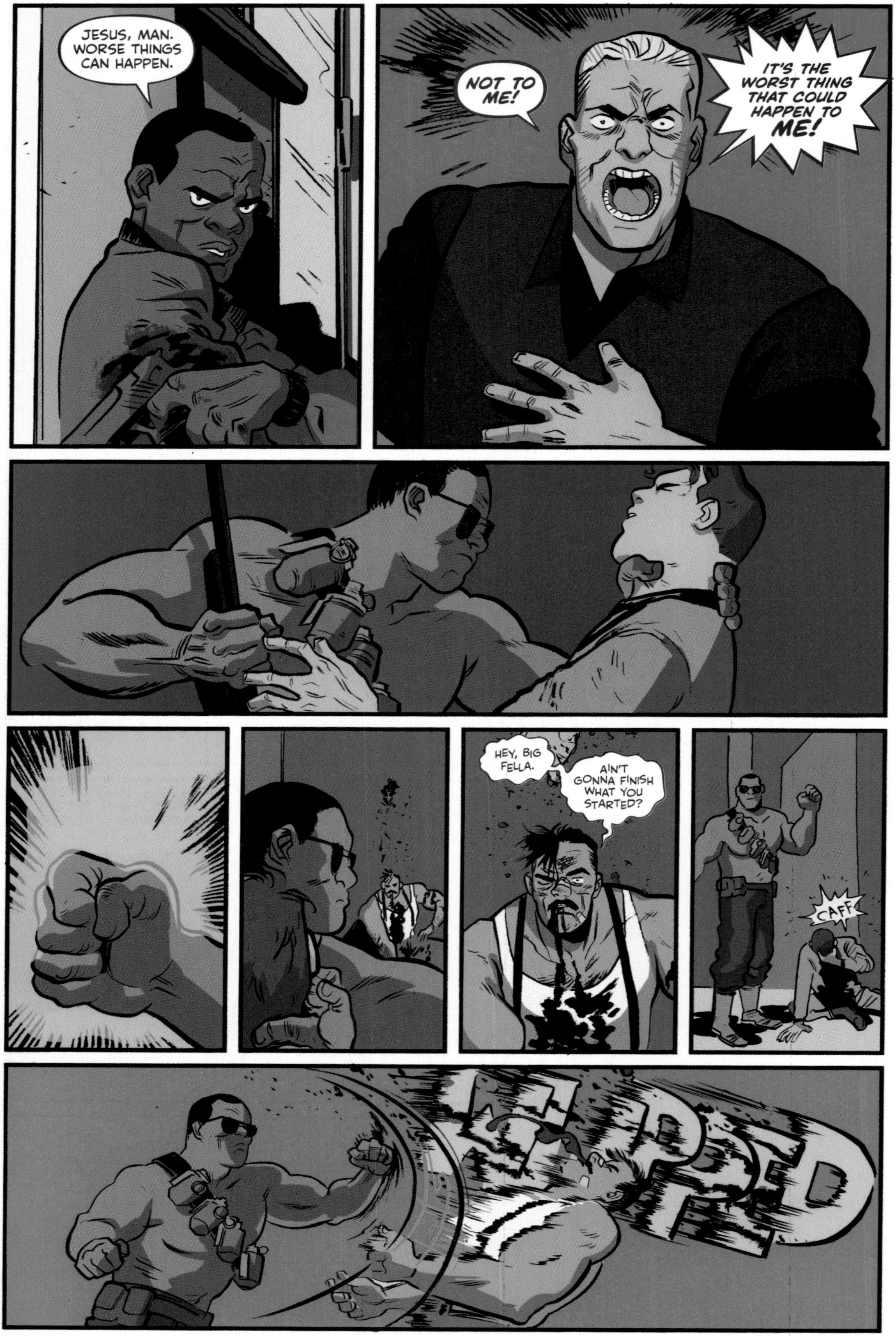

JESUS, MAN. WORSE THINGS CAN HAPPEN.
NOT TO ME!
IT'S THE WORST THING THAT COULD HAPPEN TO ME!
HEY, BIG FELLA.
AIN'T GONNA FINISH WHAT YOU STARTED?
CAFF

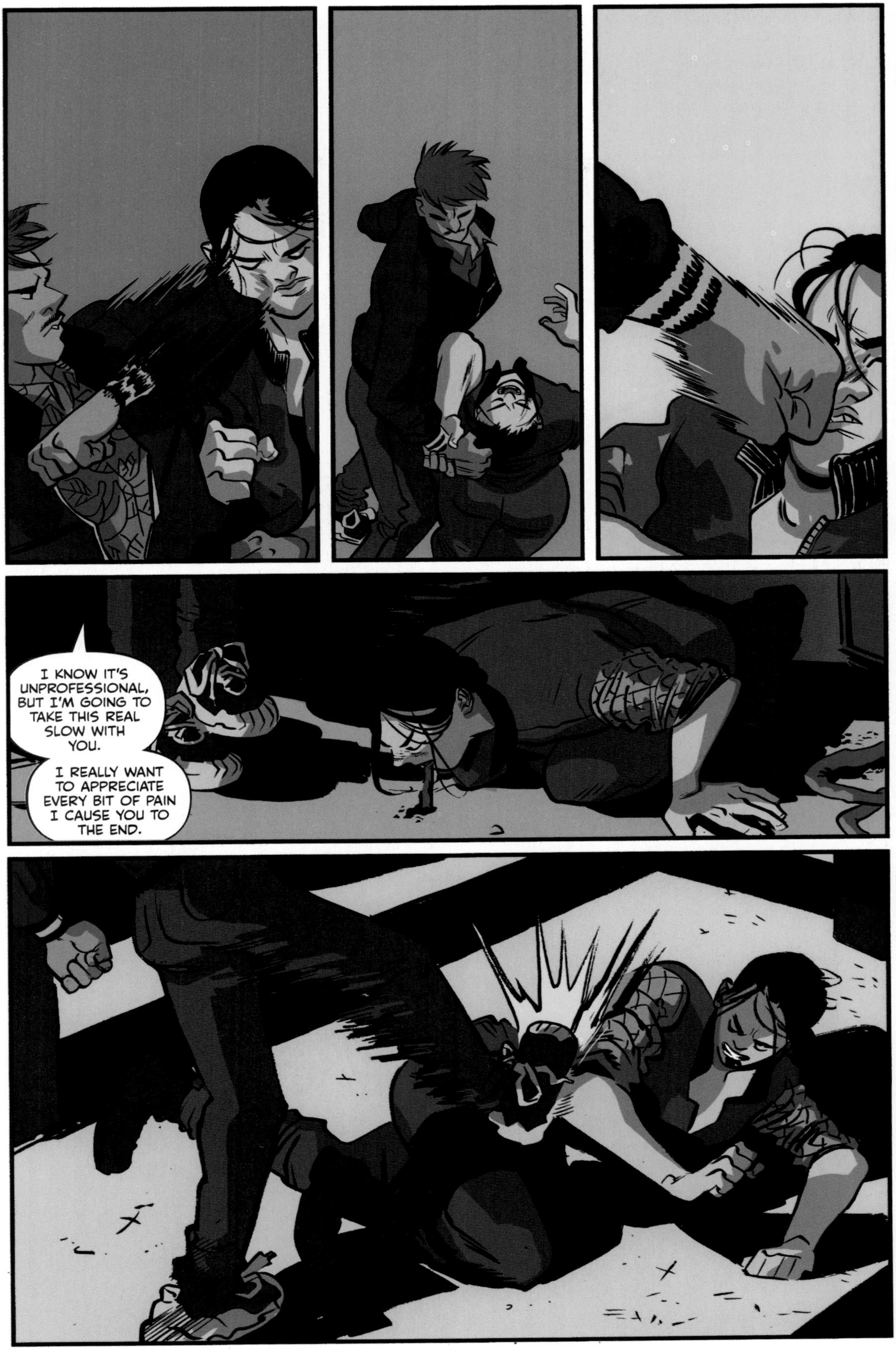
I KNOW IT'S UNPROFESSIONAL, BUT I'M GOING TO TAKE THIS REAL SLOW WITH YOU.
I REALLY WANT TO APPRECIATE EVERY BIT OF PAIN I CAUSE YOU TO THE END.

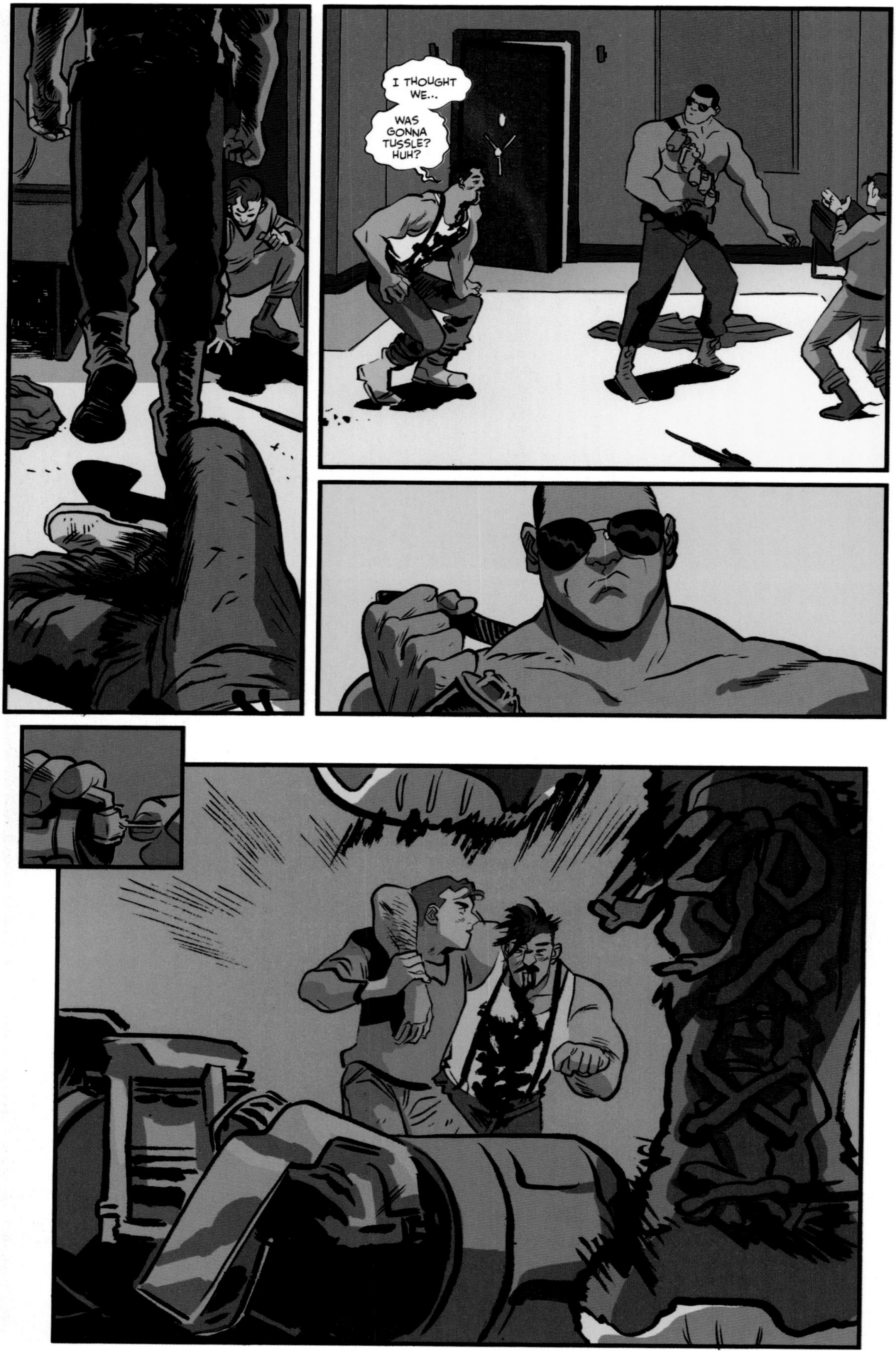
I THOUGHT WE...
WAS GONNA TUSSLE? HUH?

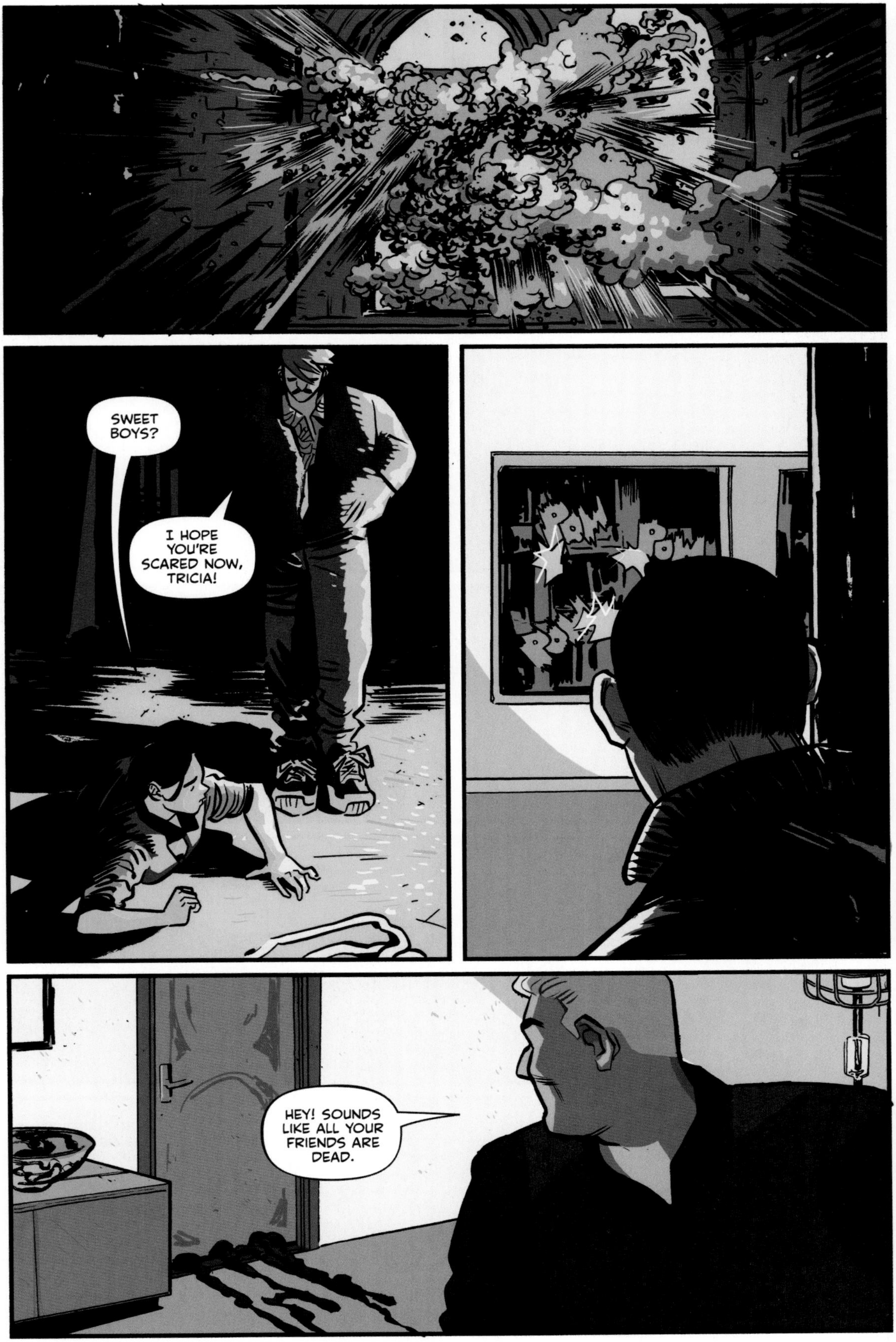
SWEET BOYS?
I HOPE YOU'RE SCARED NOW, TRICIA!
HEY! SOUNDS LIKE ALL YOUR FRIENDS ARE DEAD.

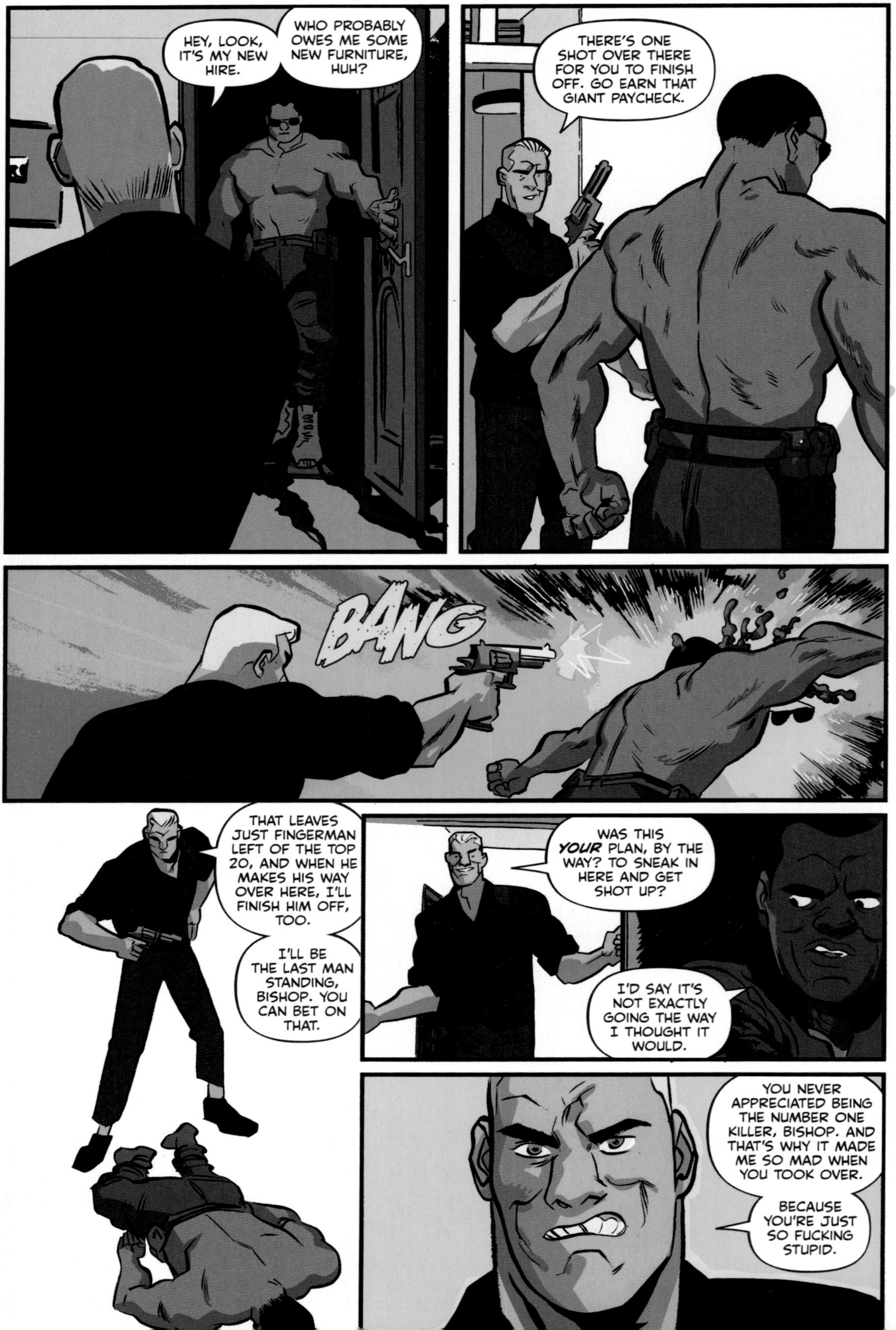
HEY, LOOK, IT'S MY NEW HIRE.
WHO PROBABLY OWES ME SOME NEW FURNITURE, HUH?
THERE'S ONE SHOT OVER THERE FOR YOU TO FINISH OFF. GO EARN THAT GIANT PAYCHECK.
BANG
THAT LEAVES JUST FINGERMAN LEFT OF THE TOP 20, AND WHEN HE MAKES HIS WAY OVER HERE, I'LL FINISH HIM OFF, TOO.
I'LL BE THE LAST MAN STANDING, BISHOP. YOU CAN BET ON THAT.
WAS THIS *YOUR* PLAN, BY THE WAY? TO SNEAK IN HERE AND GET SHOT UP?
I'D SAY IT'S NOT EXACTLY GOING THE WAY I THOUGHT IT WOULD.
YOU NEVER APPRECIATED BEING THE NUMBER ONE KILLER, BISHOP. AND THAT'S WHY IT MADE ME SO MAD WHEN YOU TOOK OVER.
BECAUSE YOU'RE JUST SO FUCKING STUPID.

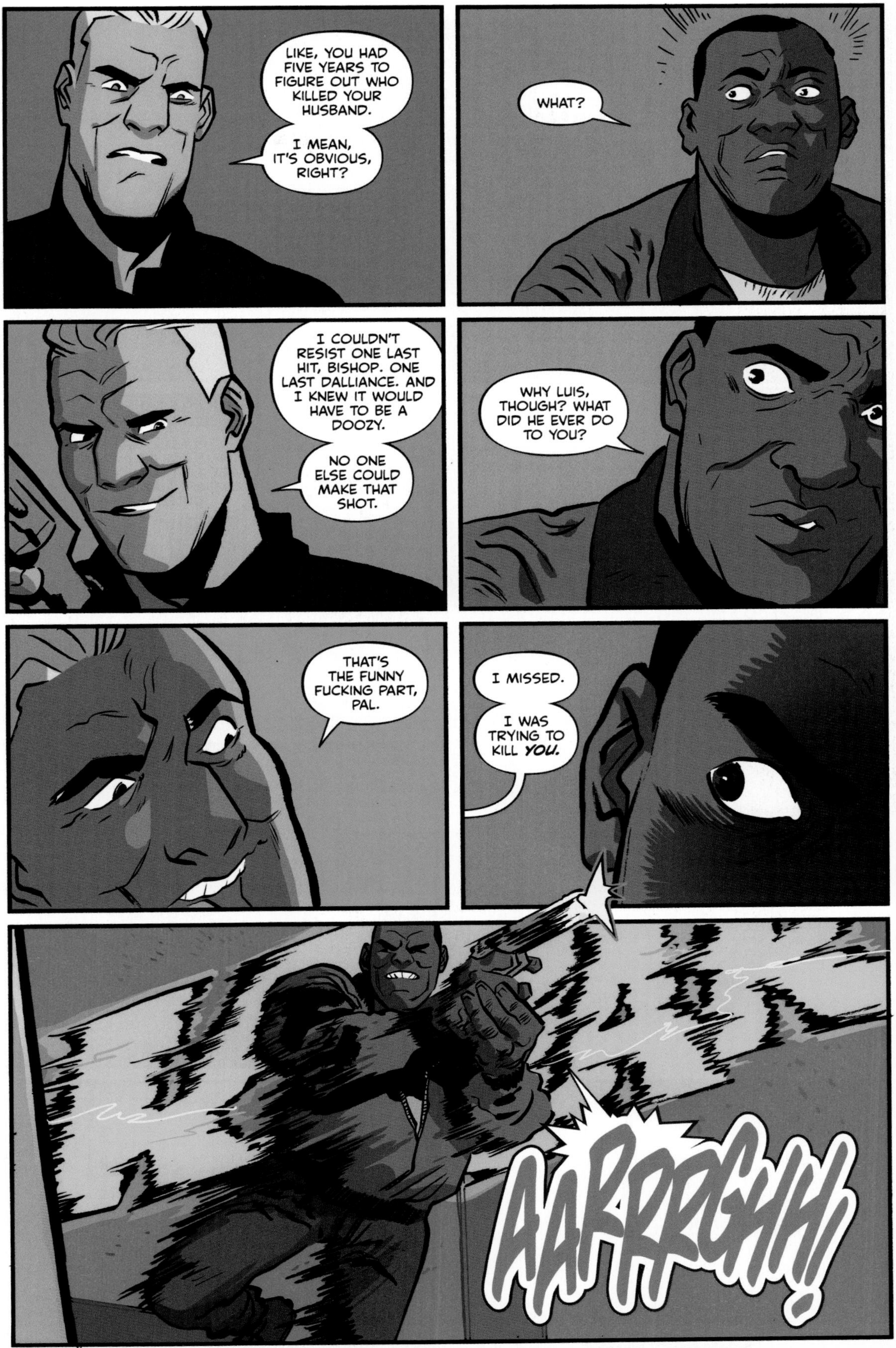
LIKE, YOU HAD FIVE YEARS TO FIGURE OUT WHO KILLED YOUR HUSBAND.
I MEAN, IT'S OBVIOUS, RIGHT?
WHAT?
I COULDN'T RESIST ONE LAST HIT, BISHOP. ONE LAST DALLIANCE. AND I KNEW IT WOULD HAVE TO BE A DOOZY.
NO ONE ELSE COULD MAKE THAT SHOT.
WHY LUIS, THOUGH? WHAT DID HE EVER DO TO YOU?
THAT'S THE FUNNY FUCKING PART, PAL.
I MISSED.
I WAS TRYING TO KILL *YOU.*
AARRGHH!

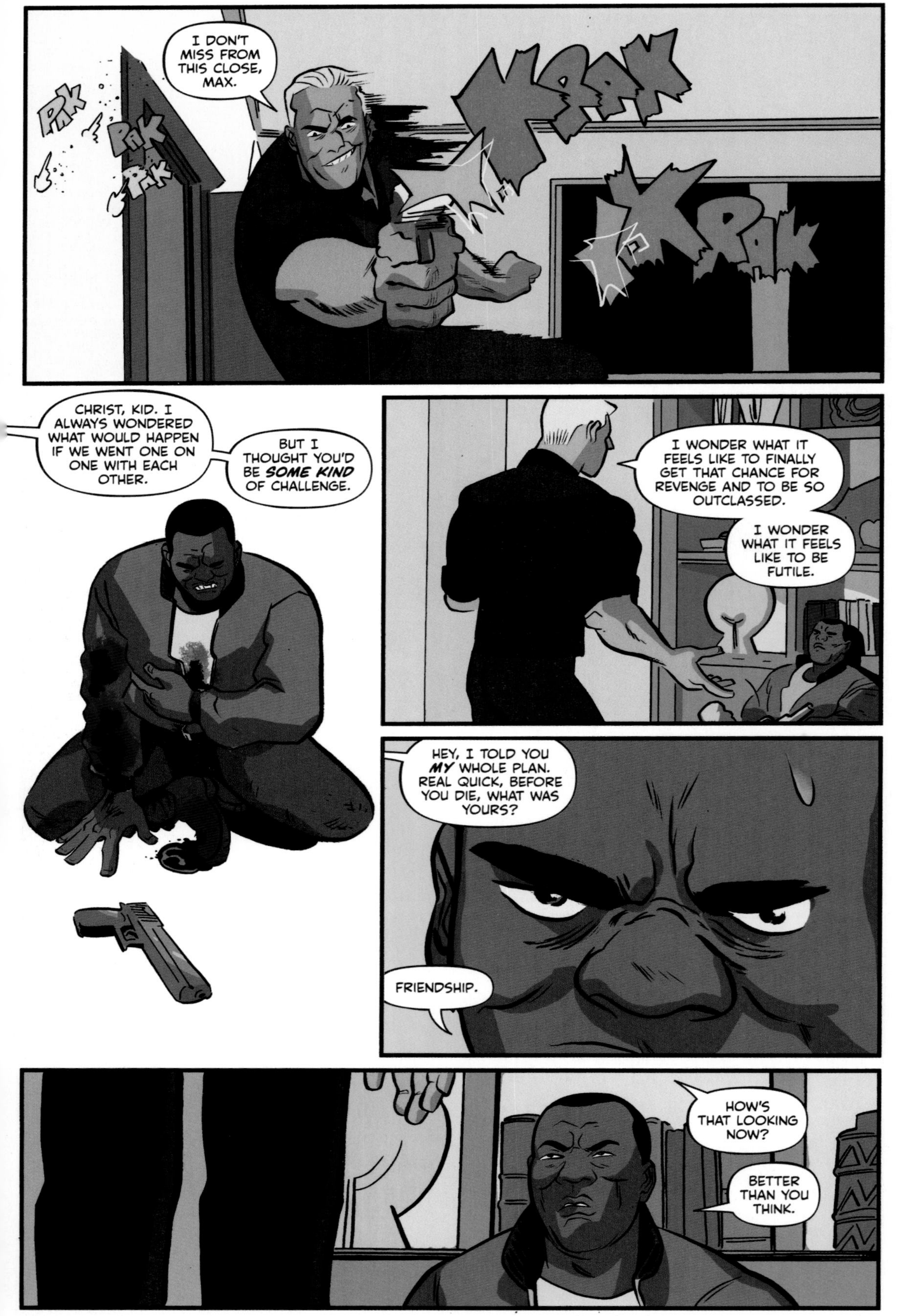
I DON'T MISS FROM THIS CLOSE, MAX.
PAK
PAK
PAK
KRAK
KRAK
CHRIST, KID. I ALWAYS WONDERED WHAT WOULD HAPPEN IF WE WENT ONE ON ONE WITH EACH OTHER.
BUT I THOUGHT YOU'D BE SOME KIND OF CHALLENGE.
I WONDER WHAT IT FEELS LIKE TO FINALLY GET THAT CHANCE FOR REVENGE AND TO BE SO OUTCLASSED.
I WONDER WHAT IT FEELS LIKE TO BE FUTILE.
HEY, I TOLD YOU MY WHOLE PLAN. REAL QUICK, BEFORE YOU DIE, WHAT WAS YOURS?
FRIENDSHIP.
HOW'S THAT LOOKING NOW?
BETTER THAN YOU THINK.

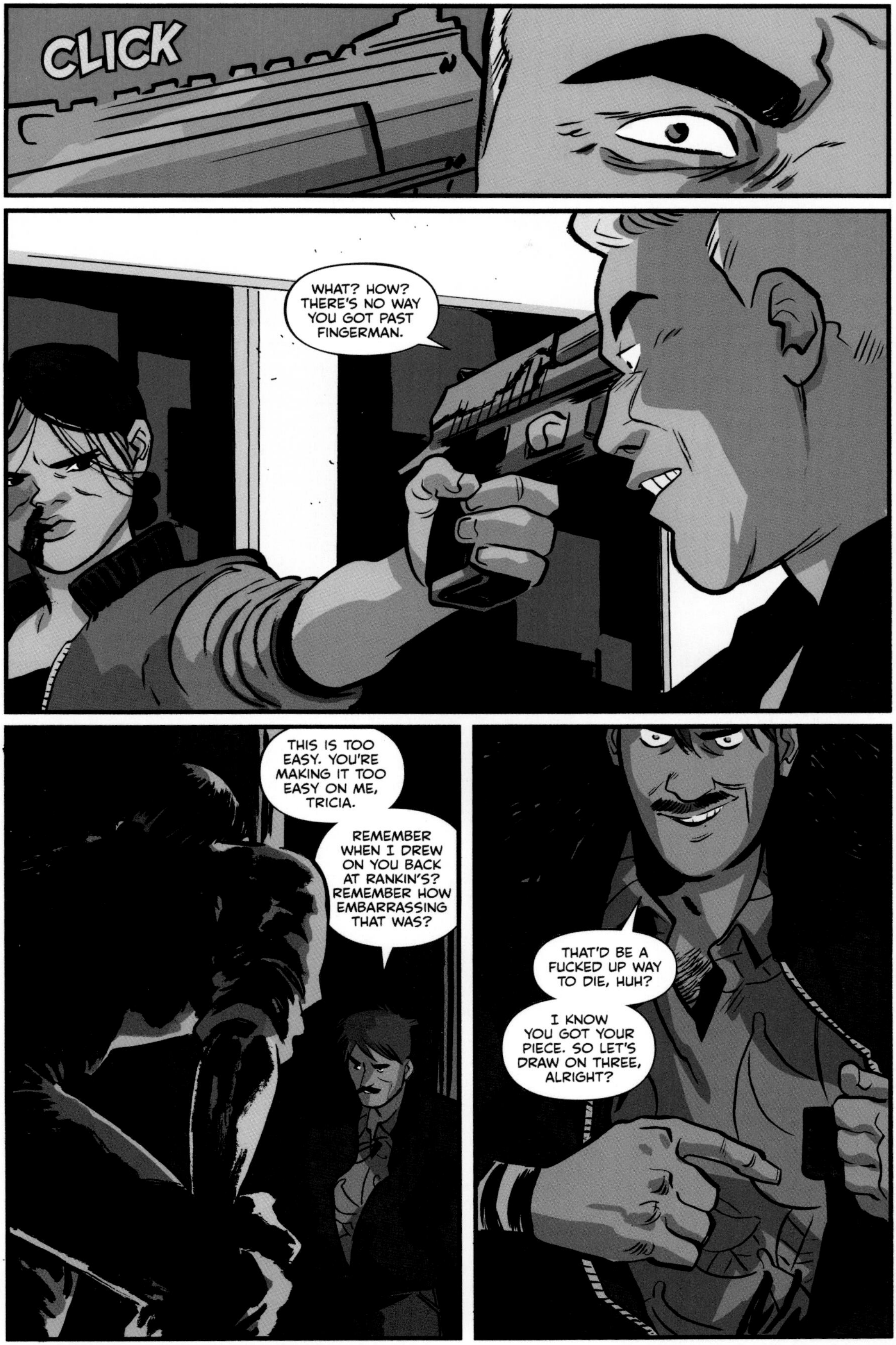
CLICK
WHAT? HOW? THERE'S NO WAY YOU GOT PAST FINGERMAN.
THIS IS TOO EASY. YOU'RE MAKING IT TOO EASY ON ME, TRICIA.
REMEMBER WHEN I DREW ON YOU BACK AT RANKIN'S? REMEMBER HOW EMBARRASSING THAT WAS?
THAT'D BE A FUCKED UP WAY TO DIE, HUH?
I KNOW YOU GOT YOUR PIECE. SO LET'S DRAW ON THREE, ALRIGHT?

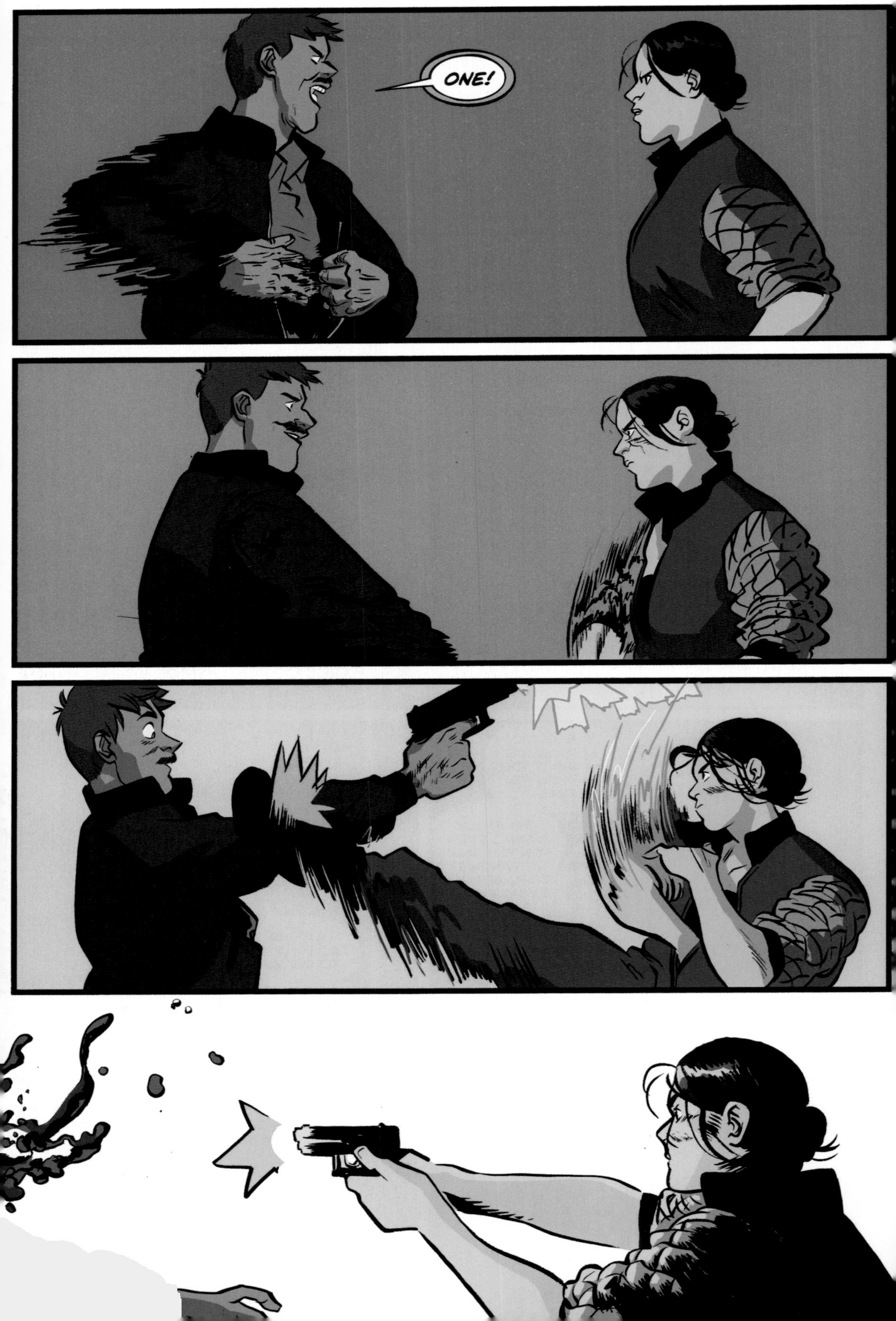
ONE!

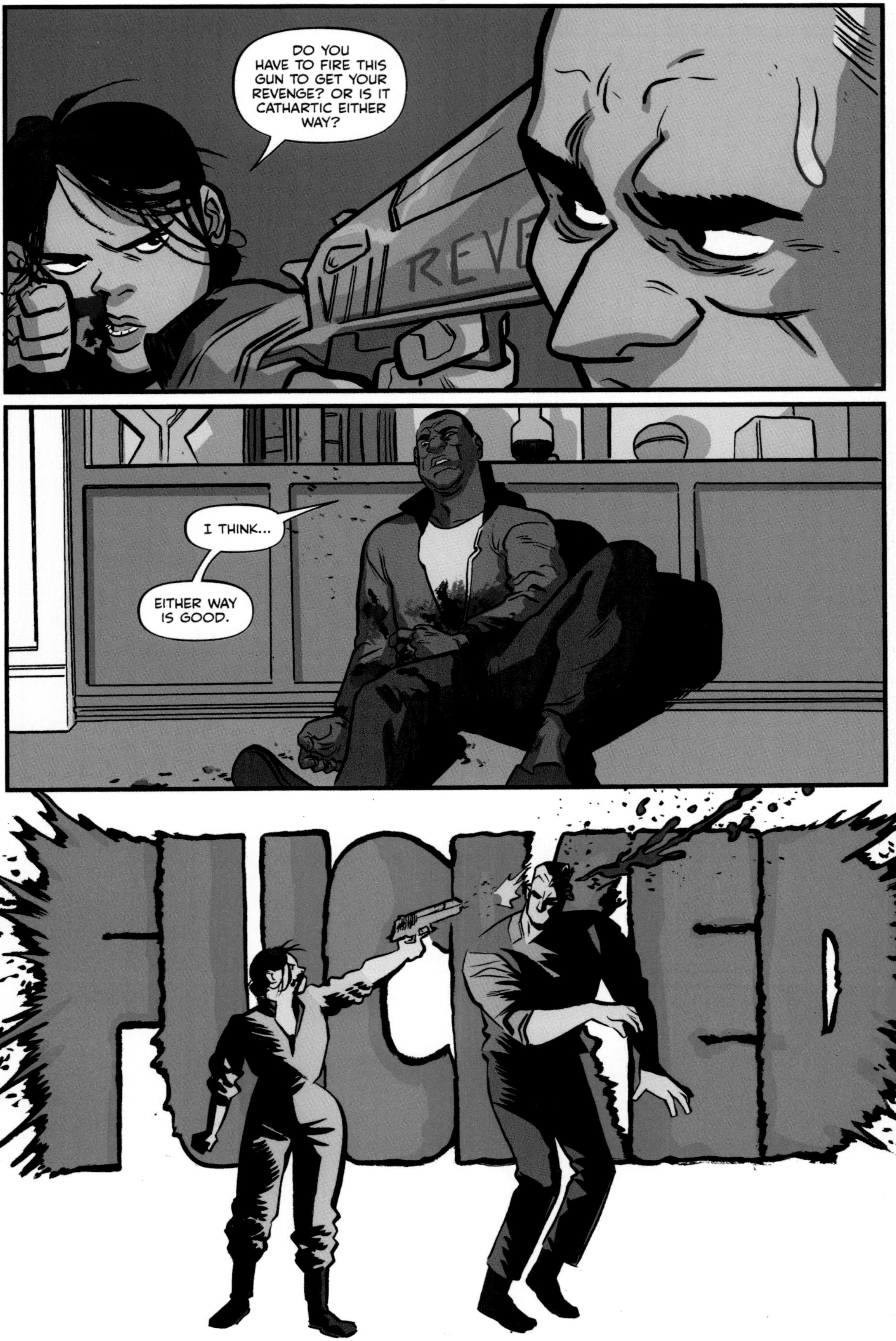
DO YOU HAVE TO FIRE THIS GUN TO GET YOUR REVENGE? OR IS IT CATHARTIC EITHER WAY?
I THINK...
EITHER WAY IS GOOD.

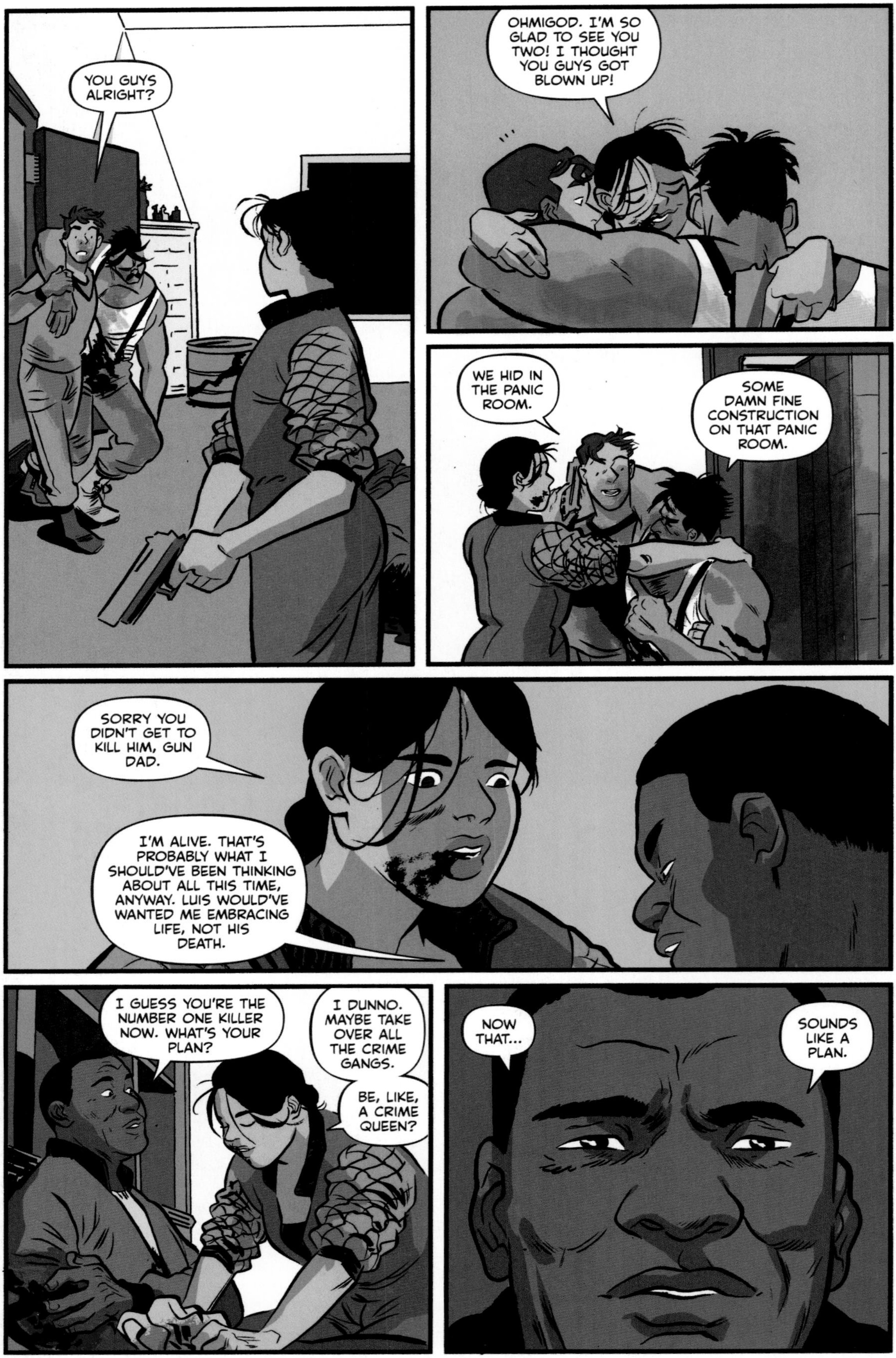
YOU GUYS ALRIGHT?
OHMIGOD. I'M SO GLAD TO SEE YOU TWO! I THOUGHT YOU GUYS GOT BLOWN UP!
WE HID IN THE PANIC ROOM.
SOME DAMN FINE CONSTRUCTION ON THAT PANIC ROOM.
SORRY YOU DIDN'T GET TO KILL HIM, GUN DAD.
I'M ALIVE. THAT'S PROBABLY WHAT I SHOULD'VE BEEN THINKING ABOUT ALL THIS TIME, ANYWAY. LUIS WOULD'VE WANTED ME EMBRACING LIFE, NOT HIS DEATH.
I GUESS YOU'RE THE NUMBER ONE KILLER NOW. WHAT'S YOUR PLAN?
I DUNNO. MAYBE TAKE OVER ALL THE CRIME GANGS.
BE, LIKE, A CRIME QUEEN?
NOW THAT...
SOUNDS LIKE A PLAN.

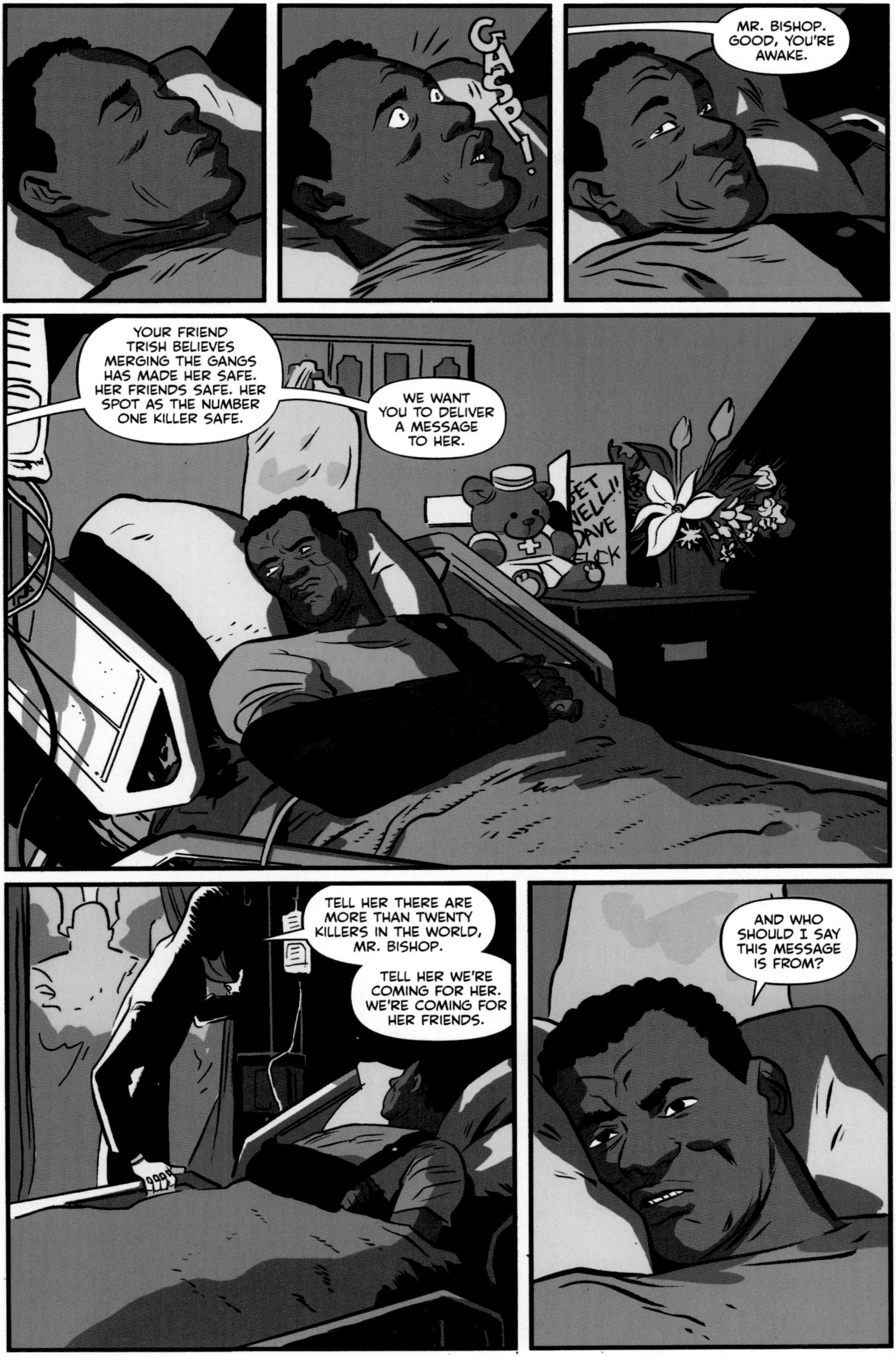
GASP!
MR. BISHOP. GOOD, YOU'RE AWAKE.
YOUR FRIEND TRISH BELIEVES MERGING THE GANGS HAS MADE HER SAFE. HER FRIENDS SAFE. HER SPOT AS THE NUMBER ONE KILLER SAFE.
WE WANT YOU TO DELIVER A MESSAGE TO HER.
GET WELL!! DAVE
TELL HER THERE ARE MORE THAN TWENTY KILLERS IN THE WORLD, MR. BISHOP.
TELL HER WE'RE COMING FOR HER. WE'RE COMING FOR HER FRIENDS.
AND WHO SHOULD I SAY THIS MESSAGE IS FROM?

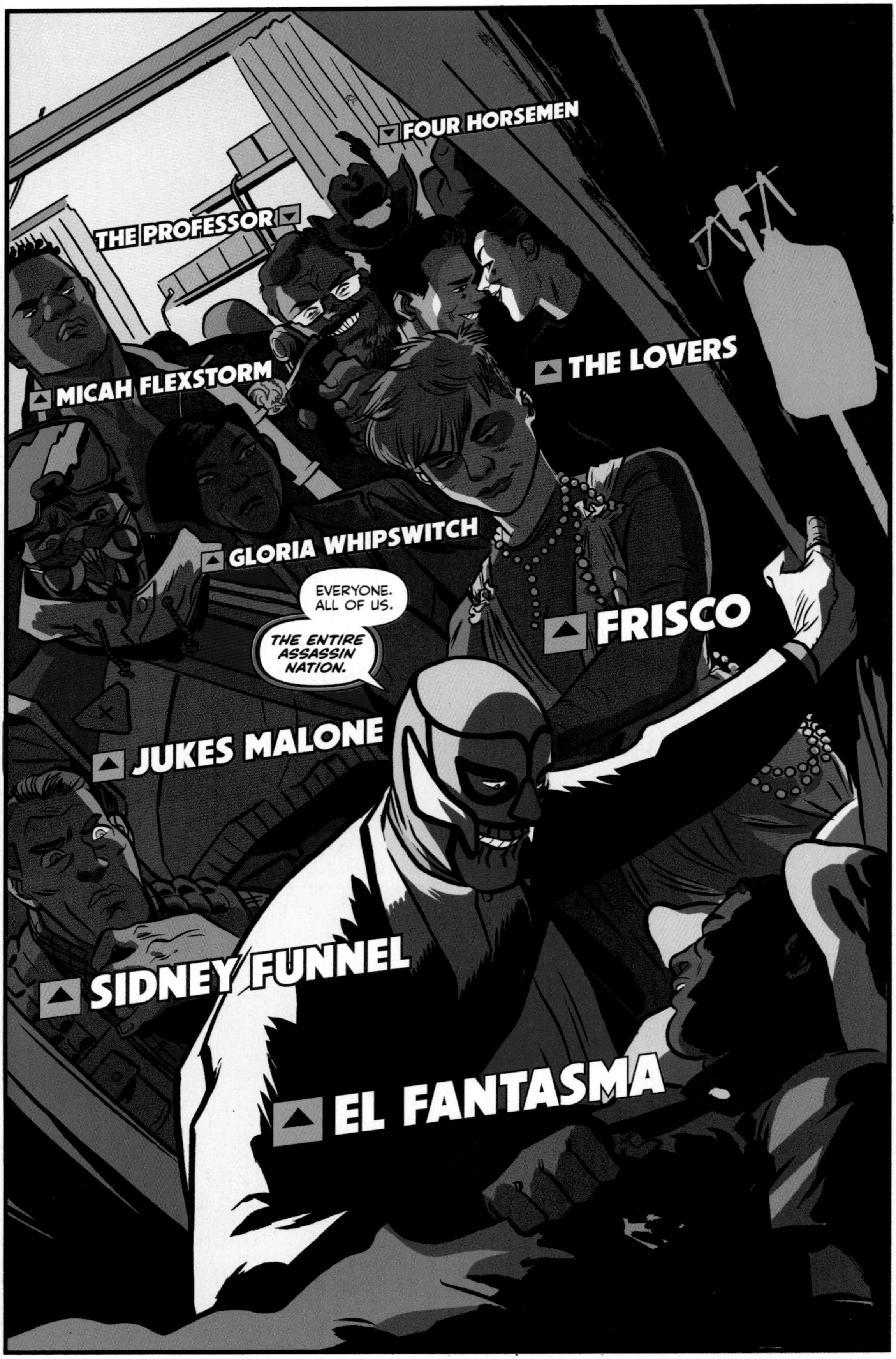
FOUR HORSEMEN
THE PROFESSOR
THE LOVERS
MICAH FLEXSTORM
GLORIA WHIPSWITCH
EVERYONE. ALL OF US.
THE ENTIRE ASSASSIN NATION.
FRISCO
JUKES MALONE
SIDNEY FUNNEL
EL FANTASMA

I CAME HERE TO
DO TWO THINGS:
GET KILLS AND MAKE
DOLLAR BILLS.